Lady Darlington

Lady Darlington

A NOVEL BY

Fred Mustard Stewart

ARBOR HOUSE
New York

*To my wife Joan, whose ideas
and help are always invaluable*

Part I

The month of May in the year 1908 was a warm one in England, and for the well-off it was a pleasant year in which to be alive. Edward VII, who had waited so long in the wings for his mother, Victoria, to die, had finally inherited the throne seven years before and, like Leo X when he won the Papacy, he had decided to enjoy it. Just the previous month, when the Liberal prime minister, Sir Henry Campbell-Bannerman, had been forced to resign because of ill health, his successor, Mr. Asquith, had had to go to Biarritz to kiss the king's hand, and the next week only the strongest pressures prevented the king from exporting the entire new cabinet to the Hotel Crillon in Paris to receive the seals of office. But if the king was enjoying himself on the Continent, so were many of his subjects at home. England was at the height of its wealth, power, and prestige; the red of the British Empire dominated maps of the world, and though English industrial preeminence was being challenged by Germany and America, English capital still financed the world. It was a good time to be an Englishman. And certainly few Englishmen had more to be thankful for than the man riding the bay mare across the green field toward the lovely country house called Ellendon Abbey.

His name was Charles Fitzmaurice August Avalon, the fifth earl of Darlington, and he was known to his friends, somewhat less pompously, as Charlie. Lord Darlington was forty-two. He had been in the House of Commons until nine years before when his father died, and he inherited the earldom which sent him to the House of Lords. In 1903 he had been brought into the Balfour cabinet as secretary of state for India, where he served brilliantly until the Conservatives were defeated in 1905. Now he still spoke frequently in the Lords, where he was considered one of the bright young Tories, the man some people said might be foreign secretary if the Tories ever came back into power which, in that high noon of the Liberal ascendancy, seemed rather unlikely. Lord Darlington was well-equipped for high office. He was what the London papers never tired of describing as "aristocratically tall, lean, and handsome," and in fact he was good-looking, with that long face so peculiar to certain branches of the English aristocracy. He had blond hair and light coloring and, thanks to tennis in the summer and riding whenever possible, he was still fit. He was attractive to women—always a political asset—and his charm as well as his social position made him one of the most sought-after guests in London. A graduate of Eton and Oxford, he was well-informed, articulate, and a good speaker. His title and family were good, and he had an income of over fifty thousand pounds a year. He was married to a daughter of one of the most powerful English dukes; he owned a mansion in London as well as Ellendon Abbey in Kent. So by any reasonable standards, the earl of Darlington should have been a happy man.

But he wasn't.

When he saw the Rolls-Royce turn into the long drive that led to the house, he turned his horse toward the automobile and galloped over to meet it. Denby, his Cockney chauffeur, stopped the car as his employer reined in his horse and looked through the rear window at the beautiful young woman in the back seat. She was wearing a gray tweed suit and a small white hat. She had soft brown hair, a classic face, and the gorgeous complexion for which Englishwomen were famous. He judged she was twenty-two or three, and in his opinion she was by far the most beautiful nurse he had ever seen. He decided his luck with nurses might be taking a turn for the better.

"Miss Suffield?" he said.

"That's right."

"I appreciate your coming down from London. Was your trip pleasant?"

"Very."

"Good. Denby, I'll race you to the house. I'll win, too," he added to the young woman with a grin. Then he spurred his horse and galloped off toward the house as the chauffeur accepted the challenge. The Rolls bumped wildly over the dirt road, sending up clouds of dust, and Margaret Suffield hung on to her hat as she bounced up and down in the back seat. She was favorably impressed by Lord Darlington. She had seen photographs of him in the papers, but they hadn't done him justice: he was much better-looking in person. She was beginning to change her mind: the trip down from London, which she hadn't wanted to make, might turn out to be worthwhile after all. When the employment agency had told her the earl of Darlington was looking for a new nurse to care for his wife, she had told them she wasn't interested. She had heard too many stories about the notorious Lady Darlington, the Harpy of Belgrave Square, as she was known among London's nurses—an arrogant and incredibly difficult woman who in three years had hired and fired three dozen nurses. She had no desire to become yet another of Lady Darlington's victims. And only the enormous salary the agency had told her the earl was offering had prompted her to go to the trouble and expense of making the trip down to Kent, where, a mile outside the village of Rockhampton, the earl's country home was located. But now she was glad she had come.

She could see Ellendon Abbey through the windshield of the Rolls. It sat at the end of the long, straight drive that bisected the field: square, surrounded by an ornamental moat and embraced by stately, new-leafing trees, beautiful in the May sunshine and at the same time solidly strong, its gray stone walls four centuries old, part of them even older. It had been an abbey at one time. Then, when Henry VIII expropriated the Church properties in the sixteenth century, it had become Crown property, only to be handed over later to one of Henry's friends, Captain Bagstone, officially as a reward for bravery, but unofficially (and more factually) as a reward to his lovely wife for services rendered to the Crown. Captain Bagstone tore down part of the abbey and rebuilt it as a country home, replete with the nonfunctional moat. The Bagstone family maintained it for more than two centuries. Then, at the beginning of the nineteenth century, the Bagstones sold it with its three hundred acres to the second earl of Darlington. This earl, the son of the first Lord Darlington, who had been born in the small nearby village, poured thousands of pounds into the place, which had fallen into some disrepair. The second earl had taste as well as money, and his restoration was brilliantly successful. He furnished the house elegantly, and added to the southeast corner a square tower which jutted dramatically over the moat and which contained an enormous two-story drawing room that was flooded by sunlight streaming through the high, leaded windows. He hired a landscape architect to lay out a lovely English garden on the west side of the building. Trees were planted, lawns limed and reseeded, and the result was a home that fitted perfectly into the landscape of green fields and gently rolling hills. As Margaret watched the earl gallop through the arched entrance a good two lengths ahead of the puffing automobile, she thought Ellendon Abbey was a fittingly romantic home for the romantic-looking fifth earl.

The Rolls chugged across the drawbridge into the square courtyard and parked in front of the stone doorway, which was flanked by potted rose trees. The earl had given his horse to a groom and was walking over to the automobile. Though his riding clothes and brown boots were dusty, still he looked well turned out and she could tell his tailor was excellent. He tapped his crop against his breeches as he waited for Denby to help her out of the back seat. Then he came over and shook her hand.

"You won," she said.

"It was hardly a fair race. They tell me the internal combustion engine is a great scientific advancement over the horse, but I'm not convinced. If you'll come in the house, we can talk in the study. Denby, you unmitigated scoundrel, you told me you were going to wash this thing."

Denby, in his gray chauffeur's uniform with the yellow piping (gray and yellow being the earl's colors) looked embarrassed.

"I got 'eld up in me work, milord."

"Undoubtedly by Helen, the upstairs maid. Denby," he added to Margaret, "is a thoroughly unprincipled man who is the nemesis of the local female population. But he's the only chauffeur in England who can change a wheel in five minutes. An extraordinarily nice day, isn't it? I think we may be in for a warm spring."

As he said this, he led her through the front door. He had an easygoing manner she liked, and he wasn't in the least stuffy or pompous. This had been an asset when he was in the House of Commons, but she thought the informality came naturally to him and had not been a pose assumed to please the voters. When they came in to the great hall of the house, a bald and dignified butler held the door.

"This is Rogers," said the earl. "Rogers, Miss Suffield, our prospective nurse."

Margaret smiled at the butler, who nodded his enormous head.

"And these are Scylla and Charybdis," continued the earl, leaning down to rough the heads of two Great Danes who had come bounding across the hall, tails wagging with excitement at seeing their master. "They look menacing, but they wouldn't hurt a flea. Are you interested in architecture?"

"Yes," said Margaret.

"This stairway is supposed to be one of the finest Elizabethan stairs in the country." He pointed to the wooden stairway, which was elaborately carved and which mounted to a landing, then turned to cross the end wall before continuing its way to the second floor. The ceiling of the wall was beamed, and the walls were smooth white plaster hung with numerous family portraits. The earl pointed to one near the bottom of the stair, a splendid painting of an eighteenth-century nobleman in wig and white satin.

"That's the first earl," he said, offhandedly. "My great-great-great-something-or-other-grandfather. He was born here in the village, a farmer's son, and went to London to make his fortune. When that didn't work out, he shipped to India with Clive and got rich in the tea trade. Would you like some tea?"

"Yes, thank you."

"Rogers, bring Miss Suffield some tea in the study, and an ale for me. Then he came back to London and bought his way into politics—the first earl, that is, not Rogers. He went into Parliament and backed that ass, George III's, stupid policies, in return for which the king made him an earl. Then he tripled his fortune in real-estate speculation and married an heiress who brought him in even more. He died of overeating at the age of eighty, and they say the bishop at his funeral called him an 'outstanding Christian,' which doesn't speak too well for the bishop's idea of Christianity. Am I boring you?"

"Not at all."

"Good. Family histories can be dull beyond belief."

"It sounds very exciting to me."

He smiled.

"You're tactful; good. You'll have to be, if you stay here. The eighteenth century was a good one for earls, but I have an idea the twentieth is going to be a bad one. Shall we go in here to talk?"

He opened a wooden door handsomely carved with linen-fold panels and led her into a book-lined room which had tall windows looking out on the sunny courtyard. A bronze-and-ebony Italian desk stood before the windows; in front of the stone mantel were two black leather chairs. The wide-planked floors were old, and the deep, rich brown gleamed. Everything in the room, she noted, was choice and kept immaculate. He gestured to one of the leather chairs, and she sat down. He took the other and propped his booted feet on the brass fender in front of the hearth. Scylla and Charybdis, who had followed them into the study, curled up on the floor next to him and went to sleep.

"Well now," he said, "the agency sent me your credentials, which I've read. They're very impressive. You come from Somerset?"

"Yes. Chewton Mendip."

"Ah, Cheddar cheese!"

She was pleased by his recognition of her village's specialty.

"Yes, we like to think we make the best in England."

"And you do, no doubt about it. I'm also partial to Mendip

snails, which you can't get around here, unfortunately. Was your father's livelihood involved with cheese?"

"Hardly. He was a vicar."

"Good Lord, I was a bit off there, wasn't I? So you're a clergyman's daughter, and a beautiful one at that. That's almost a miracle. I've never met a pretty clergyman's daughter. The daughter of our vicar here in Rockhampton has a moustache."

Margaret looked down at her gloves and tried not to laugh.

"Quite a nice one, in fact," he continued. "I told her once she should curl it. What made you decide to be a nurse?"

"When my father died, there didn't seem to be anything else for me to do. And I've always been interested in nursing."

"No local Chewton Mendip beaux?"

"None I liked."

"That's honest enough. You were graduated by the Royal Institute of Nursing, then you tended Mrs. Porter on Wilton Crescent?"

"That's right. For two years. Then I took care of Lady Millington for two more years. She passed on last month."

"I know Lady Millington's son. He's one of the most useless men in London. Might I ask what you were paid?"

"Sixty guineas per annum."

"Did the agency tell you what I'm offering?"

"They said a hundred and fifty guineas. It's quite a handsome salary."

"It's a bribe, frankly. I don't try to hide the fact that we've lost a regular army of nurses here. Ah, here's the tea."

There had been a knock on the door, then Rogers came in followed by a footman in gray-and-yellow livery carrying a silver tray.

"You can put it here, Rogers," said the earl. The butler placed a table next to Margaret's chair, and the footman set down the tray which held a tankard of ale, a pot of tea, a tray of cookies, sugar, cream, and, in a crystal bud vase, a freshly cut daffodil. Rogers poured Margaret's tea as the earl took the tankard and leaned back in his chair, taking a healthy draft of the brew.

"Being a clergyman's daughter," he said, "I hope you don't disapprove of drinking?"

"Oh, no," she replied. "My father was quite a claret fancier."

"That's good."

She wondered what he meant by that. She was conscious of his watching her as she took two cookies from the tray, and his scrutiny made her feel rather uncomfortable. Beneath his polite and cool exterior there seemed to be a forceful maleness to the man that disturbed her as, at the same time, it excited her. The thought occurred to her that the earl probably got his way with women.

When Rogers and the footman had left the room, Lord Darlington continued.

"Let me tell you something about my wife. Her brother's the duke of Suffolk. Do you know who he is?"

"I've read about him in the papers."

"He's not one of my favorite relatives. At any rate, when I married Caroline eight years ago, she had already been married once before, but her first husband was killed in the Boer War. This had had an effect on her, naturally, but she seemed in excellent health when we married. A year after the wedding, we had a child—a son—who was stillborn." He hesitated a moment, frowning slightly at the memory of something that was obviously still painful to him. "My wife was . . . well, it was a great shock to her, as it was to me. She had had no children by her first marriage, and it was my first child, and he was dead before he even had a chance to live. I think that was the beginning of Caroline's troubles. She grew quite moody; and while before then she had been active socially—in fact, she took a great delight in society—afterward she began to withdraw from the world. Then, three years ago, she had a miscarriage, and this, together with what had happened before, devastated her. She was told she could never have children, and she suffered a collapse of nerves. This seemed to provoke a general deterioration of her health, which was climaxed by a mild heart attack—and I emphasize that it was mild. I had the best Harley Street specialists, naturally, including Sir Andrew Hodge, and they all agreed that her heart is in no serious condition and that, with care, she can live to what the provincial pulpits refer to as a 'rich harvest of years.' However—and here I'm afraid I may sound a bit hard on my wife—because of the bad state of her nerves and a general tendency toward hypochondria, Caroline made herself an invalid. She took to her bed and insisted on a private nurse—this was three years ago, mind you, and she hasn't been out of bed since. All the doctors have tried to persuade her to get out of bed, but my wife can be extraordinarily stubborn, unfortunately, and the more we've tried to get her up, the more determined she's become to stay down. I don't need tell you that by leading the life of an invalid, she is in fact becoming one."

"That would be inevitable."

For a moment his face became troubled.

"It's really quite sad. I don't know how to cope with it except to go along with her wishes. As I said, she is, at times, a most difficult patient."

"In what way?"

"She's very moody. She can become petty to the point of madness, infuriatingly insulting, and quite malicious. Since she has nothing to do with her time, she tries to destroy those she comes in contact with. This is why we've lost nurse after nurse. And this is why I offer an unusually high salary for the position. With all you've heard, I wouldn't blame you for not wanting to accept it. But I'm hoping you'll consider it."

She thought a moment. He had certainly been honest about the difficulties involved in taking care of his wife, though he had told her nothing she hadn't heard from others. But she liked him, and the salary was tempting.

"Quite frankly," she said, "I can't afford not to consider it. My father had rather extravagant tastes—much more extravagant than his income—and when he died he left debts of over a thousand pounds, which I've been paying off. A hundred and fifty guineas would be a great help."

"Good. Room and board is included, of course, and I think you'll find the quarters quite comfortable. Then as far as I'm concerned, you're hired. However, the final decision is neither mine nor yours. I'm afraid you'll have to be approved by my wife. I apologize for it, but there'd be no point in your taking the position if she took a dislike to you I might add that if she does, I hope you won't take it personally."

"I wouldn't."

"Our last nurse, Miss Delafield, did. I'm afraid she was a bit fat, and my wife called her a tub of butter and the poor woman went off in a snit. I can't say I blame Miss Delafield, but I'm trying to prepare you for the worst. Happily, my wife won't be able to call *you* a tub of butter." He finished his ale and stood up. "Then perhaps we should go see her now?"

"Yes, of course."

As she got up, he said, "I hope this does work out, Miss Suffield. To be blunt, I'm most favorably impressed by you. I believe you could be a great help to my wife, as well as to me. Being in politics takes a good deal of my time—even being in the House of Lords, which some people might consider anything but time-consuming. However, it consumes *my* time. And it would ease my mind to have someone in charge of my wife whom I could trust. I believe I could trust you."

"You're very kind. I hope I'll be able to fulfill your expectations."

"I'm sure you will. Well, shall we go meet the patient?"

He started toward the door, and the two Great Danes sprang to their feet to follow him. He turned and said, "Sit!" They whimpered with disappointment, but obeyed. He said to Margaret, "My wife doesn't like dogs. She doesn't like much of anything, for that matter." The remark was short, and it struck her as rather bitter, but she said nothing. He led her back into the entrance hall, closing the door to the study. "Her bedroom's on the ground floor," he said, leading her across the empty hall toward a gallery that led to the west end of the house. "In town we have an elevator that takes her upstairs, but here there isn't one."

"Do you come to the country often?"

"During the summer when Parliament recesses. The rest of the year we're in London mostly. We came down this week because the weather turned good, but we have to be back in town tomorrow. I'm scheduled to make a speech tomorrow afternoon on the Pension Bill. The noble lords aren't too happy with the measure, and I'm trying to make them happier. Ironically, it's Caroline's brother that's leading the opposition."

"The duke of Suffolk?"

"Yes. He's a loud-mouthed boor who's mentally still in the Middle Ages. It seems to be a family trait."

Margaret thought this remark, slanted as it seemed to be at his wife, was even more bitter than the previous one. And in fact as they walked down the long corridor toward the west wing of the house, the earl's easygoing manner seemed to vanish and she could almost feel the tension building inside him as they approached his wife's room. He sank into a silence, and their footsteps echoed sullenly down the seemingly endless gallery lined with portraits, sporting prints, and cabinets filled with *bibelots* collected by his ancestors. The ceiling of the gallery was one of those splendid Tudor creations, the design incredibly intricate, the elaborately molded plaster squares well-preserved over the centuries. The leaded windows that looked out into the courtyard filled the hall with sunlight, and normally she would have been enchanted by the beautiful furnishings and surroundings. But the look on her prospective employer's face precluded her enjoying anything, and in fact she found herself becoming rather nervous. At one point, he paused in front of a life-sized portrait in a gold frame. It was of a tall, handsome woman in a white satin dress standing before a gilt French table on which rested a vase of white peonies. The style of the painting was effortlessly aristocratic, and the woman had the graceful haughtiness so admired by the noblewomen of the day.

"That's my wife," said the earl, unenthusiastically. "Mr. Sargent did the painting when we were married. She was quite lovely then, don't you think?"

"Very," replied Margaret.

"She's not any more. I don't much like vain women, but she's lost all interest in her looks. A little vanity might do her some good."

Then he continued down the corridor, Margaret in tow, the nurse glancing back at the painting over her shoulder, her curiosity heightened by his pithy and almost surly comment. By the time they reached the wooden door at the end of the gallery, she was in a state of mild apprehension as to what lay in store for her. He noticed it and smiled slightly.

"I've made you nervous, haven't I?" he said.

"A little," she admitted.

"I don't come in here too often, and when I do, I frequently get in an argument with her. So to prepare myself, I get angry before I go in. That way, I'm ready for anything. But I apologize. I imagine you must think she's some sort of monster?"

"Frankly, yes."

"Well," he said flatly, "she is." With that, he opened the door. "Wait here. I'll tell her you've come."

He went inside, closing the door and leaving Margaret alone in the gallery. She marveled at his barely concealed hostility toward his wife. Margaret's mother had died when she was twelve, and her father had been a gentle dreamer of a man who always spoke of his dead wife with nothing but tenderness. He had educated his daughter to be a lady, and though a childhood of genteel poverty had forced her to view life realistically, still what she had seen of married couples led her to assume that no matter how many quarrels a husband and wife might have, no matter how unsuccessful the marriage might be, still the appearance of domestic tranquillity was maintained. Obviously, Lord Darlington had little interest in keeping up appearances, at least in front of her.

After a moment, he opened the door and said, "Come in."

She entered a large room the windows of which were covered with blue silk curtains that kept out the sunlight. The room was furnished with French pieces, mostly of the Regency period, and illuminated by small electric lamps which gave a dim, sickly glow that accentuated the gloom and stuffiness of the place. The walls were papered with blue and white vertical stripes, but the paper was almost obliterated by the frame-to-frame landscapes, French prints, and more of what Margaret guessed were family portraits, which stretched from the white dado almost up to the high ceiling, so that the effect was like that of walking into a picture gallery. Against one wall, dominating everything, was a bed with blue silk bed curtains that swept up from the four corners to meet in a small knot at the crown. While they were elegant, they concealed the bed's occupant from Margaret's view until she had crossed the room. She noticed, as she followed the earl to the bedside, that the air was saturated with the smell of cologne, as if an attempt had been made to cover up some other, less pleasant, odor.

When she reached the side of the bed, she saw a woman propped up against huge lace pillows, eating chocolates from a box of candy on her lap and staring with dark-circled eyes at Margaret. All she had heard of Lady Darlington; everything her husband had just told her; the Sargent portrait—none of it had really prepared her for the malevolence in those two eyes peering out from the puffy, pasty face, two hot coals of suspicion and distrust in a frame of dissipation. She looked in her mid-fifties, though Margaret guessed she was not much older than her husband. The haughty grace of the portrait had turned to fat, and the earl's remark that she had lost interest in her appearance was a laughable euphemism; the woman looked a wreck. Her black hair was stringy. Her pink bedjacket edged with white down had several food stains on it, and only her hands retained any semblance of beauty. They were expressively graceful and bulging with jeweled rings, including an immense cabochon emerald.

The earl stood next to Margaret, and she got the impression he was protecting her from the "monster," an impression she liked. "My dear," he said to his wife in a tone of voice that was anything but endearing, "this is Miss Suffield."

Silence. The eyes examined Margaret coldly, like those of a butcher examining a side of beef. When Lady Darlington spoke, her voice was hoarse and unpleasant.

"She's pretty," she said. "That's a change. Come here."

It was an order. Margaret stepped up beside her. To her amazement, the woman sniffed.

"She doesn't smell," she said, though Margaret wondered how she could tell through the cologne. "That's a change too. The last one stank. Say something so I can hear your voice. I can't stand most women's voices. I can't stand most women, for that matter. Say something!"

The earl was bristling.

"Garoline," he snapped, "England happens to be a civilized country, and it is the custom to treat people with a little politeness. Why don't you try it for a change?"

She turned her eyes on her husband. "It is your opinion that England is a civilized country; it is definitely not mine. She is *my* nurse, and I'll treat her as I please. Well?" She turned back to Margaret. "I'm waiting to hear the dulcet tones of your lyric soprano?"

"Does milady never open the windows?"

"No, milady does not open the windows. And if you're going to start bullying me, you might as well leave now. I won't be bullied! I'm a sick woman who lives with constant pain, but I'm in charge here. Do you understand? My husband may try and give orders in the House of Lords, but here *I* do. He's rich and can afford to pay you a grotesque salary. In return for that, you do as you are told. Is that perfectly clear?"

Margaret glared at her. The woman's attitude had infuriated her.

"Well?" said Lady Darlington. "Cat got your tongue?"

"*If* I take the position," she said, evenly. "I, of course, would carry out whatever instructions I received."

" 'If?' " snorted Lady Darlington. "Aren't we putting on airs!" She stared at her suspiciously for a long moment. Then she shrugged and stuffed another chocolate into her mouth. "She'll do. God knows she's not what one would like, but we'll have to make do with her, I suppose. You'll come in here only when I ring for you—understand? I will not have you coming here at all hours of the day and night disturbing my privacy. But when I ring, I want you here quickly. For what you're being paid, I want service. Do you have a lover?"

Margaret's eyes widened as the earl exploded. "Dammit, Caroline, that's none of your business!"

"It certainly *is* my business!" retorted his wife. "I won't have my fragile nerves shattered by a series of backstairs liaisons and tawdry kitchen-sink amours. Well? Do you?"

Margaret tried to keep her composure.

"No."

"Hah! As if I believe *that!* Probably rolling around in some stable with a filthy groom—I know your kind. Well, my dear, you have one day off a week—Fridays from noon till midnight—and during that time you can satisfy your animal appetites in any way you choose. But the rest of the week, you are here, in this house—or in town—and you will lead the life of a cloistered nun, do you understand? Now get out. What did you say your name was?"

"Miss Suffield."

" 'Miss Suffield,' indeed! Here you are 'Miss' Nobody. What is your Christian name, assuming you had the benefit of baptism, which is doubtless a false assumption?"

"My Christian name is Margaret. And I not only had the benefit of baptism, I also had the benefit of having a vicar for a father."

Lady Darlington raised her eyebrows.

"Oh, she has spirit! A pert reply from our Margaret. Well, pert Margaret, I am not easy to get along with. I make no pretense at being 'nice.' So don't expect me to mollycoddle you. Just do as you're told and we'll get along. More than that will be a miracle. Now get out."

She glanced at the earl, who signaled her to leave. She walked back to the door alone, feeling the eyes piercing her back, and left the room, closing the door behind her. When she was alone in the gallery, she leaned against a wall and took a deep breath.

"My God!" she said to herself. The woman was worse than she had dreamed. Far worse. He had been right when he said she was a monster. It was almost amusing, or at least paradoxical, that the daughter of a duke would have the manners of a *parvenue* fishwife. She wondered if even a hundred and fifty guineas would be worth taking that kind of abuse.

When she heard the shouts, she straightened. They were coming through the wooden door, muffled by its thickness, but, nevertheless, unmistakably the earl and his wife were having a battle royal. It lasted for almost three minutes. Then silence. After another minute, the door opened and Lord Darlington came out. His face was white, and he was making a supreme effort to bottle up his rage. He closed the door and looked at Margaret a moment. Then he said drily, "Charming, isn't she?"

She couldn't help but laugh.

"She does have a way of making you like her right off."

He put his finger to his mouth in a "shushing" gesture, then took her arm and led her away from the door. "Incredibly enough," he said, "she likes you."

"She has an odd way of showing it."

"Doesn't she? But as I told you, she's that way with everybody. I apologize for what she asked you. About having a lover. It was outrageous, and I told her so just now, as you may have heard through the door—we seem to communicate best at triple forte—but you'll have to learn to ignore her. That is, if you take the position. I suppose you don't want it, now that you've seen what she's like?"

She didn't answer for a moment. She was weighing what she should do. "If I did take it," she finally said, "I can see definite problems. If she has a heart condition, she shouldn't be allowed to sit in those airless rooms stuffing herself with candy. I would think she should be put on a diet and made to take some form of mild exercise. Hasn't her doctor said that?"

"Of course. Countless times. If you take the position, I'll arrange for you to meet Sir Andrew tomorrow night, but he'll tell you the same thing I do. It's impossible to change her habits. She absolutely refuses to do what the doctors tell her."

"Then I wouldn't be able to assume responsibility for her health. I'd do everything possible to take care of her, but if she insists on doing what I know is harmful to her, I couldn't be accountable for the consequences."

"I realize that, and of course you wouldn't be held responsible."

"Might I ask why she uses so much cologne? The room seemed rather full of it."

The earl stopped, as did she. He seemed to be trying to make up his mind about something. Then he said, "Well, I might as well tell you. You'd find out soon enough if you take the job. Naturally, this is something I don't like to advertise, but my wife drinks. The cologne is to hide the smell. She drinks quite heavily, in fact—mostly champagne, though sometimes I wouldn't be surprised if she drank the cologne as well. Of course, this poses other problems."

"Do you try to keep the wine away from her?"

"No. It would mean my becoming a jailer, which I have no intention of doing if I can help it. I suppose this doesn't make you any more eager to take the position?

"I've never dealt with a drinker."

"That wouldn't matter."

She looked out the gallery window at the sun-drenched courtyard, noticing for the first time the lovely beds of daffodils that had been planted along the walls. She liked Ellendon Abbey, she liked the earl, and she liked the salary. But she disliked Lady Darlington intensely.

She turned to him and said, "I'm afraid I would be more of a hindrance to your wife than a help."

"Why? Because of her drinking? That's why I asked you if you disapproved of it."

"No, it isn't that. I'm afraid I wouldn't be able to put up with her insults. I might lose my temper, and I don't think that would be much help to her. If she has a heart condition, it might even harm her."

He looked surprisingly disappointed.

"I'll offer a hundred and seventy-five guineas," he said.

"But that's not the point. . . ."

"A hundred and eighty. I need you. It's already obvious you're by far the best-trained nurse that we've had. I'll even go so far as to ask you as a personal favor to take the position."

A hundred and eighty guineas! It was a fortune, and she couldn't resist it. She sighed and smiled. "All right. I'll do my best."

He looked pleased.

"I know you will. And I'm delighted you're staying. May I call you Margaret?"

"It seems that here I'm 'Miss' Nobody, so I think you'll have to."

He laughed, and his good humor seemed to return.

"All right, Margaret. I hope we can become friends. Where are you staying now?"

They started walking down the gallery again.

"At a boarding house on the Cromwell Road. The St. Alban's Court. I've been there since I left Lady Millington's."

"I'll have Denby take you to the station, and you can go back to London. In the morning, go to Number Ten Belgrave Square—that's my townhouse—and Mrs. Blaine, the housekeeper, will get you settled. You'll like her; she's Irish and will talk your ear off, but she's a kind woman. Tell her my wife will be there around noon—we'll motor up if the weather holds; otherwise we'll take the train."

They had reached the entrance hall, and he stopped and stared down at the stone floor a moment. Then he looked up at her and smiled, rather sadly, she thought.

"It gets lonely here. It will be nice having a friendly face in the house," he said. Then he walked across the hall and went into his study, closing the door behind him.

• • •

The first Darlington House had been built on Portland Place in 1772 by the first earl. Whatever his contemporaries thought of the first Lord Darlington's character, they universally agreed that he had left a handsome monument to his taste in the graceful townhouse, which had been designed by James Adam. The third earl, though, who was one of the great Victorian eccentrics, became convinced that the first Darlington House was infested with ants, so he sold that architectural gem and, in 1846, built a new house on the land west of Buckingham Palace then being developed by the Grosvenor family. He told his architect, Thomas Cubitt, to copy the first Darlington House, but "to make it bigger and free of ants." Cubitt had carried out this curious assignment relatively well, so that while the new house lacked the Adam grace, its pomposity and opulence were nevertheless arresting. The next morning, as Margaret walked up the stairs leading to the front door beneath the Ionic-columned portico, she stared up at the stone façade of Number 10 Belgrave Square, and decided the house was impressive but a bit over whelming, which was probably the effect the third earl had wished to convey.

She rang the bell and waited as the hack carried her three suit-cases up the steps. She was feeling exuberant. After she had paid her bill at the St. Alban's Court, saying goodbye to the boarding house's formidable owner, Mrs. Sedgwick, she had felt so excited by her new job and its staggering salary, she had decided to indulge herself in an unaccustomed luxury and told the cab driver to take her for a drive. It was another glorious spring day, and London was flowering. They had passed Hyde Park Corner and chugged down Piccadilly to the Circus, teeming with traffic and crowds; then to Trafalgar Square, teeming with pigeons; from there down the Mall to the Palace, where Margaret couldn't resist playing Royal Family and gesturing graciously to the crowds as she had seen Queen Alexandra do in the royal carriages; then down the Kensington Road past the Albert Hall and the Albert Memorial. The park was filled with strollers, the women in boaters and Gibson Girl blouses, holding white parasols; the men in blazers and new spring suits brought out by the warm weather; and the panorama was made even more lovely by the fresh leaves on the trees, the new grass, and the thousands of tulips and daffodils. When they finally reached Belgrave Square, Margaret was in a state of near euphoria that was only slightly clouded by the thought of the arrogant, drunken woman she would be tending. Lady Darlington! Margaret wondered how any woman married to such a superior man as Lord Darlington could ruin her life—as well as his—by taking to drink and false invalidism. He really was so kind, so intelligent, so handsome. Even his title was romantic sounding, though she wasn't the type to be overawed by titles and, in fact, took a dim view of "society" in general. From what she had seen of it at Lady Millington's, it was snobbish, vapid, and dull. Lord Darlington, on the other hand, was none of these things. Judging from his friendly attitude to her, he was anything but a snob. And far from being vapid, he seemed as interested in life as his wife seemed disinterested. And yet, even with a husband most women would have considered ideal, the woman drank. It was really most curious.

A bucktoothed footman answered her ring and opened the door.

"Are you the new nurse?" he asked.

"Yes."

"We've been expecting you. And from now on, use the servant's entrance."

"Ah, go on with you, Henry, you dim-witted snob!" exclaimed a plump, elderly woman in a black taffeta dress who appeared beside him. "Miss Suffield's no servant in this house, and she'll use the front door." She turned her pleasant face on Margaret, and it beamed as she drank her in. "The saints preserve us, she's a raving beauty, she is! His Lordship rang me up this morning from the country and said he'd found a prize nurse, but I had no idea you'd be so pretty! Get her bags, Henry. Don't just stand there like a clod. Come in, my dear. I'm Mrs. Blaine the housekeeper, and a better housekeeper you won't find in London, or anywhere else, for that matter."

The woman's Irish brogue and bustlingly maternal manner made Margaret like her immediately. As Henry took her bags from the hack, she stepped inside the entrance hall.

"Welcome to Darlington House," said Mrs. Blaine, examining her more closely. "Well, it's about time His Lordship was hiring a young nurse. The last one—what was her name? Miss Delafield or some such; she was gone so quick I hardly got a chance to meet her—anyway, she must have been sixty if she was a day, with a face like a prune." Margaret thought the poor Miss Delafield, being an odd mixture of butterball and prune, must have been something of a physical curiosity. "Of course," continued Mrs. Blaine, "it was a *sad* prune after ten minutes with Her Ladyship—the Lord save us from *her!*" She rolled her eyes and clasped her hands together in an expression that left little doubt as to Mrs. Blaine's opinion of Lady Darlington. Margaret was staring up at the enormous marble entrance hall, which could only be described as cavernous. Two stories high, it soared to a classic Roman ceiling, its white marble walls forbiddingly patri-

cian and classically devoid of ornamentation, as though the designer had wanted the architecture alone to make the impression,
which it did. Opposite the front door, almost forty feet away,
across the black diamond, white marble floor, was a staircase
which, like the one in the country house, rose to a landing but,
unlike the warm, wooden Elizabethan stair, it was, like the hall,
rather forbidding.

"Isn't it grand?" said Mrs. Blaine. "And cold as a potato. It
reminds me of a train station or a tomb. I never can decide which.
But when it's filled up with guests, it makes a pretty sight—not
that we have guests any more, what with Her Ladyship retiring
from the world with her nerves and whatnot. Would you like a
tour?"

"Oh yes," said Margaret, who was awed by the entrance hall.

"The rest of the house is a bit more homey, but you couldn't
exactly call it cozy," continued the housekeeper, leading her to
two doors to the right as the footman disappeared behind the
staircase to take Margaret's bags to the second floor on the
elevator. "They're a grand family, the Darlingtons, with more
money than the law allows, and the old earls weren't afraid to
spend it. This is the main drawing room, which we call the Red
Room, and you couldn't guess why."

She had opened the doors, and now she led Margaret into a
rectangular room whose walls were covered with red Spitalfields
silk. A graceful crystal chandelier depended from a circular
plaster medallion in the center of the ceiling, its chain a red
velvet rope. Four tall windows looked out on the square. The
furniture, which was covered in red silk matching the walls, had
all been made by the same designer and was in the heavy gilt
Louis XV style which, despite its ponderousness, harmonized
surprisingly well with the room.

"Like Buckingham Palace, wouldn't you say?" said Mrs. Blaine,
who seemed to take a secret pride in the house, as though years
of association with the family had made the place as much hers
as theirs. "Of course, it's a bit showy and not half as nice as
some homes I've seen in Ireland, but it's pretty good for the
English. The paintings are all of the family. There's His Lordship's father." She pointed to a mutton-chopped Victorian patri-

arch. "A fine man he was. And there's his mother—ah, a sweet woman *she* was!" Next to the fourth earl was the fourth countess, a beautiful Victorian lady in light blue seated on one of the Red Room's gilt chairs. "Looks like His Lordship, don't she?" And indeed, Margaret thought, she did. It was obvious where the earl got his looks. "Now here's the whole tribe, painted when His Lordship was twelve." She pointed to a huge canvas, one of the "conversation pieces" so popular at the time, depicting the fourth earl standing behind his wife, who was seated in a chair in the drawing room of the country house, while the older son leaned nonchalantly against the arm of the chair and his younger brother snuggled against his mother's skirts. "The young one's Arthur, His Lordship's brother—what a scamp *he* is! Goes through money like it grew on trees! And the one leaning on the chair is Charles. Wasn't he the darlingest child you've ever laid your eyes on? Look at those golden curls! I was their nanny, and they both of them could twist me around their little fingers, but Charles was the one I adored. Such a beautiful child he was, and such a handsome man he's grown up to be! And look at the wife he got stuck with! The saints preserve us!" She shook her head morosely, then lowered her voice. "In case you're getting the idea I don't like Her Ladyship, you're absolutely right." Margaret suppressed a laugh as the housekeeper bustled across the room back to the entrance hall. "Now over here's the dining room," she called, as Margaret hurried after her. They crossed the hall to two doors opposite the Red Room which Mrs. Blaine threw open to reveal a room that ran the entire depth of the house, being at least sixty feet long. Its walls were a light gray, and in each of the long walls were three white niches in which stood statues of nude Roman gods and goddesses. Down the center of the room ran a long Sheraton table with matching chairs. At the end of the room, a graceful bow window looked out on the garden.

"We can seat twenty at the table easily," said Mrs. Blaine, "and we can squeeze twenty-four. The kitchen's in the basement, and it's a beauty, with all the conveniences. His Lordship put it in when he married *her*. Renovated the whole house, he did. Put in electric wiring and the telephones and the elevator behind the stair. Those indecent statues the second earl bought in Rome eighty years ago. They're supposed to be worth a fortune, but if you ask me they should put some clothes on them, particularly the men. Of course, the fig leaves cover up the worst part, but still they don't leave much to the imagination for my way of thinking. We'll be climbing the stairs now, and I'll show you your rooms. You wouldn't be a Catholic, I suppose?"

They were headed for the stairway.

"I'm afraid not," smiled Margaret. "My father was Church of England. In fact, he was a vicar."

Mrs. Blaine sniffed.

"Well, it can't be helped. There are plenty of decent Protestants—I wouldn't want you to think I'm narrow-minded, so I won't hold it against you. This painting on the landing up ahead is a genuine Titian. It's Saint Sebastian, poor man; look at all them arrows sticking out of him, and the blood! It reminds me of my poor Ireland, and the arrows fired by the English, the terrible heathens. As much as I love His Lordship, I wouldn't continue working for him if he weren't for Home Rule, which he is, praise the Lord. Ah, we should have taken the elevator; these stairs are steep!"

They finally reached the second floor, where a long hallway ran the breadth of the house, terminating at both ends in double doors. Mrs. Blaine, panting from her climb, paused to get her breath. She pointed to the right end. "That's *her* bedroom," she said. Then she pointed to the opposite end. "That's his. You can draw your own conclusions as to how happy their marriage is." She thought a moment, then whispered in a rather shocked tone, "You're not married are you?"

"No."

"Then you probably don't know what I'm talking about, do you?"

"I'm a nurse, Mrs. Blaine. I know."

The housekeeper looked relieved.

"I wouldn't have wanted to shock your Christian sensibilities for the world, poor child. At any rate, you've met *her* and you've seen him, so I don't suppose it's any secret to you that they fight like cats and dogs. Oh, I could tell you some rare stories, I could, and I probably will, the way I rattle on. Would you like to see the ballroom?"

"Very much."

The housekeeper opened two doors that faced the top of the stairs and went into a large white room that overlooked the square. Around the walls stood small gold opera chairs, above which hung yet more of the family portraits, these predominantly eighteenth- and early nineteenth-century in style.

"We used to have some grand balls here," said Mrs. Blaine. "Darlington House used to be one of the dancingest places in London. But since *she*—" (Margaret was becoming used to the fact that every time Mrs. Blaine referred to Lady Darlington, it was always with heavy, and disapproving, emphasis) "—since *she* took to her bed with her nerves, there's hardly been a soul in the place. And if you ask me, those 'nerves' come in a bottle with a cork in it. Did he tell you about Paul?"

"No. Who's Paul?"

"Paul Rougemont, Her Ladyship's private footman." She glanced out in the hall, as if half-expecting someone to be eavesdropping. Then she lowered her voice. "He's a Swiss she hired three years ago, though no one else wanted him around. He has a police record, he does! He admits it—even brags about it, if you can imagine! Spent six months in a French jail for picking an American tourist's wallet—he'd have gotten more if he'd stolen a French wallet! Well, he's crooked as they come, but *she* adores him. He used to work in a winery, and he knows how to handle wines, and that's why she likes him. He's the official dispenser of the bubbly, and let me tell you—the empties the dustman carts away from here make *this* place look like a winery, they do! Ah, he's a wicked one, and you'll do well to keep your distance from him."

"I certainly will," said Margaret, "though I'm surprised Lord Darlington would hire a man with a police record."

"Hah! As if he wouldn't like to fire him if he could! He hates him, the insolent beggar—I hate him too. But lift a finger against Paul, and the howls *she* puts up! Well, it's not worth firing him, it isn't. See that painting down at the end of the room? That's the first Lady Darlington, a genuine Gainsborough. She wasn't much to look at, was she?"

Margaret looked at the dowdy eighteenth-century countess and agreed.

"No, she's not very pretty."

"But the second countess was a beauty. There she is." She pointed to a portrait of a woman dressed in the style of the Regency. "She was the daughter of a duke, but she acted like one, not like a certain someone I wouldn't mention."

"What was she like when she first married him?"

"Who, this one?" She sniffed. "Stuck up. La-dee-dah till it made you sick, all full of herself, her being a Cheyney and a daughter of the duke of Suffolk and what-have-you. The old duke was alive then. Well, I suppose they're very grand, but look at her now! You could find better-looking hags in Limehouse, and with better manners, too. I never could understand why a darling man like His Lordship would fall in love with a bitch like her—begging your pardon for using such an indecent word, but it's the best one I can think of to describe her. Do you know a better one?"

Margaret laughed.

"No, frankly. But he *was* in love with her?"

"Oh yes. She was pretty enough then, and he has an eye for pretty women. Not that they don't have an eye for him! Every girl in London was after that man, with guns and nets and meathooks—anything they could get their hands on! But she got him, and he's lived to regret it, he has, poor man. He goes through living hell with her! Ah, it's a mortal sin the way she carried on, and it don't do his career much good either, not that *she* cares a fig. Well, I'll show you your rooms now. They're down the hall next to her suite, and I think you'll like them. I had them all cleaned out this morning, not that they have much chance to get dusty with the turnover in nurses we have. Do you think you'll stay? Or will you be running off like the others?"

She had led Margaret back out in the hall, closing the ballroom doors.

"I'm going to *try* to stay," said Margaret.

"Well, I hope you do. Judging from the way he was raving about you on the phone this morning, I'd say he's taken a considerable fancy to you. And now that I've met you, I can see why. You're a pretty woman, and I can tell you're quality. For what it's worth, you'll have a friend in me. And frankly, in this house, you'll need all the friends you can get."

She stopped before a door that was the final one before the doors leading to Lady Darlington's suite. "This is your room," she said, taking her into a small sitting room, simply furnished but charming. Margaret's bags had been deposited on the floor. "And in here's your bedroom." She crossed the room to a door leading in to the bedroom, which had a brass bed, a full-length mirror stand, and a tall bureau with copper Sphinx-head handles on the drawers. "And the bath." This sported a huge claw-foot tub and an enormous marble basin. After Margaret had looked around, Mrs. Blaine asked, "Is everything to your satisfaction, miss?"

"Everything is perfect," replied Margaret. "And I want to thank you for the tour and all the information."

"I'm a fierce gossip, I know, but it's better you find out the lay of the land early on so you won't be making mistakes. And Paul could be a bad mistake, mark my words." She glanced out the window at the square. "I'd best be getting downstairs now. She'll be arriving soon, and she'll be fussing about *some-*thing, no doubt. She always does. The good Lord must have had a terrible stomachache when he dreamed *her* up, wouldn't you say?" She headed for the door. "You get unpacked. If you want anything, ring for Henry. He's the bucktoothed halfwit who answered the door. When Her Ladyship wants you, she rings that bell." She pointed to a small bell on the wall above the bedroom door. "But don't for the life of you go in unless she rings. That's a sure way to ask for trouble. His Lordship told me you're to report to him directly if you have any problems, and you're to have the run of the house. Ah, I've talked so much my throat's gone dry! I think I'll have a cup of tea with maybe a spot of extra nourishment in it." She smiled. "With *her* back in town, I'll need all the strength I can find."

With that, she left the room, her skirts rustling as she went through the sitting room to the hall. When she had gone, Margaret went over to the mirror and looked at her reflection. She unpinned her hat and put it on the bed. Then she smoothed her hair and smiled. "The bitch." "The monster." What a reputation Lady Darlington had in her own home.

As she started to undress to take a bath, she thought that, judging from her meeting with her yesterday, the reputation was more than well-deserved.

• • •

After she had unpacked, bathed, and put on a fresh uniform, at one o'clock she watched from her window the arrival of Lady Darlington. The Rolls-Royce had pulled up in front of the house, and Denby hopped out to hold the door as a small army of footmen, along with Mrs. Blaine, swarmed out of the house to the sidewalk for the ceremony. One footman seemed to have precedence over the others, and Margaret assumed this was the notorious Paul. From what she could see of him from the window, he was a husky six-footer with a handsome face. He leaned into the back of the car and, with some difficulty, hauled Lady Darlington out in his arms. She was wearing a lavender dress and a huge plumed hat that almost fell off as she was hoisted out of the Rolls. Hanging on to it with one hand, she tried to maintain a look of *sang-froid* as Paul carried her across the sidewalk past the line of footmen to the front door. She snapped something at Mrs. Blaine, who wrinkled her nose with obvious dislike and curtsied. Then she disappeared inside the house, the footmen in tow. It all looked so comical, with the haughty Lady Darlington bouncing in Paul's arms, that Margaret started to giggle. Then she wondered if Lady Darlington was carried everywhere by the footman, and if so, why? Certainly from what her husband had told her of her heart condition, it didn't sound so bad as to preclude her from walking. She thought probably it was a combination of laziness and hypochondriacal affectation, and she decided she would ask the doctor, when she met him, if there were any reason why the woman couldn't walk—if she could be coaxed into it. Then she settled herself in her armchair in front of the window to read the *Illustrated London News* and wait for the bell to ring.

It didn't ring until four o'clock, by which time Margaret had long since dozed off. When she heard its insistent jangle, she jumped out of her chair, smoothed her hair, and hurried to the door and out into the hall. She walked quickly to the end of the hall, but before she could reach the doors, they were opened by Paul. On closer view, she saw that he was in fact a handsome man, but he had an insolent look on his face to which she took an immediate dislike, though, from what she had been told of him by Mrs. Blaine, she was hardly predisposed to become his friend. "I'm Miss Suffield," she said.

"I know," he replied, blocking her way as he looked her over. "I'm Paul. We'll be working together."

"So I understand. Would you mind letting me through the door? Her Ladyship rang."

"What's the hurry? She just wants to talk to you. You're nice looking. Do you have a boyfriend?"

His English had a slight French accent.

"I don't think that's any of your business. Now please get out of the way."

He grinned and stepped aside, allowing her to get through the door, which she did as quickly as possible, deciding that now she definitely didn't like him. Inside the sitting room of the suite, she closed the door and looked around. It was a large room; on the opposite side was another door that was half open. "In here!" called Lady Darlington through the door. She crossed the sitting room, noticing that here, as in the bedroom in the country home, the tall casement windows were closed, although the curtains had been left open. Still, the room felt gloomy. And the richness of the furnishings seemed only to accentuate the gloom, as if they were opulent funerary ornaments in a Pharaonic tomb. The Aubusson carpet, writhing with flowers; the delicate Louis Seize furniture; the soft lavender paneling; the exquisite Coromandel screen; the crystal sconces on the marquetry escritoire; the two Watteaus on the walls; the room was a masterpiece of elegance as devoid of life as a fly in amber. She hurried through the door into the bedroom, which, like the first room, was furnished in the French style and was equally as gloomy—though here, the curtains were closed. Dominating everything was an enormous bed above which hung a huge Boucher depiction of some impossibly romantic bower through which a dimpled shepherdess was being chased by a young courtier. Beneath this sylvan scene sat, incongruously enough, Lady Darlington. She had on a clean bedjacket this time, and an elderly maid was curling her stringy hair with an electric curling iron. On a marbletopped table next to the bed was a lamp with a pink shade. Beside it stood a silver wine cooler in which was a bottle of champagne. Lady Darlington was sipping the wine from a tulip glass, and she seemed transformed from the ogress Margaret had met the previous day. She looked almost pleasant; Margaret suspected the sweetness was a by-product of the fermented grape.

"Ah, there you are!" she said. "Come in, come in. I see you've put on your uniform; don't you look smart. This wizened Cockney crone doing my hair is Maud. Maud, my new nurse, Margaret. Say something civil to her, Maud."

The maid, who was in fact quite wizened, grinned, revealing a mouth gleaming with gold inlays.

" 'Ow d'you do, mum."

"Maud is a witch," continued Lady Darlington. "So be nice to her, or she'll turn you into a toad. Pull up a chair, my dear, and sit down. I want to get to know you."

Margaret obeyed, pulling a chair next to the bed and sitting down. She felt on her guard, not trusting Lady Darlington's sudden friendliness.

"I must apologize for my behavior yesterday, but as I'm sure my husband told you, I'm subject to moods. It's nerves, of course, my wretched nerves, the constant pain I suffer . . ." She emptied the glass and refilled it from the bottle. "You must learn to put up with me, my dear, that's all there is to it. You'll find I'm really quite easy to get along with when I'm feeling good. That will do, Maud. Leave us now, before you set my hair on fire."

"Oh, milady, I'd never do no such thing!" protested Maud, removing the curling iron.

"You would and you have. Maud drinks gin when I'm not

looking, which is most of the time. She stumbles about glassy-eyed, breaking things, losing my jewelry . . . She's a wretched maid, and the only reason I keep her is she has a certain lapdog faithfulness. That will do, Maud."

"Yes, milady."

Maud gathered her haircurler and pins and scurried out of the room. When she had closed the door, Lady Darlington made a face.

"Loathesome woman," she said. "Do you drink, my dear?"

"I have an occasional sherry when I'm off duty."

"Ah yes, sherry, the 'respectable' beverage. I know several 'respectable' sherry-sippers, like Lady Jedburgh, who 'respectably' sips two bottles of sherry a day. Well, since you're bound to find out sooner or later, I might as well tell you now that I drink. My husband didn't tell you that, did he?"

"He mentioned it, yes."

"Oh? I'm surprised. The earl of Darlington, the brilliant young politician, the perfect English gentleman—he doesn't like people to know that his wife nips. But she does, she does." She sipped the champagne, eyeing Margaret over the rim of the glass. "You've met Paul?"

"Yes."

"Handsome, isn't he?"

"I didn't notice."

Lady Darlington chuckled.

"Of course, I forgot; you're the daughter of a vicar, and not interested in men. Well, for your information, he is quite handsome, which is one reason I hired him. Quite frankly, I like handsome men. I like to look at them, and any woman who pretends she doesn't is a liar." She smiled sweetly at Margaret, who didn't rise to the bait. "Paul also knows his wines. He tends my private cellar and steals some of my best vintages to sell—or drink himself. Oh, I know all about it. Paul is totally unprincipled, but it doesn't matter. I like him. He's a very important member of the household, and I would advise you to make friends with him."

"I hope to," she lied.

"So," continued Lady Darlington, draining her glass again, "What do you think of my husband?"

"I hardly know him, milady."

"Come now. You've met him. You've seen him. You've read about him. Surely you have an opinion?"

"Lord Darlington seems most kind and intelligent."

"Oh yes, he's an angel. A perfect darling, Darling Darlington! And intelligent, too. He's making a speech in the Lords this afternoon, and I'm sure it will be a wonderful speech. My husband always makes wonderful speeches, which always upset the other peers. My poor brother, for instance, is continually upset by Charles's speeches. He thinks he's a Liberal masquerading as a Conservative, which he is. Unfortunately for my brother, Charles is a good speaker, and Percy is a wretched one. Percy gets angry, and Charles is always cool. Except when he's around me. Then, as perhaps you noticed yesterday, he can get very angry indeed. It's amusing. He wants to head the foreign office, you know."

"No, I didn't know."

"Oh yes. Charles would much rather be prime minister, of course, and he might be, though it's difficult for a peer to become prime minister these days. But he'd settle for foreign secretary."

"I think he would make a very good prime minister or foreign secretary."

She drank more champagne.

"And what constitutes a 'good' prime minister?"

Margaret shifted uncomfortably.

"I'm not a political theorist."

"Anyone with a mouth is a political theorist these days. Tell me what you think."

"Well, I think a man who governs the country fairly is a good prime minister."

Lady Darlington snorted.

"That's a fine, no-opinion answer. I'll tell you what a good prime minister is: one that can hang on to power. Power, my dear! That's what it's all about. Balfour was all right—yes, he was all right—but he couldn't hang on to power. So now it's anyone's game in the Conservative party. My husband is the

Tories' leading young Liberal, which is a rather hermaphroditic position at best. My husband wants to bring the Tories closer to the little man and steal his vote away from the Liberals—though he'd make it all sound much loftier than that, talking about Disraeli and what-have-you. And he has considerable backing, too. He's good-looking, young, he speaks well, he mouths all the proper humanitarian platitudes, so the young Tories think he's god and he has become a power in the party. The old Tories, well, they don't like him; but they tell themselves he can't be too dangerous because he's rich and has a title. As if the earls of Darlington were anything! The first earl was nothing but a glorified tea merchant and land developer. But the idiots think he's 'safe'; so there's more than a sporting chance that if the Tories get back into power, my husband will get one of the richest plums. Unfortunately, there is one large, immovable obstacle in his path. Can you guess what that is, my dear?"

"I imagine it's Mr. Asquith, who seems fairly well-entrenched."

"Oh well, there's him, yes. But I mean if the Liberals ever get turned out."

"I have no idea."

Lady Darlington smiled and drained her glass.

"The obstacle is me."

Silence, as she pulled the bottle from the wine cooler and refilled the glass. Margaret thought she was well on her way to getting drunk. She wondered if she should try and stop her from drinking more, but she decided it would only cause an uproar, and not be successful.

"That shocks you, doesn't it?" went on Lady Darlington, sinking back in her pillows. "Most wives want to promote their husbands' careers. They work their ambitious little fingers to the bone to help him so they can bask in his reflected glory. But that strikes me as a cheap sort of glory. Very cheap. I don't suppose you can understand that, can you?"

"Milady," said Margaret, "I think perhaps you're telling me more than you should. I have no desire to know anything about Lord Darlington's career—"

"Liar!" shouted the older woman, bolting upright. "You're

dying to know! Don't try and fool me with this demure little goody-goody mask you wear; you're a snoop, you're going to pry every secret of this house out of me. And I know why. You're pretty and you think my husband may take an interest in you. Isn't that it? Admit it!"

Margaret stood up and looked coolly at her.

"It's not true. And I think there's little point in my staying here listening to this any longer. I'd suggest milady stop drinking if she wants me to chat with her. This is hardly my idea of a pleasant conversation."

Her patient glared at her a moment, then, as the alcoholic wind in her brain shifted, she tacked back toward the sun and smiled.

"Forgive me. Of course it's not true. You are the perfect embodiment of female Christian virtue, a lady with a lamp, and I've wronged you. I apologize. But sit down, my dear. Talk to me. I do so want to get to know you."

Margaret reluctantly sat down.

"Milady seems to be doing most of the talking. And I'll hardly have to 'pry' secrets out of you if you tell them to me point blank."

She chuckled.

"*Touché*. I do ramble on at times, I know. But I so want us to be friends." This last was almost a purr.

Margaret nodded her head with what she hoped was a degree of dignity.

"I hope we can be. But you must realize it will be impossible for us to be friends if you continue to attack my character. I don't claim to be the 'embodiment of female Christian virtue,' as I believe you called me; but on the other hand, I am neither a snoop nor a person of loose morals."

"Yes yes, I know," interrupted her patient. "And I've apologized. We'll forget I ever said it. Now, where was I? Oh yes: power. What life is all about: the ability to exert one's will on others. That *is* what life's all about, you know, though no one likes to admit it. It's too crude, too un-English. My family has had power for six centuries—six! Imagine it if you can, which you probably can't. For six hundred years the Cheyneys have had power. That's a long time to be important, my dear. It gives one a certain perspective, if you know what I mean. For instance, my family owned five castles and half a million acres—think of it! Half a million!—when the so-called Royal Family, those bug-eyed Hanoverian nobodies, were running around Germany in bearskins throwing spears. And the Tudors? Hah! A bunch of Welsh moneygrubbers. My family loaned them money to get them started, which they never paid back, I might add. No, when one is born a daughter of the duke of Suffolk, one can hardly hope to go higher. So the exercise of power, the true enjoyment of power, comes from preventing others from rising. Do you see what I mean?"

"I'm beginning to," said Margaret, quietly.

Lady Darlington smiled.

"I'm sure you do, my dear. I can tell you're swift. I'll admit," she added, a hint of melancholy coming into her hoarse voice, "that if I were able to have children, I might take a different view of things. But a capricious Mother Nature has denied me that pleasure; so what's left? Becoming the wife of a prime minister?" she made a face. "Anyone can be a prime minister these days. I, Lady Caroline Cheyney, should follow in the prissy footsteps of that tedious Mrs. Gladstone, or that ninny, Mrs. Disraeli? Not on your life. Or the wife of the foreign secretary, having to smile at hundreds of oleaginous ambassadors and their fat, foolish wives at reception after tedious reception? What a bore it would be. One would have to be so proper. The English expect their politicians to be proper, you know, so they can go on being improper." She lowered her voice and leaned forward. "But to *prevent* your husband from becoming prime minister or foreign secretary! Ah, there is the true exercise of power! There is the true pleasure! And I'm doing it, you see." She leaned back into her pillows again, smiling. "Oh, Charles could get away with an invalid wife who was sweet and charming. It would be a handicap, but he could get away with it. But an invalid wife like me, who is, alas, not charming? Who bites at people instead of meowing? Who drinks much more than is proper? No, he can't pull it off. The voters, the party potentates, the people who count: they'll never accept it. Caesar's wife must be charming, at the very least. So you see? I hardly ever leave my bed. I never entertain. I never go to the Palace, and I certainly never stand on campaign platforms and nod sweetly at the voters. But in my way, I exercise more power than all but a handful of women in London. And that, my dear, is what makes life bearable."

She drained her glass yet another time and reached for the bottle. It was empty.

"Lo, the miraculous pitcher runneth dry! Ring for Paul, will you? There's a good girl."

Margaret stood up, relieved to be able to get out of the chair. She went to the wall and pulled the bellcord, aware the older woman was watching her.

"Well?" she said. "Don't you have anything to say? No comment to make? I flatter myself that what I've just told you doesn't get said too often by the wives of ex-cabinet ministers. In fact, I rather fancy that it was almost deliciously malicious. And you have nothing to say at all?"

Margaret looked down at her.

"I don't think it's my business to make a comment."

"But make it your business, my dear. I invite you."

"Then I can only say that I would think your husband must resent your attitude?"

"*Resent* it?" She howled with laughter. "He hates me, you idiot! Oh, how he hates me! I stand in the way of everything he dreams of! But what can he do? Divorce me? Impossible. Even if he could get a divorce, he'd be ruined politically by it. Commit me to an institution? Oh, I'm sure he's thought of that. I'm sure he'd like to try. But you see, though I drink, I'm careful not to drink *that* much, and one doesn't commit a daughter of a duke unless she's an absolute raving loony. So what is there left for him but to muddle through in the time-honored English tradition?" She flicked the edge of her tulip glass, and the crystal rang like a tiny bell. She smiled. "And that, pert Margaret, is my pleasure, and my revenge."

"Revenge for what?"

To her surprise, the woman's face went very white, as if she were remembering something frightening. She closed her eyes tight, and for several seconds she said nothing. Then she said, almost inaudibly, "For all the pain."

That was all she said, but Margaret wondered if she meant the pain of the miscarriage. He had said it had been the beginning of her "troubles," and though it seemed totally irrational for her to blame him for that, in Lady Darlington's alcohol-muddled brain, rationality must have been at a premium. For a moment, she almost felt sorry for the woman. Then Lady Darlington's eyes opened and she snapped, "Well? What are you standing there for? Go find Paul! Tell him to bring me a bottle of the Perrier-Jouet ninety-three. Go on! Hurry!"

Margaret walked with deliberate slowness out of the room, no longer feeling sorry for her. Nor did she wish to become the go-between in the middle of the Lady Darlington–Paul axis. So when she saw Maud in the sitting room, she told her to go find the footman. Then she returned to her own room and sat down in her armchair to think. Her conversation with Lady Darlington had left her in an angry frame of mind. The woman was so perverse and so incredibly unfair to her husband! Whatever was the basis for her desire to ruin his career, Margaret wondered if she might not be able to root out the trouble and change her attitude. It was, admittedly, probably wishful thinking.

But she thought she would try, anyway.

• • •

At six o'clock, just as the lamps were being lighted on the square, someone knocked on the door of her sitting room. She answered it to find Paul standing in the hall. His elaborate yellow-and-gray livery looked neat, but his white footman's wig was slightly askew, and she could smell the stale odor of wine on him. She thought he must have been down in the cellar "testing" his employer's better vintages. Between him and Lady Darlington, she could see why Mrs. Blaine had said the house had turned into a winery.

"He wants to see you in the Red Room," said Paul.

"Who?"

"The mighty earl, who else? Milord. His Worship. The great Pooh-Bah. The doctor's here and wants to talk to you." He crossed his arms and leaned against the door. "You're the best-looking nurse we've had here, and we've had plenty. Do you like wine?"

"Not as well as you do, apparently."

"I've got a bottle of Lafitte-Rothschild up in my room on the top floor. Third door to the left from the stairs. Why don't you come up tonight and share it with me? We could have a nice talk, and I'll tell you all about the stinking English aristocracy. Or maybe you don't think they stink? Maybe you're a title-worshiper?"

She started to say she thought it hypocritical of him to attack the class he fed off and stole from, but decided not to provoke him into a political argument.

"I'd say offhand you're the one who stinks. And you seem to be getting in a bad habit of blocking my way. Would you mind standing aside, please?"

He didn't move.

"That's what she tells me. She says I stink. She thinks everybody who isn't a duke is dirt. Did you know that?"

She was becoming annoyed.

"Please get out of the way."

He grinned.

"I'm getting to like you more every minute. How about it? Will you come up to my room?"

"No."

"Why? Afraid? Or are you being loyal to your boyfriend?"

She decided the best way to handle him was to play games.

"Yes, it's my boyfriend."

"So you *do* have one? What's he like?"

"Well, he's older. And a bit fat. And terribly rich."

"That's nice. I mean, that he's rich. I'd like to be rich."

"Who wouldn't?"

"Do you and he . . ." He wiggled his hand suggestively. "You know."

"Oh, every night, at least."

He looked genuinely surprised.

"Every night?"

"That's right. He sends around his carriage and they take me to the Palace."

He blinked with confusion.

"The Palace?"

"Didn't you know? I'm the king's mistress."

She smiled prettily at him and gave him a gentle shove, moving him out of the way. Then she pushed by him and into the hall and walked quickly toward the stairs. When she reached them, she looked back. He was watching her with an amused expression. She knew the Swiss footman was going to be a problem.

She walked down the stairs to the entrance hall and went into the Red Room, where the earl was talking with a portly, bearded man dressed, like Lord Darlington, in a frock coat with a white carnation boutonnière, razor-creased striped pants, and spats. He looked every inch the successful Harley Street doctor and even before the earl introduced him, she knew he was Sir Andrew Hodge.

"Yes, I've heard of you, Miss Suffield," said Sir Andrew, who spoke with a slight Scot burr. "Charlie, this lass is one of the best nurses in London. And surely one of the prettiest."

"Sit down, Miss Suffield," said Lord Darlington, and Margaret noted he was careful not to call her by her first name in front of the doctor. "Sir Andrew will tell you what's wrong with my wife. Medically, that is," he added drily. "We won't get into the other problems."

Margaret sat down near the mantel as Sir Andrew cleared his throat.

"Now, Miss Suffield, there's precious little for you to do here. You'll find this is as easy a position as you've ever had, as far as your nursing duties are concerned, though Caroline's not an easy patient to get along with, as you've probably found out already. Basically, what she has is an irregular heartbeat, or what Sir James MacKenzie calls auricular fibrillation. You must check her pulse three times a day. If it's near normal, give her five minims of tincture of digitalis in the morning; this will keep it low. If it starts up, increase the dosage to ten minims four times a day until it goes down again. If it's highly irregular, or if the irregularity continues for more than a day, call me. Also, keep a chart of her pulse and show it to me when I drop around each Wednesday for my regular visit. Beyond that, there's not much to do except keep an eye on her. She's not going to get any better, particularly the way she drinks. And we must try to keep her from getting unduly excited, though I'll admit that's difficult with her temper. And that's about all I can think of. Do you have any questions?"

"Yes," said Margaret. "I see she's carried around by her footman. Is there any reason she can't walk?"

"None at all, except she's kept to her bed for so long now, it would probably take her a while to get her muscles toned up. I've told her a hundred times she should get up, but she won't have any part of it. She likes to sit in her bed and play queen-empress, and unfortunately for her own health, there's no law that says we can make her get out of it."

"I told Lord Darlington I disapprove of her habits," said Margaret, "and if you agree, I'd like to try and convince her to change them."

The doctor chuckled.

"I wouldn't even bother to try. You're a fine lass to want to, but you won't have any luck. Caroline's blissfully happy the way she is, making herself and everyone around her miserable as sin. And she won't change. Charlie, if there's nothing else you want from me, I'm off to the club for dinner and then to bed. I have to run out to Windsor in the morning and look at old General Kirkland. His horse threw him into a briar patch and he broke his hip. After forty years in the army, it's the first time he's been wounded. There's a moral there somewhere, but I'll be damned if I know what it is."

The earl thanked him and accompanied the doctor out to the hall. Then he came back into the Red Room and closed the door. Margaret had stood up, but he motioned to her to be seated.

"Don't leave," he said, coming over to the Adam mantel. "I want to hear how you're getting along with your patient. Did Mrs. Blaine get you settled?"

"Oh yes. She's very nice. She took me on a tour of the house, which is beautiful."

He stuck his hands in the pockets of his striped trousers and looked around the room. "Yes, it's a beautiful house. When I was a child, it used to be a happy house as well. It's not any more, unfortunately, and I think you know why." He smiled slightly. "My father, about thirty years ago, bought some jewels from the former French empress—this was shortly after the Prussian War, and Eugénie needed some cash. There's a tiara and matching necklace which have a number of handsome emeralds in them. Well, the story was that the emeralds had been stolen from an Indian temple, or some such nonsense, and they brought a curse to the owner. I don't put much stock in curses, though I'll admit Eugénie didn't have such good luck. But now that my wife has them, I'm beginning to believe in curses. I suppose you think it's ungallant of me to talk this way about my wife?"

"I might have before this afternoon."

"What happened this afternoon?"

She told him of her conversation with his wife, and as he listened a look of disgust came over his face. When she had finished, he said, "Like everything Caroline says, it's part fact and part fantasy. It's true I'm politically ambitious. It's also true she's a millstone around my neck. Politics is a social profession, to a certain extent, and it would be a help to me if she entertained. As far as my becoming foreign secretary goes, it's almost out of the question as long as she's my wife. Foreign secretaries simply don't have wives whose specialties are insults and drink. As far as my being a Liberal masquerading as a Conservative, that's only half true also. Oh, her brother, the duke—who incidentally is equally as arrogant as Caroline, though he's not as bright as she, and she *is* bright—Percy has called me everything from a Socialist to a radical, which, considering the way I live, is absurd. I like being an earl, and I like being rich, and I'd be hypocritical if I said I didn't. I also think the nobility has done a great deal of good for the country over the years. I think, as a class, our standards of behavior are surprisingly high, though they're not as high as they used to be. I think we tend to hold society together, even though we're prone to all the usual human faults of snobbery and clannishness. But I'm not a fool. I realize there's terrible poverty in England, and that while a few of us live like grandees, the majority can barely keep their heads above water. I also realize the House of Lords is an archaic political institution whose days are literally numbered. Mr. Asquith and Mr. Lloyd George are being very cautious now, but I have it on good authority that next spring they're going to introduce a budget with new taxes the Lords aren't going to like, and I think it very likely will bring about a confrontation between the two houses. I don't like confrontations, but I believe in the way our political institutions have developed, and if Percy and the other reactionary peers try to fight the Commons, I'll fight *them*." He paused. "It seems I'm always fighting the Cheyneys, doesn't it? If I'm not fighting Caroline at home, I'm fighting her brother in Parliament. I think I'll buy some more emeralds and put a curse on the whole clan. By the way, what makes you think you can change Caroline? In my opinion, she's as unmovable as the Rock of Gibralter, and twice as formidable."

"She's certainly formidable. I just feel if I could somehow, well, open the windows and bring in a little fresh air, she might change. I don't mean literally open the windows, though that would be a beginning. But mentally. She's just so closed in!"

"She's created a world of her own that's half alcohol, a quarter self-inflation, and quarter self-pity."

"Yes, that seems true. She talked about her family as if they were gods. But then, at the end, she became almost maudlin. Might I ask you a personal question?"

He looked at her cautiously.

"What is it?"

"She said she wanted to 'revenge' herself on you. She said it was for the 'pain' you'd caused her, and I had the impression she was referring to her miscarriage. Is it possible she blames that on you? I know it's absurd, but . . ."

She stopped. The normally phlegmatic earl was staring at her, and he looked enraged. She started to stammer an apology, and then he cut her off. "That's another of her damned fantasies."

There was an embarrassed silence which was mercifully broken by Rogers, who came into the room and announced dinner. The earl calmed down. Then, to her surprise, he turned to her and said, "Would you care to dine with me?"

It was an unusual request, since she had eaten lunch with Mrs. Blaine and Rogers in the pantry, which was where she had assumed she would be taking all her meals. But after a moment, she decided there was no point in refusing. Besides, she wanted to dine with him. Standing up, she smiled and said, "I'd be delighted to."

"Good. Rogers, set another place at the table. At my right, not at the end. I don't have a megaphone."

Rogers, looking rather startled, nodded and mumbled, "Very good, milord." Then he left the room.

The earl's composure returned.

"We have an excellent chef, so I don't think you'll be disappointed in the food. Oh, by the way," he pulled an envelope from his coat pocket, "here's a check for forty-five guineas. I thought you'd like to have your first quarterly payment in advance."

He held out the envelope to her.

"You will stay, I hope? Or is Caroline too much to put up with?"

"She's too much to put up with," she said. Then she smiled and took it. "But I'll stay."

"Well then, shall we go in?"

• ● •

Whatever the faults of the Edwardian establishment, few would deny that it acted out its role against a setting of incomparable elegance. And as the earl led Margaret into the dining room, even though the young nurse was becoming accustomed to his opulent way of life, her breath was fairly taken away by the sheer gorgeousness of the room. Down the center of the table marched a set of six Lamerie silver candlesticks whose lights, along with the candles on the sideboard and in the sconces beside the bow window at the end of the room, softly illuminated the gray walls and lent a flickering life to the niched gods and goddesses who watched, with blank eyeballs, the two diners as they were seated by the liveried footmen. In the center of the table stood a massive bouquet of red and yellow tulips, colors that were echoed on the sideboard by the Sèvres service plates, which had been made for Catherine the Great and bought by the earl's father at Sotheby's. The meal was untypical in that it was light, consisting of a consommé, lamb chops, fresh asparagus, and a custard. It was served silently and expertly by the footmen under the watchful eye of Rogers, who poured the Chambertin, Clos de Bèze, whispering the wine and the year in Margaret's ear as he poured, such being the charming custom. The ritual was stately and, at the same time, made informal by the earl, who sat at the end of the table and kept up a run of conversation. He told a joke about the prime minister's outspoken wife, Margot Asquith. He told how a whiskey baron had switched political parties to try to become a whiskey viscount. He told about the struggle to pass the Education Bill six years before, and the struggle currently going on in the Lords to pass the Old Age Pension Bill. He told how the former first lord of the admiralty had gone insane. He explained how one made polite one-sided conversation with the queen, who was deaf. He told about the king's mistress, Mrs. Keppel, and the court, where now, in contrast to the Victorian court, anything went as long as appearances were kept up and one were rich. He talked about the king's distrust of intellectuals and love of money. He talked about India, which England had united, at least superficially, but where in his opinion English snobbery and racial prejudice were alienating the maharajas as well as the Untouchables. He talked about the Germans, whom he distrusted, the French, whom he liked, and the Italians, whom he loved. He talked a river, and as Margaret listened, she thought how long the river must have been dammed as he dined in the enormous room night after night by himself, and she began to understand why he had asked her to eat with him. She also began to appreciate how damaging Lady Darlington's self-imposed isolation was to him. As he had said, politics was a social profession. The great parties in the great London houses provided a setting for deal-making and politicking, participation in which was perhaps not indispensable to an ambitious man, but exclusion from which was certainly a handicap. The earl would go to the parties alone. But as long as Darlington House remained empty, he was slowly using up his social capital.

When the dinner was finished, they went back into the Red Room for coffee. Then he said, "All right, I've gone on long enough. Now it's your turn. Tell me about yourself."

"I'm afraid that would be a disappointment," she said, "after what I've been listening to."

"You're underrating yourself. Speechmaking is part of my profession, and I need my stock of jokes and anecdotes, just like a music-hall comedian, to keep my audience awake. I'm sure you've some good stories about Mrs. Porter and Lady Millington. Or maybe it's professionally indiscreet to talk about your ex-patients?"

"Well, it is, but . . ."

"That makes it all the better. For example, Lady Millington's son?"

She stirred her coffee and smiled.

"He *is* a bit of a wild man."

"Did he try to make love to you?"

"You're being as bad as your wife."

"I know. I apologize. Did he?"

She couldn't resist him.

"He certainly did!" she said. "He practically attacked me in the kitchen!"

"Was he drunk?"

"As a lord. Oh—well, let's say he was very drunk."

He looked amused.

"I admire your tact. Go on."

"Well, I was making a pot of tea in the kitchen one day when he came reeling in and lurched at me."

"Aha! And how did you fend him off?"

"I ran."

"Always a good tactic. Did he chase you?"

She started laughing as she nodded.

"Around the kitchen table. He was whooping and howling, and the cook, poor woman, dived under the table. She was scared to death."

"And were you?"

"Of him? Not a bit. Finally, I got so angry I grabbed a frying pan and started chasing him. And that was the last time he tried any tricks with me."

"It sounds like an elegant romance. Tell me some more. Do you like sports? Besides running around kitchen tables, that is."

"I used to ride when I was a girl."

"Then you'll enjoy the country. My father built up quite a stable at Ellendon Abbey. He was a great racing fan, though his horses never won anything. I sold off most of them, but I still have a few good mounts you'll be able to ride. Do you play tennis?"

"No."

"Maybe I can teach you. My neighbor, General Carew, has a good court. How about music? Do you like it?"

"My father made me take piano lessons, but I'm tone-deaf."

"So much for music. Books? Do you read a lot?"

"Oh yes, but I'm afraid my literary taste isn't what one might call 'elevated.' I like romances."

"And I like adventure stories, so so much for elevated literary tastes. Incidentally, the library's full of wonderfully trashy novels in expensive bindings, so feel free to help yourself. How about the theater? Do you enjoy it?"

Her face lit up.

"I adore the theater! I love to see plays, particularly sad ones. I love to cry."

He laughed.

"Then I take it you don't like Mr. Shaw's plays?"

"Well, he's very witty, isn't he? But the actors all *talk* so much."

"Incessantly, like me tonight. Which reminds me that I've taken far too much of your time, as well as my own. My private secretary, Peter Sims, is dropping by to go over some papers with me, so I'll have to excuse myself. Oh, by the way, I have a ticket to the Haymarket this Friday night. I won't be able to use it—I have another engagement—and since you enjoy plays, perhaps you'd like to have it? They're doing a revival of *The*

Second Mrs. Tanqueray, so you can have a good cry. Friday is your first night off, and I imagine you'll be more than glad to get out of the house."

"Well, if you're sure you won't use it?"

"Positive. I'll have Rogers give it to you in the morning." He set down his coffee cup and came over to her. To her surprise, he took her hand. "I've enjoyed myself tonight more than I have in months," he said, quietly. "I want to thank you for a perfect evening."

"There's nothing to thank me for," she said, feeling awkward. "All I did was listen."

"That's considerably more than my wife has ever done."

He looked at her a moment. Then he released her hand and walked out of the room.

• • •

She soon settled into the routine of her new job, and, as Sir Andrew had predicted, it was professionally untaxing. Each morning at eight she went into Lady Darlington's room to take her pulse and administer the digitalis. Lady Darlington wasn't at her best in the morning, if she was ever at her best. She would be hung over, sitting up in her bed drinking hot cocoa and reading the *Times*. To Margaret's attempts at civil communication she would do little more than grunt a "yes" or "no" or "be quiet," and Margaret quickly learned to obey the last injunction. Maud would hover near the bed, straightening a loose corner, refilling the cocoa cup, and occasionally humming a snatch of a music-hall tune to herself until her mistress growled a terse "Maud!" Some mornings, Paul would be present, standing near the bed with his arms folded like a janissary guarding the sultan's throne, eyeing Margaret as she performed her morning ritual. Then she would go back to her room and wait for the summons that more often than not never came. She would check her patient's pulse again at noon, and later at four. Occasionally, Lady Darlington would ring for her during the day to issue a curt order for something trivial or complain about nonexistent drafts. Aside from that, during the first week she seemed to want to see as little of her new nurse as Margaret wanted to see of her. Margaret guessed the reason was that she didn't want to have her drinking interfered with. Whatever the reason, it was a relief, though it gave her little opportunity of "improving" the woman, a project which she began to realize would be more difficult than she imagined. It was apparent that Lady Darlington's way of life suited her perfectly. Besides, Margaret's mind was preoccupied with someone else: Lord Darlington.

After that first evening, she had seen nothing of him, to her acute disappointment. She read in the papers about the debate in the House of Lords over the Old Age Pension Bill, and saw his name mentioned in connection with the fight, so she assumed that was what was taking his time. But she wished the fight would be settled so he could spend more time at home.

She was surprised, and not altogether pleased, to find that she missed him.

• • •

She banked the advance of forty-five guineas he had given her, then sent a check for twenty pounds to Jenkins and Hawkes, the solicitors who were handling the settlement of her father's estate. She had whittled the debt down to eight hundred pounds, but it was slow going and sometimes she wished she had taken the solicitors' advice and allowed them to file for bankruptcy, which would have relieved her of paying off the debt. But she had decided against it, even though it was a severe drain on her finances and would remain so for a long time. It left her with little money for clothes, or anything else. And that Friday night as she put on her one good dress, a yellow one on which she had splurged five guineas the previous Christmas as a present to herself, she ruefully thought of the clothes she could have bought with the twenty pounds. She certainly would have liked to buy a new dress to wear to the theater, but it couldn't be helped. The money had to be paid.

She took a cab to the Haymarket. It was a bad night, raining heavily, but she didn't mind. As Lord Darlington had said, she was delighted to get out of the house after five days and nights, and she was excited at the prospect of going to the theater. The

London streets were slick and the water reflected the lights of the carriages, hackneys, and automobiles. When they turned into Leicester Square, the pavements blazed with the reflected lights of the theater marquees, creating a Whistlerian nocturne of yellows, blues, and whites. She loved London. She loved it by day, particularly in the spring, when every parish from Bloomsbury to Ilford was a dream of lilac and jasmine, and Kensington Gardens were drenched with color. But night in London was like night in no other city in the world. Night gave it mystery and a special vibrant beauty. There were, of course, so many Londons by night: the West End night with its theaters and posh restaurants; the Clapham Common night, with its thousands of tired working-class people either dozing before their fires or swilling ale at the local pub; the Limehouse night with its Oriental aura of exotic evil and its unexotic opium dens peopled by the thousands of Asians drawn to the capital of the British Empire for a try at the better life. There were the artists in Chelsea, the Russians in Stepney, the Jews in Whitechapel, the French in Old Compton Street, the bashers in Hoxton, all creating their own unique London nights, each night adding its thread to the tapestry of imperial splendor, disgusting squalor, middle-class coziness and hypocrisy, dirt, smells, light, excitement, and beauty that were London in 1908. She loved it. And as she got out of the cab and mingled with the well-dressed crowd going into the Haymarket, the men in their dress suits, the women with their egrets and opera toques—there was a law against wearing large hats in the theater—their cloaks and fur jackets and jewels, she decided, with a rush of national pride, that London was without a doubt the greatest city in the world.

• • •

When she came out of the theater, her eyes red from crying, it had stopped raining. She made her way through the crowd to the curb to hail a cab when a man came up and took her arm. It was Lord Darlington.

"I have a cab over here," he said, leading her down the pavement. "Did you like the play?"

"Very much," she said, wondering why he had come.

"Did you cry?"

"Of course."

"I hope you're hungry?"

"I had dinner . . ."

"You're going to have another with me."

They reached a hackney and he opened the door for her. As she climbed in, he said to the driver, "Clerkenwell Road. There's a restaurant there called the Petrarch."

"Right, guvnor."

He climbed in beside her as the cab clattered into the street.

"I have a very un-English love of Italian food," he said, "which I acquired when my parents took me to Florence when I was ten. You can keep all the chops, steaks, and kippers in England; give me a bowl of pasta and glass of Soave and I'm in heaven. Surprised to see me?"

"Yes, milord, I am."

"You know, I think titles are rather pleasant. They provide a romantic link with our historic past, and they secure one excellent service in restaurants and shops. But under the circumstances, I think you can call me Charlie. Not around others, mind, but when we're alone."

She gathered up her courage and said, "What are the circumstances?"

He smiled at her.

"Why, I'm falling in love with you, of course."

She thought she would faint. Instead, she remained surprisingly calm.

"Why?"

"Why? Because you're lovely and charming and available and I'm lonely."

"What makes you think I'm 'available'?"

"I meant in the sense of being near. And if you don't show a little more enthusiasm, I think I probably will stop falling in love with you."

She glanced at him. "I'm sorry. It's just that I'm frightened."

"Don't be. There's no reason to be afraid of an honest declaration."

He reached over and took her hand. She liked having him hold it; but she was still afraid.

• • •

The heart of Italian London was Eyre Street Hill and Clerkenwell Road. Here, near St. John's Gate where Goldsmith and Isaak Walton had lived and which had been the gatehouse of the priory of St. John of Jerusalem, around which the village of Clerkenwell had developed, was the Italian church; the clock and watch shops; the street-organ warehouses where the poor could hire a street organ for the day, month, or year; tenements; bakeries, with their windows filled with delicious-looking pannetonnes; an H. J. Heinz 57 Varieties warehouse; and seemingly endless numbers of small restaurants, the best of which, in Charlie's opinion, was the Petrarch. "It's never going to win a prize for its décor," he whispered to Margaret as he led her into the tiny room filled with wooden tables and the marvelous smell of cheese, "but Luigi's a great man, and his wife is the best cook this side of Brillat-Savarin. Ah, Luigi! *Como e va?*"

The proprietor was a jovial man who, judging from his girth, loved his food as much as his customers did. He beamed as he pumped Lord Darlington's hand.

"Milord Darlington!" he boomed, then shouted to the kitchen at the rear of the room, "Mama, look who's here!"

An equally fat woman leaned out of the kitchen and blew the earl a kiss.

"The good veal tonight!" she called.

"Bravo!" said Charlie, hanging his top hat on a wall peg. "Mamma's veal is . . ." and he kissed his fingers to the air. Luigi led them through the diners to a corner table which held a candle in a wax-dripped Chianti bottle. Margaret noticed that a few of the diners stared at the "milord" in the tail coat, but apparently Lord Darlington was a sufficiently frequent customer so that most of the clientele ignored him. Luigi seated them, saying. "I bring you a bottle of Soave, eh? Nice and chilled? The lady likes Soave?"

"I've never had it," smiled Margaret, removing her gloves.

"You have not lived! I bring it right away. Then you order, all right?"

"Fine."

Luigi went to the kitchen, and Lord Darlington leaned his arms on the table.

"While you were weeping at the Haymarket, I was having the pleasure of seeing the Old Age Pension Bill finally pass the Lords."

"Congratulations."

"Getting the noble peers to pass anything is a minor miracle, but getting them to pass this one is something of a triumph. My brother-in-law, the duke, nearly had apoplexy. I had the distinct pleasure of having him call me a bastard. It was the pleasantest moment of my life. Or rather, the second pleasantest. The most pleasant was when I met you. Are you still frightened?"

"Yes. Terrified."

"Don't be. Love affairs can be brutal, or beautiful. I have a feeling ours is going to be the latter."

"I've never had a love affair, and I'm not sure I want one. Even with you."

"Then I'll have to make you sure. I look forward to the effort." He smiled. "Ah, here's the wine."

Luigi uncorked the bottle and poured some of the white wine into Charlie's glass. He tasted it.

"Superb. Luigi, Miss Suffield has never dined here, so what should we give her? The veal Parmigiana, since Mama says the veal is good tonight?"

"It's not good, it's beautiful!" enthused Luigi, filling the glasses.

"Then veal it is. And an antipasto."

Luigi left them, and he raised his glass.

"To us. And your first love affair."

She drank the toast, but uncertainly. She was, after all, frightened, frightened and confused. She suspected she did love him, that it probably had begun in a romantic sense when she saw him galloping across the green fields of Kent, but had developed more substantially as she'd come to know him. But did she want to enter into what his wife had called a "backstairs liaison"? She thought of herself as a respectable woman; more important to her was her self-respect. Could she respect herself if she allowed the husband of her patient to make love to her? Did she want to join that vast army of unconnected women in the middle of the Edwardian hierarchy, the hundreds of nurses, maids, and secretaries who gave up their sacrosanct virtue to become the mistresses of their employers? Some day she wanted a husband and a family, and chastity was something men expected in their brides. She was chaste; there had been opportunities, but she had held to her virtue with the special determination of a clergyman's daughter. And now, Charlie—this beautiful, charming, lovable man sitting across from her, who had probably had dozens of women—wanted to make love to her. Even worse, she wanted him to do so.

She set down her glass.

"I think, milord—"

"Charlie."

"Charlie." How odd it sounded! "I think I had better give you my notice."

"Why? Because I'm a married man and you don't want to become involved in a messy triangle?"

"Yes. Do you blame me?"

"No. I know what you're thinking, and I respect you for it. If you were a tart, I wouldn't love you. But you're not. You're a respectable nurse who's being rushed into something by your over-impetuous employer, and I'm probably a fool to rush you. But I hate dishonesty. And I'd be dishonest if I tried to pretend I didn't feel love for you."

"But you hardly know me!"

"I know you well enough. Besides, as a confirmed romantic, I've always believed in love at first sight—or at least second sight. I'm lonely. I think by now you know enough about my life to know how lonely I am. I have a wife, but I have none of the advantages of marriage and all the disadvantages. I not only don't love my wife, I detest her—and she detests me. You've seen what kind of home I have. It's a vast, elegant mausoleum filled with empty rooms and empty bottles. And now you've brought something into it. Some warmth and life and beauty. I *want* to love you, to do things for you and with you. I want to enjoy you. I'm not going to chase you around the kitchen table, like Lady Millington's son, and I think I can keep the triangle from becoming oppressive. I don't expect you to do something you're going to be ashamed of. When it happens—if it happens—it will occur naturally. But meanwhile, I want to make you love me. And you will, you know. I can be irresistable when I put my mind to it."

"You already are. You know that. But Lady Darlington—"

"To hell with Lady Darlington."

She was startled by the harshness of his tone. She saw Luigi coming toward them with the antipasto.

"Will you let me run things my way?" he asked. "Will you trust me, at least for a while?"

She nodded.

"Good. And here's the antipasto. *E molto bello*, Luigi. *Bellissimo!*"

• • •

They stayed in the restaurant till one thirty; when they finally left, he sent her home in a cab by herself. She knew why, even though he said nothing. They couldn't afford to be seen coming home together. It was a subterfuge, just as going to a restaurant in a remote part of London where there was no chance of meeting any of his acquaintances was a subterfuge. The whole affair was clandestine from the start, doomed by its very nature to be clandestine. Was she out of her mind even considering such a relationship? As if the dalliances of the nobility weren't stock music-hall jokes! Did she think there could be any possible conclusion to it other than her being hurt in one way or another, and his walking away, on to the next conquest? And yet, and yet, there *was* something different. Why should he speak of love if all he wanted was to make love? And even if that were part of the stock dialogue, could he be such a good actor as to make dissembled feelings sound so convincing? Even more, would he run the enormous risk of making love to his wife's nurse, who was living under the same roof? If it were only a physical relationship he was after, why run any risk at all when such places as St. John's Wood were so convenient and safe? Maybe he *was* in love with her. She could believe it. Or did she merely want to believe it? She didn't know. She was miserable; and yet at the same time she readily admitted to being happier than ever before in her life.

The cab deposited her in front of Darlington House, and after paying the fare, she walked around to the servants' entrance at the side, since the front entrance was bolted after midnight. She unlocked the door and let herself into the big kitchen. The lights were on. Paul was sitting at the kitchen table drinking beer. He was in his shirtsleeves, and his footman's wig was off. He looked at her.

"Cinderella's late," he said. "It's past midnight, and her coach has turned into a pumpkin. How were things at the Palace?"

"Very nice," she said, starting across the room, trying to keep as far from him as she could without making it appear she was afraid of him. "The king was in a rare mood. We drank champagne and had a jolly old time."

"The king's in Paris, so a little bird tells me you were out with somebody else. Now who could that be?"

"If your little bird were accurate, it would tell you I went to the theater by myself."

"And stayed out till quarter of two in the morning? It must have been a long play."

She tried not to show her nervousness.

"I went to supper afterward."

"Who with?"

"By myself, of course."

"I don't believe you."

She was almost to the door, but this stopped her. She came over to the zinc-topped table and confronted him, deciding it was best to have it out with him now.

"Paul, I know I'm supposed to be nice to you. But frankly, I dislike you, and I can't be nice to people I dislike. I don't like your sneering implications about my private life, which is none of your business· and I'll thank you not to address me from now on unless it is something concerning Lady Darlington."

His face broke into a slow grin.

"But your private life *does* concern Lady Darlington. And her husband."

"What do you mean by that?"

He spread his hands. "Whatever you think it means."

He was watching her with that suggestive smile, and she was terrified he knew. But he couldn't. It was impossible.

"I think it means you have nothing better to do than bother women who wouldn't dream of having anything to do with you —a category that prominently includes me. Good night."

She started to turn when he leaned forward and grabbed her wrist. Just as quickly, she slapped him with her free hand, using all her strength. He yelped, let go of her hand and sank back in his chair, holding his cheek. Then he looked up at her and grinned.

"A fighter, aren't you? I like that."

"Don't *ever* do that again!"

"Oh, but I will. And eventually you won't fight back so hard. Paul always gets what he wants, sooner or later."

"Good Lord, you're conceited! Why, I couldn't imagine."

He shrugged. "Because some day I'm going to be a very important man."

"Oh? Are you going to buy the Kimberley gold mine?"

"My opportunity will come. Meanwhile, I'll keep working away at you."

She turned and walked out of the kitchen, trying to look cool. But when she reached her room and removed her gloves, her hands were trembling violently.

• • •

She didn't sleep all night. She lay in bed thinking of Lord Darlington, of Lord Darlington alone, Lord Darlington and herself, Lord Darlington's wife, his wife's footman—everything in her world was becoming a refraction of him. At one point she told herself that was probably one definition of love, but that was small comfort. She was certain Paul suspected something. It mattered little that she hadn't even kissed Lord Darlington . . .

Charlie (she still felt awkward even thinking of him by the familiar name). There were still grounds for suspicion; and if Paul suspected, he would tell Lady Darlington.

She tossed and turned, agonized by the prospect of facing the ogress in this new and damning position. She kept telling herself she was imagining things and that Paul knew nothing, but her guilts and fears denied it. By eight o'clock, when she went into Lady Darlington's room to take her morning pulse and administer the daily dosage of digitalis, she was in such a state of exhaustion she almost didn't care what happened. She had seen her reflection in her mirror and knew that the strain and the sleepless night were showing, which didn't help her confidence. For once, she thought she looked less healthy than her patient.

She was sitting in bed reading the *Times* as usual when Margaret came into the room. Maud was there; fortunately, Paul wasn't. Lady Darlington gave no indication of behaving any differently from any other morning. Margaret came over to the bed, said good morning, and took her pulse. Lady Darlington sipped her cocoa and said nothing. Then she gave her the digitalis. Still nothing. The ritual finished, Margaret started for the door, her spirits beginning to pick up. She was at the door when her patient spoke.

"Margaret?"

She turned.

"Yes?"

"I understand you went to the theater last night."

She tensed.

"Yes."

"What did you see?"

"A revival of *The Second Mrs. Tanqueray*."

"A tedious play. Pinero is such a third-rate playwright, don't you think?"

"I found the play enjoyable."

"Indeed. Did you by any chance see my husband at the theater? I believe he was going to attend the play himself last night."

"Lord Darlington gave me his ticket, milady. He was unable to attend. It was most kind of him."

"Ah, I see. By the way, Paul tells me you came in after midnight. Well after midnight, in fact. I needn't remind you that on Fridays you have from noon till midnight, not noon till quarter of two. I am by nature a lenient employer, but with the enormous salary you're paid, I don't much like being taken advantage of. You will see it doesn't happen again."

They stared at each other across the room. Then Margaret nodded her head slightly.

"I'll pay more attention to the time from now on."

"See that you do." She picked up the *Times* again, and then made a parting shot: "You see, my dear, I'm keeping my eye on you."

She said nothing more, and Margaret left the room. It had all been very quiet, without her usual histrionics, and Margaret couldn't be sure what it meant. But she thought Lady Darlington and Paul were playing a game with her. They were perhaps not certain; they would toy with her for a while, letting the game progress.

It was called cat-and-mouse. And there was little question as to who was the cat, and who the mouse.

• • •

She even began to wonder if Charlie were playing a game with her also.

He stayed away the entire weekend. True, Mrs. Blaine told her he had gone to a houseparty in the country at Lord Salisbury's, making it a political weekend, but still if he were as in love with her as he had said at the Petrarch, wouldn't he have found some excuse to stay home? Or was she being impossibly vain, thinking her charms would prove more attractive to him than those of the politically powerful Cecil family? It was a rainy weekend, and as she stared out the water-streaked windows of her room looking at the gray sky, she became more and more depressed. She began to wonder if Friday night had really happened, or if it had been a fantasy on her part. After all, it seemed so unlikely that a man like Lord Darlington would fall so precipitously in love with his wife's private nurse that he would take the risks he was taking. And yet it *had* happened. But where was he now?

Her depression wasn't helped by Lady Darlington, who was in a foul mood the entire weekend. She yelled at Margaret every time she was summoned into the room, telling her she was incompetent and lazy, as if going out of her way to make life miserable for her nurse. Margaret bore it as stoically as possible, although by Sunday night she was contemplating throwing it all up and quitting. Only the thought of Charlie prevented her from doing it; but why didn't he come home?

The next morning, Monday, her misery was alleviated by a pleasant surprise, although it was one that made her realize she was becoming even more enmeshed in her compromising relationship with her employer. At ten o'clock, Mrs. Blaine knocked on the door of her sitting room and came in, followed by Henry, the bucktoothed footman, who was carrying an armload of boxes. "Exciting news!" exclaimed Mrs. Blaine. "We're having company tonight for dinner. His Lordship's invited his brother and his wife—Henry, put the boxes on that table—quite a surprise it was, him not having anyone for dinner for ever so long. You'll like Arthur—that's Lord Avalon, the younger brother. He's full of charm, and an absolute devil. She's another matter: I can't say I'm too fond of *her*. Stuck-up, she is, but there—so many of the young ladies are. They seem to have lost all their Christian humility these days, the young ones. It's a godless, wicked world we live in."

Henry had set the boxes on the table and now Mrs. Blaine opened the top one.

"But why," asked Margaret, "would he want *me* to come to dinner with them?"

"Why, he enjoys your company, of course. Look!"

She pulled from the top box a beautiful blue velvet dress trimmed with white maribou and held it up for Margaret's inspection.

"Isn't it a beauty? Go on to the kitchen, Henry, and help Rogers with the silver. Go on now."

Henry shuffled out. When he had closed the door, Mrs. Blaine lowered her voice. She had an excited, mischievous twinkle in her eyes.

"It's yours," she said.

"Mine?"

"Who else? It's certainly not for me! Saturday morning, just before he left for the country, he came to me and said, 'Now Mrs. Blaine, I particularly want Miss Suffield to be at the dinner Monday night. But she doesn't have a thing to wear, does she?' And I said you only had that yellow dress that I'd seen, poor child. So he sent me around to Madame Adele—such a grand dressmaker she is, all the great ladies go to her—and told me to buy you some clothes and he'd foot the bill. But that I shouldn't tell you until you saw the dresses for fear you might take offense. But I know you wouldn't take offense, him being so fond of you and all, now would you?"

Margaret stared at the dress.

"But I couldn't accept it," she said.

"Ah, you're being a silly nit—of course you could! Here: try it on. Once you've seen yourself in it, you won't have the heart to refuse. Go on. Try it! You're dying to, I can tell."

In fact, she was. Whatever the propriety of accepting clothes from him—and she knew it was one step closer to the demimonde —she couldn't resist at least seeing it on herself. As Mrs. Blaine helped her out of her uniform, the housekeeper rattled on: "I was fairly sure of your size, and I told the Frenchie, Madame Adele, how pretty you was and how your hair is brown and your coloring so fair, and she said *oo la la* or something and brought this out. Then we got shoes to match and three other dresses—wait till you see the taupe one! Oh, you'll look grand, you will, when we get through with you. There. Now what do you think?"

She had finished buttoning the back of the blue dress, and Margaret hurried into her bedroom to look at herself in the full-length mirror. She stared with disbelief at her reflection. The dress fit perfectly and made her look like a queen.

"The saints preserve us, you look like a duchess!" gasped Mrs. Blaine, demoting her slightly in rank, but enthusiastic just the same. "Better than a duchess! Most duchesses I've seen would stop a clock. But you! Why, you'd break any man's heart in that thing, you would. Do you like it?"

"Like it?" whispered Margaret. "I've always dreamed of having a dress like this!"

"And now you've got it. Wait till you see the others; they're even more spectacular!"

"No, I don't want to see them."

"And why not?"

She turned to the white-haired woman.

"You know I can't accept these from him."

"Well now, if you're worrying about what it cost him, don't. They weren't cheap, I'll tell you that; but he's got more money than the law allows—ask the Socialists if you don't believe me—and he won't miss it."

"It's not what it cost him that bothers me. It's what it's going to cost me."

Mrs. Blaine said nothing for a moment; then when she did speak, her voice became softer. "Well now, I expected you'd take that attitude, being a good Christian girl as you are. But he'll be crushed if you don't take them. He told me he's very taken with you, not that I couldn't see what was going on with my own two eyes. Him watching you like a hawk, and you mooning around like you was going to die every moment he stays away. So what's the harm of your accepting a few gifts from him? He's not the type who'd take advantage of a sweet girl like you."

"Isn't he?" said Margaret.

Mrs. Blaine sniffed.

"Well, perhaps I'm overestimating his sense of Christian duty."

"Hasn't he had other women, Mrs. Blaine? I can't imagine he's been all alone in his bedroom for all these years."

"Well," she said reluctantly, "He *does* take an occasional outing, shall we say."

"Where?"

"It's a very respectable place, mind you! Only the toffs go there, and I understand it's very clean and high-class. But you couldn't expect the poor man to bottle it up, being in his prime? Why, he'd get headaches, and the Lord knows what!"

"Where, Mrs. Blaine?"

"Well, if you must know, there's a lady named Laura Metcalf who has a house in St. John's Wood, and I do believe His Lordship does pay her an occasional visit. But I don't see what that has to do with your wearing that dress."

She said nothing, but continued to stare at herself in the mirror. St. John's Wood. Notorious St. John's Wood. Well, it wasn't as if she hadn't suspected it.

"And what will happen," she said, "when his wife finds out he's giving me clothes?"

Mrs. Blaine sighed.

"Ah well, it would be trouble, there's no use fooling ourselves. But trouble or no, he's after you, and there's going to be no stopping him, you might as well face up to that. So you've got a choice: either you clear out of here now, before you're in too deep. Or you show up at dinner tonight in that dress."

"I see. That sounds like an ultimatum."

Silence. She could see he had planned it this way, and she could further see he was using Mrs. Blaine as his accomplice. It was unsubtle, perhaps; perhaps it was subtle. But it was the way he wanted it, and subtle or no, the decision was now up to her. Mrs. Blaine took one of her hands and patted it sympathetically.

"There now, I can see you're upset. But I don't need remind you the circumstances are unusual here. She's no wife to him; we all know that. And maybe this is the good Lord's way of fixing a bad situation. At any rate, if you want my advice, I'd say wear the dress. You can worry about making it up to God later on. They say that when people are in love, they get away with murder with the Almighty. Even Protestants."

She patted her hand again, then released it and walked out of the room.

A Christian girl! thought Margaret, still staring at her reflection. How glibly Mrs. Blaine rationalized what was going on. As if a Christian girl would even consider taking an expensive dress given to her by a man who wanted to make her his mistress. She thought of her father, who, for all his faults, had been a Christian in the strict Victorian sense of the term. He would have been horrified at the position she was in. And yet, she *did* look beautiful in the dress. For the first time in her life, she saw herself as something besides Margaret Suffield, the poor but respectable private nurse. For the first time in her life, she felt beautiful. If ever the devil was standing behind her dangling temptation in the form of these expensive clothes in front of her nose, it was now. The choice was classic. Either she could leave Darlington House and continue being the poor but respectable private nurse. Or she could wear the dress to dinner that night and become the mistress of the man she was coming to love, with all the glamour, excitement, beauty, and moral and social suicide that entailed.

As she admired her reflection, she knew she wouldn't miss that dinner for the world.

• • •

Lady Angela Avalon, Lord Darlington's sister-in-law, was the daughter of the first Viscount Bridgewater who, before he had been elevated to the peerage in 1894, was Billy Babson, the Babson Soap king. Billy was one of the self-made Victorian wonders who clawed his way out of a Manchester slum by selling soap with such zeal that, by the age of twenty-eight, he was able to buy a small factory and start manufacturing his own product. Babson Soap was no better or worse than any other soap on the market. But Billy realized the power of advertising, and his advertisements and campaigns, fabulous by the standards of the 1870s and 1880s, soon made Babson Soap one of the three most popular soaps in England. Billy never lost his Manchester manners and gusto. But such is the power of a title that his daughter —who as plain Angela Babson might have been a nice, well-bred, self-centered rich girl—was transformed into an insufferably haughty snob when her father became Lord Bridgewater. Gone were the slum antecedents a mere generation away—or at least forgotten. Now, as Lady Angela Avalon, she affected the elegant languor and drawl of a Plantagenet. The difference between her languor and the fishwife mannerisms of Lady Darlington, who, after all, was a genuine blueblood, would have amused a sociologist (a breed which, though fathered by Comte in the preceding century, was, happily for the Edwardians, still not much in evidence in 1908).

Her husband, Arthur George Fitzmaurice, Baron Avalon, was thirty-six years old. While, thanks to the laws of primogeniture, he had inherited neither the main family title nor the family fortune, he had inherited his father's love of racing and the family looks, though Margaret thought he was too thin and not nearly as good-looking as his older brother. When she came down to the Red Room that night in her new dress and was introduced to Lord Avalon by Charlie, Arthur gave her a look that immediately set her against him. She felt defensive enough wearing the dress. But Arthur's look, as he drank her in, struck her as offensively suggestive as Paul's expression Friday night in the kitchen. It seemed to say, "As if we don't all know what *you're* up to!" What he actually said was, "We've heard about you, Miss Suffield. But nothing we've heard led me to expect so beautiful a creation. The nursing profession has just climbed several notches in my estimation."

"The first rule to learn about Arthur," said Charlie, "is to listen to everything he says. The second rule is not to believe a word of it."

Arthur smiled. "I'll admit to a certain basic insincerity, Charlie. I think insincerity does wonders for one's character. But I'm always sincere with beautiful women. And I hate to be given lectures in sincerity by a politician."

"Ah, but the difference between us, Arthur, is that I'm sincerely political. You're politically sincere. It's a substantial difference, don't you think?"

"Not especially."

They smiled at each other, and Margaret thought there was little love lost between the two brothers.

Charlie then led her over to a sofa where a tall, thin woman in a white satin dress was sitting. She had a long face with a birdlike beak of a nose which, coupled with her ostrich-length neck banded by a diamond dog collar, and her somewhat hyperthyroid eyes, gave her the appearance of a not-very-friendly buzzard.

"This is my sister-in-law, Angela," said Charlie.

Lady Angela extended a bejeweled hand and fixed on Margaret a smile that was as false as her diamonds were real.

"How do you do?" she said in her high, birdlike voice. "I do think it is so charmingly novel of Charlie to have Caroline's nurse dine with the family, as it were. One can only hope it will be a broadening experience for all of us."

Margaret stared at her, struck dumb by her supercilious rudeness, but Charlie was master of the situation.

"It's almost as charmingly novel as becoming the brother-in-law of a soapmaker's daughter," he said. "And I'm sure it will be twice as broadening."

Lady Angela shot her brother-in-law a look.

"You are not amusing!" she snapped.

"Nor are you." He turned to Margaret. "Angela will do everything in her power to snub you, and you must do everything in your power to ignore her," he said, pleasantly. "Remember, your father was a vicar. And I believe the Church is an infinitely more aristocratic profession than soapmaking."

There was a massive silence which was broken by Rogers, the massive butler, who came up to Charlie and bowed.

"Dinner is served, milord."

"Good," he said, offering Margaret his arm. "And what with everyone starting off at each other's throats, I'm sure dinner will be a complete disaster. Shall we go in?"

If she had loved him for no other reason, Margaret would have adored him for the beautiful way he had put his arrogant sister-in-law in her place.

• • •

In fact, the dinner was not much of a success. Lady Angela sat opposite Margaret and stared at her, forked her food, sulked, and said nothing. Arthur sat next to Margaret and said next to nothing. Margaret was too nervous to eat much, and Lady Angela's bird-eyes boring into her were hardly calculated to improve her appetite. Only Charlie seemed completely at ease, if not actually enjoying himself. He rattled on pleasantly all through the meal, talking mostly to Margaret as if challenging his brother and sister-in-law to think what they pleased, but *he* was treating the nurse as not only an equal but a favorite. She was wondering if he had noticed the dress, and the implication that went with her wearing it, when, halfway through the entrée, he casually remarked that the dress was beautiful. She thanked him. He had noticed. She assumed he had drawn the proper, or improper, inference and that the inevitable consequence would soon follow, perhaps even that night. At this point, she was anxious for it to happen. Having made up her mind, she now wanted him more than she had ever wanted anything.

• • •

In fairness to Arthur and his wife, Lord Darlington was flouting every rule of Edwardian society by having Margaret dine with them. If Margaret had been fat and ugly it still would have been an unthinkable infraction of the rules to invite a nurse into the family dining room. But she was not ugly, she was beautiful, and this made it far worse. He was leaving himself most vulnerable to gossip, which was particularly dangerous for a politically ambitious man such as himself. As Arthur watched the lovely young nurse in her expensive blue dress during dinner, he kept asking himself why his older brother was behaving so foolishly. It wasn't possible he didn't know that Angela, who disliked him even before his preprandial insult and was now seething with ill-concealed outrage, would have the story all over London by lunch the next day. The only conclusion Arthur could draw was that his older brother was so infatuated with the nurse he didn't give a damn. It didn't make much sense, but neither did any alternative supposition.

She *was* beautiful, he reflected as he sipped his wine. Damned beautiful. And the way Charlie was directing ninety percent of his conversation toward her, and the way she hung on his every word, left little doubt about what their relationship was. Arthur decided he would have a talk with his brother after dinner.

Arthur didn't like Charlie. Margaret had been correct in surmising that. Arthur had expensive tastes and Charlie had inherited
all the money—it was that simple. Not only the money but
Darlington House and Ellendon Abbey. Of course, Arthur had
landed an heiress in Angela. Angela wasn't much to look at,
she wasn't very bright, and she put on laughable airs, but she
was rich. Or at least her father was. Billy Babson was worth two
million if he were worth a penny. But unfortunately, Billy
refused to die. Even worse, the year before, he had remarried a
divorced woman who, Arthur knew, was a fortune-hunter of the
most blatant sort, and both he and Angela were becoming in-
creasingly nervous that the new Lady Bridgewater, who had
old Billy wrapped around her finger, might inveigle him into
changing his will, if not entirely, at least partially in her favor.
That would not be pleasant. Angela spent money as wildly as
Arthur would have liked to, and they were forever short of
funds. They were, in fact, heavily in debt, and their credit depended on Angela's inheritance. If that went, or if it were
severely reduced, they would both be in a sticky financial
position.

So Arthur was always looking for new sources of money; and
as he watched his brother and the nurse, he began to see new
veins to mine. He would start small, or relatively small. There
was something he wanted; something expensive, but not that
expensive. Something exciting, dangerous, new and even faster
than horses or motorcars.

He would see if he could get his brother to buy it for him.

• • •

"She's quite beautiful," he said after dinner as he and Charlie had
cigar over their port. Margaret had excused herself and gone
airs. Angela had gone back into the Red Room to sulk, leaving the two brothers alone in the dining room.

"Isn't she?" replied Charlie. "I thought she looked particularly
beautiful in that dress. I bought it for her, you know."

"I didn't know, but I guessed as much. It looked too expensive
for a nurse's salary. Don't you think you're being a bit foolish?

After all, Caroline's nurse . . . having her to dinner with us? It doesn't look very good."

Charlie exhaled a cloud of cigar smoke.

"It doesn't look very good to have Caroline sitting up in her bed drunk every night either."

"I'll grant you she's no plum, but still I think you're being a bit indiscreet."

"There's nothing going on between us."

Arthur shrugged.

"Perhaps. But who'd believe it? Now personally, if you want my fraternal advice, which I'm sure you don't, I have nothing against your having an affair with Miss Suffield or whomever. But let's keep it in the family. Angela has a wicked tongue, and I'm sure she's sitting in the next room making up a list of people she'll call in the morning. You *weren't* very clever with her, after all. She can be cajoled. But anyhow, if you want, I'll keep her quiet. I'll tell her family honor and all that. She'll see the point and simmer down. But you'll have to be a bit more careful. It won't do if you start having people outside the family in for dinner with the pretty young Miss Suffield. It won't do at all."

Charlie tapped his ash.

"Your fraternal solicitude never fails to move me, Arthur, though I don't quite see why you're getting so nervous about my reputation now. You never have before. In fact, I hear from my friends that you never miss an opportunity to talk about me behind my back, and the talk is generally unflattering, if not downright nasty. So why are you being so solicitous now? Is this a late-blooming burst of brotherly love? Or—and far be if from me to sound cynical!—or could it be that you're about to put the touch on me in return for helping keep the nonexistent skeleton in the family closet?"

Arthur looked at his brother.

"You don't mince words, do you?"

"I try not to. I don't like mincing in men. How much do you want?"

Arthur sipped his port, then put the glass down.

"Five hundred pounds."

"Ah, we get to the point. What's wrong this time? Tailors'

bills? Gambling debts? Or do we want a new motorcar to race all over the countryside in, scaring people and horses and generally making a nuisance of yourself?"

"Well, you're going to think this is foolish, but I want an aeroplane."

For the first time, Charlie looked surprised.

"A what?"

"An aeroplane." He took on a genuine look of excitement. "Charlie, I've flown eight or ten times—my God, it's like a whole new world up there! They're building them as fast as they can over in France and in the States, and they've finally started here, too. It's the most thrilling thing I've ever done! I've been taking lessons from Bob Marquand, and he's got a friend who has a biplane he'll sell for five hundred quid. I'd give anything to buy it!"

Charlie burst into laughter.

"My God, I knew you were a rascal, but I didn't think you were crazy too! You mean you'd risk your neck going up in one of those flying coffins?"

"They're as safe as automobiles. Well, almost. And it's certainly safer to risk your neck flying than it is to risk your political neck getting into a messy situation with a common nurse."

"So you'll save my political neck if I buy you a plane?"

"That's right. A fair exchange. Angela and I are unusually tight right now—old Billy's spending all his money on that new wife of his, and she's going through it with something approximating the speed of light. So I think it would be a suitable quid pro quo, so to speak, if you buy me the plane and I shut Angela up."

Charlie leaned forward.

"In the first place, Margaret's not 'common,' as you put it. She's a gentle, charming, beautiful woman, a species that seems to have died out in London society. In the second place, I don't give a damn if Angela writes a letter to the *Times* about us; nothing is going on that either I or she is ashamed of."

"You buy her clothes. That's not a normal perquisite of the nursing profession."

"I buy her clothes because I enjoy buying them for her."

"Then you *are* in love with her?"

Charlie drew in the cigar smoke, then blew it out again slowly. "Yes, I think I am."

Arthur smiled.

"I've thought you were a lot of things, Charlie, but I never thought you were an ass. It seems you're proving me wrong."

"I've thought you were a lot of things, Arthur, but I never thought you were a blackmailer. It seems you're proving *me* wrong. Now I think we'd better end this discussion before I shove this cigar down your throat."

He stood up from the table. Arthur knew better than to push his brother any further. He stood up also, and they went out of the dining room without saying anything more. But Arthur couldn't understand it. His brother really *didn't* care what was said about him and the nurse.

It really was incredible. Unless, he thought, there was something he wasn't seeing.

But he had no idea what it could be.

• • •

As he and Angela were driven in their limousine from Darlington House to their home in Portman Square, Angela finally let go the resentment she had been storing up all evening.

"Did you *see* how he treated her?" she sputtered. "Why, he was practically kissing her at the dinner table! And right in front of *us*, his own family! It was indecent! Perfectly indecent! And poor Caroline upstairs not able to defend herself while this filthy charade goes on in her own home!"

"Poor Caroline," said Arthur, "was probably upstairs passed out."

"It doesn't matter: Charles has no right to carry on that way. It's disgusting. Why can't he go to his fancy woman in St. John's Wood? Bringing that hussy of a nurse right into the dining room! And that remark he made to *me!* As if there's anything wrong with making soap! *Your* family started out in tea leaves, if I remember correctly."

"You do. And it was pretty rotten tea, too. No, there's something going on behind all this. Charlie's sly, and he's much too cool emotionally to fall head over heels in love with a nurse without caring two figs about what people say."

"Charles is a fool for women; he always has been and always will be. And he's at that age when men start behaving like idiots over pretty faces."

"That age begins at puberty."

She sniffed.

"I'm sure. It's *she* that's leading him on. You can tell; that quiet, mousey type is always the worst kind. The vicar's daughter, indeed! I've known quite a few vicars who made a habit of *not* practicing what they preached!"

Arthur was sunk into the corner of the seat, staring out at the passing houses.

"Oh, there's no doubt the Church is a hotbed of sin. I hear they have orgies at Lambeth Palace."

"Arthur! There's no need to be sacrilegious."

"Sorry."

"Well, I fully intend to let Caroline know what's going on. I shall write her a note tonight. I shan't actually *say* it, of course, but I'll certainly let her know that it seems *very* peculiar that her private nurse is dining with her husband. *Very* peculiar indeed."

Arthur said nothing, but continued to stare out the window of the automobile, trying to comprehend the "peculiar" behavior of his brother. The more he thought about it, the more he thought Angela was probably right. It was the nurse, not Charlie. The nurse must be a fantastic actress, putting on that demure front that had so obviously enchanted her employer, while at the same time leading him by the nose down the primrose path. What a tricky little baggage she must be, he thought. He also thought he would give a good deal to have her trick him, at least once.

• • •

Margaret had not undressed when she came upstairs after dinner. She had closed the door of her sitting room, turned out the lights, then gone over to the window and sat down to stare out at the square. It somehow composed her thoughts, and if ever they needed composing, it was now. She was sure Charlie would claim his "prize" that night; and eager as she was to see him, still her nerves were in an advanced state of shock at the thought of giving herself up to a man for the first time. She was a moral woman, but she was in love. And fearful as she was of the consequences of giving herself to Charlie, she was even more fearful of what would happen if she didn't. She couldn't bear the thought of leaving him now that he had become such an integral part of her life, and she was afraid if she continued to reject him, ultimately he would reject her. It was a vicious dilemma she was faced with, and as she waited for his knock on the door, she was torn with fear at the prospect of taking the irretrievable step downward, or laterally in the direction of notorious St. John's Wood, while at the same time, being only human and in love, she was keyed up with anticipation.

The knock came at eleven fifteen. She stood, smoothed her skirt, and tried to appear calm. Then she crossed the room, switched on the lights, and opened the door. He was standing in the hall, still dressed in his white tie and tail coat, looking elegant and handsome and woefully desirable.

"Might I come in for a moment?" he said, so charmingly that he might have been commenting on the weather rather than, as she assumed, about to launch a seduction.

She stood aside and he came into the room. She closed the door, turned and looked at him, her eyes wide and her face white. Despite her attempt to look composed, she was breathing heavily. He went over to the window and pulled the curtains. Then he turned, stuck his hands in his pockets, and looked at her.

"My brother tried to blackmail me," he said nonchalantly. "Arthur works fast. Of course, he's leaped to a few conclusions in the process, but that doesn't matter to Arthur."

"You mean, he tried to blackmail you about me?"

"It certainly wasn't Mrs. Blaine! He told me I'm risking my political career by being so open about you, and then very casually said if I would give him five hundred pounds to purchase an aeroplane—of all things—he'd stop Angela from gossiping about us. Arthur has the finely tuned moral sensitivity of a ravenous Bengal tiger. At any rate, I told him to go to hell."

"I shouldn't have come to dinner," she said. "And I should never have worn this dress."

He smiled.

"But I see you did."

"I know. But I shouldn't have. And you mustn't buy me any more."

"Nonsense. I like beautiful women to wear beautiful clothes. I can afford to buy them for you, so why shouldn't you wear them? As far as my political reputation is concerned, people are bound to talk about us no matter what we do. The more innocent we try to appear, the more guilty they're going to assume we are. So we might as well appear guilty and enjoy ourselves. Or do you think that's foolish?"

She came away from the door.

"I don't know," she said, quietly. "It's your reputation that's important, not mine. It's up to you."

"Of course, we can't flaunt ourselves. But I reserve the right to dine with whom I please in my own house, and if Angela wants to puff that into whatever she'll puff it into, it can't be helped. Isn't she the queerest-looking woman you've ever seen? I always expect her to hop up on a perch and begin cawing like a sick crow. You know, I'm about to kiss you. You look so beautiful, I don't think I can hold back any longer. Would you mind very much if I kissed you?"

She entwined the fingers of her hands to keep them from trembling and looked at him.

"No," she said.

He came up to her and took her hands.

"I don't usually ask," he said, with a smile. Then he raised her hands to his mouth and kissed them. She watched him with fascinated awe. Then he put his arms around her and pulled her to him as he put his mouth against hers and kissed her. She sank into the warmth of his body, and her fears began to vanish.

He smoothed her hair and whispered, "You're frightened, aren't you?"

She nodded.

"Do you want me to leave?"

"Yes." Then, after a beat, "No."

He released her.

"Poor Margaret," he said. "Caught in our damned double standard. I can do what I like, but it's not so easy for you. Well, perhaps I *should* leave." He pulled a cigar from his coat pocket and lighted it with a gold lighter. She watched as he puffed it to life; then he exhaled a cloud of strongly odored smoke. "Perhaps," he said, "I should go off with Laura. You know about her, I suppose?"

"The woman in St. John's Wood? Yes, I know. What's she like?"

"Funny. Warm. Enjoyable. Everything a woman's supposed to be and my wife isn't. She's also expensive, but well worth the price."

"How long have you been going to her?"

"Since Caroline's miscarriage. I haven't touched my wife since then."

He frowned at the memory, and she remembered the look on his face that first evening in the Red Room when she had asked him why Lady Darlington seemed to blame the miscarriage on him. Then it had been a look of anger; now he looked more hurt. He went over to the chair in front of the window and sat down, stretching his long legs in front of him. She watched him while he puffed the cigar, wondering if he was going to tell her. Then he looked up at her.

"I used to be," he said, "what we English like to think of as a highly moral man. Oh, at Oxford I had the usual number of shall we say 'experiences,' and in my bachelor days I wasn't exactly a monk. But I believed in the sanctity of the English marriage and all that's supposed to do with it. And when I married Caroline, I firmly intended to be a faithful husband as I assumed she would be a faithful wife. Needless to say, I was a bit naïf." He slowly blew out more cigar smoke. Then he continued: "My best friend, at Oxford and afterward, was a man named Harley Jackson. Harley was bright, funny, rich, a terrific athlete, and good-looking as the very devil. We were very close.

He was an usher in my wedding, and I was an usher in his. We were both married within a month of each other, and afterward he and his wife and Caroline and I continued to be thick as thieves. It was like one, long, jolly houseparty. They had children; Caroline lost our first child, but we kept trying for more. And then, three years ago, she became pregnant again, which delighted us both."

He paused, rubbing his eyes a moment, as if recalling the events was painful to him. Then he continued: "That October, I was among a party of politicians that went out to India for the installation of the new viceroy, Lord Minto. Caroline couldn't go, of course, being pregnant, but I assumed I would be back in London in time for the birth of the child. Well, it didn't quite work out that way. I'm the world's worst sailor, and the ship wasn't three hours away from the dock until we ran into some rough weather. I became violently seasick; and since the weather continued bad and I continued filling up bucket after bucket, it was finally decided to put me ashore and send me home, which they did. Of course, I wasn't two minutes on land until I felt fine again, but that didn't matter. The trip to India was out, and there was nothing for me to do but go back to London, which I did."

Again he paused, inhaling the cigar.

"I arrived here at the house at nine thirty in the evening. Rogers let me in, and I remember he looked startled to see me. Poor man, I suppose he wanted to warn me, but didn't have the nerve. At any rate, I sensed something was wrong and came directly upstairs to our bedroom—the one that Caroline now reigns over in solitary splendor. I went into the bedroom, and there she was. And there he was."

"Harley Jackson?"

He nodded.

"I think if it had been anyone but him, I probably wouldn't have minded so much. But we had been such close friends—he was the closest friend I ever had; much more of a brother to me than Arthur, whom I really don't like—and he had been sleeping with Caroline for almost a year. Of course, I only discovered that later. But then? Well, to put it mildly, I was angry. I'm normally a well-controlled man, I think; but seeing them there together, in the bed, I went quite berserk. I don't remember exactly what happened, but I almost killed Harley. And in the brawl, I struck Caroline so hard she fell out of the bed onto the floor. And that was when she miscarried."

He tapped the cigar ash in a china pin dish.

"And that was the beginning of the war. The long war between Caroline and myself. She blames me for killing our daughter. I blame her for cuckolding me with Harley—who, by the way, now lives in France. The war never gets anywhere, and divorce is impossible. And that's why I go to St. John's Wood. And that's partly why I'm here with you."

Silence as they looked at each other across the room. Then she came over beside the chair and took his hand.

"I'm sorry," she whispered.

"I'm sorry too. I'd like a happy marriage. I'd like to have children. I'd also like to be foreign secretary. Instead, I have nothing but bitter memories, Caroline's bottles, raging scenes, and that human scum, Paul, lurking around. I've even wondered if she goes to bed with him, but the odd thing is I don't care enough to bother to find out."

"Why don't you fire him?"

He shrugged. "I'd love to. I will, if the right opportunity ever comes."

He ground out his cigar in the dish and stood up, taking her hands. "You're the only good thing that's happened in this house for three years," he said, quietly. Then he took her in his arms and kissed her. "God, I love you so much!" he whispered. "I want you so much. I don't want us to hide. I want to be able to show you to the whole world, just as if you were my wife—if I had a real wife instead of that Gorgon . . ."

"Charlie?"

"What?"

"Either leave right now, or . . ."

She couldn't finish saying it, but he said it for her.

"Or spend the night?"

"Yes."

He held her away from him, looking into her eyes. Then he

said, softly, "You're quite a woman, Miss Suffield. Let's turn the lights out. That way it will be easier for you."

He released her and went over to turn off the switch. Then he opened the curtains, and the lamplight from the square flowed softly into the room. He came back to her and kissed her again, rubbing his strong hands over her back. Whatever resistance she still had was crumbling.

"Let's go in the bedroom," he whispered, taking her hand and leading her to the door. He bumped into a table, mumbled "Damn," then made it to the door where he stopped and kissed her again.

"I love you," he said. "It's going to be quite beautiful, you'll see."

Then they were in the bedroom, where again the light from the square spilled through the window, casting a long, rectangular glow on the floor and the opposite wall. She watched him as he took off his coat, then sat on the bed to remove his shoes. She was crying as she began unbuttoning her dress, thankful for the mask of shadow behind which she could hide while she undressed, something she had never done before in the presence of a man. Charlie was less demure. He stood up and removed his white tie and boiled collar. Then he took out his pearl cufflinks and removed the matching pearl studs.

"Charlie," she whispered, "get out of the light. Someone might see you from the square."

"Let them look," he grumbled, but obeyed nevertheless, stepping into the shadow. She could hear the crinkle of his boiled shirt as he took it off, then his pants dropping to the floor. By the time he crossed the room to the bed, his trim, golden-haired body appearing for a moment in the light, she had removed all her clothes too. She could hear him pulling down the bedspread, then the blankets, then the slight squeak of the bedsprings as he climbed in.

"Margaret," he said quietly.

She was standing by the wall, trembling slightly. Now, slowly, she started toward the bed. If she was indeed ruining herself, at the moment she was too much in love to care.

• • •

"For Lady Darlington," said the footman, handing the crested envelope to Rogers at the front door of Darlington House the next morning, then returning to the automobile at the curb. Rogers looked at the envelope and recognized the handwriting and crest as belonging to Lady Angela. He handed the envelope to a footman. "Give this to Paul," he said.

The footman nodded and went off to find Paul, who was always given Lady Darlington's personal mail. He found him in the pantry and handed him the letter. "For Lady Darlington," he said. Paul looked at the envelope, then put on his coat and went upstairs. Knocking on the door to her suite, he went into the sitting room where she was stretched on her chaise, eating chocolates. He gave her the letter and she opened it, munching on the candy as she read the elegant round hand. My dear Caroline, it began,

> Far be it from me to pry into your personal affairs, but believe me I do so only through motivations of sisterly affection. As you may know, Arthur and I came to dinner last night at Charles's invitation. We were seated in the Red Room chatting before dinner when, to my surprise, Charles announced that your nurse—Miss Suffield, I believe, is her name—was to dine with us. And indeed, a few minutes later, Miss Suffield came downstairs and proceeded to join us. I do not mean to imply that anything sordid is going on between Charles and this woman; but I need hardly tell you, dear Caroline, that such an arrangement looks distinctly peculiar. And I felt it my duty to call this fact to your attention.
>
> Affectionately,
> Angela

Lady Darlington finished reading the note, then tapped the corner of the note paper thoughtfully on her coverlet. After a moment, she looked up at Paul.

"Paul," she said, "do you find Miss Suffield attractive?"

"Oh, I suppose."

"Of course you do: don't be coy. She's a pretty woman, and you're an alley cat. I'm sure you find Maud attractive, for that matter. How would you like to earn some extra money?"

His blue eyes glittered.

"How much?"

"Ah, the thrifty Swiss! Never quite so alert as when money is mentioned. Fifty pounds."

He grinned.

"I'd do a lot for fifty pounds."

"I'm sure. Happily, I think you'll find what I want you to do pleasant. In fact, knowing you, I think you'll find it *quite* pleasant."

• • •

The next morning, Margaret was surprised to receive a letter from Percival Jenkins, the senior partner of Jenkins and Hawkes, informing her that her father's debts, including the solicitors' fees, had been entirely paid off by the earl of Darlington. She was stunned. And when he came home that evening, she went to his study, closing the door behind her.

"You *can't* do this," she said, handing him the letter. "It's too much. Eight hundred pounds is a fortune. I can't allow you to do it."

He placed the letter on the desk, then put his arms around her.

"It's already done, so there's nothing you can do about it."

"Then I'll pay you back the money. You can deduct it from my salary."

He smiled and ran his hand over her hair.

"All right. Half a crown a year for the next hundred years. Including interest."

"Don't joke—please. I'm serious. I feel guilty enough about accepting the dresses from you . . ."

"I want to give you things!" he interrupted, with sudden annoyance. "Can't you understand that? For God's sake, forget your country parsonage scrupulousness about money. I'm a millionaire five times over. The money means nothing to me, but making you happy means everything; so accept it and forget it."

"But it's wrong!" she persisted.

"What's 'wrong' in this life and what's 'right'? What society says? Society says it's wrong for me to love you because you're not my wife, and it's right for me to love my wife. But you're lovable, and my wife's anything but; so much for society's conception of rightness and wrongness! I'll tell you what's right and wrong: giving people pleasure is right, and giving them pain is wrong. You give me pleasure by letting me pay off your debts, so it's right. You give me a pain by trying to stop me from spoiling you, so that's wrong."

She was dizzy from his generosity and his refusal to listen to her objections. After a lifetime of penny-pinching, to have eight hundred pounds without a blink was overwhelming. Yet, despite his rationalizations, she knew accepting the money was wrong, as wrong as accepting the dresses and letting him make love to her. He was an ardent lover, the Prince Charming out of a million shopgirl fantasies, and he was hers. But she was beginning to understand he had a wonderfully facile way of explaining away all ethical objections to what he wanted, just as she was beginning to have a facile way of responding to him.

"All right," she said, reluctantly. "I'll forget my 'country parsonage' upbringing and accept the money."

"You don't look very happy about it."

"Do you expect me to? Oh, I don't mean to sound ungrateful, but I feel just like a tart. That night at the Petrarch you said I wasn't, but I've let you make love to me and you've paid me for it; so the 'respectable' Miss Suffield, when you get right down to it, really is just that: a tart. And a very highly paid one at that. I can't help feeling ashamed."

He took her face between his hands.

"You're not a tart. We love each other. That makes all the difference."

She looked into his eyes.

"Does it?" she asked, quietly.

He didn't have an answer.

• • •

He was out of the house for the next few days, and she went about her normal duties, missing him desperately and realizing how her whole existence was depending more and more on him. She literally ached to see him. Whatever the chemistry of love— a blend of sex, charm, mutual loneliness, and pleasure—she had been filled with it. Yet her guilt was spoiling it. And her apprehension at what would happen when his wife found out made her miserable. If Lady Darlington knew, and Margaret felt she did, despite the care she and Charlie had taken on the night he came to her room, she was pretending not to know. What the purpose of this game was, Margaret wasn't sure. Then, on Thursday morning, something happened that meant the game was entering a new phase. At ten, Margaret answered the bell to find Lady Darlington seated on the chaise lounge in her sitting room. Paul was standing beside her. She looked up as Margaret came in.

"Ah, here you are," she said. "Did you read in the papers yesterday about the terrible fire in the nursing home in Earl's Court?"

"Yes, I did. I knew one of the nurses who was killed."

"A shocking tragedy. Twenty-two of the patients burned to death. Shocking. It set my mind to thinking, and I realized how helpless I would be in case of a fire here. Consequently, I've given instructions to Paul—dear, faithful, Paul—who has sworn to come to my rescue in case of a fire. This morning we're going to have a fire drill, and I want you to be my stand-in, if you will. It would be too strenuous for me to do, and I'd appreciate it if you'd help."

She was being unusually affable.

"Of course, milady," Margaret said. "What shall I do?"

"Well, I think the most probable time a fire would occur would be in the middle of the night. So Paul is going to go upstairs to his room. Then, when I ring the bell to his room, that will be the signal for the beginning of the fire. He will run down here and get me out of my bed and downstairs to the ground floor. Except he'll be getting *you*, because you're standing in for me. Or rather, lying in. I'll sit here and time the whole procedure. We'll run through it twice. The first time we'll pretend it's a serious fire, and Paul will go as quickly as he can. The second time, we'll pretend the fire isn't so serious, and Paul will get my jewels out of my safe. All right, Paul, you go up to your room. And Margaret, you go into my bedroom and get in my bed. There's a good girl. You'll take off your shoes, if you don't mind?"

She smiled at her nurse, who went into the bedroom and closed the door. The bed had been made by Maud, so she took off her shoes and lay down on the white spread, where she waited for Paul, wondering what scheme her employer had in mind. Five minutes passed. Then she heard someone running through the sitting room toward the bedroom door. The door was opened and Paul charged in. "Fire, milady!" he cried as he ran to the bed and scooped Margaret into his arms. "Put your arms around my neck," he said, lifting her off the bed. She obeyed and he winked at her. "Cozy, isn't it?"

"Not particularly."

He carried her to the door, then out into the sitting room, where Lady Darlington was watching them, a clock in her hand.

"Very good," she called. "Take her out to the elevator, then bring her back."

Paul carried Margaret down the marble corridor to the elevator; then he put her down, puffing from his exertions. "We make a great team, don't we?" he said.

She said nothing, and they returned to the sitting room where Lady Darlington checked her clock. "Excellent. You delivered me to the elevator in a minute and a half. I can't imagine that wouldn't be ample time to get out safely. Margaret, you were a very good stand-in. Now, my dear, if you'll go back to the bed we'll try a slower drill. Paul, back upstairs with you; this time, we'll pretend a fire has started in the kitchen, say, and there is no immediate danger. We would try to save the jewels, at least, and whatever else could be carried out of the house in time."

Margaret returned to the bedroom and lay back on the bed again. After a few minutes, Paul reappeared at the door, though this time he wasn't running. He came into the room, closing the door behind him, and walked over to the rear wall of the room where he removed a small painting, revealing a safe behind it. Margaret watched him as he turned the dial.

"I'm surprised Lady Darlington doesn't keep her jewels in a bank," she said.

"She does. Her important ones. She keeps a few trinkets here, though. She likes to look at them every once in a while." He opened the door and reached in to pull out a large black leather case embossed with a gold coronet. "Want to see them?" he asked. Not waiting for a reply, he carried the case over to the bed and opened it. Margaret watched as he pulled out a thick diamond and ruby bracelet and held it up for her inspection. "A nice trinket, isn't it?" he said, twirling the bracelet slowly so the light sparkled off the jewels.

"It's not what I'd call a 'trinket,'" said Margaret. "And frankly, I'm surprised she trusts you with the combination."

He glanced at her, but didn't take offense. "Oh, she trusts me completely. More than anyone else, you know. Look here; isn't this beautiful?" He replaced the bracelet and pulled out two immense diamond eardrops, each containing a large Ceylon ruby in the center. "What do you think of these?" he said. "Here, try them on." He held them out to her, but she shook her head.

"Paul, let's get this over with," she said impatiently.

"We have time. Go on. Try them."

"No."

"Paul!" The voice was Lady Darlington's, calling from the other room. Paul dropped the jewels back in the case and hurried to the door, leaving the case on the bed. He opened the door. "Yes?"

"What's taking so much time?" she called. "This is a slow drill, admittedly, but we'd all be cooked by now! Hurry up."

"Yes, milady."

He came back to the bed, shrugging at Margaret, then closed the case and handed it to her. "You carry this while I carry you." She took it; then he picked her up again and carried her into the sitting room. Lady Darlington was scowling.

"What *were* you doing in there?"

"I had trouble with the safe combination."

"Well, hurry! Take her to the elevator."

Paul obeyed. By the time he reached the elevator, he was red in the face and sweating from his exertions. He put Margaret down, then leaned against the wall to catch his breath.

"You should lose a few pounds," he puffed.

"I just have," she said, loading the heavy jewelry case into his hands. Then she walked down the stairs and proceeded to the kitchen for a cup of tea.

• • •

At three that afternoon she was sitting in front of the window reading *Lorna Doone* when someone knocked on her door. She went over and opened it. Rogers and Henry were standing in the hall.

"I beg your pardon, Miss Suffield," said the butler, who looked upset, "but I'll have to ask you to allow us to search your rooms."

"For what?"

"Two diamond and ruby earrings are missing from milady's jewelry case. She has given us instructions to search the entire house before calling Scotland Yard."

She began at least partially to see what Lady Darlington's scheme had been.

"Paul had the case last," she said. "I gave it to him after the fire drill."

"I know. We are searching his room too. All our rooms are being searched. It's most distressing. This has never happened in Darlington House before."

The dignified butler looked genuinely embarrassed. Margaret stood aside.

"Come in."

"We'll try not to disturb anything," he said as he entered with Henry behind. She said nothing, but watched with growing apprehension as they searched the sitting room. Then they went into the bedroom. She waited. A few minutes later, Rogers appeared in the door, his huge face startled.

"I think," he said, "we should go see Her Ladyship."

"Why?"

He held out his hand. In his palm were the diamond eardrops. She stared at them.

"Where did you find them?" she asked.

"In your pillow case."

Now she saw the whole plot, and she was furious. She went into the hall and ran to Lady Darlington's suite, bursting through the door without knocking. Her patient was on her chaise drinking champagne, but her eyes were cold and sober. She watched her nurse impassively as she confronted her.

"You put them in my room!" Margaret said, trying to keep from shouting. "The whole thing was planned—"

"What *are* you talking about?"

"That fire drill! You planned it with Paul, then had him put the earrings in my room!"

"So *you* took them!" she said, sitting up.

"You know I didn't! Do you think I'd be so stupid as to steal your jewels and then put them in my pillow case?"

"I have no way to assess your criminal skill," snapped her employer, "but I'm beginning to reassess your honesty." She looked past her to Rogers, who had just come in the room. "Rogers, did you find the earrings in Miss Suffield's room?"

"Yes, milady."

He came up to the chaise and showed her the jewels. Lady Darlington took them, then looked up at her nurse.

"Have you done this with your previous employers?"

"I have never stolen anything! And why would I steal your earrings?"

"Because they're valuable, of course."

"Then why not Paul? Why not accuse *him?* Because he was acting on your orders!"

"And why would I tell my own footman to steal my own jewels?"

"So you could have a good excuse to fire me."

She smiled and sipped her champagne.

"My dear, I don't need a good excuse to fire you. I don't even need a bad one. But since you seem to believe this bizarre fantasy, I'll ring for Paul and you can accuse him to his face. After all, we want to be fair." She put down her glass and pressed the bell to Paul's room. Then she turned to the butler. "Rogers, tell the staff the jewels have been found. Tell them it was all a mistake. Now that they've been recovered, there's no need to start a rash of gossip."

Rogers nodded and left the room.

"So you think I tried to 'frame' you, as I believe they call it in the *romans policiers?*" she said to Margaret. "And why would I have wanted to do that, my dear?"

Margaret was cooling down. She decided it was best not to answer, for Charlie's sake as well as her own. Her employer smiled.

"Cat got your tongue? Ah well, I thought you might think twice about that particular accusation. And here's Paul." The footman came over to the chaise and glanced at Margaret. "Paul, we have located the earrings in Miss Suffield's pillow case. However, Miss Suffield seems to feel *you* stole them and put them in her room, oddly enough. Did you steal them, Paul?"

Paul's face took on a look of wounded innocence.

"Of course not."

"Then, let me put it this way: did Miss Suffield have any opportunity to steal them?"

"Naturally. During the fire drill."

"*You* had the jewel case!" snapped Margaret.

"No, you did. You held it when I was carrying you. Remember?"

"Ah, he has you there," said Lady Darlington. "I distinctly remember seeing it in your hand as he took you through here to the elevator."

"And she had it even before that!" exclaimed Paul. "I had opened it to show her what was inside. Then when you called, I went to the bedroom door and left the case with her on the bed. It was open, and she could have easily slipped the earrings in the pocket of her uniform without my noticing it."

"Isn't it possible and much more likely, considering the fact you have a police record—"

"That's *hardly* fair," interrupted Lady Darlington sanctimoniously. "Paul has paid his debt to society."

"It's not fair what you're doing to me!" she exclaimed. "He

could have taken them when I gave him the case at the elevator, then when I went down to the kitchen, he could have gone into my room and put them in my pillow."

"But why would I do it?" smiled Paul. "I have the combination to the safe. If I wanted to steal the jewels, I could do it any time. And I certainly wouldn't steal them just to put in your pillow case. Now, that doesn't make any sense at all, does it?"

Silence. She was caught in a neat pincer, and she knew it.

"I will expect you to be out of this house within an hour," said Lady Darlington, quietly. "Whatever your reasons for doing this criminal act—and I must say, it makes something of a mockery of your self-advertised moral righteousness—I am not vindictive and do not intend to tell the police. That is, if you leave quietly. However," and here she smiled slightly, and Margaret thought she had never seen such a look of smug malevolence in her life, "if you try to see my husband again, I shall contact Scotland Yard and prosecute you. I have a whole house full of witnesses. When I am done with you, you will never work in London again—that is, after you get out of jail." There could be no doubt now; she knew, and this had been her crudely elaborate way of getting back. "Now get out," she said, adding, in a tone of sheer viciousness, "you slut."

The word was like a slap in Margaret's face. It almost literally stung. She wanted to hit back, to scream at this terrible woman who had so maliciously trapped her. And yet she held back because the word was the truth. The weight of all her guilt and fear of the past few days tumbled in on her and broke the back of her anger. She turned and hurried out of the room, running down the corridor to her room to pack her bags and run out of Darlington House as soon as she possibly could. A slut. She, Margaret Suffield, a slut. If she had only not gone to bed with him, she could have fought back. But she had gone to bed with him, and in her mind she could not defend herself.

There was nothing left for her but to run.

• • •

"You mean she *left?*"

Lord Darlington had come home at six to find a tearful Mrs.

Blaine in the hall. She took him into his study and told him what had happened.

"She *had* to! Rogers told me the whole thing; Lady Darlington was going to call Scotland Yard if she didn't leave immediately. Ah, it would be a terrible scandal! Terrible!"

She dabbed her eyes with her handkerchief. Lord Darlington looked confused.

"Why Scotland Yard?"

"Because your wife, Lord love her, paid Paul to plant her ruby earrings in Miss Suffield's bedroom, so she could accuse her of stealing them. I know, because Paul's drunk and has been going around all afternoon bragging about the talking machine he bought with the money, and a pile of trashy American songs. Oh, it was a wicked thing to do! The poor girl was in tears when she left, she was. She packed her things and was gone in half an hour. She told me to tell you she had left the clothes you bought her. I've been a wreck since she left! A wreck!"

"Did she tell you where she was going?"

"She did, though she didn't want to. Back to the boarding house on the Cromwell Road where she come from she went—the St. Alban's Court's the name of it. And *her!*" Mrs. Blaine rolled her eyes. "Sitting up in her room getting drunk as a lord with Paul, celebrating their victory! It was a cruel thing to do to that poor girl, it was."

Charlie started toward the entrance hall.

"Are you going after Miss Suffield?"

"I'm going after my wife," he said. His voice had been flat, but Mrs. Blaine had no doubt there was going to be another of the fights between husband and wife that periodically shook the walls of Darlington House. Except, from the look on his face, this one promised to be a holocaust.

• • •

When he reached the second floor, he heard a record playing "Meet Me in St. Louis" coming from his wife's suite. He hurried down the hall to the door and listened. His wife's voice was singing a drunken accompaniment to the record, seconded by Paul joining in occasional snatches. Someone was also stomping on the floor and clapping hands in a staccato rhythm that sounded like some weird tap dance. He opened the door and went into the sitting room. A new crank-up talking machine with an enormous lily horn was standing on a table beside a pile of thick recordings, one of which was on the turntable. Lady Darlington was sitting on her chaise, swaying slightly as she attempted to sing the lyrics of the song, a tulip glass of champagne in her hand and the bleary look of advanced drunkeness in her reddened eyes. In the middle of the room was Paul. His footman's coat was off, thrown over the back of a chair, and his shirt tail was out. The shirt was open, and his bare chest was streaming with sweat as he stomped and clapped his way through a vigorous Swiss *schuplatten*, ignoring the tempo of the waltz tune grinding scratchily out of the lily horn. When he saw his employer, he stopped the complicated dance and a look of confusion came over his face as he panted for breath. Lady Darlington stopped singing, but the voice of Nora Bayes on the record droned placidly on.

"Get out," said Lord Darlington.

Paul wiped his face with sleeve, but didn't move.

"I was showing Her Ladyship the *schuplatten*," he slurred. Then he giggled. "Or was I showing Her *Schuplatten* the Ladyship?"

Caroline burst into laughter.

"That's it!" she shouted. "You were showing Her *Schuplatten* the Ladyship, that marvelous old Swiss folkdance that's sweeping London! Soon everyone will be doing the Ladyship—"

"Get out," repeated Lord Darlington quietly, starting toward the footman. Paul backed away.

"I was invited in here," he said, defensively. "She asked me to bring my new talking machine. She'd never seen one . . ."

Lord Darlington grabbed his arm and shoved him toward the door.

"Let him alone!" Caroline said from the chaise. "Get your hands off him!"

Her husband ignored her.

"You're fired," he said, giving the footman a final shove that sent him stumbling against the doorframe. "Pack your bags and get out."

Paul pulled himself up.

"You can't fire me. Tell him he can't fire me!" he called across the room to Caroline.

"Of course he can't," she said. "Charles, you're behaving like an ass. Paul stays. He is *my* servant and he stays. Paul, go change the record. Put on 'A Bird in a Gilded Cage.' That's me," she added, waving her hand in gesture of alcoholic moroseness. "A poor bird in a gilded cage . . ."

"You're a *drunk* bird," snapped her husband. "And of all your despicable tricks, what you did to Margaret was the worst."

"Oh yes, dear, lovely Margaret—your *mistress*," roared Caroline, snapping out of her moroseness with sudden fury. "Don't bother to deny it. That idiot sister-in-law of yours wrote me a note; it's all over town! They're shouting it from the towers of London Bridge! You and that simpering bitch of a nurse—you haven't even good taste in women!"

"Obviously. I married you. Paul, I told you to get out of here."

The footman was halfway to the talking machine. Now he turned on Lord Darlington.

"Don't order me around," he said with new-found bravado. "You think you're so high and mighty, the great earl of Darlington . . . 'milord,' 'your worship' . . ." He made a mocking bow. "All the world bows and scrapes to the great English nobleman! Well, Paul doesn't."

"Paul," snapped Caroline, "that's enough class warfare. Change the record."

But Lord Darlington was already at the machine. He took "Meet Me in St. Louis" off the turntable and skimmed it across the room, where it smashed against the opposite wall. Then he picked up the other records and started throwing them, one by one like discuses, through the air. As they smashed against the wall, Paul threw himself at his employer and tried to grab the remaining records out of his hand. To his surprise, he gave them to him. Then, as Paul stared with confusion at the stack of records in his hand, Lord Darlington smashed him on the jaw with a right hook that sent him sprawling on the Aubusson carpet in a clatter of smashed Tin Pan Alley ware. He groaned, then lay still, unconscious.

Caroline reached to the wine cooler beside her chaise and pulled the champagne bottle out of the ice.

"Filthy bully," she said.

He turned to look at her as the heavy green bottle sailed through the air toward his skull. He tried to dodge it, but he was too late: it hit his right cheek, just below the eye.

"I'd kill you," she said with conviction. "I'll kill you, just as you tried to kill me. . . ."

He was holding his cheek. Blood started to ooze through his fingers. He pulled a handkerchief from his pocket and held it against the cut.

"This is a lovely scene, isn't it?" he said. "The peerage of England at home amidst surroundings of elegant tranquillity."

She was staring at the blood.

"You're bleeding," she said.

"That usually happens when one is hit by flying champagne bottles."

Suddenly, irrationally, she started to cry. He watched her, his face impassive as the blood turned the handkerchief scarlet. After a moment, she sank back in the chaise and truly began to sob. He walked over and looked down at her.

"I'm so miserable. Oh, Charlie, I'm so damned miserable."

"You're drunk and maudlin."

She looked up, tears streaming down her puffy cheeks. "Why do you treat me so rottenly?"

"*I* treat *you* rottenly? For years you've made my life a considerable hell, and now you lock yourself in here with that cheap—"

"Cheap?" she interrupted. "And what about Miss Suffield?"

"Miss Suffield not only has the marks of a lady, she is one."

"I believe you and your *lady*—"

"And you and Paul?"

She looked surprised.

"Him? Do you think *I* would allow a common footman to make love to me?"

"Frankly, I think you'd allow the dustman to make love to you."

"You're making up more filthy lies to intimidate me," she said.

"I've never done a thing with Paul. Good Lord, he doesn't bathe!"

"Nor do you—except in alcohol."

"But Miss Suffield bathes, doesn't she? She *squeaks* she's so clean."

"Kindly leave her out of this—especially after what you did to her, and on no grounds at all except a note from that bird-brain, Angela."

"I have *ample* grounds for suspicion, not the least of which is that you're so angry she's gone. You bought her dresses, you had her for dinner in our dining room, you took her to the theater—and don't try to deny it. Besides . . . I simply don't like her."

"You don't like anyone except Paul, and the bottle. You can forget Paul, he's through. And if you insist on behaving like a fishwife, the bottles will go too. That's no empty threat. I've never tried it with you, but I'm fully prepared to turn this place into a prison, if necessary."

"You wouldn't dare!"

"Try me and see."

"You lock me in here, and I'll tell the world that you killed my child—"

"That's a lie, and one I'm especially sick of hearing."

"It's not a lie. You attacked me. You tried to kill me, just as you tried to kill Paul."

"If you recall the circumstances, beloved wife, I walked into your bedroom to find you in a somewhat compromising position with Harley Jackson—"

"He hadn't touched me."

"He had his mouth on your neck. I assume he wasn't a vampire? And considering the fact you both in bed, naked—"

"All right, we were lovers. What of it? But you—after going into a most unbecoming rage and hitting him, you tried to strangle me." She put her hand to her throat in a drunkenly melodramatic gesture. "You choked me . . . you would have killed me—"

"I accidentally knocked you off the bed. Please get your facts straight."

"Yes, and killed the child. My poor, unborn baby. You are a murderer!"

He slapped her so hard she fell back into the cushions of the chaise again, where she stared at him with a dazed look of half pain, half shock. "Don't ever," he said tightly, leaning over her, "don't ever again say I killed my daughter." He straightened and looked at the blood-soaked handkerchief. Then he put it back against his cheek.

Caroline whispered, "I *detest* you."

"Believe me, my dear, the feeling is heartily mutual."

He looked at Paul, who was still sprawled on the floor in the middle of his broken records.

"I'll send Rogers up to sweep up the trash. God knows, I should have done this years ago. I suggest you go in the bedroom before the servants come up. I'm sure they've heard everything, but it might be amusing to try and maintain a shred of dignity. After all, you know, we *are* supposed to set an example."

He started toward the door, determined to try and bring Margaret back to Darlington House, no matter what Caroline's objections would be—and he knew she would object. But, he thought as he stepped over a broken record and walked out of the room, Caroline could say what she liked. He really didn't give a damn any more.

• • •

Mrs. Sedgwick, the owner of the St. Alban's Court boarding house on the Cromwell Road, was as forbidding as the ugly red-brick façade of her building. When, from the window of her parlor, she saw the taxi pull up in front of the St. Alban's Court that evening at nine o'clock, and when she saw the well-dressed gentleman emerge from the back (his face, despite the bandage on his right cheek, looked familiar), her face became even more sternly forbidding. Mrs. Sedgwick rented only to respectable young ladies. However, some of her respectable young ladies were attractive, and periodically gentlemen would come to 'call,' at which time Mrs. Sedgwick would summon her reserve troops of righteousness and thinly veiled moral outrage and head the gentlemen off at the pass—which, in the case of the St. Alban's Court, was the stairway. So when she spotted the earl of Darlington (and by the time he was halfway to the front door she had remembered his face from pictures of the noted politician she had seen in the newspapers), she lost no time in getting to the hall to take her post by the stair as Ethel, her maid, answered the bell.

"I believe there's a Miss Suffield staying here," said Lord Darlington, whose right cheek was considerably swollen beneath the bandage.

"That's right, but visiting hours are over," said Ethel in a high-pitched Cockney voice.

Lord Darlington looked annoyed.

"This is rather important."

Ethel glanced back at her mistress, who shook her head in a slight, but nevertheless unmistakable, "no." Ethel turned back.

"I'm sorry, sir. Would you like to send up a note?"

Lord Darlington pulled a card case from his pocket and jotted something on one of his cards, which he handed Ethel along with a half-crown piece.

"Tell Miss Suffield I'll be outside," he said, shooting Mrs. Sedgwick a disapproving look as he started back down the stairs. Ethel closed the heavy frosted glass and carved walnut door, then hurried to the stair.

"Would you look 'oo 'e is?" she whispered, showing the card to Mrs. Sedgwick. "A bleedin' *earl!*"

"I know who he is," sniffed Mrs. Sedgwick, who had egalitarian tendencies, "and just because he's an earl doesn't mean he's any better than you or I. In fact, he's probably much worse. They usually are. Now go on up and deliver the card."

Ethel ran up the stairs, thinking that Lord Darlington, no matter what his character, could have her any day of the week. Any day of the week at all.

• • •

Lord Darlington waited for ten minutes outside the St. Alban's Court. It was a balmy evening, and a number of strollers passed by, taking advantage of the pleasant spring weather. Then, as he watched from the sidewalk, she came out the door of the boarding house. She was wearing a blue cloak, and as the gas light of the lamp to the right of the door fell on her face, he could see she looked exhausted. She came down the steps and walked over to him, looking at the bandage on his face. "What happened?" she asked.

"My wife," said Charlie. "Dear, sweet, gentle, well-bred Caroline hit me with a champagne bottle."

She looked concerned as she examined the puffed blue-black cheek.

"It cut you, didn't it?"

"I bled like a stuck pig. But I had Sir Andrew look at it; he says I'll survive. Will you walk with me a while? I want to talk to you."

"I don't know if I should."

"Dammit, I've had a hell of a fight with Caroline," he said with sudden irritation. "Please, don't *you* fight with me."

Despite his tone, she couldn't help but feel sorry for him. He looked thoroughly miserable. She took his arm.

"All right. But let's get away from Mrs. Sedgwick's prying eyes."

He glanced at the parlor window to see the woman in question duck behind the curtain.

"Yes, she's a definite charmer, isn't she?" They started down the sidewalk. For a while he said nothing.

"I want to apologize for what Caroline did to you," he finally said.

"It doesn't matter."

"Yes it does. It was typical of her: underhanded and vicious. I think I've come to the end of my patience with her."

"I assume she told you she knows about us?"

"That was part of it, of course. Then there was a lot of other hysterical caterwauling. If we'd been two drunk beggars in Shoreditch we couldn't have put on a more inelegant performance. By the way, I fired Paul. That was the one good—I'd even say 'glorious'—moment of the day. I also had the distinct pleasure of knocking him out cold. She paid him to put the earrings in your room, you know."

"I know. But we were as much in the wrong as she."

"Why?"

"Well, we are lovers. Or were."

"Does that mean she has the right to compromise you with a false larceny charge and threaten to send you to jail? Besides, there's nothing wrong in our being lovers."

She smiled. "That's the difference in our viewpoints. I'm the vicar's daughter, remember? And when she called me a slut, it hurt. Oh, I'm not blaming you. I could have said no, but I didn't. I wanted you, and now . . ." She gestured wearily with her free hand. "Now it's all over."

They walked in silence for a moment as an elderly silk-hatted gentleman passed them, tipping his hat and saying "Good evening." When he was out of earshot, Lord Darlington said, "I thought you'd feel that way, but I don't happen to think it's all over."

"It is as far as I'm concerned."

"I want you to come back."

She looked surprised.

"You don't honestly think I'd even consider that now?"

"I think you might once you've heard my proposition. You see, I've been toying with the idea for some time now. It's a fairly bizarre idea, and a frightening one. But I keep toying with it."

"What are you talking about?"

He didn't answer for a moment. Then he said, "Do you trust me?"

"Yes."

"Can I trust you?"

"Naturally."

Again, he remained silent.

"Charlie, what *is* it?"

"Well," he began, "I first had the idea when I was interviewing you, that first day. The idea popped into my mind and then popped out again, but it was definitely there. You were so beautiful, and so intelligent and efficient, that it occurred to me you might be the one."

"The 'one' to do what?"

He turned toward her. His face looked entirely calm.

"The one to kill Caroline."

She didn't think he was joking, but she wasn't quite sure.

"Are you serious?"

"Quite serious. In fact, deadly serious, to make a feeble pun."

"You mean *murder* her?"

"The semantics don't interest me, and I'm sure they wouldn't interest Caroline. But if you insist, all right—yes, murder her. I thought you might murder her for me, if I could make you fall in love with me, which I flattered myself I might be able to do without too much trouble."

She felt sick.

"Then all the pretty speeches, and the dresses—it was all a trick?"

"Not exactly. I wasn't that calculating. It was more a game, really. I wanted to see how far I'd go. I really didn't think I'd ever go this far, but after this afternoon I decided why not?"

She stared ahead of her.

"And how was I supposed to murder her?"

"There are enough ways for a nurse to do in her patient, particularly a drunken patient with a heart condition. I'm sure it's done quite frequently, except that people never find out about it. If you had balked, which I thought you might, then I was prepared to offer you a large sum of money—say, ten thousand pounds placed in a French or Swiss bank. It would have been well worth it to me to get rid of Caroline. *Well* worth it. But I made a mistake. I actually did fall in love with you."

"You don't have to lie," she said, her eyes filling with tears. "There's no point keeping up the game any longer."

"I'm not lying. I *did* fall in love with you. And I made love to you, and bought you dresses, and had you to dinner with Arthur and Angela, and flaunted you to annoy them, and the inevitable happened: I tipped my hand. Caroline found out, and then, all this today. Plus, you feeling miserable and guilty. Oh, I mucked it up beautifully. But now at least you know the truth."

Her eyes were dry again as she stared at him. "You really *could*," she said slowly, as if she could hardly assimilate the fact, "murder her."

"Easily. Well, not easily. I'm actually a gentle enough man, and murdering one's wife may be something a lot of men dream about, but when you start to translate wishes into action, it becomes another matter. I've wanted to get rid of Caroline for years. She really is a millstone around my political neck, and divorce is out of the question. But lately it's become more than just the career. I hate her. I actively, passionately hate her. As long as she lives, I'm dead, for all purposes. And until she's dead, I can't really start to live."

They passed two elderly ladies deep in conversation. When they were out of earshot, he continued. "Of course, she might kill herself drinking, in which case why risk murdering her? But she also might live to be eighty. My great-aunt did, and she drank as much as Caroline. For that matter, Caroline's father was a drunk, but he lived to be sixty-seven. Caroline is forty-one. If she only lives five more years, I'll have lost my sanity. And if she lives as long as her father, which she might, well, let's just say my life would be finished. And I don't intend that my life should be finished. I shock you, don't I?"

"You frighten me."

"I frighten myself. Except when you begin to become accustomed to the idea of taking someone's life, it doesn't seem quite so terrifying. One adds up the pros and cons of the situation. The cons are obvious: the risks of getting caught, the struggle with one's conscience—and I do have a conscience, though I wouldn't blame you if you didn't believe me. But then one considers the pros: her life against mine. I love life. I think I lead a useful life. I helped get the Pension Bill through the Lords, and that alone will benefit thousands of people. I could have a fairly spectacular political career if I could get rid of her, and since I'm an ambitious man, that's a definite pro. So I consider my life worth something. Caroline, on the other hand, leads one of the most useless existences I know of. She doesn't love life; she loves the bottle, and the anaesthesia it produces in her brain. So she's already half dead, and I can't honestly believe her life is worth much. Of course, there's something of a difference between half dead and dead. Most religions and philosophies teach that human life is sacred; but in all frankness one has to admit that there are people whose death would benefit the human race. Caroline is, in my opinion, one of them."

"You sound like you're trying to convince yourself of something you can't really accept."

"Yes, you're right in a way. The idea still terrifies me. I suppose I'm almost hoping you'll talk me out of it. Will you?"

"I think it's more a question of your talking me into it. After all, it seems I'm the one who has to do the dirty work."

"Yes, that's one of the less attractive features of the plan, from your viewpoint. Would I be able to talk you into it?"

She stopped and disengaged her arm. "I think I'd better get back," she said.

"You haven't heard all of my proposition.

"I don't want to hear any more. I love you, but I'd never do that for you or anyone else."

He took her hand and whispered, "If you don't kill her, *I'm* going to. I'm quite finished with having my life ruined by her."

"I think you're bluffing. You're either bluffing or insane."

"I might be both, that's conceivable. And even if you agreed to help me, I might back out at the last minute. But I think not. Caroline's driven me to the point where one goes over that thin line of conscience, or fear, that keeps most of us, most of the time, from becoming killers."

They stepped aside to let a group of students pass. Then, when they were gone, Charlie started back with her toward the St. Alban's Court. She said, "And what if you were caught?"

He shrugged.

"I go to the gallows. Being a peer, I'd get a silk rope, which might be some consolation. But I'd try my best not to get caught, needless to say. My chances of getting away with it would be immensely improved if you helped me."

A carriage clattered by and for a moment she wondered if she were dreaming. This calm discussion of a murder seemed so impossible, and yet it was happening. Death was the ultimate reality. Lady Darlington's death. Charlie's death, if he were caught. Her death if she helped him and they were both caught.

A breeze rustled the fresh leaves of a small tree in front of one of the houses they were walking past. The breeze was balmy, but to her it felt cold.

"Now," he said, "I have something else to offer you beside the ten thousand pounds."

"No. Please! I'll forget you told me any of this, but I don't want to hear any more."

"But you're going to."

"Charlie I wouldn't do it! If for no other reason, I don't have the nerve to do something like that!"

"How much nerve does it take not to give her her digitalis? Sooner or later she's bound to have another heart seizure. All you'd have to do would be not to give her the medicine."

"That wouldn't necessarily kill her."

"Then slip something in the digitalis that would. You're a nurse. You know the tricks of the trade."

"The 'tricks of the trade,' as you put it, are designed to keep the patient alive," she said. "And I wouldn't do it! Don't you understand that? I'm *not* a murderer!"

She had stopped and said it with a great deal of quiet force. An automobile chugged past them as they looked at each other. Then, when its noise had died away, he said, "Even if it meant your being the next Lady Darlington?"

She was taken completely by surprise, and he knew it. He took her arm and they started walking. "That's my proposition," he said. "Oh, of course we'd have to wait a while. We couldn't rush into it; it wouldn't look so good. But after a few months, we could get married. I love you. Even if I didn't, you'd still make me an excellent wife. You're attractive and charming, and even though you're perhaps a bit unaccustomed to the ways of London society, you could catch on to them quickly—God knows, they're simple-minded enough. And being the countess of Darlington would have certain definite advantages for you. We could have children, which since her miscarriage has been out of the question for Caroline. Would you like to carry my children?"

"Charlie, stop it!"

"Wouldn't you?"

"You know I would. But stop tempting me. . . . Please!"

"Life is one great temptation. To really live, that is. To try for everything you want. The temptation is always there and you either give in to it and try for everything, or you back away and accept whatever a whimsical destiny has assigned you."

"You're arguing against your better convictions again—or rather, in this case, mine."

"Perhaps."

They walked in silence for a while. Life. Death. Murder. Cold-blooded murder. How neat and easy he made it all sound.

"You're considering it, aren't you?" he asked.

"No."

"Yes you are. And the next thing you'll wonder is, if you agree to help me, how can you trust me to marry you afterward? The answer to that—aside from the fact that I love you—is I have everything to gain by marrying you and everything to lose—including my neck—by not. As my wife, you could never testify against me. Nor I against you. It would be our secret, and to hell with the world. But if we weren't married, you could turn against me."

"And you could turn against me."

"But I'd be a fool if I did. As Mr. Franklin said in another context, we either hang together or we hang separately. And in our case, the danger of hanging separately would be considerable."

They had reached the St. Alban's Court, and they stopped and faced each other, their profiles silhouetted against the gas lamp by the door.

"I'll leave you now," he said, quietly. "You think it over. If you're with me, come back to Darlington House in the morning. Caroline won't like seeing you back, but I can force her into accepting you. If you're not with me—and I'll understand if you're not—then we'll never see each other again. Either way, I want you to know that I love you. Despite my lying. Can you believe I love you?"

She paused before answering, searching his eyes.

"I don't know," she finally said.

He took her hand, raised it to his mouth and kissed it. Then he whispered, "Goodbye, my darling." He released her hand and walked away, down the street. She watched him go. Then she slowly climbed the steps to the door of the boarding house.

She already knew what she would do in the morning.

Part II

Violet, Lady Bridgewater, was what her contemporaries called—behind her back—an "adventuress." Her origins she kept purposefully hazy, though they were respectable enough. She had been born fifty-one years before, the daughter of a Latin master in one of the small church schools in the Midlands. Because she was unusually pretty, the Latin master's daughter had attracted the attention of every male in town; by seventeen, she was already married to her first husband, a husky local squire with considerable acreage, but not much money in the bank and even less intelligence in the skull. Three years of married life with the squire and she was going out of her mind with boredom. Unfortunately, or fortunately from Violet's viewpoint, the squire was killed in a hunting accident. The widow sold the farm and moved to London where, through the good offices of a maiden aunt, she manipulated her way into the fringes of London society. At a ball she met a Polish prince who was sixty, ugly, and the owner of a hundred thousand acres near Cracow. He fell in love with her and proposed; she accepted and moved to Poland, which she detested. She existed in Poland for ten years, at which point her husband died, leaving everything but a small sum to his son. Violet was furious. After ten years of what she considered hard labor in the Polish wasteland, to be cheated of the prize was a cruel blow, and she determined never to let it happen again.

She didn't count on the weaknesses of the flesh, however.

Moving to Rome, she fell in love with a handsome young tenor who milked her of her last penny, then vanished. Undaunted, Violet borrowed some money and returned to London where she met a retired admiral whose wife had just died. True to form, Violet captivated the admiral, who proposed, married her, then, eight years later, conveniently died. This time, she fared better: the admiral left her a hundred thousand pounds in the Funds, enough to keep her comfortable for life.

But Violet wanted more than comfort. Her life in Poland had whetted her appetite for luxury, and she had a passion for jewelry that only a millionaire's income could satisfy. So she cast her net for a millionaire. And she capped her dizzying matrimonial career by landing Billy Babson, the Babson Soap king. Billy wasn't much to look at and he was pushing seventy, but every time a housewife bought a cake of Babson Soap, Billy's coffers swelled; and this was what warmed Violet's heart. Plus, he had a shiny new title, a townhouse on Eaton Square, a yacht, and a huge, ugly country home in Scotland called Ayre Hall, which he had built in 1885 in an architectural style that could best be described as Jacobean-Victorian.

Ayre Hall had a superb location. It was set on a hill overlooking the River Dee only a few miles from Balmoral Castle, and few places on earth could match the Dee Valley for scenic beauty. The view was breathtaking. But Ayre Hall itself was a red brick monstrosity bristling with chimneys, turrets, mullioned bays, terraces, and, everywhere, lead statues of dogs, deer, woodchucks, squirrels, and even, incredibly enough, a small sculpture of a cake of Babson Soap placed in the kitchen garden. The place was a masterpiece of bad taste but Billy loved it, and his former neighbor, Queen Victoria, had thought the lead statues were "charming."

The following August, Billy had invited his daughter and son-in-law for a week at Ayre Hall, and though Angela detested her stepmother and Arthur hated Ayre Hall (as well as his father-in-law), because of their concern over the possibility that the infatuated Billy might change his will in Violet's favor, they decided it would be wise to go north. Their fears about Billy's will were founded on something more substantial than anxious guesswork. Since he had married Violet, a coolness had developed between Billy and his daughter which Angela was convinced was Violet's doing. Billy wasn't overly fond of his son-in-law, whom he considered a titled loafer (which he was). Angela knew Violet's history; she knew how she had been "cheated" out of her Polish husband's estate and she was convinced Violet was using Billy's dislike of Arthur as a wedge to talk him into leaving the bulk of his estate to her instead of his daughter, and thus not be "cheated" out of another husband's largesse. The previous month, Arthur had learned from Billy's solicitor that the old man had made a new will, which intelligence sounded most ominous; so when the annual invitation to Scotland had arrived, Arthur and Angela had wasted little time in packing their bags.

The first night of their arrival, they ate dinner with Billy and Violet in the big, paneled dining room, the dark walls of which bristled with stag heads the soap magnate had shot before arthritis had forced him to stop slaughtering the local wildlife. The aging industrialist was mummy-thin, and gauzelike white hair cascaded from the top of his rather pointed skull. Arthritis had stooped him and swollen the knuckles of his hands; asthma gave him a perennial wheeze and cough, which had been made worse by a cold he had caught that afternoon. On top of everything else, he was half deaf; so every time he wheezed, coughed, or cupped his hand behind his ear, Angela was unpleasantly reminded of his mortality. She hated herself for being so mercenary as to brood about her father's will, but in the three months since she had written the note to Lady Darlington, her, and her husband's, finances had gone from bad to worse, and only the previous week they had been forced to borrow another thousand pounds just to pay their household expenses. Credit was easily advanced to peers and peeresses in 1908, particularly peers and peeresses with wealthy parents. But even so, Arthur and Angela had pushed their credit about as far as they could. And they were both convinced their financial future lay in the well-manicured hands of the charming Lady Bridgewater.

She sat opposite her husband, and as Angela watched her she grudgingly admitted to herself the woman was beautiful. Even at fifty-one, Violet's skin was still practically unmarked by time. Her figure was good, her hair expertly dyed, and her taste in clothes was excellent. She had style, she had charm, and she was a mistress at the art of small talk. Old Billy could hardly take his bleary eyes off her.

"And how is your brother?" she said to Arthur, as the footmen passed the partridge. "We saw him at Mrs. Morley's reception last June. He's such a delightful man. I do think he's the Tories' best bet, but then it does seem the Tories are going to be out for some time, doesn't it? Perhaps he should switch over to the Liberals, though that probably wouldn't go down well with his friends."

"I think it would go down very badly with his friends," said Arthur. "In fact, I think they would probably hang him. But Charlie's fine, as far as I know. I haven't seen much of him lately. He's gone to the country."

"The Liberals are going to raise the taxes, damn them!" shouted Billy, who talked at the top of his voice to compensate for his deafness. "Mark my words, they're going to tax the rich out of existence! It'll be the ruin of England—" He went into a coughing fit that cut short his remarks, to no one's dismay. Billy Babson was a confirmed Benthamite, and everyone had heard his economic opinions at least a hundred times. Lady Bridgewater signaled one of the footmen to pound her husband's back. Then, when the old man had stopped coughing, she turned back to Arthur.

"Then your brother is at your family place in Kent?"

"Yes, Ellendon Abbey."

"General Carew has a place not far from there. He and his wife were here two weeks ago, and Mrs. Carew told me how well Lady Darlington looks."

Arthur smiled.

"Mrs. Carew obviously takes an optimistic view of Caroline's health. I doubt if she even saw her. Caroline never leaves her bedroom."

"You're quite wrong there. At least, according to Mrs. Carew. She said Lady Darlington was taking the air on the lawn and even walking. She said it was quite a miraculous transformation.

Apparently she has a new nurse who's done wonders for her."

Angela raised her eyebrows.

"Oh, that's our dear friend, Miss Suffield," she said. "We know all about *her*."

Lady Bridgewater looked at her stepdaughter, whom she disliked not only because she was a rival for Billy's estate, but because she was so plain. In fact, Angela looked remarkably like her father, which complimented neither of them.

"And what do you 'know' about Miss Suffield?" she asked.

Angela thought a moment how to phrase it.

"She's an adventuress," she said, sweetly. "And I dislike adventuresses."

Lady Bridgewater didn't miss the implication, but she was far too experienced at this sort of dagger play to look concerned.

"You mean there's something going on at Ellendon Abbey? How delicious. Tell us all about it."

"I don't choose to spread gossip," said Angela, who was dying to, but since her stepmother wanted to hear it, she refused to give her satisfaction. Just then, old Billy went into another coughing fit, this one worse than the last. Angela looked at her father with concern.

"I think you should see a doctor," she said.

"What?" The old boy cupped his ear.

"A *doctor*," she shouted. "That cough sounds terrible."

"I'm in perfect health," he yelled back.

"Doctor Fraser is coming around in the morning," said Lady Bridgewater to Angela in a firm tone that implied "*I* call the doctor in this house, not you."

"Don't you think he should look at father tonight?"

"No." The short answer left no room for argument. Angela simmered as her stepmother turned the charm back on and smiled at Arthur. "Then perhaps *you'll* spread some gossip. Is this Miss Suffield pretty? One usually thinks of nurses as being rather formidable."

"Oh, she's a stunner," said Arthur. "And shrewd as they come, in my opinion. Except I'm really surprised that Caroline's out of bed and walking. She hasn't moved for years. Of course, now that Paul's gone . . ."

"Who's Paul?"

"He was her footman, who used to carry her around, quite literally. My brother fired him several months ago. Oddly enough, I saw him last week. He came around to the house and asked to see me. The poor chap was really on the skids—hadn't shaved for days and looked like the very devil—and he told me since my brother had refused to give him a recommendation, he couldn't get a new job. I asked why Charlie had fired him, and he said it had something to do with some of Caroline's jewelry. He didn't look too eager to go into it, so I didn't push it any further. But he begged me to hire him, or at least recommend him to someone who would. Well, I wasn't about to take on another footman—our payroll's stiff enough as it is—and I didn't want to recommend him, looking the way he did. But I gave him a few pounds and told Cook to feed him. And that was the end of it. But I wonder if Miss Suffield had something to do with his going."

"Why?"

"I know Caroline liked Paul. And perhaps he was gumming things up for Miss Suffield."

Lady Bridgewater laughed.

"I'm intrigued, but hardly enlightened. Gumming up what?"

"Oh well, that's very simple," sniffed Angela. "The footman was undoubtedly carrying tales to Caroline, and so he had to go."

"You mean tales about Miss Suffield and Lord Darlington? Now it's getting most interesting!"

"Well, this is all guesswork," said Arthur.

"Which is why it's fun," said Violet. "But if this Miss Suffield is involved with your brother, and getting rid of footmen who 'gum up the works,' why is Lady Darlington apparently blooming with health? It would seem it would pay the nurse to keep the patient in bed so she could walk the lawns with the patient's husband, which would be much more to the point, I would think."

Arthur wiped his mouth with his napkin.

"Perhaps we've misjudged Miss Suffield. Perhaps she's a dedicated nurse who has the misfortune of being pretty. Dedicated nurses should definitely be plain; otherwise, it's too difficult to take them seriously."

"The manufacturers are the backbone of this country!" shouted old Billy, who was still a bit behind in the conversation. "Tax industry and you kill England!"

Lady Bridgewater sighed and signaled to the butler to serve dessert.

• • •

"Arthur, we must *do* something!" said Angela that night in their bedroom. She was seated at the vanity in her peignoir, brushing her hair as Arthur sprawled in a wing chair smoking a cigarette. The bedroom was roomy, dark, and over-furnished. Against one wall stood a giant bed, the headboard of which was a jungle of carved vines and birds, some late-Victorian furniture-designer's idea of pseudo-rustic tranquillity. Outside the mullioned windows a storm was blowing up, and the north wind whistled around the corners of the house, creating a mood that was anything but tranquil. Arthur stared at the clouds scuttling in front of the moon and inhaled on his cigarette.

"Do something about what?"

"You know very well 'what.' That horrible woman! Did you see father coughing?"

"I not only saw him, I heard him. He looks fairly wobbly, doesn't he?"

"He looks dreadful, the poor dear. And *she* sits there like the cat who swallowed the canary, waiting for him to go—it made me furious! I *know* she's got him to change the will! Call it feminine intuition if you want, but I know it! And we must do something to protect our interests."

"And what do you suggest?"

She turned to her husband.

"We must try to have a child."

Arthur tapped the cigarette ash.

"We've tried."

"We must try *again*. Sir Andrew says there's absolutely no

reason I can't have perfectly healthy children; it's just that we've had rotten luck. But if we had a child, I *know* father would change his mind. If he had a grandchild, he wouldn't want to disinherit it. It's the only possible weapon we have against Violet. Besides . . ."

She hesitated.

"Besides what?"

Her plain face took on a sad look. "Well, I want children. I want them very much. Don't you?"

Arthur didn't answer for a moment. He was thinking of Gladys. In the six years of his marriage with Angela, they had slowly drifted apart, their sole common bond being money, or more precisely, their lack of it. Arthur wasn't attracted to his wife, and he found his husbandly duties an unpleasant chore. He infinitely preferred making love to Gladys Denning, a lovely young actress he had met three years before and whose rent he paid in return for bed privileges. Angela knew about Gladys, but she was resigned to it, and, typically, had decided to maintain face by ignoring her husband's extracurricular activities. Thus, as far as Arthur was concerned, their childlessness hadn't particularly disturbed him till now. Children meant governesses, which meant further expenses, which meant more trouble. But now? Well, he thought, the old girl may have a point. A bouncing baby boy might bring old Billy around.

"*Don't* you?" persisted Angela.

"Yes, I want children."

"Then . . ." She couldn't bring herself to beg. She knew she was plain and that Arthur didn't enjoy her. It hurt her to admit it, but she knew it was true. And what made it worse was that she was so in love with him. She adored his blond, thin good looks at the same time she deplored his lack of character. She hated to beg for his attention and she had guessed, quite accurately, that the best way to command it was to link it with her father's fortune, which was, she knew, what had attracted him in the first place.

She watched him as he stubbed out the cigarette and stood up. He undid his white tie and said, with a slight smile, "If he's a boy, shall we name him Billy?"

• • •

The tight little world of the English upper classes has always provoked emotions ranging from adulation to detestation. Yet no matter what one's attitude toward them, it would take a cold heart not to admire their country homes. They had a love of the country, and a genius for enhancing the natural beauty of the land with houses, the names of which evoke a way of life that will live in the memory of civilization as something supremely graceful. Knole, Easton Neston, Castle Howard, Warwick Castle, Blenheim, Hatfield—the list is long, and each jewel in the necklace is unique, creating a heritage the country has reason to be proud of. Their owners for the most part adored them. And though it might be argued that the wealth poured into the construction and decoration of these homes might have been more equitably spent to alleviate the poverty of the day, still anyone with a sense of beauty will secretly rejoice in the pleasure assured by their erection, and selfishly forget their sociological pricetags. Of course, not all the homes were gems, nor all the past beautiful. The poor had their noisome slums, and the rich had their monstrosities such as Ayre Hall, though even its vulgar exuberance had a certain aesthetic appeal.

But few of the beautiful homes could surpass Ellendon Abbey for harmonious proportions and a happy marriage of brick and stone with grass, trees, and flowers. And a week after the dinner at Ayre Hall during which Lady Bridgewater had told about Lady Darlington taking the air, Margaret seated her patient in a wheelchair and pushed her through the courtyard over the bridge spanning the ornamental moat to in fact "take the air"—which, on this late August day in Kent, was invitingly warm and well worth taking. Lady Darlington had changed during the past three months. She had lost twelve pounds, thanks to the strict diet Margaret had forced her to adhere to. The diet excluded her beloved chocolates, but more importantly, Margaret had managed to force her patient to restrict her intake of alcohol to three glasses of sherry a day. This had not been an easy accomplishment. Lady Darlington had howled with rage; but Margaret had persisted. And, after a week of enforced total abstinence, Lady Darlington had meekly—for her—given in. She had no alternative. With Paul gone and Margaret in total charge, the only way for her to get alcohol would have been to distill it herself in her bedroom, which was a bit impractical. Besides, Margaret had noticed that the irascible and imperious Lady Darlington seemed to lose some of her fight when Paul left. He had not only supplied the alcohol, he had been a sort of partner in maliciousness. He was an *eminence grise,* whose cynical opportunism, as well as cold sexuality, must have fueled the destructive side of Lady Darlington's personality. Certainly without him she became much less formidable. She still retained her bark. But, removed from Paul and alcohol, her bite was blunted. She complained, but she had also begun to evince an interest in life that Margaret flattered herself was a product of the more healthful regimen she had forced on her. The sunshine, the open air, the daily exercise of walking was beginning to work its magic; and not only had the older woman lost weight, but her face was losing its dissipated puffiness and actually taking on color. She became interested in the garden at Ellendon Abbey, and after the second month of Margaret's regime, Lady Darlington actually began to look forward to her airing, and would grouse when bad weather prevented it.

Now, as Margaret pushed her chair across the moat, her patient, dressed in a yellow skirt and white blouse and wearing a large straw garden hat to ward off the sun, pointed to the lily-choked water below and said, "Why hasn't Evans cleaned out those lilies? Didn't I tell him to last week?"

"Yes you did," replied Margaret. Evans was the gardener. "But he's been fertilizing the dahlias, and there were those five rose bushes you told him to take out. The ones with the fungus."

"Oh yes, I forgot. Well, we mustn't push Evans. He's a gem of a gardener, and like all good gardeners, he's temperamental. Margaret, do you suppose I could walk from here?"

Margaret stopped the chair at the end of the bridge. Usually, she pushed her patient to the garden where she would get out of the chair and walk slowly, but with increasing strength and certainty, within the confines of the garden wall.

"Do you want to try?" she said.

"Yes. It's such a gorgeous day, and I'm feeling repulsively healthy. Besides, this thing bumps so! Let me try walking it. If I fall in the moat, you can fish me out."

Margaret braked the chair, recalling with amusement how Lady Darlington had roared when Margaret insisted she buy the chair three months before; then the howls when, after she had gotten used to becoming mobile in the chair, Margaret insisted she begin walking. Now she could hardly be restrained from hopping out of the chair; and Margaret wondered how long it would be before the chair would be relegated to a closet. As she had known all along, there was nothing preventing Lady Darlington from leading a normal existance except her devotion to the bottle (which aggravated the indolent side of her character) and her perverse desire to punish her husband. Now she helped her to her feet. She stepped out on the grass, leaning on Margaret for support. Then she rather irritably pushed her nurse's arm away. "I can do it myself," she snapped, forcing a gruff show of independence.

"Take the cane," said Margaret, removing the Malacca stick from its bracket on the back of the chair.

"I don't need it. That thing makes me feel like the village crone. I can do nicely without it, thank you."

As Margaret watched, Lady Darlington straightened her back and took a few tentative steps. Then she looked back, her face beaming with pleasure like a child with a new toy. "You see? In another month I'll be doing jigs. I'll race you to the garden." She laughed. "Well, we shan't race. What a glorious day! What an absolutely glorious day!"

She walked slowly along the edge of the moat as Margaret followed her, pushing the heavy wooden chair. They had gone almost to the corner of the moat when she heard hoofbeats. She looked around to see Lord Darlington coming toward them on his bay mare, Maryann. He was wearing his riding clothes, which were covered with dust, and Maryann was glistening with sweat from a twenty-minute canter. He reined the horse and looked at his wife without excessive affection.

"Bravo, Caroline," he said. "We're going to have to enter you in the Olympics."

Lady Darlington looked up at her husband.

"There's no need to be facetious," she growled. "If there's anything I detest, it's false cheerfulness with sick people."

"But you're no longer sick."

"No thanks to you," she sniffed. Then her high spirits got the better of her and she smiled. "Oh Charlie, I'm walking further every day! It really is most extraordinary. I hate to admit it, but I'm actually feeling quite good. No, that's wrong. I'm feeling marvelous!"

He smiled slightly.

"I'm sure you *do* hate to admit it. Gushiness isn't exactly your style."

"But I feel gushy. And I think everyone has a right to gush periodically, don't you, Margaret?"

"Definitely."

"So I shall gush. Mind you, you'll all pay for it later on. I shall make a point of being particularly nasty tonight at dinner. I shall complain bitterly about the food and make everyone thoroughly miserable. But right now, I gush."

Charlie's smile remained fixed, but his eyes shot to Margaret.

"And whom will you make miserable at dinner?" he asked.

She put her hand to her hat to protect it from a sudden breeze.

"Why, you and Margaret, of course. Didn't she tell you? I'm sick to death of eating alone in bed, and you two have had the dining room to yourselves far too long. So I'm dining with you from now on. Come along, Margaret. I see Evans, and I want to make sure he doesn't put too much fertilizer on the dahlias. Oh, and remind me to ask him about the chrysanthemums. I particularly want the yellow ones for the border."

She started off in the direction of the garden again. Charlie watched her until she was out of earshot; then he said to Margaret, "I'd like to see you in the library when you get back from the garden."

He spurred his horse and galloped off toward the stables to the north of the house. Margaret knew he was angry.

And she knew why. When, two hours later, she walked across the entrance hall to the library and knocked on the linen-fold paneled door, she had prepared herself for a difficult meeting.

"Come in," came his voice through the door. She did. He was standing at the window looking out on the courtyard, with Scylla and Charybdis, the two Great Danes, asleep on the floor beside him. He turned and gestured to the two leather chairs in front of the fire. "Sit down," he said. She went over to the right chair; he took the other and, as on that first day she had met him, he propped his boots up on the brass fender. He picked a pencil off the table next to his chair and ran his thumb over the sharp point. Then he said, "So Caroline is going to eat with us from now on?"

Since her return to Darlington House, Margaret had been taking her meals with Charlie when he was home. When they moved to the country, the practice had continued, though he had been gone a great deal of the time, including three times to Vienna for what he vaguely referred to as "some government business," though she had read in the papers that he and a group of other peers interested in foreign affairs had been conferring with diplomats in Vienna and Paris on the brewing Balkan crisis over the disposition of the former Turkish provinces of Bosnia and Herzegovina.

"Your wife," she said, rather formally, "told me she felt up to eating in the dining room, and I saw no reason why she shouldn't."

"Oh, there's no reason why she can't turn somersaults. You've turned her into the picture of health. She blooms!"

"I've only been trying to do my job."

He gave her a skeptical look.

"Margaret, something tells me you haven't been exactly truthful with me these past few months."

"I've been very untruthful. I was wondering when you'd bring it up."

"When you came back to Darlington House that morning, I assumed you were going to help me. But you had no intention of helping me, did you? In fact, you've been working against me the whole time. Am I right?"

"Yes."

"Why?"

"To save you."

"From what?"

"Yourself." She leaned forward and lowered her voice. Even though the walls of the ancient house were well over three feet thick, she still instinctively spoke in a near whisper. "If I hadn't come back, you might have tried to kill her. Or get someone to do it for you. And I couldn't let you do it."

"You had no right to make that decision for me," he snapped.

"Charlie, you were like a madman that night. Walking down the sidewalk talking about murder as if you were talking about putting a cat to sleep—it was insane! Oh, I don't know if you would have had the nerve to try it, but I couldn't take the chance. I had to protect her, and I had to protect you."

He looked disgusted. "You've protected her, all right, but who's going to protect *me* from her? My God, now you've got her walking! She's going to come to the dining room and plague me even more. I preferred having her in bed drunk—then at least I didn't have to see her. What in God's name gave you the idea to *improve* her?"

"Because life is sacred. You said that night it wasn't, but you're wrong. If one life is cheap, all life is cheap."

"I'm not interested in sermons."

"I think you could stand a few, frankly. Oh, I saw the dilemma you were in. She was horrible—no one knew that better than I. Good Lord, she tried to send me to jail! But just because she was a horror didn't mean we had the right to kill her. When you left me that night, I decided the only thing to do was to make her *less* horrible. I thought that with Paul gone, I might be able to get her off the bottle and help bring her back to a more normal life, in which case she might not be so difficult for you to live with. And I've done it. A lot of it was Paul. He was a terrible influence on her."

"What makes you think she wasn't a terrible influence on him? She was attracted to him—"

"I don't believe it. She's in love with you."

"She's in love with herself, and *no* one else!"

"That's not true! That's how I got her to stop drinking and go on the diet: you know how furious she was when I came back, but I told her the only way to save her marriage was to stop drinking, and she believed me. She loves you enough to have abstained for almost three months now."

"I don't want her love," he almost shouted. "She doesn't love me anyway. And why in God's name didn't you tell me the truth?"

"Because you would have interfered. Just as you are doing now. Except that I'm not going to let you, if I can help it. Paul was able to substitute for you because you were never around. Now she's got something to fight for. And I don't care if you're furious at me or not; this way is better than my trying to slip arsenic in her soup, or whatever other mad scheme you might have dreamed up. Charlie, she can be a good wife to you. There's no reason she can't help your career, but only if you meet her half way. You have to give her some love and attention. You have to encourage her. And if you do, there's no reason why both of you can't be happy."

He looked at her with dry skepticism.

"The noble, sacrificing Miss Suffield, mending the frayed marital knot. And what about you and me?"

She shrugged. "That was out of the question from the start."

"I thought we loved each other?"

She looked at him resentfully. "So did I. But I think you probably were lying to get me to do your dirty work. It hasn't been a pleasant realization for me."

"And that's why you haven't let me come to your room?"

"That, and other things. It hasn't been easy. But if I was to exert any influence over your wife, I could hardly leave myself open to her suspicions. Besides, as I told you, I don't want to be your mistress. You can call me sanctimonious if you like, but I think it's rather cheap. And as you now know, your price for marriage was considerably higher than I could entertain."

He put the pencil down.

"Well. It seems I've pegged you all wrong, doesn't it?"

"It would seem so."

"Of course, I knew something was wrong when you kept putting me off with those feeble excuses: headaches and whatnot. And getting Caroline to cut down her drinking seemed rather odd for someone who was presumably waiting for an opportunity to send her to what one might call an eternal binge. But I really didn't see that this was an elaborate attempt to 'save' me, as you put it. I'm not sure I like being saved, and I definitely dislike being tricked."

"You tricked me, didn't you?"

"Yes. I also invested eight hundred pounds and three months' time in you."

"I'll pay you back the money."

"You're a cool one, aren't you? You know, I think you're still in love with me."

"Yes, I am. Too much in love with you to let you make the worst mistake of your life."

"Ah, there you go again, saving me. Margaret, you've inherited from your preacher father a most unpleasant streak of the redeemer." He stood up and wandered to the window. "You see, the basic difference between us is that you have a favorable view of human nature, and I don't. Oh, we can pass legislation and alleviate misery and increase social justice and publish moral tracts and build churches, but human nature is never really altered. As Mr. Darwin says, we are descended from animals, and when our backs are against the wall, we behave like animals. You think Caroline can be 'redeemed' or 'reformed.' I don't. Caroline has always been a selfish, destructive woman, and she always will be. Caroline's wonderful rehabilitation that you think is going to restore domestic bliss to Darlington House is nothing but a change of tactics on her part; but because you like to think you're 'saving' me, you flatter yourself that you've improved her character as well as her health. Well, you're wrong. Caroline's stopped wallowing in bed with her bottle because she's realized she can no longer afford to. When I started fighting back at her—when I fired Paul and threatened to stop her supply of alcohol—she saw I'd taken about enough of her. She didn't stop drinking because she loves me. She stopped because she saw it was her most vulnerable point—her Achilles' heel where I could conceivably really hurt her. And now she wants to eat with us—why? Because she knows it's the only way she can separate us."

"That's not true. She knows there's nothing going on between us. I'm sure of it. We're already separated."

He turned on her and said, angrily, "But we're not, dammit! If you'd get over your damn moral squeamishness—"

"We *are* separated!" she persisted. "Don't you understand? There's no future for us. Your future is with *her!*"

"I'd rather be dead."

"You will be, if you don't listen to me." She got out of the chair and came over to the window beside him. "Don't you think I was tempted that night? You say I'm so morally squeamish; well, I'm human. I was tempted. I wanted you, and I wanted to be Lady Darlington. But I'm realistic too. And the only realistic way out of your mess is to try and change her—and I think I *can* change her! I think you're wrong: her mind is changing, as well as her health. You can change people's nature for the worse, and you can change it for the better—and I'm doing it with her."

"And what happens to you if you succeed?"

"I go away."

"I don't want you to go away. And I don't think you want to."

"No, I don't. But it doesn't matter what I want."

He suddenly took her in his arms and tried to kiss her. She wriggled free.

"No. *Please.*"

"You're lying to yourself. You want me as much as I want you."

"No!"

She moved back away from him, watching the coldness come into his eyes. "All right," he said. "I won't try that again." Then he laughed. "I suppose the joke's on me, isn't it? Women! My brother told me I was an ass to fall in love with you, and he was right. And I was an idiot to trust you, too. I suppose you're going to try and blackmail me now?"

"You know I wouldn't."

He looked at her a moment.

"No, I suppose you wouldn't. You're too 'moral' to do that,

happily. Well, this is a joyful day for moralists everywhere, isn't it? It proves that killing one's wife is not an easy proposition."

"It's nothing to joke about."

"That's your opinion. But don't worry: I've learned my lesson, so you can relax. I won't steal into her bedroom and strangle her. I probably wouldn't have had the nerve to go through with it anyway. I talk a good murder; but I suppose I'm not the type, really." He picked up a sheaf of papers from the desk and began leafing through them. "I have some work to do if you don't mind."

She waited for him to say something else. When he didn't, she left the room.

• • •

By the time of the ascension of Edward VII to the throne, the strict morality which has become synonymous with his mother's name had already been eroded, though the majority of the public still observed the Victorian ground rules of behavior. There had always existed a "velvet underground" in nineteenth-century London. The great courtesans reigned in Paris, but one of the greatest of them, Cora Pearl, was English, being the daughter of a Plymouth music teacher named, incredibly, Crouch, and many of her only slightly less successful sisters stayed home and did almost as well as Cora in London. Victoria could write in 1870, "the animal side of our nature is to me—too dreadful"; but in the same year, her son was involved in the divorce case of Lady Mordaunt, a member of a socially exclusive international set. By the nineties, public morality and "delicacy of feeling" were even further jolted by the Wilde case, with its revelations of purple goings-on in the back streets of London. So by the first decade of the new century, what Lady Longford called the "cozy havens" of Victorian morality had been thoroughly aired, and the incredible prudery of the former century was on its way to a well-deserved demise.

Thus, Charlie's quiet trips to St. John's Wood were very much in the tradition of the day; and considering his disastrous home life, it was hardly surprising that he looked for solace, as well as emotional and physical release, in the cheerful red brick cottage that belonged to one of the more successful Edwardian "*grandes horizontales*," Laura Metcalf. Laura, like Cora Pearl and Lady Bridgewater, came from respectable beginnings—in her case, the family of a Brighton dentist. Unlike Lady Bridgewater, who chose the more socially acceptable path of fortune-hunting matrimony, Laura moved into the demimonde, where she achieved success perhaps more honestly than Lady Bridgewater, if not as genteelly. Certainly Laura's clientele believed they received good value for their money. And none of her customers—all of whom came from the upper levels of society—were more devoted than Lord Darlington. He not only thought Laura was one of the most beautiful women in London, which she was, but he also enjoyed her company. She was funny, warm, and generous, and she was a wonderful listener. He had thought he had found some of these qualities in Margaret. But when his wife's nurse turned against him, locking him out of her room and, even worse, becoming the champion of Caroline, he had no alternative but to return to St. John's Wood and Laura Metcalf, in whose plump, pink arms he was lying the night after Margaret had told him she had become, as far as he was concerned, the enemy.

He had just made love to Laura and was now staring up at the circle of pudgy cherubs she had hired an out-of-work artist to paint on the ceiling. From the outside, Laura's house looked cozily unprepossessing. But on the inside she had let her passion for overdecoration run rampant, and the parlors and bedrooms were choked with every conceivable gimcrack as well as overstuffed chairs, gilt and marble tables, ferns in brass jardinières, palms in porcelain tubs, china animals, Oriental rugs, gilt-framed landscapes (or worse, imitation Landseers)—and in her bedroom, above the enormous bed with its gilt-swan headboard, the riot of rosy cupids on the ceiling. Charlie thought the cupids were bilious, but he liked Laura too much to tell her his opinion of her taste.

She ran her hand slowly over his chest and said, "So Margaret has gotten Caroline off the bottle?"

He considered Laura a discreet woman, so he had kept her informed, though for obvious reasons he hadn't told her what he had wanted Margaret to do for him regarding his wife.

"Yes, damn her. Miss Suffield has turned out to be a moralizing disaster."

Laura chuckled. "You're just angry because she's locked you out of her bedroom."

"That's only part of it, but it's the most ridiculous part. Can you imagine her trying to save her virtue after she's already gone to bed with me? It's not only idiotic, it's impossible."

"You're confusing virtue with chastity. I lost my chastity *years* ago. But I still think I'm a virtuous woman. I'll grant you the archbishop of Canterbury might argue differently."

He laughed and kissed the palm of her hand. "You *are* a virtuous woman, Laura. More virtuous than half the women in London, I'll wager."

"Don't overestimate me. I'm not *that* virtuous."

"Well, half the women in London society, then."

"That's more believable. But I still think you're fond of this nurse."

Silence. She tickled his ear. "Tell Laura the truth. Are you in love with her?"

He brushed her hand away from his ear lobe, but still said nothing.

"You're sulking, aren't you?"

He sat up.

"Do you blame me? I did everything for the woman: bought her clothes, paid off her father's debts—which wasn't cheap—and what does she do in return? Gets Caroline out of bed. Turns her into the picture of health—Good God, the *last* thing I want!"

Laura smiled.

"You ought to have gotten her to put Caroline away instead."

Charlie blinked.

"Well, I hadn't thought of that."

He felt slightly clammy. Laura sat up and kissed his bare shoulder.

"I think Miss Suffield sounds like a very *good* woman, and she's probably an excellent influence on you."

"That's your opinion."

"I also think you're in love with her."

"I was. I'm not so sure now."

"Do all members of the House of Lords lead such a complicated love life?"

"I have no idea. I'm sure you're better informed on the love life of the peerage than I am."

She laughed and got out of bed to put on her black silk robe embroidered with pink flamingos.

"Oh, I am. I'm planning to write a book about it someday. After I retire, of course."

He shot her a curious look. "I hope you wouldn't use any names?"

She piled her long chestnut hair on top of her head and began pinning it.

"Oh, it wouldn't be fun if I didn't use names." She smiled at him, then pulled the bellcord by her vanity. "I hope you're hungry. We're having pressed duck for dinner."

Charlie sat on the bed watching her, feeling not only naked but suddenly rather exposed. The uncomfortable thought occurred to him that perhaps Laura Metcalf wasn't as discreet as he had always assumed. Nor as virtuous.

But then he decided—or hoped—she was pulling his leg. It was odd. He didn't enjoy her as much as he used to. And despite his resentment at what Margaret had done, he missed the beautiful young nurse. Perhaps, he mused, it was her tricking him that made her that much more desirable. Perhaps he was, after all, in love with her, as Laura said. He certainly thought he had been until she turned on him. Despite his anger at her, if she had walked into Laura's bedroom, which was unlikely, he thought he probably would forgive her on the spot. He could understand her behavior. She was, as he had told Caroline, a lady, in the last analysis, and to continue sleeping with him would only serve to make her miserable, and him too, in the bargain. But Caroline was a "Lady," for that matter. He was surrounded by ladies, either with a capital *L* or a small one, and they were driving him insane. He probably had been half insane to suggest murdering his wife to her nurse, and yet what had been the alternative? The situation he was in now, and had been in for the past three years: going to Laura. Except that now he had the added misery of missing Margaret.

To hell with all of them, he thought. If he couldn't find satisfaction with his wife or Margaret or even Laura, he'd put them all out of his mind and concentrate on politics. They had been dull this past year, since Mr. Asquith had taken over the premiership after the death of the former Liberal prime minister the previous April, and the only activity of any interest in which Lord Darlington had participated had been the trips to Vienna. He had been flattered that the foreign secretary had included him in the informal group chosen to try mediating the Balkan mess; he did, after all, belong to the party out of power, and it had been a tribute to his knowledge of foreign affairs to have been asked to go. But the situation seemed insoluble at that point. And though the group was scheduled to go again the next month, Lord Darlington had little hopes for their attaining any success. The real battle that was shaping up was the budget battle in the spring. Already rumors were flying about the new taxes Lloyd George would introduce; and though no one knew any details, it was generally conceded the taxes would cause a bitter fight in Parliament, a fight that might end up in the House of Lords. This was interesting to Charlie. And as he watched Laura fixing her hair, he decided he would skip dinner with her and go to Mona Morley's instead. The leading Conservative hostess was having a musicale at her townhouse on Pelham Crescent. The usual group of important Tories would probably be there, including Caroline's brother, the duke of Suffolk, who was the leader of the reactionary peers in the Lords; and Sir Reginald Hamilton, the leading Tory in the House of Commons and Charlie's rival for the foreign secretaryship when and if the Tories ever were returned to power. The talk would be about the budget, and the duke would probably pressure Charlie into taking a position against the Liberal proposals, whatever they turned out to be. Charlie didn't look forward to seeing his brother-in-law. But he thought it would be intelligent for him to put in an appearance.

Besides, Fritz Kreisler was going to play the Beethoven *Spring* Sonata, and he wouldn't have wanted to miss that.

Laura came back to the bed and kissed him.

"What are you thinking about?" she asked. "Love?"

He shook his head.

"Politics."

She made a face.

"How dull."

Charlie laughed.

"With my miserable love life, politics aren't only an escape, they're a relief."

• • •

Margaret assumed she had lost Charlie now, and while it at first had made her spend night after sleepless night alternatingly crying and hating herself for having taken the path she had chosen, she had slowly become resigned to the fact he was gone. She had known sooner or later he would find out what she was doing, and now that he had, now that she had told him there was no future for them, he had understandably enough drifted out of her life. He remained civil to her, but that was all; the fire was out. In the ensuing month, he spent less than five days at Ellendon Abbey, claiming politics required his time in London, and during those five days, he spent most of the time by himself, either riding, playing tennis at General Carew's house down the road, or working in the library. When he was with Margaret, they both studiously avoided any mention of what had happened. She felt virtuous for having stopped his scheme to do in his wife; she felt professional pride for having rehabilitated Lady Darlington. But as is so often the case, virtue and pride make lonely bed companions, and she was anything but happy. She finally began to think the best thing for her to do would be to leave Ellendon Abbey. She had achieved her goal; she didn't think Lady Darlington needed either her protection or her nursing. And she began to think about her future, a future that was apparently no longer going to include the earl of Darlington.

If he was angry over what she had done, Sir Andrew Hodge, on the other hand, was overwhelmed. She had told the doctor at the beginning what she had hoped to accomplish, and asked him to say nothing to Charlie about it until she had some signs of success. Though he was skeptical of anyone's ability to stop Caroline from drinking, he acquiesced. And when, at the end of September, he came down to Ellendon Abbey for his weekly visit and was met by Caroline in the drawing room rather than her bedroom, he was frankly amazed. "You've accomplished a miracle!" he enthused to Margaret, as she walked him to the entrance hall after leaving Lady Darlington. "A genuine miracle! Why, her blood pressure's practically normal, and her pulse is regular. You haven't been giving her the digitalis?"

"Only once every three days. She doesn't seem to need it more often."

"That's good. And the whiskey? Is she still off it?"

Margaret nodded.

"Three glasses of sherry a day: one at lunch, one at dinner, and one before she goes to bed."

"I told Charlie he should have dried her out years ago, but he always said it couldn't be done. And here you've done it! I think it's remarkable. And she walks everywhere now! Do you use the chair at all?"

"Only when she gets tired, which isn't often any more."

The doctor shook his head in wonder.

"I knew you were a fine lass, but I had no idea you were a miracle worker. The only problem is, I think you're doing yourself out of a job. If she keeps improving like this, I can't see why she'll need a nurse at all."

"I know. And I was wondering if you could keep an eye out for any possible openings for me."

They had reached the entrance hall with its great wooden staircase. A beautifully carved heraldic lion stood on top of the newel post, over which Sir Andrew had hung his silk hat. Now he lifted it off and put it on his head. "As a matter of fact, one of my patients, a Mrs. Addison, may be needing a nurse soon. She's getting on in years, and her only daughter is about to get married. When the times comes, I'd be glad to recommend you.

She's well-fixed, but I don't think she could pay what Charlie's paying you."

She stared past him, seeing a ghost on the stair, the ghost of her past, of tending another elderly lady, of scrimping her salary to pay Charlie back the eight hundred pounds. Once it had seemed like a fulfilling life for her. Now, after Charlie, it seemed miserably drab.

"What do you think she might pay?" she asked, quietly.

"Oh, the going rate, I imagine. Fifty, maybe sixty, guineas. Shall I ask for you?"

She forced a weary smile.

"That would be most kind."

"Good. Well, I'm off to the station. My regards to Charlie when you see him."

"I hardly ever see him these days."

He caught the sadness in her tone, and looked rather surprised, as if seeing something about the nurse he hadn't seen before. Then he picked up his bag and headed for the door.

"Yes, he hasn't been around much lately, has he? Well, good day to you."

When he had left, she walked slowly to her bedroom, which, as in the London house, was next to her patient's. She felt miserably depressed. Leaving Charlie, which she had only contemplated before, now, with the prospect of new employment, seemed a reality. She went in her room and opened the closet where the blue velvet dress he had given her was still hanging. She took it out and held it up in front of her, looking at her reflection in the mirror on the back of the closet door. It had been so beautiful, at least for a short while. He had been the only man she had ever loved. It was odd she could love a man who had lied to her, a man who had wanted her to murder for him.

And yet she had. Even worse, she still did.

• • •

The beautiful late-summer weather continued into autumn, which brought a crispness to the night air but left the days unusually warm. And on the last Thursday of September, Lady

Darlington told her nurse she wanted to take lunch in the garden. Margaret went to the kitchen to tell Mrs. Blaine; when she arrived, the housekeeper handed her a letter which had just been delivered. Margaret ordered the lunch, then opened the letter. It was from Sir Andrew, telling her he had spoken to Mrs. Addison about hiring a nurse, and the elderly lady would be pleased to meet Margaret any time she was in London during the next few weeks. Margaret folded the letter and put it in the pocket of her uniform, then she started out of the kitchen when Mrs. Blaine stopped her.

"It wasn't bad news, I hope?" said the housekeeper.

"Oh no."

"You looked so gloomy, I thought perhaps a relative had passed on."

Margaret smiled.

"It was just a note from Sir Andrew. He has a new position arranged for me in London."

"You mean you're leaving us?"

"Perhaps. There won't be much need for me with Lady Darlington doing so well."

Mrs. Blaine glanced at the nearby cook, then motioned to Margaret to follow her into the pantry, which was empty.

"You've had a falling out, haven't you?" she whispered. "You and him?"

Margaret chose her words with care.

"As far as I know, His Lordship is quite pleased with what I've done."

"Ah, go on with you! Don't feed me that blarney: don't you think I see what's going on? Him blowing his top because you've got the old bitch out of bed and healthy as a twenty-year-old debutante? And now you're leaving us! Do you think it'll be any better when you're gone? Do you think that woman will turn into a sweetheart? The one chance of happiness he had was you, and now you're leaving him. Ah, I don't understand you. It must be because you're English, acting so queer."

She might have been angry if the housekeeper's words hadn't expressed some of her own thoughts of the past few days. Now instead of anger, she found her eyes filling with tears.

"What else can I do?" she whispered. "I can't stay! I love him too much to stay."

Mrs. Blaine took her into arms and patted her shoulder sympathetically.

"There, there, now don't you cry, you poor dear. I know. I knew from the beginning it probably wouldn't work out, you being a clergyman's daughter and all—even though he was a Protestant clergyman. And he hasn't been much help either, staying away in London and the Lord knows what he's been up to *there*. Still and all, I think he's sweet on you."

"No he's not," she said, straightening and drying her eyes with a handkerchief. "He's too selfish to love anyone."

"I think you're being a bit hard on him."

"No I'm not." She stuck her handkerchief back in her pocket. "Selfish men don't love people: they use them."

"Well, maybe so. I suppose he is selfish, but if you want to know the truth, I've never met a man who wasn't selfish. So if you be looking for one, you're going to be looking for a miracle, and good luck to you."

Margaret smiled in spite of her depression.

"You know, I think you're absolutely right."

"Sure I am. Don't think the late Mr. Blaine wasn't as selfish as they come, particularly when it came to sharing his whiskey! Ah well, God rest his soul, I suppose it's the nature of the beast to be selfish." She shook her head. "Men! It's hard to do with them, and even worse to do without them."

• • •

Rogers filled the crystal goblet with golden sherry and handed it to Lady Darlington. She took a sip and smiled.

"Lovely. Quite lovely. The one nice thing about temperance is that it makes one appreciate so much more the few liquid crumbs one gets. That will do, Rogers. You can leave us. Miss Suffield and I will lunch alone."

They were seated at a white wrought-iron table in the middle of the garden. The table had been set with crystal, china, and silver, and Rogers and a footman had served the cold chicken luncheon. Now the butler bowed and motioned the footman to follow him back to the house. Lady Darlington, wearing a flowing white garden dress and her straw hat, relaxed in her chair and gazed around at the flower beds which blazed with color in the sun; the stock, the dahlias, and the chrysanthemums formed a rainbow of beauty, all carefully calculated to give the informal look that is the genius of English gardening. The flowers had little time left, and they were using their borrowed time to advantage. A last few white roses climbed the low brick wall, and in the center of the enclosure was the lawn, so level and smooth it was often used for croquet. A honeybee buzzed busily around the table. Lady Darlington waved it away, snapping, "Don't ruin my sherry." The bee, apparently intimidated, headed for the roses for its lunch.

"Well, my dear, I'll be sorry to see you go," said Lady Darlington to Margaret. "And I frankly never thought I'd say that. Who is this Mrs. Addison?"

"I don't know much about her yet," answered Margaret, who had told her patient of her plans.

"If you don't like her, don't take the position. You're free to stay with us as long as you wish, you know."

"That's very kind of you."

"Not at all. I owe you a great debt. You've quite literally changed my life, and I appreciate it." She sipped more sherry. "I used to despise you, you know. I absolutely detested you when you first arrived. Of course, I can say that now because I've become so very fond of you. It's interesting how people change, isn't it? Help yourself to the chicken."

"Thank you." Margaret took a thin slice of white meat and a spoonful of salad.

"I firmly believe," continued her patient, "that all human relationships should begin with lies and end with truth. That is the definition of friendship, really. And I fear I was terribly false with you at the beginning. Oh, not that I ever gushed with love for you. But I concealed what I was really thinking."

"Which was?"

"That I was jealous of you. Quite insanely jealous. You were young and very pretty, and I know my husband—he likes young and pretty women. You're in love with him, aren't you?"

Margaret looked startled. Lady Darlington smiled. "Oh my dear, don't worry: I've known it all along. And I can't blame you. He's terribly attractive. And quite unprincipled, which is why he's such a good politician. Not that I suspect anything, mind you; if I weren't sure that you and Charles weren't being naughty, I'd never confide in you the way I am. Charles met his match in you, which is why he's being so studiously unpleasant now, I suspect. And of course, you wouldn't have been so eager to rehabilitate me if you were involved with him, would you? So I trust you now. But then, I was jealous; and of course, Paul fed my suspicions. Dear Paul! I missed him for a while, but there— he really was unscrupulous, wasn't he? A charming rascal. Why is it the most attractive men are so thoroughly rotten? At any rate, Paul fed my suspicions, and then that note from the bird woman, Angela . . . Well, I decided to take my revenge on you, which was dreadful of me. But I do hope you've forgiven me for the fire-drill business? I wouldn't blame you if you didn't, but I hope you will."

"Of course," she lied. "I'd forgotten all about it weeks ago."

"Ah, you have a charitable nature, which I admire. A truly Christian nature. You've returned good for evil, and that is the definition of Christianity. Dear me, I seem to be defining every- thing today, don't I? But the reason is, I've been defining myself lately, and I've come to a rather major decision which I wish to discuss with you. More chicken?"

"Yes, thank you. It's delicious. But you must eat some too."

"In a moment, my dear. I'm savoring the sherry; when one is rationed, one likes to linger. Now where was I? Ah yes: my decision. You undoubtedly recall that rather drunken conversa- tion I had with you the first day you arrived? When I babbled on about power and my taking my revenge on Charles and the Lord knows what else?"

"Yes, I remember."

"You could hardly forget. I was being terribly vespine, I fear. I *did* once think that way. I *did* want to hurt Charles." She paused a moment, and, for a moment, she dropped the casual chatty tone she had been speaking in and became almost morose. "It's terrible to want to hurt one's husband, isn't it? And yet he had hurt me."

Margaret watched her as a fly buzzed around the table. Then Lady Darlington waved it away and continued. "At any rate, I was wrong. I can see that now. And you helped me to see it. How right you were to tell me to stop drinking. As long as I drank, I was weak, and I prefer to be strong. It is always important to be strong, isn't it? Particularly when one wants to be a good wife—one who is a help to her husband. And that's what I've decided I want to be."

She smiled, and Margaret had the feeling her patient was being a touch too friendly, too unaccustomedly confiding.

"Marriage, for all its faults," continued Lady Darlington, "is still the foundation of our society, isn't it? You've helped me realize that, and to see that it's a matter of give and take. And of course I've done nothing but take for years. Now I intend to give. More specifically, I'm going to open Darlington House and become the hostess Charles needs in a wife."

No matter what Margaret's feelings toward her, or toward Charlie, she could only be delighted at this news, if it were true.

"Does that please you?" asked her patient.

"Very much. And I'm sure it will please him."

"Yes, I think so. I'm going to give a ball before the opening of Parliament. Of course, we shan't say anything to my husband —he's going to Vienna next week, and I want to surprise him when he returns. I'm giving it in honor of Sir Reginald Hamilton. Do you know who he is?"

"He's one of the leading Tories, I believe."

"More than that. He's Charles's leading rival in the party. He's a perfectly dreadful man, and that perfectly dreadful woman, Mrs. Morley, who fancies herself a sort of political kingmaker, has been having an affair with him for years. Oh, it's all done with great politesse, of course, and he and Charles attend the same dinner parties, but he'd give anything to do Charles in, politically, as would Mrs. Morley. Well, there's no defense like a good offense. And by giving a ball in his honor, it will make Charles look magnanimous and put Reggie Hamilton one down in the score. Besides, it will open the season on a dramatic note. Everyone will be dying to come, and I fancy it shall be quite brilliant. I'll wear my jewels and a new gown, and the whole world will see the new Lady Darlington. And of course, *you* must come."

"Me?"

"I insist. If it weren't for you, I could never give the ball; and this is my small way of showing my gratitude to you. I shall buy you a new gown, and I think you'll be quite a dazzling success. You will come, won't you?"

She was more than a little taken aback.

"Well, if you want me."

"Of course I do, or I wouldn't have said it. However, I'll admit there's another reason I want you. A rather selfish reason, in fact. Do finish the chicken, my dear. There's a good girl."

Margaret shook her head. "No, I've had enough. And you must eat something."

"I'll have the salad and nothing more. No, the reason is there has been a certain amount of talk circulating about you and Charles. Most of it has been spread by Arthur and Angela, I imagine: she likes nothing better than gossiping about her in-laws—I suppose because no one would bother talking about her, or that repulsive stepmother of hers, Lady Tapwater, or whatever. Well, my point is, there's no better way to kill the gossip than to have you at the ball with me. It's irregular, of course, but I shall explain that I need you nearby because of my heart, or whatever. What matters is that they will all see how close we are; and that should stop the gossip. It would be a great service to Charles if you'd do it. It would clear his name of suspicion, and I would be even more indebted to you than I am now. Society is malicious, particularly a society involved so deeply with politics, like London society. You and I know there's no truth to the gossip; but I think you can see the wisdom of stifling it. Will you come?"

How peculiar, she thought. How ironic that I should be put out on display to save Charlie's reputation when, after all, he *did* make love to me. And how odd that she, of all people, would ask.

"Of course I will," she said. "I'd be delighted to."

Lady Darlington smiled and reached across the table to squeeze her hand fondly.

"Ah, my dear, you are a jewel! I can't tell you how happy you've made me. I promise you it will be a night you'll never forget! Never. And now I think I'll have some salad."

As she heaped the greens on her plate, Margaret wondered. Despite what she had said about forgetting the fire-drill incident, she really hadn't forgotten her outrage at being pincered into a dangerously compromising situation by Lady Darlington and Paul; and now she wondered if Lady Darlington could really have forgotten so completely her admitted former jealousy. She was being wonderfully glib, but not entirely convincing. And yet people did change, as she had said. Margaret herself had argued to Charlie that his wife had changed in the past three months. Why did she now find herself having doubts? Was Charlie right when he had told her she wanted to believe Lady Darlington had changed because she had set out to change her? And yet everything the woman had just said seemed reasonable enough.

As Margaret watched her eating the salad, she told herself it really didn't matter whether she had changed or not. She would be leaving soon, and Lady Darlington would no longer be her concern.

Yet she couldn't help but wonder.

• • •

The household returned to London the next week, and shortly thereafter the newspapers and periodicals began filling with articles about the countess of Darlington's ball. It had been a placidly uneventful summer and autumn, and the opening of Darlington House after so many years, as well as the re-emergence of Lady Darlington into an active social life, gave the reporters something to write about and the London public something to read. The fact that the ball was being given by the wife of one prominent politician for his rival helped build the fires of public interest, and it seemed people couldn't get enough printed speculation about the guest list, the decorations, who would wear what, and a mountain of similar glamorous trivia. It was said the king and queen would be attending, which wasn't true. It was said the prime minister was attending, which was. It was said Lady Darlington had ordered ten thousand orchids to decorate Darlington House, which wasn't true; but it was true she had ordered the construction of a glass conservatory on the rear of the house to contain the overflow of guests, which was accurately estimated at five hundred. It was reported that she would wear the famous Darlington emeralds which Charlie's father had bought from Eugénie. This was true enough, and sketches of the jewels were carried in several magazines, the suite including a tiara and necklace blazing with diamonds and cabochon emeralds as big as small eggs. The extravagance of the stones as well as the reputed cost of the gala brought forth rumblings in some sections of the press and pulpits reminiscent of the uproar caused by the ball given in New York three years previously by the son of the founder of the Equitable Life Assurance Society, an event that had caused that worthy to emigrate to France under a cloud of what many considered well-deserved approbrium. However, at first the general tone of the articles were sympathetic, if not breathless. Charlie was popular; the fact that his wife was emerging from a prolonged illness (the specific nature of which was left unmentioned) gave the occasion a certain convalescent cachet the public liked; and by and large, the event was looked forward to with anticipation.

But if the public was looking forward to the ball, Charlie was infuriated by it. When the army of workmen had descended on Darlington House to clean the building from attic to basement and begin contruction of the conservatory, he had been back in Vienna. When he returned home, after a month's absence, he found not only the ground floor swarming with workmen, but his wife closeted with her seamstress in her bedroom, having a fitting of the dress she was going to wear. He slammed into the library and sent for Margaret. A few minutes later she came in and closed the door. He was standing in front of the fireplace, puffing on a cigar and looking as if he were about to explode.

"Has she gone crazy?" he blurted out.

"Not that I know of."

"This circus she's putting on! And all the publicity—it was even in the Vienna papers! Listen to this bilge . . ." He picked a newspaper from the desk and turned to the middle pages. When he located the article, he read aloud:

> Your reporter has gathered from a reliable source a few of the statistics about the countess of Darlington's ball, which has caused so much comment recently. The main floral motif will not be orchids, as reported earlier, but roses instead: £3,000 worth, which should satiate even the most ardent rose fancier.

"Three thousand pounds!" He sputtered. "My God, the woman's out of her mind!" He continued reading:

> The dinner, which will be served at midnight as a buffet, will include quail in aspic, *les médaillons de foie gras en timbale à la gelée de Porto*, and, naturally, caviar. The champagne will be magnums of Pol Roger, and we are told Lady Darlington has instructed her staff not to limit the guests to a quart each, as done at some of the larger parties. The champagne is to flow until the last titled stomach is filled. And what will all this cost? The estimate we heard is £25,000. *That* should show New York!

Charlie threw down the paper.

"Of all the cheap, vulgar idiocy—twenty-five thousand pounds for a party! Does she realize what this makes *me* look like? I fought to get a Pension Bill through Parliament that would give thirteen pounds a year to the indigent, and my wife throws a ball costing twenty-five thousand pounds. If this doesn't make me look like the most callous, hypocritical cretin in Europe, I don't know what will!"

Margaret was shocked by his reaction, assuming, as she had, that he would be delighted by his wife's re-emergence as a hostess. Obviously, he wasn't.

"Most of the publicity has been good . . ." she volunteered.

"This sort of publicity is never good for a politician! The

society columns may be tittering and clucking about it now, but the radical press will be howling soon enough and have a field day at my expense. I'd stop it if I could, but it's too late now—everyone would say I was trying to save face. 'Champagne flowing till every tilted stomach is filled'—good God, the Welsh miners barely make a living wage, and *she's* filling titled stomachs with bubbly. She *knew* this would hurt me. She *planned* it."

"Charlie, you're wrong. She told me she wanted to help your career—"

"You naïve little fool, you *believe* her! I told you she'd never change. I told you she means to destroy me—I told you that the first day you came here. But no, you think she's brimming over with the milk of human kindness! Reggie Hamilton is already making political hay out of it. He and Mona Morley are telling everyone in town they're embarrassed to come, even though the party's in his honor. Oh, they'll come, all right. And they'll drink the champagne. But they'll cluck and shake their heads and say what a tragedy it is Charlie Darlington is so irresponsible and socially indifferent—*damn* her." He threw the cigar in the fireplace and tried to calm himself. Margaret waited a moment before speaking.

"She's asked me to go to the ball," she said, quietly.

He looked up, surprised.

"Why?"

"To show everyone there's nothing to the rumors your brother and his wife have been spreading about you and me. She's even buying me a dress to wear. I'm leaving the next day."

"Where are you going?"

"I'm taking another position. There's no need for me here any longer."

"But you *can't* leave."

"I really don't think you'll miss me."

For a moment he didn't move, and she thought he looked genuinely upset by the news.

"You're wrong," he finally said, quietly. "This is a bit late for apologies, I suppose, but you were right to come back and stop me. I've thought a lot about you these past few weeks in Vienna. I really have missed you. Have you missed me?"

She couldn't lie, and she didn't think he had.

"Yes," she said.

"But you're still leaving?"

"Yes."

He put his hands to his eyes and rubbed them wearily.

"Well, I don't blame you. I haven't exactly been pleasant to you. So." He removed his hand from his eyes, looked at her and forced a smile. "She wins. Caroline wins all. I suppose it was inevitable she'd defeat me, wasn't it?" He went to his desk and sat down. "Now she's even going to bankrupt me with her stupid parties. What a wonderful wife I have. What a wonderful, loving wife. At least it's all ending with a properly Wagnerian finale: Lady Darlington's twenty-five-thousand-pound fiasco. I hope you'll save me a waltz?"

She stood up. She had never seen him look so defeated before, and she felt sorry for him for the first time in weeks.

"Since I'm supposed to be there to stop gossip about us, I don't think my dancing with you would look very good."

"But with Caroline watching us, who could say anything? Besides, at this point, I don't give a damn. Do you?"

"No," she said. At that moment, she didn't.

• • •

Lord Darlington was right: by the week of the ball, the radical press had started to howl, and even the conservative *Times* had mumbled against the "extravagant excesses of the rich, which in these times seem peculiarly tasteless." The day of the party, a thick fog rolled in, covering the city with an unusually heavy blanket of almost opaque soot, and a few of the reporters decided to attribute this to some vaguely divine sign of displeasure at Lady Darlington's folly. Nevertheless, none of them was deterred by either the fog or moral indignation from showing up at Belgrave Square. And by eight o'clock, a considerable crowd of onlookers had gathered in front of Darlington House to witness the show.

And a show it was. The lights of the huge house blazed through the fog, and they were echoed by the blurred carriage lanterns and automobile headlamps as the unending stream of luxurious vehicles stopped at the curb, their chauffeurs and coachmen leaping out to open the doors as the guests stepped out, the tail-coated men with their stars, ribbons, and decorations providing almost as glittering a spectacle as the women in their furs, egrets, and jewels. The duke and duchess of Connaught; the marquess and marchioness of Lansdowne; the prime minister and his wife, "Henry" and Margot Asquith; Daisy, princess of Pless; the infamous "double duchess" of Devonshire, who had been the mistress of one duke while married to another; the "Socialist" Countess of Warwick, a beauty who had shocked society by espousing left-wing causes; Mrs. Keppel, the king's mistress; a pride of Rothschilds; Reginald McKenna, the first lord of the admiralty; Sir John Fisher, the controversial first sea lord; Mr. and Mrs. Lloyd George, the chancellor of the exchequer, who was already preparing the revolutionary budget estimates of 1909; the monkey-faced marquis de Soveral, the popular Portuguese ambassador; Sir Ernest Cassel, the millionaire friend of the king who, with the Rothschilds, had broken the anti-Semitic prejudice of the Court and been admitted into the most intimate royal circles; Prince Louis of Battenberg, who was shortly to become second sea lord (only to be forced out of office during the war because he was German) and whose grand-nephew would become the duke of Edinburgh; the duke and duchess of Marlborough; Herbert Gladstone, the son of the grand old man of Victorian politics who had just resigned as home secretary because of a brouhaha over a Catholic procession through London, an event that had aroused the ire of the Protestants; the "yellow earl" and his wife, Lord and Lady Lonsdale, he being one of the most flamboyant figures of the era, who at one time went several rounds in the ring with John L. Sullivan; the fantastically wealthy duke of Westminster, owner of more than two hundred and seventy acres of London real estate; Spanish grandees, Hungarian magnates, a sprinkling of Prussian Junkers, Austrian archdukes, and Russian grand dukes; Boni de Castellane, the impoverished French nobleman who wooed and won Jay Gould's daughter, then proceeded to squander the ill-gotten Gould millions in an orgy of spectacular

parties, much to the delight of everyone but the Goulds; Lord
Curzon, the ex-viceroy of India; a maharaja; Count Albert de
Potaki of Poland; and a leading Swedish socialist of royal blood.
The whole glittering panorama of London's cosmopolitan society
debouched from its carriages and limousines in front of Darlington House, presenting a display of international power, privilege,
and panache, a distillation of centuries of European civilization,
that was unique to London and which was soon to be blasted
from the face of history by the murderous bloodletting and
revolution that was a mere half-dozen years in the future and
yet which seemed, except to a few of the most prescient, as
improbable as a typhoon in Trafalgar Square. The crowd ogled
and applauded. The horses whinnied and the primeval motors
coughed. The fog swirled. And the guests continued to pour
into Darlington House where, in the marble entrance hall blazing
with light, Lord and Lady Darlington, stationed on the landing
beneath the Titian Saint Sebastian, received them as they climbed
to the ballroom on the second floor.

Margaret, watching the scene from the top of the stairs,
thought she had never seen Charlie look so distinguished. As he
shook and kissed hands, he gave no hint that he thought the party
a disastrous mistake, and gave rather the impression of urbane
charm. Nor did his wife give any indication she had on her mind
anything other than being a successful hostess—though, of
course, if she had intended to embarrass Charlie by the expensive
party, the damage had already been done. She looked astonish-
ingly healthy. She was wearing a white dress against which the
emeralds of her necklace showed with brilliant intensity. For
once, her stringy hair was set—so set, in fact, that Margaret suspected she was wearing a hairpiece. The diamond-and-emerald
tiara, nestled like a huge, expensive bird in its nest of soft hair,
was dazzling. And when Margaret thought back to the dissipated
wreck Lady Darlington had been when she first met her, she
could feel a twinge of justifiable pride at the transformation she
had achieved. Lady Darlington looked almost as well as she did
in the Sargent portrait in the gallery at Ellendon Abbey. Of
course, the price of this transformation had been the loss of

Charlie; and the thought that this would be the last night she would ever see him filled her with anguish. Perversely enough—or perhaps naturally enough—now that she was leaving him, she wanted him more than ever. Once he glanced up and saw her watching him. Her instinct was to turn away, but she did not. She kept her eyes on him, wondering if he might be thinking about her the same thing that she was thinking about him, wondering if he had actually missed her, as he had said. What if she had misjudged him? What if he really had been in love with her, and was not just using her for his own purposes, as she had convinced herself. While she wished it were true, she told herself she was indulging in wishful thinking. And even if it were true, it would change nothing. She still was obliged to leave.

Her spirits weren't improved by her strange sense of foreboding. Lady Darlington's character rehabilitation, about which she had once been so sure, she now was having grave doubts over. The whole affair—the ball; the announced desire to be a "good wife" and help her husband's career; her kindness to Margaret and her insistence that she come to the ball; even the admittedly breathtakingly lovely white satin gown she had bought for her from Mr. Worth (the sweeping low neckline of which made her feel rather naked)—it all seemed somehow too tidy, and reminded her uncomfortably of the way she had been maneuvered during the fire drill. She felt quite certain there was a special design to all this, but she couldn't for the life of her figure out what it was, beyond what Charlie had already told her. She could only sense that something unpleasant was going to happen in the midst of all this elegant glitter.

A handsome woman in her mid-forties, wearing a yellow dress and carrying a plumed fan, came up the stairs and smiled at Margaret. She was accompanied by a tall man with a prognathous jaw, whose frame was so burly he looked as if he might split out of his dress suit at any moment, sending his blue Garter ribbon and medals flying over the marble floor. To Margaret's surprise, the couple came over to her.

"And you are the miraculous nurse we've heard about," smiled the woman, who had brown eyes, brown hair, pink skin, and a honeyed voice. Three strands of pink Burmese pearls were draped around her throat, and on her head was a matching pink-pearl-and-diamond tiara. "I'm Mrs. Morley."

The kingmaker extended her hand and shook Margaret's. Then her companion bowed his head slightly.

"Sir Reginald Hamilton," he said. "And the guest of honor insists on a dance later on with the miraculous nurse."

"Reggie, don't push," said Mrs. Morley. "You're to be congratulated," she continued to Margaret. "From what we understand, this evening would never have been possible without you. Caroline looks marvelous. Simply marvelous. My poor husband has a nurse who is, I'm convinced, totally ignorant of medical science. Mrs. Morley suffered a stroke several years back and requires constant attendance. I don't suppose I could lure you away from Caroline to take care of my husband?"

"I'm afraid I've already committed myself to a position with someone else," said Margaret.

"Oh? I didn't know that. So you're leaving Darlington House?"

"Yes. Tomorrow, in fact."

"From what I hear," said Sir Reginald, "you'll be terribly missed."

The remark sniffed of innuendo.

"On the contrary." Margaret smiled. "It is I who will miss Lady Darlington."

"Of course," said Mrs. Morley. "Caroline is a source of constant amusement. London will be so much more interesting now that she has been returned to our midst—somewhat," she added with a slight smile, "like Lazarus rising from his grave, as it were. Ah, Signor Gabrielli's orchestra, I believe. I do so adore Italian orchestras, don't you? I imagine Charles hired them. He is so passionately fond of Italian things. I understand he spends a good deal of time at Italian restaurants." Again, the smile; then Sir Reginald led her away to the ballroom, where the orchestra had started a waltz.

Margaret decided she liked neither Mrs. Morley nor her escort. In fact, she disliked them both intensely.

• • •

"Charlie, I don't think you bought enough roses," said Arthur, pointing to the staircase balustrade which was entwined with hundreds of the flowers. "For three thousand pounds they should have thrown in Kensington Gardens. But really, old boy, don't you think you've gone a bit overboard? You should leave vulgarity to American millionaires. They do it so much better."

"Not at all," replied Charlie. "We English can be every bit as vulgar as the Americans. I see no point in being outclassed by foreigners in anything. And when it comes to vulgarity," he glanced at his wife standing next to him on the stairway landing, "Caroline knows no peer, foreign or domestic."

"It's amusing being vulgar," said Caroline, undaunted. "And when one has so many vulgar friends and relations, it becomes a moral and social obligation. How *are* you, dear Angela?

She smiled and kissed her sister-in-law's cheek. Angela, who had not missed a word, bit her lip but said nothing.

"By the way," said Arthur, "congratulations are in order. Angela and I are going to be parents."

"Wonderful!" said Charlie, kissing Angela. "I've very pleased for both of you."

"Thank you," said Angela. "We're both so thrilled. Arthur's convinced it's going to be a boy. If it is, we're going to name him after father."

"If it's a girl," purred Caroline, "you must name her after your dear stepmother, Lady Passwater, isn't it?"

"*Bridge*water," snapped Angela.

"Oh yes, how stupid of me. Dear Emilia! I'm so delighted you could come!"

As Caroline kissed the next guest, Arthur and Angela continued on up the stairs, Arthur barely able to conceal his amusement.

"It *wasn't* funny," said Angela.

"Oh yes it was!" her husband replied.

"Look at all the faces," said Charlie, an hour later. He was standing next to Margaret at one end of the ballroom watching the elegant crowd dance. They each had a glass of champagne. "Or rather, look at all the masks. Watching any social event in London is like watching a convention of living lies. Everyone out there on the floor is lying to someone. I lie all the time. I've lied to you, I lie to Caroline, she lies to me. . . . I wonder what would happen if everyone suddenly told nothing but the truth?"

"I imagine," said Margaret, "it would be the end of the British Empire."

"And the beginning of a bloody fight. If people told each other what they really thought, there'd be a lot of black eyes—and cut throats. Sometimes I get sick of the whole thing. I mean the political maneuvering. And I get definitely sick of the domestic maneuvering with Caroline. Sometimes I'd like to chuck it all and go off to some Pacific island and sit under a palm tree to watch the sun set."

"Then why don't you?"

"Because I'm ambitious, I suppose. And because while one part of me sneers at all this, another part of me loves it. I'd be lying even more if I said I didn't enjoy being what I am. And our snug little hypocritical club we call society does put on a glittering show when it feels like it. Like tonight. It's vulgar. It's immorally expensive. It's probably making me political enemies. But as much as I detest Caroline for putting it on, I like seeing it. I suppose that's childish of me, isn't it?"

"I think it's natural enough. I like seeing it too. That crowd outside on the sidewalk was enoying it also."

"Oh yes, bread and circuses. This is definitely a circus, though one wonders why they don't resent us even more. Maybe they do, but still like to watch the glitter. It's odd."

"I met Sir Reginald and Mrs. Morley."

"What did you think of them?"

"I didn't like them."

"One doesn't like Mona Morley, but one should respect her.

She's a remarkable woman. She has a great deal of political influence."

"She made a snide remark about Italian restaurants."

"Doesn't she like spaghetti?"

"The implication was that you went to Italian restaurants for something besides spaghetti. I believe I didn't let her see that I was frightened by her remark, but I was."

"Don't be. She hears a lot of loose gossip and makes a few inspired guesses, but she has nothing definite to go on. For that matter, I don't think Sherlock Holmes himself could find anything going on at present between you and me. We're probably the most antiseptic lovers since Cyrano and Roxanne. I'm not sure I enjoy being antiseptic. Do you?"

She said nothing as he looked at her.

"I like your dress," he went on, glancing at her bosom which the low neckline exposed as far as fashion would permit. "Is that the one Caroline bought for you?"

"Yes."

"I find it rather amusing that she's buying you dresses now instead of me. By the way, you said you'd waltz with me, and Signor Gabrielli is playing *Kunstlerleben,* one of my favorites. May I have the honor, Miss Suffield?"

She put down her glass of champagne. "I don't think we should," she said, glancing around the packed room.

"Life's sweetest moments are made up of what we shouldn't do," he said, leading her out on the floor.

• • •

"Don't they make a handsome couple?" asked Caroline, nodding toward her husband and Margaret. Mrs. Morley, who was standing beside her at the edge of the dance floor, raised an eyebrow.

"Much too handsome, I would think, for your peace of mind," she replied. "The nurse is most attractive. And that's a very seductive dress she's wearing."

"Isn't it?" replied Caroline. "I bought it for her. Charles seems to think it's seductive too."

Mrs. Morley looked at Caroline curiously.

"That doesn't seem to bother you?"

"On the contrary; I planned it that way."

"I beg your pardon?"

"I'm planning on Charles seducing her. Of course, one can never be certain about these things. But Charles is furious at me for giving this ball and would like to get back at me some way. And dear Margaret is leaving us tomorrow. So, what with one thing and another, I think the chances of Charles seducing her tonight are quite good."

Mrs. Morley smiled in disbelief.

"I believe you're having a laugh at my expense."

"Hardly. And if you and Reggie stick by me, you may see some excitement later on. Charles is looking singularly reckless."

Mrs. Morley closed her plumed fan noiselessly.

"Why are you doing this to your husband?" she asked.

"What do you care so long as you and Reggie profit by it?"

"I don't care. But I'm curious."

Caroline shrugged. "To ruin him."

• • •

"I think it would have been interesting if we *had* murdered Caroline," said Charlie as he waltzed Margaret around the crowded floor.

His partner looked shocked.

"Charlie, please—keep your voice down!"

"No one can hear with all this noise. But seriously: I suppose my idea was unprofessional, but I'll wager we could have succeeded. And think how exciting it would have been afterward. You know, wondering if we'd be caught, watching everyone nervously, wondering if they suspected. I think it would have been damned good sport, much better than the way things are turning out with you leaving and Caroline growing healthier by the minute.

"Charlie, I think you have a basically criminal nature."

He laughed.

"Of course I do. I'm descended from a long line of criminals.

Most of the peerage started out as thieves or murderers, and the Avalon family was no exception. Neither is Caroline's family, for that matter. The first Cheyney made his fortune by braining more defenseless peasants than anyone else in the army, and the first duke of Suffolk was known as the best embezzler in England. So crime is very much an aristocratic tradition, along with Eton and Harrow. And I think I would have made a first-class murderer."

"Well, I hope you're not changing your mind? I mean, about trying it? Because, if you are, I'll have to stay on to protect your wife."

"My wife. Poor, 'defenseless' Caroline. That's a laugh. If threatening to dispatch Caroline to that distant shore would persuade you to stay, I'm off to the chemist to buy some arsenic."

"Charlie, please. It's not funny."

"Yes it is. The idea of Caroline crossing the bar is quite hilarious. And I definitely believe you *should* stay, because the way I feel toward her tonight, her life is in real danger." The lightness, she thought, was suddenly out of his voice. Was he once more *serious* about it? "Besides, I want you to stay."

"I can't. It's all arranged. I start at Mrs. Addison's tomorrow. My bags are all packed."

"I think you're being unreasonable."

"Not at all. I'm being sensible."

"That's not one of my favorite words. Especially tonight. In fact, I feel very unsensible tonight."

She didn't say anything for a moment. Dancing with him was reviving all her longing for him, and she felt sad, desperately sad, that this was the last time she would be with him. She had kept up a conversation with him because she didn't want him to see her true feelings, but she really preferred not to talk. She wanted to be alone with him, away from the brilliant, noisy throng of dancers. She started to tell him, when she glanced to the side of the room and saw Mrs. Morley watching her. The woman made her nervous. She was so sleek, so well turned out, so expectant. Yes, that was the word. She was expecting her to do something foolish, and Margaret knew she didn't dare let her guard down. "You're feeling unsensible," she said to Charlie, trying to sound anything but the way she felt, "because you've been drinking too much champagne."

"Not at all. It's because you're so beautiful. I want you, Margaret."

"Charlie, please."

"When I think of you going off to tend some elderly biddy, it makes me want to shoot Florence Nightingale. This city's filled with nurses—I should know, I've hired enough of them. Let them take care of Mrs. Addison. Let me rent you a flat somewhere—"

"No. Charlie, can't you see I feel miserable? And you're just making it worse for me. Please dance with someone else now . . ."

"I want to dance with you."

"Please!"

"Who's there to dance with? Caroline? She steps on my toes. She always has been a terrible dancer, consistent with her overall performance as a wife."

"Then dance with your sister-in-law."

"Angela? Good God, I'd rather dance with a vulture. Besides, she's pregnant."

"Well, someone. Please take me back. Can't you see Mrs. Morley is watching us?"

"Let her watch! I don't give a damn."

"But you should!"

"Margaret, I don't want to lose you! I love you. You're the only thing I really have in this world. . . ."

"You have your career. You have your social position, and there's no room in either of them for me."

"I'll make room, if you'll let me."

Her eyes were filling with tears.

"Charlie, if you don't take me off the dance floor, I'll have to leave by myself."

"Why are there tears in your eyes?"

She tried to look away.

"Why?" he persisted.

"Can't you guess?" she said.

"You don't want to leave, do you? Any more than I want you to."

"Oh God, stop it!"

"Tell me the truth."

"Of course I don't want to leave you. But I have to."

"Will you have dinner with me tonight?"

"You mean, the buffet?"

"Yes. At midnight."

"All right. But only if you stay away till then."

He smiled, waltzed her once more around the floor, and then left her alone at the side of the room.

• • •

His wife had said he looked reckless, and in fact he felt reckless. As he stood at the end of the room an hour later watching a gathering of the most powerful and glamorous people in London dancing in the ballroom of his house, he would like to have felt a sense of justifiable pride, or at least satisfaction. And he did, to a degree. He liked playing host to the prime minister and the other peers and potentates who had come to Darlington House that night, no matter what they might think or say about the extravagance of the occasion. But he wasn't exhilarated, by any means. As he had told Margaret, a part of him would have chucked it all, even his career. Politics hadn't provided him the escape or relief he had believed it would, after all. He was no romantic fool, but he was no Disraeli either: he couldn't find satisfaction in the pursuit of political power alone. He needed a woman, and he wanted Margaret. He was amazed at how much he wanted her. He had contemplated setting her up in an "establishment." This, though not the most satisfactory solution to his marital dilemma, would have at least been a solution. But he knew she wouldn't have any part of it, which only made him want her more. And the inevitability of her walking out of his life the next morning left him feeling not only frustrated, but lonely as well. He had money, position, and a certain amount of political influence. But none of these was of any use when it came to bending what was turning out to be one of the most unmovable forces he had ever encountered, Margaret's damned moral squeamishness. She had allowed him once, but she wouldn't twice, and there didn't seem to be anything he could do about it. He had never scoffed at the power of women; the wreck Caroline had made of his life would have been more than enough tangible evidence of that power, even if he hadn't been aware of the enormous influence women exerted in the political and social life of his day. But the power Margaret was exerting on him that night totally bemused him, for by walking out on him, the nurse from Somerset was reducing him to a state of morose frustration. He would not play the fool by trying to force himself on her in front of such a distinguished company. He knew Mona Morley was watching them.

But he would have liked to.

A footman passed with a tray of champagne-filled glasses. He finished the glass he was holding and took another. He wasn't normally a drinking man, but tonight he felt like getting drunk. And when he saw Arthur approaching him, he knew damned well he needed another drink. In his present mood, he didn't think he could put up with his brother without the crutch of alcohol.

"What made you and Angela decide to have a child?" he said by way of starting a conversation when Arthur had come up beside him.

"We thought it was time to produce a proper heir to the family debts," replied Arthur, hooking a glass of champagne for himself from the retreating footman. "We also, I confess, thought a grandchild might bring the light of love into old Billy's eyes— and, more importantly, into his check-signing fingers. As usual, Angela and I are barely one jump ahead of our creditors. I don't suppose you'd loan me a few thousand?"

"I won't have anything to loan after I pay for this extravaganza. Don't worry: you'll get what's left eventually. Caroline's never going to have children, and I'm never going to get rid of Caroline. So some day it will all be yours, dear brother. And you can dance a jig on my grave."

"You're not by any chance planning to die in the near future?"

"I'm afraid I'm not going to be that accommodating."

"No, you look fairly healthy. Well, I'm not going to do any

jigs yet. I can see a number of pitfalls before baby Billy becomes the sixth or seventh earl, not the least of which is his starving to death while his parents languish in debtors' prison. Now, if you could see your way to making an investment in the infant's upbringing—"

"Arthur," interrupted Charlie, irritably, "I'm in no mood to have you put the touch on me. I've loaned you enough money, and I've seen how you spend it. I won't loan you any more."

"I didn't buy the aeroplane," said Arthur, defensively.

"A superb economy. How about that actress. Gladys what's-her-name?"

"Denning? Well, if that's all you're objecting to, you'll be glad to hear Gladys and I have parted. She fell in love with a juggler and they ran off to Australia to work up an act with a koala bear, I believe. No, I've been the very model of the faithful husband lately. Angela has no reason for complaint."

"Arthur, you're almost as big a liar as I am. I know you've been to Laura Metcalf's three times in the past two weeks."

Arthur looked amazed.

"How did you know that?"

"Laura told me, of course. It's none of my business if you cheat on Angela. But if you're so hard up, I think you might go to someone a little less expensive than Laura."

"Oh, it's all right if *you* go to her, but *I'm* supposed to make do with the kitchen maid!"

"Your love life, Arthur, is a matter of supreme indifference to me. And as far as Laura's concerned, I'm giving her up myself. In fact, I'm seriously considering joining a monastery."

Arthur grinned. "Having troubles with the lovely Miss Suffield?"

Charlie shot him a look. "Please leave her out of this."

"Ah, chivalry is not yet dead. Sir Charles will tilt his lance at anyone who besmirches the reputation of the fair Lady Margaret."

"Arthur, you're beginning to be unpleasant."

"Sorry. It's my damned envy, you see. I envy your ability to throw intimate soirées like this—soirées which would make Nebuchadnezzar blush—while Angela and I are continually scrounging to pay the gas bill. I realize it's petty of me, but what can I do? I'm a petty person, Charlie."

"I've noticed." He finished his champagne, then walked away. He wasn't in the mood to take any more of his brother.

Someday I'll shove it all in your face, Charlie, thought Arthur as he watched him leave. It was such a childish thought, one he had had countless time since his first memories of his older brother, the older brother who had always received all the attention as well as the inheritance. But like most childish thoughts, it retained its potency well past childhood.

Someday I'll shove it all in your face, Charlie. All of it.

• • •

At eleven thirty, Signor Gabrielli's orchestra broke into a lively polka. Caroline, who had been dancing with the Portuguese ambassador, excused herself, saying she wasn't up to the strenuous dance, and retired to the side of the ballroom where she was joined by Mrs. Morley. The two women watched the dancers whirling by, the parquet floor shuddering at the rhythmic thump of the many feet. Charlie came along with a tall, spare, sophisticated-looking woman with sharp features.

"There goes Charles with Mrs. Asquith," said Mrs. Morley. "She adores him, you know, even though he's a Tory. So many people adore your husband, my dear. Sometimes I quite despair for Reginald's political future, with such a popular man as Charles in the same party."

Caroline continued watching the dancers.

"Reggie's future will look much brighter after tonight."

"Perhaps. However, Charles seems to be behaving in exemplary fashion. Except for that one dance, he hasn't even talked to the nurse."

"Don't be so eager, Mona. You might accidentally bite someone."

"I can't help being eager, Caroline. You're offering me such a juicy plum. Of course, if Charles *doesn't* do anything tonight, it won't make that much difference, will it? I'm sure you have

some tangible evidence of the affaire? Billets-doux, for instance?
A love letter from the earl of Darlington to his wife's nurse
would make fascinating reading to a goodly number of dis-
criminating people."

Caroline gave her a faintly contemptuous look. "Dear Mona,
you really have such an unimaginative mind. Billets-doux sound
like something out of French farce."

"English politics often resemble French farce."

"Nevertheless, my husband would never stoop to scribbling
love letters. He's no fool, after all. No, if one wants to catch
Charlie, one must catch him *in flagrante*. Besides, if one sets out
to destroy a husband, it should be done with a little style. I need
hardly remind someone as adept at political blackmail as you that
anyone can intercept love letters. That hardly requires talent. So
do try to be a little patient. And meanwhile, be grateful that
I'm being so accommodating."

Mona Morley took stock of her benefactress: the well-cut
profile observing the crowd; the magnificent tiara and necklace;
that stature that, despite her weight, left no doubt she was the
daughter of a duke. How curious that she would go to such
lengths to ruin her charming husband.

"You must hate him very much," she said quietly.

Lady Darlington, remaining silent, never took her eyes off the
dance floor.

• • •

Lord Darlington's spirits were reviving.

Mrs. Asquith, the prime minister's wife, had, while dancing
with him, broadly hinted that if he would change parties and
support the Liberal policies in the Lords, there might be a
junior cabinet post in prospect for him. Of course, he knew this
was tactics on her part: what she was after was a commitment
from him to support the budget proposals in the spring. Though
he would never commit himself this early (just as he would never
switch parties), still the fact that the prime minister, through his
wife, thought enough of him to dangle an office in front of his
nose buoyed his spirits. And when, at midnight, the footmen

passed through the crowd announcing the buffet was being served in the dining room, he moved off to search for Margaret, determined to make their last night together at least pleasant, and hopeful that he might be able to arrange some sort of future relationship with her, though how he would manage it he wasn't sure.

The hundreds of guests began to make their way down the stairs from the ballroom to the dining room, where a magnificent display awaited them. The long dining-room table had been set with the vermeil service the second earl had bought in Paris in the 1820s, and three enormous gold-and-crystal epergnes heaped with fresh fruit stood in the center, alternating with four gigantic vermeil candelabra, each with eight lights, each a masterpiece of the goldsmith's art. The candelabra and epergnes were set on a long vermeil *surtout-de-table* which ran the length of the center of the table; placed between the bases of the big pieces were small vermeil-and-cut-crystal bowls banked with ferns and yellow roses. On the sideboard two immense crystal vases held more of the lush yellow flowers, and the bay window was filled with three ranks of tiered rosebushes.

But magnificent as the service was to behold, the gold glittering in the candlelight, the food itself as displayed on the table was enough to bring tears of joy to a gourmand's eye. Caroline had hired M. Escoffier himself to supervise the banquet, and the master's touch was everywhere in evidence. The roasts, squabs, trout, salmon, oysters—everything was prepared with an eye toward visual stimulation as well as excitation of the gastric juices, and the skill with which the glazes and aspics had been manipulated to simulate fruits, baroque designs—even, on the mutton, the crest of the earls of Darlington—was breathtaking. As the dozens of footmen and chefs served the crowd, no sooner would a dish become one quarter consumed and picked over then it would swiftly be replaced by a new dish. It was a bravura gesture of typical Edwardian excess, but it worked; during the hour and a half it took to feed the five hundred guests, the buffet never lost its fresh, untouched appearance.

Lord Darlington had been cornered by Admiral Sir John Fisher, the bulldog-faced first sea lord, who was berating him about the importance of the British navy's keeping a healthy lead over the German fleet. The advantage had been lost by the recent introduction of the giant new dreadnought class of battleship, which rendered almost all existing naval vessels obsolete and gave Germany the opportunity to become the world's leading naval power. Charlie, who had heard it many times, pretended to listen to the long-winded admiral while his eyes searched the crowd for Margaret. Finally breaking free from the navy, he made his way to the dining room where he was apprehended by the dowager duchess of Mandeville, a fat octogenarian in black lace and amethysts who was a distant cousin and who wanted to hear all the details of "dear Caroline's miraculous recovery. Had her doctor discovered a new tonic?" With strained politeness, Charlie assured her Caroline's recovery had been an act of God, which sent the duchess into an ecstasy. "She found religion!" she enthused. "How thrilling! I must go find the bishop to tell him: he'll be so pleased." She vanished to search for the bishop while Charlie continued to look for Margaret. She wasn't in the dining room; he headed back to the Red Room. He was collared by General Carew, his neighbor in Kent, who told him he'd shot a "damned fine fox" the previous weekend. Charlie nodded and moved on, amused by the fact that the general never seemed able to remember he was honorary chairman of the Society for the Suppression of Blood Sports. He looked for Margaret in the Red Room. Again, there was no sign of her. Becoming irritated, he started for the entrance hall when the French ambassador spotted him and asked what he thought Russia would "do next" in the Balkans. "Deceive us," said Charlie knowingly, and moved on.

Reaching the entrance hall, he started to head up the stairs; but when he saw the throng coming down he changed his mind and hurried around to the elevator behind the staircase. Stepping into the brass cage, he pushed the lever and glided to the second floor, which was nearly empty. He glanced briefly into the ballroom, but he knew she wouldn't be there. By now he was certain where she was. And, after checking the corridor to make sure no one was watching him, he made his way down the hall to Margaret's door and knocked.

When she opened the door, she was in her bathrobe. Her hair was let down, and she was obviously about to go to sleep.

"I thought you were going to have dinner with me," he said.

"Mrs. Morley had her eyes fixed on me all evening. It made me nervous, and I decided to go to bed. I should have told you, but I knew you'd make a fuss so I just came upstairs. This way is better. Really."

He looked down the hallway. Two footmen and several guests were at the top of the stairs, but no one was looking in his direction. He stepped inside the door, closing it behind him. "Another noble sacrifice from Margaret?" he said.

"Charlie, please don't stay. It's dangerous."

"But you don't know what you're missing. Monsieur Escoffier really outdid himself with the buffet."

"I saw it. Mrs. Blaine showed me an hour ago. It's beautiful, and you're rather beautiful as well, but I'm not going to ruin everything my last night here. So *please* go."

He didn't move. She looked so delicious standing there, her long hair down over her shoulders, her face so fresh and innocent and lovely. He not only wanted to make love to her. He needed to.

"At least let me go down and get us two plates and some champagne. I'll bring it up here and we can dine together. We're safe here. And no one will miss me in that crowd."

She wanted to. She was dying to, in fact. But her common sense kept telling her every moment he stayed in her room was dangerous.

He saw the hesitation in her face and came over to her. He took her hand and raised it to his lips to kiss.

"Don't be afraid. I don't think even Mona Morley can see through doors."

He took her in his arms and kissed her mouth. She responded for a moment, then tried to push him away.

"Margaret, for God's sake, relax!"

"I *can't*. I'm afraid!"

"You're afraid of your feelings, not Mona Morley. She's my problem. Margaret, I love you. There's nothing wicked about our loving each other."

"But it's impossible . . ." She leaned against his chest. "Oh Charlie, please just let me go. Just let me walk out of here to-morrow and forget me, and let me forget you. What's the use of our sneaking about London, meeting in tea rooms and all the other trashy devices we'd be forced to? That's not a real life—"

"It's better than the life I have now."

"Perhaps for you, but not for me. Do you think I've wanted to close you out of my life? Do you think I've been happy these past months? There hasn't been a minute I haven't thought of you, wondering where you were, wanting you. But what's the use of wanting someone you can never have?"

"But we *can* have each other. I could set you up in a flat—it's done all the time."

"No." She shook her head and tears started to run down her cheeks. "It's no good. I don't want that. I want to have a life too. I want to have children and a family some day—can't you under-stand that?"

"Bravo!" said a voice from the door. "A rather overwrought speech, but one that quivers with conviction. You're to be con-gratulated, my dear."

They stared at Caroline who was standing in the open door-way. Behind her, looking at Charlie and Margaret, was Mrs. Morley. Charlie's face turned white. He let Margaret go, and put his hands in his pockets, almost like a boy caught stealing cookies. Caroline saw the gesture and laughed. "You see, Mona, my husband has that prime necessity for a successful foreign sec-retary. He never shows emotion. Look at his face. You'd never dream he'd been caught red-handed, as it were."

Charlie said nothing, but just stared at them. Mrs. Morley watched him a moment, then walked away down the hall. Caroline came into the room, closing the door and leaning her back against it. Her smile was most pleasant, even friendly.

"Afraid?" she said. "Don't be. She won't tell more people than is absolutely necessary. Just the party leaders. The important men. That's all. So don't worry, Charles dear. It won't be in the papers."

"Get out," he said, "before I kill you."

"And wouldn't you love to. Oh yes, dear Margaret, he's tried it before, you know. He tried to strangle me and killed our baby instead."

"Get *out*."

Margaret took hold of his arm. "Charlie, the guests will hear. . . ."

"That's right, Margaret, we must try to protect Charles from his perfectly fiendish temper. And he is a fiend, you know." She smiled. "Beneath that beautiful, angelic face is a killer. And it has given me exquisite pleasure to kill him. Or rather, his career. And I'd do it again. Thanks to the blooming health our Margaret has given me, I'll be around for a long time, Charles. And I intend to make you *crawl*. It's going to be such fun. Such wonderful fun." She opened the door. "Won't the two of you come downstairs for dessert? It's *fraises glacées à la Reggie*. I named it in honor of dear Reggie, which I consider most thoughtful of me. But then, I'm always thoughtful. And I'm *always* thinking of you two."

She closed the door slowly, her grin, like the Cheshire Cat's, seeming to be the last thing to vanish. When she was gone, Charlie stood in the center of the room staring at the door. He looked numb. Margaret took his hand but said nothing.

Then he shrugged, and forced a half-hearted smile.

"Well," he said, " I suppose at this point the good sport accepts defeat gracefully and says something asinine like, 'It really doesn't matter,' or 'I really didn't want to be foreign secretary.' Except it does matter. And I *did* want to be foreign secretary. God. Judging from the way I fumbled this, I probably would have had us in a war within two days." He let go her hand and went to the door.

"Where are you going?" she asked.

"Back to the party. I think I may get roaring drunk. What else better is there left to do?"

He opened the door and looked at her for a moment.

Then he left the room.

• • •

She heard Lady Darlington's bell at four ten that morning. And perhaps—she couldn't be sure, the distance between their rooms muffling the sound—Lady Darlington's voice momentarily calling out.

She hadn't slept. She had lain in her bed, weeping at what had happened, weeping for Charlie, and furious at his wife. She had known it was going to happen. She had tried to prevent it from happening, and it had happened anyway. She had never hated anyone in her life, but now she hated Lady Darlington. She was indeed a monster—a monstrous, vicious bitch of a woman. Everything Charlie had said about her was true, and she had been a fool to doubt him. She didn't care that by conventional standards Lady Darlington's behavior was justified. She didn't care about convention or standards at this point. All she could think of was that vicious smile on her face as she had left the room, delighted that she had vengefully ruined two lives.

And then the bell above the door had rung.

She sat up and stared at it through the darkness. Outside the windows she could see the oily fog swirling, blurring the street lights on the square to fuzzy blobs. Not since she had come to Darlington House had the woman summoned her in the middle of the night. And tonight of all nights she couldn't imagine why she would possibly want her.

It rang again, shortly, insistently. Then it stopped.

She didn't want to go. The last thing she desired was to see her again. But she got out of bed and put on her bathrobe, turning on the bed light. All right, she *would* go. She would tell her to her face she was a monster. It was useless, of course, but at least it would make her feel better. By the time she had gone through the sitting room to the door, she was almost glad the bell had rung.

She opened the door to see someone running down the hall toward the stairs. It was Paul Rougemont. He was carrying a satchel in his left hand. When he saw Margaret, he slowed down. The lantern in the stairwell was on, as usual, and it threw enough light on his face so that she could see he was startled by her appearance and frightened by it. She stood there, gaping at him, wondering why he was there. Then he started toward her. She screamed and ducked back into her sitting room, slamming the door.

Silence. She was terrified. She leaned against the door expecting him to push it open and attack her—but why? What was Paul doing running down the hall in the middle of the night with a satchel? It was absurd, insane. And then she remembered. The Darlington emeralds. The publicity. The wall safe in Lady Darlington's bedroom, which Paul knew the combination to. She had never changed the combination after Paul had left, or at least, if she had Margaret didn't know about it, and certainly Paul didn't. And the bell! She must have awakened while he was opening the safe and rung for the nurse. Of course! Paul didn't know she had stopped drinking. He would have reason to assume she would have passed out from champagne, just as she had nearly every night when he had been her footman—particularly after a ball where the papers had said champagne would be flowing like water. He would have assumed he could get the jewels with little trouble. And he still might have his key to the servants' entrance.

Except that she had wakened and rung the bell.

Silence. She strained her ear at the door. She could hear his heavy breathing on the other side, but as yet he'd made no attempt to force it open. And then, running footsteps. He was apparently going to the stairs, thank God! It was more important to get out of the house and escape than—what? Kill her, a dangerous witness? She listened to the diminishing sound of footsteps hurrying down the marble stairs; then silence again. She waited a moment, opened the door, and looked out into the hall.

Empty.

She went out into the hallway and ran down it to the door of Lady Darlington's suite. It was half open, and a dim light was visible in the sitting room, though she knew before she entered that the light was coming from the bedroom beyond. She ran across the sitting room. The bedroom door was open, and she could see that the light was coming from the bedlamp, which had been knocked off the bedtable onto the floor. Even before she reached the door, she could smell what she immediately recognized to be chloroform. And when she reached the door, the view stopped her cold.

Lady Darlington was sprawled across the bed on her back, her head hanging over the side, an inch away from the marble top of the bedtable. There had clearly been a struggle: the bed-clothes were half on the floor, and one of the pillows had been thrown across the room. A red handkerchief covered her mouth and nose, and as Margaret hurried across the room to the bed, she realized Paul must have chloroformed her. A foresighted villain, after all. When she reached the bed, she saw the blood. It was coming from the back of Lady Darlington's head, dripping to the floor. There was a slight smear on the edge of the marble top of the bedtable; she must have struggled with him as he chloroformed her, and in the fight banged her head against the table. Margaret removed the handkerchief from her mouth and gently lifted her head onto a pillow. Then she took her wrist and felt her pulse. It was fluctuating violently, and she knew that the excitement of the struggle and the shock of the blow, though superficial, on the back of her head, had put her heart into fibrillation. Quickly, she pulled open the drawer of the bedtable and pulled out the bottle of digitalis.

She usually administered the medicine by spoon, but she realized that Lady Darlington would be unable to swallow normally, being unconscious, and the danger of her choking was too great to try to forcefeed her. The only alternative was to use a medicine dropper and place the drops under her tongue. This way the digitalis would mingle with saliva, and because she would swallow occasionally by reflex, the medicine would eventually get into her system. It was slow, but she knew no other way. She filled the dropper with the solution, then gently pried Lady Darlington's mouth open and stuck the dropper under her tongue, squeezing a drop out. Then she removed it and closed her mouth to wait for the first dosage to be swallowed.

She heard someone come into the sitting room, then run across it to the bedroom door. It was Charlie. He was wearing a bath-robe and looked as if he were just now becoming fully awake.

"I heard a scream?" he started, and then he saw his wife. He came into the room, staring at her. "God," he whispered, "what happened?"

"Paul broke in to steal the jewels. She must have wakened while he was opening the safe, and he chloroformed her. She hit her head on the table—I suppose in the struggle while Paul was giving her the chloroform. I met him in the hall and I screamed." She realized she was talking with nervous rapidity, though she was trying to keep calm. She also realized she had yet to look at the safe. Now she did. The door was half open. "Get me a damp towel so I can clean the wound," she continued, "then ring up Sir Andrew. Tell him to get here as fast as possible. Her heart's fibrillating badly, and I'm giving her digitalis, but I can only give it to her a drop at a time."

He had come up to the bed and was standing over her. Now he reached down and took an iron grip on the wrist of her hand that held the medicine dropper.

"Charlie!"

"Let her die. Paul has given us our chance. All we have to do is call Scotland Yard and tell them we came in here and found her already dead. You tried to give her the digitalis but it was too late."

The light from the bedlamp on the floor was hitting his face from below, throwing his features into dramatic chiaroscuro. She looked at him, then back at his wife's face. It was twitching slightly, and the blood from the wound was turning the white pillowslip scarlet. Her breath was coming in short gasps. It would be simple, she knew. As much as she hated the woman, as much as she wanted Charlie, it was tempting.

She shook her head.

"Margaret," he insisted. "Let her die!"

"No."

He grabbed the dropper with his left hand and twisted it out of her grasp, almost breaking it in the process.

"Charlie, give it to me!"

He was backing away from her; she got up from the bed and tried to retrieve the dropper. He put it behind his back.

"Give it to me!" she repeated.

"Go back to your room."

"Charlie, there isn't much time!"

He didn't move.

"Please don't do this!" she begged. "Please!"

No answer.

"I'll tell them," she whispered. "I'll tell them you murdered her."

"Then," he said, calmly, "you send me to the gallows."

There was nothing more she could do except try to bluff him. She started toward the sitting room. "I'm calling Sir Andrew," she said, hoping this would frighten him.

"It's too late," he replied. "Look."

He nodded toward the bed. She turned and looked. Lady Darlington's arm had fallen over the side and was dangling limply. Her eyes were shut.

She knew even before she went over to feel her heart that Lady Darlington was dead.

Part III

"*Countess* of Darlington Murdered!" was the headline when the story broke in the papers the next day, and London bought up all editions to devour the facts of the sensational crime.

Mona Morley heard about it when her maid hurried up the stairs of her townhouse at Number 3 Pelham Crescent to give her the newspaper. "Oh, ma'am." she said, bursting into the bedroom, "Lady Darlington was murdered!"

"Murdered?" exclaimed Mona, putting down her coffee.

"Yes, ma'am. Early this morning. I thought you'd want to read about it."

"I certainly do!" She took the newspaper, adjusted the pince-nez she used for reading on the thin bridge of her nose, and plunged into the article.

> The Countess of Darlington, wife of the noted Conservative peer, the fifth earl of Darlington, and sister of His Grace, the duke of Suffolk, was the victim of foul play in the early hours of the morning, shortly after the conclusion of a ball given by Lord and Lady Darlington at their home, No. 10 Belgrave Square, which was attended by, among other notables, the Prime Minister and Mrs. Asquith. At about four o'clock this morning, Miss Margaret Suffield, private nurse to Lady Darlington, was awakened by a bedroom bell used by her patient to summon her. Miss Suffield went out into the hall to go to her patient's room when she met a footman formerly in the employ of Lord

Darlington, a Swiss named Paul Rougemont. He was running from Lady Darlington's suite toward the stairs, carrying a satchel. Upon seeing Miss Suffield, the man moved to attack her. The young nurse screamed and managed to escape back into her room, whereupon Rougement ran out of the house. Miss Suffield then hurried to her patient's room where she found her sprawled upon her bed. Based on testimony from Lord Darlington and Nurse Suffield, Scotland Yard's reconstruction of events is as follows: Lady Darlington had apparently wakened and discovered Rougemont in the act of removing some valuable jewels from a wall safe in her bedroom. The former footman then placed a chloroform-soaked handkerchief over her mouth to silence her; during the ensuing struggle, Lady Darlington struck the back of her head on the marble top of her bedtable. When Miss Suffield came into the room, she found her patient unconscious and her heart in dangerous fibrillation. Lady Darlington was known to have a history of heart ailment. Before Miss Suffield could administer the appropriate medicine, her patient died. Lord Darlington immediately notified Scotland Yard, and Inspector Hadley Mayhew was placed in charge of the case. Among the jewels missing are the so-called Darlington Emeralds, a matching diamond-and-emerald tiara and necklace which once belonged to Eugénie, the former French empress. Lady Darlington had worn the jewels the night before at the ball. . . ."

Mrs. Morley put down the paper a moment to fit a cigarette into her black-lacquer holder and light it. All she could think of was how wonderfully convenient this was for Charles. She remembered the look on his face when Caroline had opened the door to the nurse's sitting room. It was a look of fear, yes. But there had been something else in his face, something much more deadly. There had been rage. It was no secret among those who knew Charles and Caroline that they most certainly didn't get along, which was putting it mildly. But she had never realized the intensity of the ill feeling until the night before, when Caroline had purposefully exposed her husband's affair with the nurse. And now Caroline was dead. Murdered. As far as Charles and the nurse were concerned, it surely couldn't have happened at a more convenient time.

She returned to the article:

A manhunt has been started to apprehend Rougemont, whose police record includes arrest in France four years ago on a charge of stealing a wallet. Meanwhile, expressions of sympathy are beginning to pour into Darlington House. The bereaved earl was unavailable to the press for comment.

The bereaved earl. Mona smiled. Charles was undoubtedly doing a jig of glee. A thought crossed her mind, an intoxicating, irresistible thought. Was it possible Charles had hired the footman to kill his wife? That the whole affair had been, so to speak, staged? Or perhaps the footman had never been there at all. Perhaps Charles had gone into his wife's bedroom and killed her—possibly after a violent argument over the nurse—and then staged the theft of the jewels to throw the police off his trail. It did seem improbable Charles would risk his neck by actually killing his wife. Yet it seemed even more improbable that Caroline would be conveniently dispatched so short a time after the scene in the nurse's sitting room.

Whatever the truth, she was now especially glad that she hadn't told anyone what she had seen. She hadn't even told Reggie Hamilton. She had filed away the information in her mind, to be drawn out later on at the proper time. But now, she thought, there was even better reason to keep it to herself. It might be much more valuable than she had ever imagined.

She again picked up the newspaper to read the conclusion of the article. But her mind kept playing with the enticing speculation. Yes, it was improbable, she supposed.

But it was most definitely possible.

• • •

Arthur had heard the news earlier.

That morning at seven thirty, Mrs. Blaine had rung him up and told him about the murder. The Irish housekeeper and former nanny of the two brothers had seemed remarkably in control of herself when she made the report, and it occurred to Arthur there were going to be few authentic tears shed at Darlington House over the demise of his sister-in-law.

He told Angela, who registered conventional shock, then put

on a black dress, and the two of them drove over to Belgrave Square, where the big house, which the night before had been the scene of such festive elegance, now looked appropriately somber. There were two policemen on the sidewalk. Arthur identified himself. Then he and Angela climbed the stairs and rang the bell.

Mrs. Blaine admitted them into the entrance hall. The house-keeper's face was glum. "A terrible tragedy," she said. "Terrible. It's a wicked world, isn't it?"

"Definitely," agreed Arthur, handing his silk hat to a footman. "Where's my brother?"

"Went to the funeral home with the body, he did. The poor man's terribly shaken up."

"I imagine."

"He should be back soon. You can wait in the Red Room for him. The house has been crawling with detectives all morning, asking everybody a million questions. I knew that Paul was no good. The man was a born murderer—you could tell."

"How?" asked Arthur, as he followed Mrs. Blaine and Angela into the Red Room.

"His face! Evil eyes, he had, and a bad mouth. I've always said he looked like Jack the Ripper."

Arthur and Angela sat down on a sofa.

"Considering the fact that no one knows what the Ripper looked like," he said, "I think that's remarkably perspicacious of you, Mrs. Blaine."

She sniffed. "You can make fun of me if you like, but I was right, after all. Look what the scoundrel did! I hope they catch him and hang him from the nearest tree. I won't be pretending I was too fond of Her Ladyship: she had her faults, there's no denying. But killing . . . well, now, that seems to me going too far. You ought to have seen her! What a mess! Blood dripping all over the place, there was!"

"Please," said Angela, her face turning white.

"Oh, I forgot you're in a delicate condition. Sorry. Would you two like some tea while you're waiting?"

"Yes, thank you."

Mrs. Blaine headed for the door.

"Cook's got the kettle on. I'll bring you some nice muffins, too. Ah, it's a wicked world, it tis."

"Mrs. Blaine," said Arthur.

"Yes?"

"Where's Miss Suffield?"

"In her room. The poor girl was terribly shook up, she was, as were we all. When they took the body out, I thought she'd pass right out on the floor. Ah, murder! In *this* house! Your poor father, God rest his soul, and your mother, God rest hers, must be turning in their graves at the disgrace."

Shaking her head, she left the room. Arthur stared at the large painting of his parents and himself and his brother, remembering when it had been done, so many years before, and the safe, secure world all had seemed to him then. Mrs. Blaine was right: his parents would have been horrified at the thought of the family being dragged into a tabloid scandal. Curiously, the publicity didn't bother him, though. He could think only of one thing, and it wasn't the disgrace attendant upon a brutal murder.

Angela whispered, "Do you think she's right? Do you think it was Paul?"

"Probably. He looked hungry enough to commit murder when he came around to see me a few months ago. I can imagine him trying something as desperate as robbing Charlie."

"It's all too dreadful," sighed Angela. "*Too* dreadful."

"The dreadful thing is what's going to happen to us."

She looked at her husband. "What do you mean?"

"Inheritance, my dear. Caroline would never have had any children, so I might have inherited the earldom one day. Certainly our son would have. But now that Caroline's gone to meet her Maker—who, I imagine, is having mixed emotions about the introduction—Charlie is free to remarry. And that means Charlie will doubtless have children. Which means that any chance I ever had to inherit the estate has just gone up the flue."

Angela frowned. "I suppose you're right. I hadn't thought of Charles remarrying."

"You can begin thinking about it, and I doubt he'll wait too long, either. He hated Caroline, and I don't think the noble earl is going to pine too long for the dead countess. In fact, I wouldn't be surprised if he didn't lead the winsome Miss Suffield to the altar before very long."

Angela looked shocked. "He wouldn't dare! Why, she's a nobody! She has neither family nor position."

Arthur gave his wife a dry look.

"Neither did you."

She turned beet-red: the remark had hurt.

"That's not fair, Arthur. And at least I had money—which you were *very* aware of!"

"Oh yes. I was aware of it, as I'm aware of our lack of it now. Painfully aware. At any rate, Charlie has position enough for two. And he's in love with our buxom young nurse, whose healthy good looks suggest inevitable fertility. So I think we can discount baby Billy becoming the next earl of Darlington."

He walked across the room and stared up at the huge conversation piece, remembering his parents and cursing his luck at having been born after Charlie.

He hadn't told Angela, but two days before he had learned that old Billy Babson had yet to make out a new will in favor of him and his heir.

• • •

Mrs. Blaine was right. Margaret had come very close to fainting when she saw the covered litter being carried down the hall from Lady Darlington's suite by the two ambulance attendants. It was macabre, watching the white sheet under which lay the body of the woman she had come to detest, that incorporation of so much vicious arrogance, deceit, and destructiveness that had been the countess of Darlington, but who was, nevertheless, a human being. After the corpse had been taken out, she had been summoned downstairs to the library where the inspector had questioned her again. She repeated what had happened—leaving out the one vital fact that altered the entire matter, and marveling at her ability to lie so conveniently. He had thanked her, and she had gone upstairs to her room where she collapsed on the bed. She was horrified at what Charlie had done, and terrified by the fact that she had protected him. But what could she do? Tell the inspector the truth? Watch him be taken off to prison, tried, and hanged for murder? She loved him, and she couldn't bring herself to betray him. And yet, she knew that by keeping silent she was incriminating herself as well. If Charlie was a murderer—and he was by his act of preventing her from administering the digitalis—then she, by covering up for him, was an accomplice to the crime and subject to a prison sentence. The thought made her skin crawl. She lay on the bed waiting for Charlie to return from the funeral home, wondering if someone would guess the truth, half expecting that any moment the moustached Inspector Mayhew would come into her bedroom and arrest her.

But it was Charlie who came in, instead.

At twelve thirty, he slipped into her sitting room without knocking and came to the bedroom door. She sat up, marveling at his composure. He looked as cool as he had the night before when he stood on the landing of the stair with his wife, greeting the guests. He was wearing a morning coat and had already put a mourning band on his sleeve.

He came over to the bed and sat down beside her.

"Have you talked to Mrs. Addison yet?"

Mrs. Addison? She had totally forgotten that she was supposed to report to her that morning for her new position.

"No."

"I think you'd better ring her up and tell her that in view of what's happened—she's probably read about it—you'll be a bit late and see her this afternoon. Then pack your things and leave. It's better that you go to your new job, just as you'd planned: it will seem more normal. And Mrs. Addison will be dying for all the details. By the way, I have something for you." He reached into his pants pocket and pulled out a small black velvet box. Opening the lid, he removed the cabochon emerald ring she had seen so often on Lady Darlington's finger. He offered it to her. "This has been in my family for God knows how long. I gave it to Caroline as an engagement ring, and I took it out of her bedroom this morning. It's one of the few things Paul overlooked when he cleaned out the safe. Don't wear it, needless to say, but keep it. I won't be seeing much of you for a while. But in three or four months' time when all the furor has died down and I can stop the hypocrisy of looking bereaved, we can announce our engagement. People will cluck, of course, but to hell with them. Try it on, unless, of course, it makes you feel uncomfortable."

She stared at the beautiful jewel. Then she looked up at him. "You don't have to marry me."

"Of course I don't, but I want to."

"I mean, I didn't tell the inspector this morning, and I won't tell him later on. I can't. I think what you did was very wrong, and yet knowing what I know, and having seen what I've seen, I suppose I can't blame you. And I certainly can't send you . . ." She started to say "to the gallows," but couldn't get it out. "At any rate, you don't have to marry me to protect yourself. You're safe."

"I know I'm safe," he replied. "I know you well enough to feel quite comfortable, and I'm contemplating living to a ripe old age surrounded by dozens of grandchildren. I'm also perfectly aware I've committed murder, at least in a strictly legal sense, and quite frankly I'm really quite surprised at how completely guiltless I feel. Considering the fact I had a conventional Church of England upbringing, I think this speaks very badly for Christian education in this country, and I'm considering making a speech about it in the Lords."

She winced. "Charlie, don't. For God's sake, don't joke about it!"

He reached over and took her hand. "Why not? I'm free, for the first time in years. I can start living at last. I can marry you and have a normal life, after having gone through those years of bloody hell. And if you think I should feel sorry for what I did last night, you don't know me very well."

She said nothing for a moment.

"But what if . . ." she whispered, "they find out?"

"They won't. I'd go so far as to say it appears we've committed the perfect crime, except I don't consider it a crime."

"But I do."

"I realize that. But in time you won't. You'll forget it. I intend to *make* you forget it. In a few months' time I'm going to lay the world at your feet and make you the happiest woman alive.

We're going to redefine the meaning of happiness, and after what I've gone through, I believe I thoroughly deserve it." He leaned over and kissed her. Then he got off the bed and to his feet. "Now I think you'd better ring up Mrs. Addison. That will be a good place for you to be the next few months. By the way," he smiled, "you haven't said 'yes' to my proposal. I hope you're not going to turn me down?"

Murder without guilt. It was, to her, unimaginable. And yet he quite plainly felt totally free of any sense of it. He had never looked happier, in fact. It chilled her. She remembered what Lady Darlington had said the night before, in her sitting room. That beneath his angelic face lay a killer. And now she, Margaret Suffield, was not only protecting a killer, but was considering marrying one.

"What's troubling you?" he asked quietly.

"Nothing."

"You're telling yourself this is all wrong, aren't you? That somehow we should have to pay the piper?"

She nodded.

"I wish I could pass it off as easily as you," she said, "but I can't. I feel afraid, and I feel guilty. I keep thinking of her being carried out with the sheet over her, like a thing instead of a person. And I can't help feeling to blame for it."

"I was to blame for it, not you. And there's no longer any point in our lives being ruined because of her, especially when we can avoid it. Margaret, she was murdering me, in her own way, and I can't for the life of me feel badly about what I did. She very much got what she deserved. I genuinely believe that. You still haven't said 'yes' to my proposal."

She nodded her head and said, flatly, "Yes."

"That's better." He pointed at the ring. "Try it on."

Reluctantly, she put the ring on her finger. It fit perfectly, and caught the light from the window in its green depths.

"Very nice," he said. "You're going to make a spectacular countess."

He went over to the door, then looked back at her.

"By the way," he whispered with a grin, "I love you."

He blew a kiss to her and walked out of the room. Did he?

She wondered as she sat on the bed staring at the emerald. Or was he marrying her to protect himself, to sew her up, as it were. The last neat stitch in the perfect crime, the crime he felt no guilt for. She remembered that night in front of the St. Alban's Court when he had said they would either hang together or hang separately. On the other hand, he must believe she wouldn't tell. So perhaps he genuinely loved her. She didn't know. All she really knew was that she loved him, despite everything that had happened.

She held her hand up and inspected the stone from another angle. A countess. A spectacular countess. Margaret, Lady Darlington. And Charlie . . . having him for the rest of her life . . .

No matter how guilty she felt, she didn't have the strength to turn him down.

• • •

Lady Darlington's funeral was held three days later at the small church near Ellendon Abbey. It had begun to snow heavily the night before, and by the time the black horse-drawn hearse slushed to a stop in front of the church, at least half a foot of snow had fallen, depriving the landscape of color and presenting a suitably funereal backdrop for the ceremony. Charlie had wanted a small family service; consequently there were few outside guests. Arthur and Angela were there, as was Mrs. Blaine, Rogers, and a number of the older family retainers. Caroline's brother, the duke, came down from London, although his wife, the duchess of Suffolk, was in bed with a cold and couldn't make it. A few of the Tory leaders made the trip out of respect for Lord Darlington and the duke. And, to Charlie's surprise, Mona Morley came. He wasn't too happy to see her, considering what she had witnessed the night of the ball; but she made no mention of Margaret at all and was nothing if not conventional in her expressions of sympathy. Whatever she was up to, he thought, she was concealing it well.

Inspector Mayhew attended the service also, which at first alarmed Charlie. But when the bland, bureaucratic-faced detective expressed his condolences in the most sympathetic fashion, adding quietly that the Yard was convinced Paul had gone to the Continent to try to dispose of the jewels and that they were confident of catching him sooner or later, Charlie decided, with relief, that the police still had no inkling of his involvement with his wife's death.

After the service, the casket was carried out to the adjacent churchyard where Charlie's family had been buried for generations. As the crested coffin was lowered into the grave, he stood with head bowed in prayer and wondered if he did, in fact, feel no guilt at what he had done. He probably shouldn't have shocked Margaret the way he had, but he had felt so exhilarated at his release from what he considered life imprisonment, he couldn't bother with a moroseness which, then, he hadn't felt. But now? He, after all, had taken a life, and the fact was disturbing. Yes, she had been a horror, and yes, he wanted Margaret. They were mitigating factors. But still, he had killed.

He sprinkled a handful of earth on the coffin and felt a chill run through his body that had nothing to do with the snow-whirling north wind. He was a murderer, and he would secretly carry the stigma to his own grave.

Still, he thought as he walked away from his wife forever, if he had it to do over again, if Caroline—vicious, hateful Caroline—were alive and the opportunity to kill her presented itself again? He at least was no hypocrite. He would have done the same thing twice.

• • •

As he walked down the church path to his carriage, he saw the duke of Suffolk hurrying out of the church and coming toward him. Charlie wondered if he could reach his carriage before his former brother-in-law caught up with him, then decided he couldn't without losing his dignity, and today he very much wanted his dignity.

Percival Peregrine Guy Peter Cheyney, the seventh duke of Suffolk, was in many ways a prototypical Edwardian duke. Inheriting the dukedom ten years before, at the age of thirty, he had settled into a way of life that seemed inexorably entwined with the horse and the gun. When not hunting the fox, he was shooting the grouse; and on any subject that was not involved with these mated passions, his views were so narrow as to be fossilized. He thought all the Victorian social reforms since the Reform Bill of 1832 were odious mistakes; and to him the ideal society flourished somewhere in the first third of the eighteenth century when the great landowners such as himself held sway over the country, and the rest of the population "knew their place." Because of his wealth and social position, he was a power in the Lords, and though he was not overly interested in politics (which he considered a "nuisance") he was sufficiently interested to keep abreast of what was going on, and he never failed to make his predictable views known in the loudest, bluntest possible fashion. Now as he caught up with his former brother-in-law, to Charlie's surprise the duke, who had grown portly and was gaining a double chin as he lost his sandy hair, launched into a discussion of the naval estimates.

"Now Charlie," he said, taking his arm, "you know you've got to take a position on these damned dreadnoughts. You can't shilly-shally around any longer, you know."

"I think we might let the funeral end first—" began Charlie.

"Yes yes, I know. Terrible tragedy. Terrible. I hope they catch the blackguard who did it and draw and quarter him. But Caroline's gone now, poor woman, and we can't bring her back. We have to face reality, Charlie, and reality is the Liberals and their naval estimates. Now, mind you, I don't like the Germans any more than the next man, and I don't like the idea of their building more battleships than we build. On the other hand, if we panic and start building ships right and left, you know what the result's going to be. More pressure for higher taxes. There's pressure enough, thanks to that damned Pension Bill you helped push through—"

"Percy," interrupted Charlie, "out of respect to your late sister and my wife, I would prefer not talking shop until they've at least put the dirt on her coffin. My position on the naval estimates right now is that I have no position. I'm in mourning.

And it seems to me rather tasteless of you to worry about what I think of the German navy and the Liberal budget when I am carrying the strongest grief a man can bear: the loss of his beloved wife."

All things considered, thought Charlie, there was a certain amount of amusement in that remark. But it worked. The duke harrumphed. "All right," he said, "I'll talk to you about it later. But we have to take a position soon. The Lords have to be united on this issue."

"We're not going to be united on the naval estimates—you know that as well as I do."

"It's not the estimates, it's the budget that madman, Lloyd George, is drawing up! He's talking about land taxes, damn him, and a surtax of sixpence on the pound—now that's nothing but robbery of the rich! Outright robbery! It attacks the most stable elements of society."

"You mean, I assume, us?"

"Of course I mean us! Who else? We've got to stop them, Charlie! Once the doors open an inch, they'll be able to push them all the way open and drown us."

"When you've finished mixing your metaphors, Percy, you may realize you're being a bit of an alarmist. Now if you don't mind, I'd like to go home."

He walked away from the red-faced duke. As he climbed into his carriage, he noticed Mrs. Morley watching him from her carriage behind his own. He again wondered why she hadn't told Percy—or anyone else, apparently—about Margaret and himself. If nothing else, she would consider it a fascinating piece of gossip. Unless, of course, with fine sensibility, she was sparing his feelings so soon after his loss. A contingency which was not, he thought, bloody likely.

• • •

Inspector Mayhew sat in the compartment of the train returning to London from the funeral and wondered about the nurse.

Hadley Mayhew had an excellent record with the Yard, and

being placed in charge of the Darlington case had been a form of recognition of that record and a testimony to his reputation of being thorough and—perhaps more important, considering the prominence of the people involved—tactful. His superiors knew Mayhew would handle things well. And since the earl of Darlington was not without political influence, this was important.

Mayhew thought the case looked cut and dried. But as with all cut-and-dried cases, he was suspicious of its very neatness. He had learned from the members of the household that Rougemont had known the location of the safe as well as its combination. He had kept a key to the house—the butler had neglected to retrieve it from him when he had been fired. He had a police record and a bad reputation among the servants. The publicity given the ball and the presence of the jewels had afforded him an irresistable opportunity. So it all seemed logical.

But the nurse bothered him. He had checked out that she had been planning to leave Darlington House for some weeks to take a new position with an elderly lady living at Number 134 Park Lane. And she had gone, as planned. But this struck him as odd. Under the extraordinary circumstances, wouldn't she have rung up her new employer and said she had to stay on at Darlington House for a few days? True, there was no reason why she should stay, but wasn't it human nature to want to remain at the scene of so much excitement? Mayhew had a young daughter about the same age as Miss Suffield. He was certain she would have wanted to stay. And in the turmoil, wouldn't she more naturally have stayed to help out? No, the nurse's departure seemed rather too "normal."

And there was the added fact that she, after all, was the only person in the household who had seen Rougemont. The entire story rested on her testimony, and if nothing else, she would be the key witness for the Crown in the trial if he were apprehended. It was possible the crime had been committed by someone else—someone she might have let into the house in return for a cut—and her story concocted to throw the blame on a likely suspect. Or she might even have been in collusion with Rougemont, then changed her mind after the fact. Mayhew didn't seriously believe in these theories, but he thought it would be wise to assign one of his men to watch Miss Suffield for a while.

Just in case.

• • •

Three months passed—three cold, wintry months.

The time passed pleasantly enough at Mrs. Addison's. She was a kind lady who did petit point and was no trouble to take care of. Her house was charming, situated a block from the Marble Arch and overlooking Hyde Park, and under normal circumstances Margaret would have found her new position a welcome relief from the tensions of life at Darlington House. But the circumstances weren't normal, of course. She still felt the guilt of what had happened, but, as Charlie predicted, time began to blunt its sharpness, and the dust of forgetfulness began to settle on her memory. More and more, when she would think of it, she would shift the blame from Charlie to Paul, who, after all, had attacked Lady Darlington, struggled with her, been responsible for her head banging on the table, and caused her heart to go into its gyrations. Very likely, she told herself, the woman might not have survived even if she had been able to give her more of the digitalis. There were all sorts of "ifs," "ands," and "buts" in the situation, the extenuating circumstances of life that were overlooked in the courts, where the stern concept of blind justice had to be served. And surely it would have been inhumanly cruel to send Charlie to a degrading death for what he had done. That she couldn't have done. Ever.

She missed him. He rang her up a few times, but otherwise she neither saw him nor heard anything from him. Sometimes she would become nervous because of his prolonged absence and begin doubting his commitment to her. Then she would take the emerald ring from the bureau drawer and look at it for reassurance. He was merely being careful, she would tell herself. And when she noticed the man from the windows of the house, she was glad Charlie was keeping his distance.

The man was about forty, rather nondescript in appearance, well-dressed, but not ostentatiously so. He would be standing on Park Lane watching the house, and when she took walks she sometimes noticed him following her. She was certain he was a detective. She rang up Charlie to tell him. He took the news calmly enough, telling her to pretend to ignore the man and not to worry; the police wanted Paul, and if they were watching her it was only because she would be their key witness. She decided he was probably right, but still the man made her nervous.

She began to have trouble sleeping at night.

Then, one day in March, she went for a walk in the park. It had turned warm, and the first hint of spring was in the air after the long winter. She felt exhilarated by the weather and, after walking for twenty minutes, she sat down on a bench to rest. She hadn't seen the detective; she hadn't even looked for him. But she assumed he was around.

Charlie came up the walk looking beautifully dapper in his beaver-collared coat and shiny silk hat. The mourning band was gone from his sleeve. He was carrying a gold-tipped walking stick and wearing new spats. He came up to the bench, tipped his hat and smiled.

"I've missed you," he said.

As he sat down next to her, she wanted to cry with joy.

• • •

On the third floor of the lumpish building on the Thames Embankment called Scotland Yard was located Inspector Mayhew's office, and a month later Wilson, the plainclothes man who had been watching Margaret, was seated before his superior's desk while the inspector read his latest report. "It would seem, Wilson," said the inspector, "that you would make an excellent society reporter, or better yet a writer of romantic fiction. This report reads like a pulp romance.

> On the fifth of March, the earl of Darlington met subject on a bench in Hyde Park. They talked fifteen minutes. Subject returned to 134 Park Lane. March 6: subject left house at six o'clock, took cab to the Café Royale where she dined with Lord

D. Afterward, they went in the earl's limousine to Covent Garden and attended a performance of *Tosca*. After the opera, the Earl drove her to Marble Arch. Subject walked home. March 9: Subject leaves house at six, takes cab to Rules where she meets Lord D. They dine. Afterward, they go to Drury Lane to see *Mrs. Dot*. Lord D. drives her back to Park Lane. March 12: Subject is picked up at house by Lord D. They dine at Simpson's, then attend a performance of *Midsummer Night's Dream*.

Et cetera, et cetera, ad nauseum. I assume you've enjoyed yourself?"

Wilson grinned. "I've gotten a bit hungry watching them eat."

"I can imagine." The inspector put down the report. "Well, what do you think?"

"I think there was something going on between them *before* his wife was killed."

Inspector Mayhew pulled a handkerchief from his pocket and blew his nose. "And?"

"Well, assuming they were having an affair, and the wife found out about it, it's conceivable they might have tried to kill her, isn't it?"

The inspector returned the handkerchief to his pocket. He agreed with Wilson: it was conceivable. Also, it was possible the earl's romance with the nurse had nothing to do with the crime at all. It all depended on Rougemont's testimony, whether he had a good alibi or not, whether he had the jewels or not. But the inconvenient fact was that Rougemont continued to elude the police, even though a five-thousand-pound reward had been offered for his capture. But Wilson's not altogether farfetched theory, together with his report, did justify his own uneasy feeling about the nurse. There could be no doubt now that she had not been entirely truthful with them. There was even the possibility she and the earl had been involved with the death of the earl's wife. And if that were true, he could understand why the earl was being so aggressively romantic.

If he married the nurse, she could not, as his wife, testify against him.

"Shall I keep watching them?" asked Wilson.

Mayhew didn't hesitate in answering. "Definitely."

• • •

On the fifteenth of April, 1909, Lady Angela Avalon climbed into her automobile with some difficulty—she was in the seventh month of her pregnancy—and her chauffeur drove her to her father's house on Eaton Square. Angela rarely went out now. She was quite large with child, and it was considered improper for pregnant women to display themselves publicly. But she had wrapped herself in a voluminous cloak to conceal her swollen belly, and during the past week she had made several trips to visit her father, who was recovering from a severe cold. Her relations with old Billy had improved considerably since the aging soap king had learned he might be a grandfather—she had been correct in surmising that—and though no mention of the will had yet been made, Billy had given Arthur and herself, on the previous Christmas, a check for four thousand pounds. This bonus had been entirely unexpected. And though it fell far short of relieving their financial woes, it did pay off their most pressing debts and improved their credit. So her hopes for salvaging her inheritance were rather high. And while her stepmother, Lady Bridgewater, was behaving ever more arcticly as her standing with her father improved, Angela didn't mind. In her opinion, Lady Bridgewater's irritation was the best indication that her cause was winning.

Eaton Square, southeast of Belgrave Square, was laid out at about the same time as the square on which Darlington House stood, principally by the same architects—Lewis and Thomas Cubitt—though the architectural inspiration seemed to decline steadily from Belgrave through Eaton and Chester Squares, then to Eccleston Square, Warwick Square, and finally to the back end of Pimlico, which was quite unpretentious. But if Eaton Square were less inspired than its sister square, Belgrave, it still possessed a pleasing simplicity and a quiet elegance. And while Billy Babson's house was not ornate, it was distinctly handsome.

Angela climbed out of her automobile and, assisted by the chauffeur, made her way to the front door, where she was admitted by Gadsen, the butler, who had worked for the Babson family years before old Billy became Lord Bridgewater.

"And how is my father today?" she asked as Gadsen took her cloak.

"He seems much improved, Miss Angela," said Gadsen, who half the time referred to her as if she were still a child. "Quite alert and even high-spirited."

"That's good. May I go in and see him now?"

"Of course."

"Is Lady Bridgewater with him?"

"Yes."

That wasn't pleasant news. Angela was hoping her stepmother might be out shopping. But it couldn't be helped, and she followed Gadsen to the rear of the house where a back parlor had been converted into Billy's bedroom, thus obviating the necessity of his climbing stairs. The previous year, Lady Bridgewater had redecorated the house in the Art Nouveau style that had become so fashionable in Paris and Brussels, and the rooms were filled with writhing lily-stem lamps, writhing purple lotus-leaf wall-paper—everything writhed as in some florid, artificial jungle. It was a style that Angela disliked heartily; she considered it decadent, showy, and thoroughly un-English. The fact that her stepmother loved it didn't improve her opinion of it. However, she had to admit that the back bedroom was rather attractive. It had been done entirely in white and blue—surprisingly enough, considering that its occupant, Billy, was partial to dingy Victorian browns—and for a sickroom it was pleasantly sunny and cheerful.

When she came in, Lady Bridgewater was sprinkling some red geraniums on the windowsill. When she saw her step-daughter, her handsome face smiled with ill-concealed displeasure.

"Dear Angela," she said. "How nice of you to drop by again. How are you?"

"Quite well, thank you. Hello, father. How are you feeling?"

Billy was propped up in his bed, a white nightcap on his head, a copy of the *Financial Times* spread before him on the counter-pane. He looked almost cheerful.

"Better," he shouted, though without the usual fortissimo "Much better."

She came over and kissed him as he eyed her protruding stomach.

"How's the baby?" he asked. "Kicking?"

"Not yet." She sat down on a chair next to the bed.

"You shouldn't be gadding about, you know. Your mother never moved from her bed when she was carrying you."

"The more advanced doctors don't approve of that any more," said Angela. "It's considered more healthy to take some exercise. You're looking quite good, father."

"What?"

"I said, you're looking *good!*"

"I'm feeling good. Quite good, except I shouldn't read the papers. It's coming, I tell you!" He shook his head. "I can see it coming."

"What's coming, father?"

"Socialism! It's all here in the papers." He tapped the *Financial Times*. "This damned Lloyd George is going to raise the taxes. Budget Day's the twenty-ninth, and it's going to be a black day in English history, mark my words. A black day."

"Father, you mustn't let the budget upset you," replied Angela, removing her gloves. "We'll all survive somehow, I'm sure."

Lady Bridgewater had come to the foot of the bed, hovering, Angela thought, like a hawk ready to pounce on her if she became too intimate with her own father.

"Tell us all about the wedding," she said. "We couldn't go, of course, with Billy being ill. But I read about it. Was St. Margaret's packed?"

"Surprisingly enough, yes."

"Whose wedding?" said Billy.

"Lord Darlington and the nurse's," replied his wife. "Of course," she continued to Angela, "I could hardly believe he'd do it. I suppose Arthur was devastated."

"Oh, he took it in stride," said Angela, forgetting for a moment her dislike of her stepmother as she gave herself up, like an addict to opium, to the joy of gossip. "But I personally was shocked beyond words. It was most brazen of Charles. A common nurse, and Caroline barely six months in her grave, poor woman. Of course, Charles has no sense of decency. None at all. I dislike speaking harshly of my brother-in-law, but he had nothing but contempt for poor Caroline, and I imagine this is his peculiar way of getting back at her. In my personal opinion, he was actually quite delighted she was killed. He's really not very English," she added as the ultimate indictment. "And there's always been a streak of perversity in the family. His grandfather was quite mad. He was convinced he was being pursued by millions of black ants."

"I hope," said Lady Bridgewater, suggestively, "that Arthur has not inherited the family perversity?"

Angela glared at her.

"Arthur is quite rational, thank you," she snapped.

"But lazy," growled her father. "And now that his brother's remarried, they'll have children. And there goes my grandson's chance for a title and a fortune."

"We've thought of that," said Angela. "Naturally, we both had hoped the title could have gone to our child. But there's nothing we can do about it." She thought that her fading hopes for her child inheriting the Darlington money might kindle her father's desire to leave it his own. Lady Bridgewater seemed to be thinking the same thing, because she brought the subject quickly back to the wedding.

"And the reception? How was it?"

"Quite nice. Everyone came. I must say the new Lady Darlington didn't come off so well as a hostess. She looked completely awed by all the grand guests, though Charles carried the load for her, so to speak. And then off they went on their honeymoon, and Arthur and I had to play host and hostess for the rest of the evening."

"Where did they go?"

"Italy. Charles is quite mad about Italy, you know. Florence, Rome, Venice, though why anyone would want to go to Venice is beyond me. So unsanitary! At any rate, they'll be back next week, in time for Budget Day, as a matter of fact." She smiled at her father. "It may turn out to be a black day for England, but Charles seemed most determined to be on hand for it."

"I suppose he's for raising the taxes," said her father, who had been brooding about something.

"Oh, I don't know. I don't follow politics that closely," said Angela. "But I imagine poor Caroline's brother will be against it."

"I told you not to marry him," said old Billy, suddenly changing the subject.

Angela looked confused.

"I beg your pardon, father?"

"I said, I told you not to marry Arthur. The man's no good. He never has been and he never will be. A lazy, titled beggar who was after my money. That's all he wanted. He didn't want you."

Her cheeks stang.

"Father, *please* . . ."

"Oh yes, you looked shocked," continued the old man, undeterred. "But I'm for plain speaking. You could have gotten a decent husband, but you were dazzled by his fancy title and his good looks. You were a fool, Angela. A damned, silly fool."

She stood up, trying to keep her composure before the unexpected attack, cringing with embarrassment that it was happening in front of Violet.

"Father, you're not being fair. I love Arthur. He loves me. He has faults, of course, but—"

"Faults?" snorted the old man. "What's his financial situation? Oh, you don't like to discuss that, do you? Well, I can tell you what it is. I've checked it out. He owes almost twenty thousand pounds! A fortune! And he has no income to speak of, and no prospects of any now that his brother's remarried. That's what you married, my dear, and don't ever say I didn't warn you. And *that's* to be the father of *my* grandchild."

She stared at her father. "I won't deny we're having difficulties. . . ."

"Don't talk like an idiot," he said. "You're in worse than difficulties. And what about me? Who do I have to leave the company to? The company I built up by myself—and don't ever think that was easy! Don't ever forget that if it hadn't been for what I did in my life, you'd still be back in Manchester with no fancy title and no airs of being a great lady. I slaved to make us rich, and who gets the company? A damned pack of slick, whey-faced Oxford parasites, that's who's running it now—when *you* could have brought me a son-in-law with some guts who could have kept the management in the family. You disappointed me, Angela. You severely disappointed me. You went for the glamour of fancy titles, when the real strength of England lies in the men who are willing to work."

She said nothing for a moment, but she felt she must somehow answer him.

"Perhaps, if I have a son, he can run the company some day."

"Perhaps," said Billy, dubiously. "But I won't be around to find out, will I?" He gave her a long, searching stare, one that seemed to Angela full of accusing disappointment. Then he picked up the *Financial Times* and buried himself behind the paper.

She looked at Violet, whose face was smiling ever so slightly, then she put on her gloves.

"Will you stay for tea?" asked Violet, in a smug tone.

"No, thank you," snapped Angela. She walked over to the door, then turned and looked back at the bed.

"Father," she said, softly, "I *do* love him, you know."

The *Financial Times* never moved, and the voice, coming from behind it, was wintry. "Bravo. Now let's see that love pay your bills."

It was her finest moment. Without responding, she left the room and walked to the front hall, where Gadsen fetched her cloak.

"He is looking better," said Angela coolly.

"I think the warm weather has improved his spirits," said Gadsen, putting the cloak over her shoulders, then opening the front door. "He has always like the spring, and the winter was unusually cold."

"Yes, it was a dreadful winter, and today is most especially nice." She stood at the door a moment, breathing in the warm April air and wondering if her father's blast inevitably meant that the progress she thought she had achieved in the past months had been illusory. Then she smiled at Gadsen. "You're looking fine yourself, Gadsen."

"Thank you, Miss Angela. Might I inquire when the blessed event will be?"

"Oh, not for some time yet. Late May, perhaps."

The butler lowered his voice. "Mr. Babson—Lord Bridge-water, I mean—is most pleased, you know. Most pleased."

She knew he was on her side, and that he was trying to cheer her up. She smiled sadly. "Yes," she said, "he seems pleased." Then her chauffeur came to the door to help her to the automobile.

She ensconced herself in the back seat and waited while the chauffeur cranked the engine to life, quite certain that her private war with Lady Bridgewater had been lost. The engine backfired a few times, then turned over and caught. As the chauffeur climbed in front, she looked up to see Gadsen reappear in the doorway. His face looked stricken, and he was waving at her.

"Wait a moment," she said to the chauffeur. Gadsen hurried down the steps to the sidewalk and came over to her.

"Miss Angela," he said, "you'd better come back inside."

She knew from the look on the old man's face what had happened. She closed her eyes a moment. As much as she had been hurt by her father, his death saddened her, and its suddenness shocked her. She thought of the child she was carrying, the child whose future had probably just been decided.

• • •

She had never thought any human being could be so happy. He had said he would redefine the word, and he had.

First there had been the wedding, which, coming as it did after months of doubt as to the sincerity of his proposal, months of recurring waves of guilt about her and Charlie's role in the death of the first Lady Darlington, months of living in the shadow of the plainclothes detective—all this made the wedding seem almost unreal, the release from a nightmare, though its unreal quality didn't prevent her from enjoying it. Rather, she went through the ceremony in a state of cloud-skipping euphoria. And that night, on the boat-train to Paris, when he had made love to her in their compartment and she could enjoy him for the first time as his wife, the euphoria was intensified by the realization that it had actually happened to her, and she was undoubtedly the luckiest woman alive.

They saw Paris. After Paris, the south of France. Then Florence, which Charlie knew as well as London and loved perhaps even more. A week of Florence, seeing the sights: the Duomo, so ugly at first viewing and then, on second and third viewings, so majestic; the house where the Brownings had lived; the English cemetery where they were buried; the Pitti, the Uffizi, the Ponte Vecchio, the shops and restaurants; a *fête champêtre* in the countryside above the Arno; it was all sublime. Then Venice and Vicenza, then on to Rome. And everywhere, Charlie. Charlie buying her endless gifts: some cheap trinkets, others expensive jewels and dresses. Charlie playing jokes on her. Charlie making love to her—and it seemed his passion couldn't exhaust itself, as if, after years of his sterile relationship with Caroline, he had recovered the heat of his youth with his new, young, and most receptive bride. She never dreamed existence could be so beautiful. She told herself it couldn't last, that the honeymoon would end and his ardor would cool, but she didn't believe it. It was a time of emotion, not rationality. And though the ghost of her Victorian father was undoubtedly clucking with otherworldly disapproval, she was certain, that such total capitulation to the gratification of the senses could only be good, or else how could she possibly be so blissfully happy.

One hot afternoon in Rome, as they lay naked in each other's arms on the bed in their suite at the Hôtel de Russie, she brought the subject up.

"Charlie?"

"Um?"

"I think you're turning me into what my father used to call in his sermons a sybarite."

"There is that distinct possibility. I'm an advanced sybarite myself."

"But I think it's probably quite wrong. Even though we're married. I mean it's wrong for us to enjoy each other so much."

"I'm sure it's terribly wrong; but in case you hadn't noticed it before now, I have a rather elastic sense of right and wrong. That's why I married you. I need your superior moral fiber to save me from total moral ruin."

She laughed and rubbed her hand through his hair. "I don't know if I can save you if I become an advanced sybarite myself."

"Shall we worry about that later? It *is* hot, isn't it? The one thing I don't like about Italy is the blasted heat. One would think the Pope would do something about the climate."

"Now Charlie, be serious."

"Why? In Italy, nothing should be taken seriously except love."

Love! She was so in love with him, so totally in awe of him, she wondered at her own sanity. Sometimes she thought of that night in Darlington House, of the look on his face when he had said, "Let her die." There could be no doubt he had meant it. And yet there was so much good in him. He was so kind, so generous, so warm, so passionate. How could one man combine such wonderful, loving qualities with the . . . other?

He sat up and stretched, and she made love to every inch of his body with her eyes.

"I think I'll take a long, tepid bath and cool off," he said. "Where do you want to go for dinner tonight?"

"I don't know."

He looked at her.

"What's the matter?"

"Oh, nothing."

"You're worried about something. I can tell. What is it? Our becoming advanced sybarites?"

She pulled the sheet up to her chin and lay back in the pillows.

"I know you laugh at my country-parsonage morality, but I can't help being what I am."

He leaned over and kissed her.

"I don't laugh at it," he said. "I adore it. Don't you know that? Why do you think I married you instead of some chinless Lady Somebody-or-other with an overweight mother itching to palm her daughter off on the rich earl of Darlington?"

"I don't know," she whispered, smiling. "Tell me."

"Because you're honest and good. And you're going to make

a wonderful mother for the sixth earl. And you can stop feeling guilty about our lovemaking. I've waited too long already to have children, and I intend to spawn a dozen. And I'm told to spawn children one has to make love first. So brace yourself, Lady Darlington: I'm going to continue making love to you morning, noon, and night until we produce a little brat. And if you think that's immoral, then God save England from the moralists."

Her eyes lighted with excitement.

"Oh Charlie," she said, "I hope it happens soon."

He straightened and got off the bed.

"Well," he said, "I'm doing the best I can."

He winked at her, then went into the bathroom to turn on the tub.

• • •

The next morning, they sat on the balcony outside their room and sipped their coffee. The unseasonable heat had been broken by thunderstorms, which had been followed by cool air, and the city sparkled in the sunlight. It was a lovely view of Rome, and Margaret drank it in with her coffee as Charlie opened a cablegram the waiter had brought.

"I'm afraid we're going to have to cut short the honeymoon," he said.

"Why?"

"This cable from Arthur. Old Billy Babson died yesterday of a stroke. We'll have to go back for the funeral."

She tried to hide her disappointment.

"Of course," she said. "I'll begin packing after breakfast."

"Damn," said Charlie, who wasn't hiding his disappointment. "The old goat picked an inconvenient time to die. He never liked me, you know, and I never liked him. But I respected him."

He picked up his coffee again and sipped it.

"It's odd," he continued. "He was one of the greediest men I ever met, and I detest greed. His whole life was dominated by moneymaking, and he never gave an inch to his employees unless he had to. But he had an extraordinary vitality I couldn't help but admire. He started out with nothing and he beat the world, and there's something admirable in that, isn't there? The sheer vitality of the man was amazing." He stared out over the rooftops of the city a moment. "I sometimes think we'll never see that kind of vitality again. Perhaps it's just as well, but I wonder."

He put down his coffee cup and stood up. "I'd best make arrangements for the tickets," he said, and went into the bedroom.

• • •

The constitutional crisis brewing in that spring of 1909 would result in a final showdown between the hereditary peers, as represented by the House of Lords, and the House of Commons. It would eclipse the power and prestige of the British aristocracy and profoundly alter the fabric of British life. But this "upper ten thousand," as it was sometimes called, was still a potent force, socially and politically, when Charlie and Margaret returned to England that April. And it included numerous families without titles, whose lineage was nevertheless considerable. These families were often lumped together under the catch-all label, the "Squirearchy." And among the most prominent of the Squirearchical clans were the Morleys.

Augustus Morley owned twenty thousand acres of rich farmland in Hampshire, acreage that had been in his family since the sixteenth century. On this property were a hundred thirty tenant farmers, many of whose families had also been on the land since the sixteenth century. The Morley country home, Braceton Hall, was one of the handsomest examples of Jacobean architecture extant, and over the years it had been filled with treasures collected by generations of a cultivated and art-loving family. That none of the Morleys had ever acquired even a baronetcy didn't bother Augustus Morley in the least. In an age when the scramble for titles had become an international joke —when a soap king like Billy Babson could buy a viscountcy and when American tycoons sold their daughters into noble slavery to link their shiny new millions with the mellowed gentilty of historic-sounding titles—Augustus Morley considered a title almost common. He was too secure to worry about labels.

In 1893 he had married the daughter of another squire, Mona Sinclair. She had been a beautiful, intelligent girl, apparently enamored of nothing more controversial than Chopin nocturnes, with whom Augustus, who was considerably older, had fallen deeply in love. To his surprise, this sweet and seemingly unspoiled country girl had begun to yearn for the glamor of London. And Augustus, who loved the country and disliked the capital, had finally given in to her and bought a handsome town house on Pelham Crescent, a formal but almost perfect urban unit built in the 1840s by George Basevi. Mona bedeviled her husband into spending more and more time at Pelham Crescent and less at Braceton Hall. She decorated the townhouse with French furniture and began to entertain. Her parties were never large—she was too clever to compete with the great houses —but they were always interesting. Mona was a born *salonière*, a spiritual descendant of the marquise de Rambouillet, whose salon had captured Paris in the seventeenth century. She knew how to bring witty dilettantes together with profound thinkers and make the wit more profound and the thinking wittier. There was always good food, excellent wine, accomplished music, and, above all, talk. Talk of scandal and gossip, naturally, but also talk of business, art, and literature. Unlike America, where the political capital has always been separated from the artistic and business capital, to the detriment of both, London had always been the center of everything, enabling a kind of cross-fertilization to occur between the various important areas of human thought and activity. And while it was true there were "sets" in Edwardian London—literary, artistic, and political cliques that saw little of each other—there were also places like Number 3 Pelham Crescent, where the leaders of all fields could mingle, talk, and perhaps even learn something from each other.

By the end of the nineties, Mona's salon had become so popular that she succeeded in attracting one of the most powerful political figures of the day, Arthur Balfour, the nephew of the prime minister, the marquess of Salisbury. Balfour was young, a bachelor, good-looking, impeccably connected (being a Cecil), a golf addict, and so unflappable people sometimes wondered if he were awake. He was. He had an excellent mind and he liked Mona Morley. He became a frequent guest at her parties. And when, in 1902, he succeeded his uncle as prime minister and head of the Conservative Party, Mona acquired her reputation as king-maker. It became general knowledge that if Mona liked you and put in a word for you to the prime minister, your chances of getting what you wanted were immensely improved. Not that Balfour was corruptible; he wasn't. But he was, like all politicians, open to suggestion. And throughout the three years of his premiership, during which Lord Darlington had been secretary of state for India, Mona Morley's influence was unsurpassed.

Her husband, meanwhile, dazzled and dismayed by his wife's thrust to power, had gradually retired to the sidelines, spending most of his time in the country and leaving Mona to her own devices in London. His retirement was made permanent when, in 1905, he suffered a paralyzing stroke. And while Mona was always good to him, making sure he received the best attention and never failing to visit him in the country at least once a week, she was hardly devastated by Augustus' disappearance from the scene. It enabled her to become what she had always wanted to be: a completely free agent, able to maneuver in the corridors of power as she wished. Her enemies, who were many, called her heartless. She didn't care. If she had been a man, she would have pursued politics herself. Being a woman, she pursued politicians instead.

On the evening of April 29—the black day in English history predicted by Billy Babson only minutes before his death two weeks before—a number of influential politicians assembled at Number 3 Pelham Crescent to discuss the momentous budget proposals made that day in the Commons by Lloyd George, the chancellor of the exchequer. The Cabinet had been arguing for weeks over the proposals, and for months people had been talking about the radical new tax impositions which everyone knew constituted a genuine revolution. The Liberals were, in-deed, out to "tax the rich," though the Liberals—themselves hardly revolutionaries—were basically cautious men and, if they were thinking of a revolution, it was only in terms of the gentlest possible interpretation of the phrase. They had little choice. The expanding government functions of the past decade, as well as the cost of keeping the navy from being swamped by the German fleet, forced them to find new sources of revenue. And the only place to find them was in the vast resources of the wealthy classes.

It was a politically lopsided gathering. Mona's salon, which had started out apolitically, had gradually become more conservative. And when the Liberals came into power in 1906 and rival Liberal hostesses began salons of their own, any attempt at bipartisanship had been discarded. Mona Morley was a Tory, and Number 3 Pelham Crescent, while still retaining its artistic cosmopolitanism, had become a Tory house. Thus Caroline's brother was there, along with Sir Reginald Hamilton, each of whom led certain factions of the conservatives, the duke in the Lords and Sir Reggie in the Commons. There were other Tories there of varying shades of conservatism. But it was the duke who was the most incensed and, as was typical, the loudest. As they gathered in Mona's small but elegant white drawing room, the duke held forth in front of the mantel while Mona, looking lovely, as usual, in a lavender gown, sat in her favorite *fauteuil* and listened as she smoked cigarette after cigarette through her black-lacquer holder.

"You realize what it's going to come down to?" said the duke. "The Lords will have to reject the finance bill."

"Impossible," said Sir Reggie, who was drinking Madeira, of which he was overly fond. "The Lords haven't been able to block finance bills for two centuries. It's out of the question. It would force an automatic dissolution of Parliament and a new election, which would get us nowhere. The Liberals would still come back with a majority in the House, and whatever public sympathy the peers might claim to have would be finished, probably forever. You can't reject the bill. It would be a disastrous move."

"No more disastrous," said the duke, "than approving this damned budget! If we don't fight now, we'll never have a second chance."

"Percy, please," said Mona. "There is no need to bellow. We're all quite capable of hearing you."

"Besides, you're jumping the gun," continued Sir Reggie. "The bill hasn't passed the Commons yet, and it will probably be months before it does. The best thing for us to do is whittle it down while it's in committee. We have allies. The Irish aren't going to be happy about the whiskey duties, for instance, since it knocks a hole in the Irish whiskey trade. Everyone has a soft spot when it comes to taxes, and the thing for us to do is get all the soft spots together and modify the bill. It can be done. I'm sure Lloyd George and the Liberals don't think they can get it through without compromises; but meanwhile, they can take all the glory of having made the proposals. Even if they can't get them through, they still get the publicity, which is all they're interested in."

"You're wrong," said the duke. "Lloyd George and Asquith won't compromise. They like the publicity, but they have the dangerous streak of the idealist in them and they're not going to back down. Which is why I say we must assume the bill will pass the House in its present form, and begin now lining up the peers to reject it."

"I agree," said the marquess of Plymdale, a middle-aged, mild-mannered man who was an expert on Chinese porcelains. "I think the Lords have to take a stand on this, whatever the consequences."

Lord Saxmundham, the earl of Chitterdon, Viscount Rosedale, and Lord Plymouth chorused their approval. Sir Reggie looked at them.

"And what," he said, "if Asquith gets the king to create new peers, just as William IV did in 1832?"

"Preposterous," snorted the duke. "He wouldn't dare. Besides, Edward's on our side."

"You can't be sure. It's happened before and it can happen again. I tell you, it would be madness for the Lords to reject a finance bill. Worse than madness. It would be suicide."

The duke scowled. "All right," he said. "You go your way in the House, and good luck to you. We'll support you as we can, needless to say. Meanwhile, we'll go our way in the Lords.

Perhaps we won't have to reject it—God knows, I hope it doesn't come to that sort of confrontation. But we have to be prepared for it if it does. And judging the temper of the Lords today, I'd say we can get a majority to agree to rejection if we have to."

"You're forgetting one person," said Mona, quietly.

"Who?" asked the duke.

"Your former brother-in-law."

The duke looked disgusted. "Darlington? Well, yes, he'd be against rejection. But he doesn't have that much influence."

"I think you underestimate him," said Mona, fitting another cigarette into her holder and leaning forward for Sir Reggie to light it. "The handsome earl is popular, both with the young Tories and the people. Particularly now that he's made the lavishly democratic gesture of marrying his nurse, the public thinks he can do no wrong." She exhaled.

"I'll grant you he's popular, in a cheap sort of way," said the duke, grudgingly.

"Well, then, isn't it better to get him on your side if possible?"

"I doubt if it's possible. He's more a Liberal than a Conservative. Always has been, damn him. I never understood what Caroline saw in him."

Mona laughed. "You would if you were a woman, Percy. Believe me. Might I make a suggestion?"

"Of course."

"Why don't you leave Lord Darlington to me?"

The group of men looked at each other knowingly. Lord Plymouth laughed. "I'll be damned, Mona, are you going to seduce him?"

"I'd certainly like to try," she smiled. "But I think there are other ways to handle Charles. Perhaps even better than seduction."

"Like what?" asked the duke, intrigued.

"Why, Percy," said Mona, "surely you wouldn't expect a woman to reveal all her secrets?"

"Arthur, wake up!"

Laura Metcalf leaned over her swan-bed and shook Arthur's arm. He had passed out an hour before, and she had another customer waiting in the drawing room.

"What?"

"Wake *up!*"

Arthur sat up in the bed, trying to locate himself. His head split with pain, his stomach felt bilious, and he was still more than a little drunk. He blinked at Laura, who was standing by the bed, swimming in his vision, as did the cupids, jardinières, palms, and gilt that decorated the garish room. Then he began to remember. The reading of old Billy's will which had sent him on a three-day binge. He had never gone on a binge before, but he had been so depressed by the will's contents he had sought the escape of alcohol to forget.

"Can't I stay the night?" he mumbled, running his hand over his skinny, upset stomach.

"No," said Laura, who was looking uncharacteristically annoyed. "What's more, you can't come back till you pay your bill. I'm not running a charity here, you know."

He hiccoughed, and for a moment thought he would throw up.

"You're not being very hospitable," he slurred.

"I become more hospitable when my accounts are paid."

"How much do I owe you?"

"Ninety guineas."

His eyes widened. "Ninety? You must be out of your mind."

"I must be to give *you* credit. Now, hurry. Get dressed. I have a *paying* customer waiting."

A grumbling Arthur got out of the bed and weaved toward the bathroom. She watched him with ill-concealed dislike as he closed the door and disappeared inside. What a difference from his brother, she thought. And how she wished Charlie would come back! The exchange of the charming, paying earl for his uncharming non-paying younger brother had been one that was definitely to her disadvantage. She took Arthur's clothes off the chair and spread them on the bed. Then she went back out to the drawing room to entertain the city banker who was waiting.

Arthur got dressed, left by the back door, and caught a hackney to take him home. He didn't want to go home, but he was at the end of his string, and he barely had cab fare. His memory of the past three days was hazy at best. The binge had started at his club and ended at Laura's, and what had happened in between was a blank. His dress suit was filthy and he needed a shave. He felt like a beggar, but then he was a beggar, a penniless beggar, practically.

Well, not penniless. Billy had left Angela ten thousand shares of Babson Soap preferred stock, which was currently quoted at ten pounds a share on the Exchange and would yield something around four thousand pounds. Arthur owned the house on Portman Square, which had been given to him by his father, and he had an income of about a thousand pounds from various holdings. So he wasn't penniless. But he owed twenty thousand pounds, and he spent, with the most rigid economies—at least by his standards—eight thousand pounds a year. Where was the money to come from? Not old Billy. He had left his millions in a trust, the usufruct of which was to go to his wife for the duration of her lifetime. Violet had won.

Yes, it was true the trust would ultimately go to his child; to this extent he and Angela had won. But not till the child reached maturity. Meanwhile, there would be a driblet to pay for the child's education, but none of this helped Arthur now. The bills lay in piles about the house, ranging from the greengrocer's to Laura's staggering ninety guineas (how in God's name, he thought, did I run up *that* much with her?) and he needed cash now. Moreover, word would get out to his creditors that Lord Bridgewater's millions were frozen in a trust, and they would be descending on him like vultures on a dead cow. He didn't know what to do or where to turn. He was frightened, sick, and exhausted.

When he got home, it was eleven o'clock and Angela had already gone to bed. He let himself into the empty front hall, just as glad it was late since he had no desire to be seen in his present condition, and he certainly wasn't looking forward to answering Angela's inevitable questions concerning his whereabouts for the past three days. He locked the front door, put the key back in his pocket, then, out of habit, picked up the pile of mail on the hall table. Bills, of course. He sifted through the envelopes listlessly, wondering if there was anyone in the world who would ever write him a letter, instead of a bill.

The next to the last envelope was different: apparently someone had written him a letter after all. The envelope was of cheap paper, and the penciled address was crudely lettered, almost as if by an illiterate's hand or, perhaps, a child's.

He tossed the other mail back onto the table and opened the envelope. Inside was a plain piece of lined paper, such as was used in notebooks. The message, written like the address in pencil, read:

> Sir:
> If you are interested in recovering the Darlington emeralds, be at the Schooner Pub, Bankside, at 11:00 P.M. this Monday. Ask for Mrs. Green. Do not bring the police. You will be watched. Wear workman's clothes.

He looked skeptically at the unsigned message and decided someone was attempting a hoax, and a rather stupid one at that. He wasn't about to go to an East End dive and be attacked, which was probably what would happen, even if it weren't a crank note.

He stuffed the note in his pocket and went into the drawing room, turning on a light. He fixed himself a brandy and soda, which he didn't need, and slumped into a chair. The brandy cleared his head somewhat, and he began to wonder about the note. It had been months since the emeralds were stolen and Caroline murdered, and with all his troubles, he had nearly forgotten about them. He knew, of course, that Paul was still at large, but he had read he was supposed to be on the continent. Was it possible he had come back to England? Or never left it, for that matter?

He began having second thoughts about the note. Paul had come to him before, when he was looking for a job, and while he hadn't helped him find employment, he had fed him and given him some money. So it was possible Paul would come to him again. But why?

He didn't know, but another thought had occurred to him. There was a five-thousand-pound reward for Paul, and the insurance company had put up an additional three thousand, making a total of eight thousand pounds. Tempting. Eight thousand pounds was very tempting. He took the note from his pocket again and looked at it. The Schooner Pub. It sounded like the worst sort of dive. Mrs. Green. That sounded wonderfully fictitious, probably a signal of sorts—green for emeralds, or something equally ludicrous. Still, Paul was no Professor Moriarty. It might be just the sort of thing he'd concoct.

Arthur finished his brandy and wondered if he could borrow an outfit from Ian, his second footman. Ian was his size; and from what Arthur had seen of Ian's taste in haberdashery, his clothing would look most suitable in the Schooner Pub.

• • •

The May sunshine beat down on the broad terrace of the Victorian-Gothic Houses of Parliament, where a number of M.P.'s were having lunch. The terrace overlooked the Thames, and was a favorite lunch spot for the lawmakers, many of whom were entertaining their wives, friends, important constituents, and, in one case, an opera star. The women wore the enormous picture hats that were the fashion, which not only created a charming scene but helped protect their complexions from the sun. Mona Morley's hat was white, as was her dress, though the latter had a small pale-yellow bow below the left shoulder, and she looked not only charming but stunning as she sat opposite Lord Darlington at the small table by the balustrade. He wondered why she had asked herself to lunch.

"And how is the new Lady Darlington?" she began in a pleasant voice as she sipped her *vin blanc*.

"Down in the country at the moment," he replied, prepared to go along with her game for a bit—after all, she was a charming lunch companion. "She loves the country, you know."

"And Ellendon Abbey is such a lovely place. So rural. So less complex than life in the city, isn't it?"

"Well, I should say cities do tend to be more urban," Charlie replied with a straight face.

"Everyone, of course, has remarked on the marvelous gesture you made, marrying her," Mona persisted. "One feels the upper classes have become much too ingrown and cliqueish, and an infusion of new blood is only to be welcomed. Of course, for a man like yourself who at one time aspired to high political office—the foreign office, if I recall correctly—in utter candor, one cannot call your marriage a brilliant one. Or do you disagree?"

At last, she's getting to the point, he thought.

"I'm no longer interested in being foreign secretary, Mona. I gave that up the night Caroline brought you into Margaret's sitting room."

Mona smiled. "You're honest, at least."

"Somewhat more than you're being. What is it you want from me?"

She sipped the wine. "Oh, several things."

"You're looking extremely pleased with yourself. By the way, why haven't you told anyone?"

"That's simple enough. Knowledge is power only as long as one doesn't disseminate it. If everyone knew what I know, there'd be no point in our having lunch."

"I'm not sure there is, in any case."

"Oh, there is, there is."

He leaned forward on the table. "Well, now, let me guess, if that's what you'd prefer. It couldn't by chance have something to do with the budget?"

"It could, and does."

"I thought as much. You want me to vote for rejection of the Finance Bill when it comes to the Lords, and in return for that you won't open Pandora's box. Correct?"

"Partially."

"Oh? There's more?"

"There's more. But I think I'd like another glass of wine before I come to it."

Charlie signaled the waiter, ordered, then leaned back in his chair. "I'm listening, Mona."

She looked around her: the adjacent tables were empty. Then she looked out at the river, as if searching for help in saying it. "The Thames," she finally said, "that broad, majestic river that flows through our national history like a silver thread. How much it has seen! How many wars, elections, intrigues, scandals, executions, catastrophes." Then she looked back at him and smiled. "And murders."

He nodded. "You'd make an excellent tour guide, Mona."

"I think I might. Normally, I dislike anything but clear speaking, but one must careful when one only suspects. However, suspicions have a certain power of their own. For instance, if it were suggested to the home secretary that the police might be searching for the wrong man in a certain recent celebrated murder case, why that mere suggestion alone might bring about a complete reevaluation of the case, which in its turn could possibly lead to the apprehension of the real murderer. So suspicions do have some value, if you catch the drift of my remarks."

He smiled. "The 'drift,' as you put it, is more like a tidal wave so far as subtlety is concerned. Let me translate what you're obviously too cautious to put bluntly. You have the idea I had something to do with Caroline's murder. I'll grant there's reason for you to suspect that. You and Caroline caught me red-handed, as they say, with Margaret, and a few hours later Caroline is killed. Cause and effect: I, in a rage—or perhaps more insidiously, I, with cold-blooded cunning—whack the back of Caroline's head on the marble table so that she dies of heart failure, then stage-manage the chloroforming and the robbery and blame all on a phantom burglar. Q.E.D. Now, you hope to put me in a sweat of apprehension by threatening to alert the home secretary of this plot most foul unless I go along with Percy and those other idiots in the Lords in their attempt to reverse the practice of two centuries by rejecting a finance bill which, if they had any brains or political finesse—not to mention compassion—they'd support. Am I close so far?"

She was more than a little surprised by *his* frankness. "Yes," she said.

"Well, Mona, I hate to break this fine web of intrigue you're trying to weave, but for your information, Scotland Yard already suspects me and have had plainclothes men watching me and my wife for six months. So far, they have neither been able to 'get the goods,' as they say, on either of us, nor have they been able to lay hands on Paul Rougement, the real murderer. So not only does your cheap threat not frighten me, but for your information, I'm seriously considering making a speech in the Lords asking for an investigation of a police force that doesn't seem capable of catching the flu, much less my wife's murderer. Now, having made my point and yours as well, do you see any reason, charming as you are, for our continuing this lunch? I think, under the circumstances, conversation would be strained at best."

She was—rare for her—at a loss for words. Then she laughed. "My dear Charles, you are a superb player. My congratulations."

"Thank you. I try."

"You've truly surprised me. I almost believe I was totally wrong about you."

"Almost?"

"Almost. There still, sad to say, lurks the suspicion that perhaps you're bluffing. Of course, you could dispel that easily enough."

"How?"

"By finishing lunch with me, of course." She smiled, and now it was his turn to laugh.

"Mona, I'd be delighted."

The waiter brought more wine, and Charlie ordered lunch.

• • •

The new Lady Darlington preferred the country to London for the simple reason that Darlington House depressed her. The coldly elegant townhouse held too many unpleasant memories, associations that reminded Margaret her present happiness had been made possible by something she would much rather forget. Ellendon Abbey, on the other hand, was not so haunted. The west wing that Caroline had lived in was closed off, and the remainder of the beautiful country house held few mementos of the past for Margaret. Thus, after their return from Italy, she moved to the country. This meant seeing Charles less than she would have liked, but it was the price she was willing to pay for her relative peace of mind.

Besides, she loved Kent and she loved Ellendon Abbey. Life was simpler in the country, and this appealed to her as well. It was fun being a countess, but she neither enjoyed nor felt comfortable in London society, where she knew she would encounter both snobbishness and personal snubs. And here in the pleasant green hills, she could live informally, take up gardening and riding, read, manage the household, and involve herself in the life of the small village a mile from the Abbey.

The people of the town were enchanted by the lovely new Lady Darlington, who was such a refreshing change from the former countess, and when Margaret went into town to browse in the shops, she found to her delight that she was almost immediately accepted. She attended the local church, and befriended the vicar, Dr. Filbert, whose daughter (the one Charlie had said had a moustache) had, happily, found a beau. Dr. Filbert had known Margaret's father, which was a pleasant connection, and when she invited him to dinner at the Abbey, the vicar was won over completely and spread the word to his parishioners that the earl had chosen a wife of exemplary charm and character —though most of them had already come to the same conclusion.

Charlie was amused by Margaret's popularity, and he joked with her about becoming dowdily respectable, but she knew he was pleased. And after a month of her residence in the mellow old house, the only item of contention between them was her refusal to go up to London. Not that he insisted, but he did urge. He said he was lonely without her in town. And though she never was explicit about the reason for her reluctance to go, he knew and didn't insist.

Still, it was a cloud on the otherwise sunny marital horizon

She assumed she was being watched in the country as she had been in town. But here the plainclothes man was much less conspicuous, which only reinforced her desire to stay in Kent. She had heard that a "single" gentleman had rented a cottage not far from the Abbey. She even saw him a few times, riding a horse near the Abbey grounds, and Evans, the gardener, told her that one day the gentleman in question had engaged him in a casual conversation. Of course, this didn't prove he was a detective, but she thought it likely he was. It was unpleasant, but she had become used to it and the threat of police seemed much less real here in this beautiful country of green trees and rolling hills.

She took a great liking to Evans. He lived not far from the Abbey in a small stone cottage, and Margaret several times rode over to take tea with his wife. They were both middle-aged, simple people who worked hard, Evans' only distinguishing quality being his real genius for gardening. He could coax sick plants to health, healthy flowers to glorious bloom, and his knack with lawns was something close to miraculous. Since Margaret loved gardening and the gardens at the Abbey, she became a pupil of the soft-spoken, taciturn man, and their friendship bloomed with the flowers. She liked his wife, Edna, equally as well, and she fell completely in love with their nine-year-old son, Sidney. He was a beautiful child, full of life and mischief, and she asked Evans to bring him to the Abbey to play, which the gardener was happy to do. The pleasant spring days afforded her many hours to be with Sidney, playing on the lawns, and her enjoyment of the child further whetted her desire to have one of her own, something that, to her disappointment as well as Charlie's, still had not happened. Meanwhile, though, there was Sidney. And because Charlie had given her a handsome allowance, she was able to buy toys for the boy, which excited him and delighted her.

One day she rode over to the Evans' cottage to find Sidney in tears, and his mother in a state of embarrassment. When Margaret asked what the matter was, Mrs. Evans said, "The boy has gotten spoiled, that's what, by your Ladyship's kindness. He woke up this morning and said he wanted a pony cart, of all things, and when I told him he couldn't have it he went into a state."

Margaret kneeled down and put her hand under Sidney's chin. "Dear me, Sidney, I had no idea I was spoiling you. And now you're turning into a crybaby as well."

Sidney snuffled and looked at her defiantly. "I'm not a crybaby. And I still want a pony cart."

Margaret stood up and exchanged looks with his mother.

"Well, it seems to me that only very good boys deserve pony carts. And very good boys don't cry."

Sidney wrinkled his face in a look of disgust at this argument. But he stopped crying.

"You mustn't worry, milady," he said to Margaret. "You haven't spoiled me. Honestly."

Margaret laughed, though Mrs. Evans shook his shoulder.

"Here, don't you talk that way," she said. "The devil's in that child," she added morosely.

"Oh, I think Sidney's not *too* wicked," said Margaret.

"Then will you give me a pony cart?" he said, choosing the direct method. His mother gasped.

"But I don't know where we could find one," said Margaret innocently.

"I know. Mr. Baintree has a red one for sale with a beautiful pony, all for eleven guineas."

"You go in the house," snapped his mother. "I'll deal with you later!"

As Sidney scampered inside, looking unrepentant, Mrs. Evans turned to Margaret. "I'm so embarrassed!" she said. "I've never known him to be so bad."

Margaret smiled.

"Please don't apologize. He's adorable and I can't resist him. I'll ride into the village and see Mr. Baintree this afternoon."

"But you mustn't!"

"Nonsense. When I was his age, I would have given the world for a pony cart. And you can't deprive me of the pleasure of giving Sidney one now."

She returned to her horse, leaving Mrs. Evans secretly pleased that her son was going to receive the gift, but shuddering at the thought of his reaction to it.

That night at dinner Margaret told Charlie about giving Sidney the pony cart. Charlie had come down from town late that afternoon, and she had put on a lovely green dress he had bought her in Paris and told Mrs. Blaine to fix fresh asparagus with the mutton because she knew he especially admired the dress and that asparagus was one of his favorite foods, and most important of all, she wished to please him. But she had sensed something was wrong the moment he arrived. He said nothing out of the ordinary, but she could sense that he was worried. She hoped he would mention it later, and meanwhile at dinner in the comfortable walnut-paneled dining room with the beautiful view of the gardens, she enthused about Sidney.

"Oh, darling, you would have died laughing at the way he has his way with me," she said. "Of course, I know I'm spoiling him but I can't help it. And I don't think I've ever seen any child more thrilled than he was when he saw the cart and the pony. The cart is beautiful—all red and shiny—and the pony's cute, though he's not very well-groomed. But Sidney just stood and stared at it, his eyes large and getting larger. Then he got in the cart and took the reins and drove around the cottage just as fancy as you please! It was such fun!"

"Mmm," Charlie said, forking his mutton.

"The Evanses are such nice people," continued Margaret, her enthusiasm diminishing. "All the people here are so nice."

"Yes. Fine people."

"We had seven inches of purple snow this morning."

"Really?"

"And then the moat flooded and Rogers was drowned."

"You don't say?"

She put down her fork. "Charlie, what's wrong?"

"Wrong? Nothing's wrong."

"You haven't listened to a word I've said. I just told you we had seven inches of purple snow, and you said, 'Really?' Darling, what is it?"

He smiled. "I suppose I haven't been very attentive. I'm sorry. It's this damned budget business, that's all."

"Are you sure it's nothing else?"

"Oh no. Really. This asparagus is excellent. Did it come from the garden?"

She looked at him curiously. There was something, she knew, something he wasn't telling her. She'd thought they had achieved that state of total honesty with each other that both had agreed was the only basis for a lastingly successful marriage. If nothing else, the nightmare evening in Darlington House had accomplished that. And yet now he was hiding something from her. She said nothing more, hoping he would eventually tell her, after all.

But the small cloud already on the marital horizon was now threatening to become somewhat larger.

• • •

The Schooner Pub was located on the river in the heart of the grimy East End and was, as Arthur had suspected, a dive, although its etched-glass booth-separators, its elaborate Victorian bar, its tin ceiling, and its tile floor might, in a later age, have earned it the label "quaintly charming." As Arthur came into the smoky room, however, he saw it for what it was; and the clientele, composed mostly of dock workers in varying stages of inebriation, were anything but quaint or charming. He decided the author of the anonymous note had been wise to recommend he wear "workman's clothes." A dress-suited swell would have stood out like a sore thumb in this dingy crowd, and Arthur felt more comfortable in his footman's plaid suit and cap, though even this looked comparatively flashy. He made his way to the bar and ordered a whiskey. The barman, a burly gentleman with a luxuriant moustache, didn't seem to take notice of him.

When Arthur paid for the drink, he quietly said, "I'd like to see Mrs. Green." The barman shot him a look but didn't hesitate. "Up those stairs," he said, pointing to a curtained doorway at the back of the room.

Arthur drank his whiskey, then made his way to the stairs. They were narrow, atilt, and dark, but he hardly expected a grand stairway. He climbed them to the second floor. The walls were covered with peeling paper smeared with soot, and a gas jet flickered by a door. Seeing no other door, Arthur knocked. After a moment the door was opened by a woman in a soiled dress who, on second glance, had, to Arthur's surprise, a certain refinement of features. He thought that if she would fix her hair and wash, she might be pretty.

"Mrs. Green?" he said.

She looked him over, then stood aside. "Come in."

He entered a room that seemed a combination sitting room, bedroom, and kitchen. It was cheaply furnished and dirty, though an attempt to brighten the place was evidenced by a number of theatrical posters pinned to the wall as well as by photos and chromos of Ellen Terry, Mrs. Patrick Campbell, and other stage stars. Otherwise the barrenness of the room was depressing, whispering the presence of a crushing poverty that made Arthur uncomfortable.

"Sit down," said the woman, pointing to a chair. "Would you like a cup of tea?"

There was a kettle on a gas burner on the bureau. She spoke with a slight East End accent which seemed to have been polished either by a partial education or elocution lessons. He thought she couldn't be over twenty-five or six, but there was a quiet bitterness about her that seemed ingrained in her soul as well as her face and which made her seem older. The combination of the theatrical posters, the pretty face, and the consciously polished diction led him to believe she was probably an unsuccessful actress.

"No tea, thank you," he said, sitting down in the tattered chair the woman had indicated. "I didn't contact the police," he remarked.

"I know. If you had, you wouldn't have gotten this far."

"Are you threatening me?"

She sat on the bed.

"Maybe. We have to be cautious."

"Who's 'we'?"

"Who do you think?"

He took his crested gold cigarette case from his coat pocket, reflecting that it hadn't been so wise to bring it, then extracted a cigarette and tapped it on the lid.

"Not being an expert in melodramatic skullduggery, I haven't the foggiest," he said, lighting the cigarette. "Although I'd venture an educated guess that Paul Rougemont is lurking in the background somewhere." Perhaps, he thought, even behind the curtain next to the bed, which covered what he assumed was a closet. He had noticed the curtain moving slightly as he came into the room.

"Paul's in Holland," said the woman shortly, "and has been for the past six months."

"I take it he has the emeralds still?"

"That's right. He can't sell them. They're too hot. That's why we've contacted you. Paul wants to make a deal."

"I see."

"He'll return the emeralds for the three thousand pounds the insurance company's put up for his head. You're to be the go-between."

"Why me?"

"He trusts you. You was kind to him once."

"What makes Paul think the insurance company would go along with this?"

"It's going to cost them a lot more if they have to pay off your brother."

True. He thought a moment. "I assume Paul intends to take the three thousand quid and flee to America, to lose himself in the anonymity of the New World? Or perhaps to the back reaches of the Amazon, where the long arm of British justice can never reach him for the murder of my sister-in-law?"

He noticed the curtain beside the bed rustle again, and he more strongly suspected that someone in fact was standing behind it. If it were Paul, it represented eight thousand pounds on the hoof. He pretended not to have noticed.

"Paul didn't murder your sister-in-law," said the woman.

"I'm sure that's what he says. The police take a different view of the matter."

"He didn't!" she exclaimed in an abrupt show of anger. "He

told me she woke up while he was opening the safe, and she rang for the nurse. That's when he gave her the chloroform. He thought she'd probably be passed out drunk like she always was before, but to make sure, he brought the chloroform and it was a good thing he did. Oh, she put up a fight all right, and banged her head a touch before he put her to sleep. But it wasn't much more than a tap even if there was some bleeding. Paul made very certain of that. When he left the room, she was alive!"

"Barely. Her heart was giving out."

"Oh yes, the 'heart' story. We read that one in the papers and got a good laugh. A very convenient story for *her*, wasn't it?

"You mean the nurse?"

"Who else? She tells the police that when she comes in the room, she tries to save her patient but, alas, she's too late. A very nice story for her, and she can let Paul hang for it. But Paul didn't want Lady Darlington dead. Just the opposite. Better for him to be a thief than a murderer. All *he* wanted was the jewels. But *she* had a reason to kill her."

"What do you mean?"

"Who's the countess of Darlington now?"

Silence. The woman got up from the bed and came over in front of Arthur.

"She was sleeping with your brother. Paul knew that, and so did your sister-in-law. That's why Paul got fired—because he helped the first Lady Darlington try to get the nurse out of the house and your brother got furious at them for doing it. The nurse had him wrapped around her finger and he brought her back. And now she's married to him and living in luxury. Do you really think when she went in that bedroom and found the woman whom she had every reason to want out of the way unconscious, she didn't do something to make sure she'd never wake up?"

Arthur hesitated.

"What, for instance?"

The woman shrugged. "The heart medicine was right there, easy for her to get at. And she must have got to the room right after the accident and Paul left—he saw her in the hallway when he was running out. She said she went straightaway to Lady Darlington when she heard the bell and after seeing Paul. Either she lied about that, or she was mighty slow about giving her the medicine, or maybe she never even tried. Maybe she put a pillow over her face and helped her through the Pearly Gates that way. There were lots of things she could have done. And you don't believe she's so innocent yourself, I wager, not any more than Paul and I do. But she'll let *him* hang so she can go on being a great lady, with the help of the likes of you, and no one will suspect her because now she's a la-dee-dah countess and everyone in this bloody country worships the nobility and thinks they can do no wrong. You have a cigarette?"

Arthur's thoughts were racing so fast he didn't hear. "What?"

"A cigarette." She held out her hand.

Arthur fumbled in his coat and pulled out the cigarette case, offering her one. She took it, then went over to the gas burner to light it.

"You mean to tell me you never thought of this?" she said, exhaling.

"No, frankly, I haven't," he said, and he meant it. The idea had dumbfounded him.

"And I suppose you're going to tell me you don't think a sweet person like Miss Suffield—pardon me, Lady Darlington—could do such a terrible thing as murder her patient?"

He didn't answer. He was remembering that first evening he had met her at Darlington House. The evening Charlie had brought her to the dining room and Angela had been so upset. Then he had thought she was a tricky little baggage, up to something he couldn't quite see. Now he was beginning to wonder if his first instincts hadn't been correct after all.

He looked up at the woman. "I think you and Paul have every reason to attempt to put the blame on Miss Suffield, or rather, my sister-in-law."

She shrugged. "Granted."

"And I think most of this is bluff based on wild supposition."

"Maybe yes, maybe no. But I know Paul didn't kill that woman intentionally. He had no reason to! *She* did. And I'm not going to let Paul hang for something he didn't do. He stole the jewels. All right, now he's ready to give them back. For a price. The insurance company won't starve."

Arthur stood up. "You take a rather—shall we say biased—view of the ethics of the situation."

"I'm not interested in ethics. I'm interested in getting out of this bloody rotten country."

"I see. I take it you're in love with the dashing Paul?"

She didn't answer.

"And you intend finding happiness with him in whatever backwater of the globe you assume the three thousand quid will get you to in style?"

"You can think that if you want. Will you help us?"

He glanced at the curtain and wondered what would happen if he said "No." He had the uncomfortable feeling he might not get out of the room alive. However, he had no intention of saying "No." The information he had received had opened up a dazzling new prospect to him; and if he had the nerve to go through with it—and if it worked—it would be to his advantage to help the former footman and his girlfriend or wife, or whatever. Their formal relationship was unimportant. Of real importance was getting them out of the country where they could never tell what they knew—as well as strongly, convincingly suspected. Such information was much more profitably restricted to himself.

He ground out his cigarette in a dish which was filled with Dutch cigarette butts.

"Yes, I'll help you," he said. "The emeralds are family heirlooms, and we'd be sad to see them lost forever. But you must give me some time."

"How much time?"

"A month."

"Two weeks."

"My dear Mrs. Green, or whatever your name is, I'll be assuming considerable personal risk to help a man who is wanted by the police of three continents. You're in no position to dictate terms."

"Yes, we are." Her face was cool. "You don't want Paul

caught any more than I do. He might tell the truth about what happened that night and make some nasty trouble, bad publicity at least, for your 'distinguished' family. I know how you toffs think, anything to keep the family name clean, particularly since your brother's a politician. Two weeks."

Arthur was privately amused by how far off the mark she was there. "All right," he said, "I'll work as fast as I can. I assume I can contact you through the gentleman behind the bar downstairs?"

"That's right."

"Is he your father?"

"No."

Arthur suspected he was. He walked over to the door and opened it. Then he looked again at the curtain by the bed. It wasn't moving. He glanced at her.

"Might I ask what your name is?"

"Mrs. Green."

"Well then, your first name."

She hesitated, gauging whether to reveal this much. Then: "Alice."

"I see. Well, Alice, you're a very pretty girl. Paul's taste in women, if nothing else, is admirable."

She said nothing. He walked out of the room and closed the door behind him. He was excited and, at the same time, frightened. An invaluable weapon had been placed in his hands. Now the question was, would he have nerve to use it for all it was worth?

As he descended the dark stairs, he thought he could hardly afford not to.

• • •

She heard about it from Mrs. Blaine.

Margaret and Charlie were playing croquet on the garden lawn. It was a Saturday morning, and Charlie had just sent her ball to the end of the court. "That's not fair!" she complained, holding her broad white hat with her hand to prevent it from blowing off in a sudden breeze.

"All's fair in love, war, and croquet," said her husband, sending his ball through the middle wicket, then aiming for the next one at the corner. He hit the ball with the mallet, and it rolled across the smooth lawn, coming to a halt two feet in front of the wicket. Then he ambled across the grass, swinging his mallet nonchalantly over his shoulder. "I sometimes think I missed my true calling," he said. "When it comes to croquet, no one is my master."

"Conceited," sniffed Margaret, aiming for the middle wicket again. "I'll beat you yet."

He leaned on his mallet and watched as she missed the wicket by a good three yards.

"Hah! It will take you at least two strokes to get back in position. You might as well give up now and accept a graceful defeat. I'm known to be magnanimous in victory, and might conceivably open a bottle of Chablis for lunch if you concede to my superior skill."

"I'd die first. Now quit bragging and play."

"There's no competition," he grumbled. "Oh, well, here goes yet another superb shot by Darlington of the all-England team."

Click! The ball sailed through the wicket. As he set up his next shot, Margaret saw Mrs. Blaine hurrying into the garden.

"Milady!" she called, her taffeta skirts flying as she ran toward them.

"What's wrong?"

"The Evans child—Sidney!" The housekeeper was puffing. "There was an accident!"

Margaret looked alarmed, as did Charlie.

"What happened?"

"The pony cart you bought him! He was riding in it and the pony took off at a run and the cart overturned!"

"Oh, no! Was he hurt?"

She nodded. "Broke his leg. I just heard about it from the vicar, he rang up. Dr. Quarles set the leg but the poor child's in terrible pain—"

"Charlie, we must drive over right away," said Margaret, dropping her mallet on the lawn and starting for the house. Her husband hurried after her. When they reached the courtyard, where Denby was polishing the automobile, they piled into the back seat, Charlie ordering him to drive to the Evanses as quickly as possible. They reached the cottage in ten minutes. Mrs. Evans was standing in the door with her husband. Her face looked strained and she had been crying. Margaret and Charlie hurried up the path to the door.

"When did it happen?" asked Margaret.

"About two hours ago."

"May we see him?" asked Charlie, who looked concerned.

The woman nodded, trying to hold back her tears, and stepped aside as Margaret and Charlie came into the front room of the cottage.

"He's in back," said Evans, leading them across the clean stone floor to a small bedroom where Sidney lay on the bed in his nightshirt. His right leg had been wrapped in a splint, and he was sobbing. Margaret went over to the bed and took his hand. Sidney seemed a little cheered by her presence.

"Epsom Downs ran away," he said—he had named the pony after the track—"and the cart turned over."

"But you're a brave lad, aren't you?" Margaret smiled, leaning over to kiss his forehead. "And you're going to be all right."

"I hope so," said Sidney dubiously. "But my leg hurts terrible bad."

Charlie had come up beside his wife. "Broken legs mend," he said, "and then you'll be up and about, running twice as fast as before. You'll see."

Margaret was looking at the splinted leg. There was something odd about it.

"Mrs. Evans," she said, "where did the doctor say the break was?"

Sidney's mother was standing with her husband at the foot of the bed. Now she pointed to the lower leg, just above the ankle. "There, milady," she said, "the doctor said it had split clean in two."

There was a bulge just above the ankle. Margaret studied it a moment, then smiled at Sidney and squeezed his hand again. "Is the cart broken?" she asked.

"The axle is."

"Well, we'll get it fixed. Meanwhile, you stay in bed and get well."

She released his hand and went back into the front room, followed by the others. She signaled Evans to close the bedroom door, then said in a low voice, "Charlie, we must find another doctor. Dr. Quarles hasn't set the leg correctly. Is he old?"

Charlie nodded. "An antique."

"It doesn't surprise me. He's done a shocking job. Oh, don't worry, Mrs. Evans. It can be reset easily enough. Where can we find another doctor? One who's been to a medical school in the past half century, that is."

Silence. The Evanses looked blank, as did Charlie. Then the latter said, "The nearest one I can think of is old Dr. MacLeish in Ivesbury, but he's not much of an improvement over Quarles. Can you reset it?"

Margaret hesitated. "I can if necessary. But I'd rather have a doctor do it. Let's ring up Sir Andrew. He could come down on the noon train. It's trickier resetting a leg than setting it, and I'd feel better if Sir Andrew did it."

Charlie agreed; and after reassuring the Evanses Sidney was in no danger, they drove back to the Abbey. On the way Margaret said, "Charlie, we should do something about this. We should try to get a new doctor in the village."

"I think probably you're right. Quarles was adequate in his day, but I hear he's got cataracts and can barely see what he's doing."

She thought that was obvious from the terrible job he had done on the leg. But as she thought about it, she began to wonder if more than a new doctor weren't needed. Though in his budget speech, Lloyd George had called for health insurance, if this were passed she knew it would probably be restricted to the trade unions, and even if it encompassed wider coverage, still in the small villages like Rockhampton, which for centuries had been dependent on local doctors for medical care—if not witches —it would be unlikely that any extensive medical facilities would be available for years. She asked Charlie about this and he agreed it probably was true. Then she said, "But if in the meantime there were a bad epidemic? Or a flood, or who knows what catastrophe? These people have no medical help at all. Oh, I know this isn't the only place in the same fix; there are hundreds of villages like Rockhampton. But we could *do* something here."

"Like what?"

"Well, we might set up a small clinic."

She looked at him cautiously, trying to gauge his reaction to this idea. He thought about it a moment, then reached over and took her hand. "You really are a compulsive do-gooder, aren't you?" He grinned.

"I suppose I am. But I've become very fond of the people here. They've accepted me, allowed me to be their friend. Now I'd like to do something for them."

"Well, I rather fancy the idea of a clinic," he said. "Nothing grandiose, of course, but with whatever new equipment would be needed for a place this size. When Sir Andrew comes down, why don't we talk to him about it?"

Her face lighted with excitement.

"Oh Charlie, may we?"

He nodded and she kissed him. The notion of building a clinic delighted her, and the thought that Charlie would support her in the project gave her an especial feeling of satisfaction. Gone was the cloud on the marital horizon; whatever incipient doubts she had had about their relationship dissolved in a surge of love for him. There was so much good in him . . . despite what he had done that night. She had always believed it; she could never have loved him so much if she didn't. Certainly he was no saint, she well knew that. He could be bitter, cold, and she knew he viewed his fellow humans as, in general, hopelessly imperfectible —which prescription he doubtless used to justify something less than admirable behavior. On the other hand, he could be unexpectedly kind and generous. The unfortunate in life could arouse his compassion; he had championed them in Parliament, and today she had seen his genuine concern for Sidney. He was a strange admixture of good and bad. And what had first struck her as a paradox, now that she was more accustomed to it, she was beginning to accept. Again, she was convinced that by protecting him she not only had done what she had to do because of her love, but what in the long run would prove right as well.

At least, she hoped so.

• • •

In fact, Charlie took to the idea of the clinic with considerable relish.

Sir Andrew came down to the village and reset Sidney's leg, which job indeed had been botched by the incompetent local doctor. Afterward, he came over to the Abbey for dinner. And after congratulating Margaret for having detected the mis-set bone, he listened as Charlie proposed the idea. It had grown since Margaret had suggested it that morning. Now Charlie wanted to build a hospital that could handle not only the village of Rockhampton, but the surrounding countryside as well. After expressing his surprise and delight at the suggestion, Sir Andrew threw himself wholeheartedly into the scheme, volunteering to devote his spare time to locating a qualified architect who could design a hospital incorporating the latest advances in medical science. The cost, he said, would be considerable, but Charlie had already decided how to finance it. The insurance company had been sluggish about paying the claim for the stolen emeralds, some fifty thousand pounds, in the hope that the jewels would be recovered. But the previous week they had told Charlie they were ready to settle; and to Margaret's delight, Charlie proposed turning over the entire settlement to the construction of the hospital. She was surprised when he further proposed naming the hospital for Caroline, which under the circumstances struck her as being a touch morbidly ironic. But when he winked at her across the dining-room table, she could hardly suppress a smile. And she couldn't have cared less if he had named it after Paul, so long as it got built. The important thing in her mind was that good was coming out of bad.

The project launched and dinner completed, Sir Andrew prepared to leave for the train station. Charlie had been called away to the phone, so Margaret accompanied the doctor to the door alone. He paused before leaving and said, "You both seem quite happy."

"We are." She smiled.

"Well, I'd be a liar if I pretended I didn't think you were a glorious improvement over your predecessor." He put on his top hat. "You don't go up to town much, do you?"

"Hardly at all."

She wondered why he had made the remark, and was perplexed even further by the frown on his face. After a moment, he said in a low voice, "Do you know a Mrs. Morley?"

"I've met her. Why?"

"I attended her husband, Augustus Morley. The poor man passed on two weeks ago. He was an invalid, and it was only a matter of time for him. At any rate, while I was at Braceton Hall, their home, I overheard a telephone conversation between Mrs. Morley and someone in London. She was in the sitting room next to her husband's bedroom, and she either failed to realize I was there or didn't think to close the door. Her husband was in a coma, so she hardly needed to be concerned about him. I'm not, I hope, the sort who snoops but I couldn't very well suddenly afflict myself with deafness, and so I heard portions of the conversation. She was arranging a dinner engagement with the man, and it was certainly a man."

Margaret remembered the glacial woman with the plumed fan she had met at the ball. She could well imagine a woman like that arranging to meet another man for dinner even while her husband was dying in the next room. It would take veins full of ice to do it; but Mona Morley looked icy-veined.

"It doesn't sound as if she were exactly grief-stricken over her husband, does it?" she said.

"Hardly." The doctor looked toward the library door behind which Charlie was still talking on the phone. Then he turned back to Margaret. "The man's name was Charles," he said quietly.

She stiffened.

"Now," he continued, "there are lots of Charleses in England; but I don't know too many who live on Belgrave Square. I'm very fond of you, Margaret, and I don't want you to be hurt.

That's why I'm telling you this, not because I wish to start rumors or cause trouble. But I think you should know, and perhaps you should begin spending a little more time in London. *Verbum sapienti,* if you see my point." He patted her hand, looking into her eyes a moment. Then he left the house.

For several moments she stood alone in the great entrance hall. The information had stunned her, and for a while she simply couldn't believe it. Her first instinct was to run after Sir Andrew and slap him for even suggesting Charlie could be unfaithful. Then she reminded herself the doctor most certainly wasn't the sort to pass on such information if he weren't sure it was accurate, and that in fact he had been trying to help her. No, it must be true.

Her whole world seemed to collapse into dust. The clinic, which Charlie had accepted with such easy enthusiasm—merely a device to keep her even more firmly entrenched in the country, leaving him free to maneuver in London with Mona Morley? She quite literally felt ill. She had banked everything on his love, and her love for him. She had protected him from the law, risked imprisonment, and undergone God only knew how many sleepless nights for this man she adored. And now, with one stroke, the whole superstructure of faith had been undermined. She felt too numb to move, too hurt to cry. She could only stand there, alone in the large hall.

At last she began to pull herself together.

She was rushing to conclusions. After all, simply because Charlie dined with Mona Morley hardly proved he was having an affair with her, any more than when she herself had dined with Charlie at Darlington House it had meant she was having an affair with him then—though ruefully she had to admit the dinner had indeed led to involvement. Still, she would not be another Caroline. God, no! She would give Charlie every benefit of the doubt and behave with dignity. The more she thought about it, the more certain she became that there was, after all, a reasonable explanation. Her husband was an honorable man. They loved each other. Their marriage was solid, no matter what its basis had been.

He came out of the library, telling her the call had been from

Sims, his secretary, and that he would have to go up to town first thing in the morning. She said nothing, trying to show nothing, but inevitably wondering if he were lying and whether the call had been from Mona Morley instead. They proceeded into the drawing room and sat for a while discussing the hospital, Charlie full of enthusiasm, Margaret forcing a show of interest though her mind was elsewhere. Then they went to their bedroom and undressed. She put on a blue peignoir and brushed her hair. She knew, under the circumstances, it would pay to look her best. When she came out of her dressing room, he was sitting in bed.

"You're looking most seductive," he said. "I hope you're planning to seduce me."

She came across the large room to the four-poster bed and sat on the edge beside him. "That depends," she said.

"On what?"

She decided not to fence—too much was at stake. "On whether you've been having an affair with Mona Morley."

His handsome face remained composed. "Who put such an idea into your head?"

"Sir Andrew. He told me he overheard a telephone conversation between Mona and you. 'Arranging a dinner engagement' was the way he put it."

He smiled slightly. "I think you're jealous."

"Of course I'm jealous."

He leaned back on his pillows, crossing his arms over his chest. "Yes, I have been seeing Mona. Quite a lot, as a matter of fact."

"And why haven't you told me?"

"Because husbands customarily don't tell their wives when they've been dining with other women."

She looked down at her hands. "Are you in love with her?"

"Madly. Beneath Mona's icy exterior beats a heart of tropic passion. She dances naked on table tops while I lash her with whips. It's extraordinarily sensuous and very un-English of both of us."

"Charlie, I'm serious!"

He laughed and took her hands, pulling her over to him. Then he kissed her

"If you must know, jealous little wife, Mona put the fear of living God into me. She asked herself to lunch a while back and in her charmingly cool way tried to blackmail me into voting with Percy against the Finance Bill."

"Blackmail you? How?"

"By suggesting she might hint to the home secretary that the police have been looking for the wrong man."

She stared at him. "Does she know?" she whispered.

"She's guessing, but is uncomfortably close. I think I was able to bluff her, but felt it would be only prudent to at least take her to dine a few times. And apparently it's worked. At the risk of sounding immodest, I do believe the devastating Mrs. Morley has fallen head over heels in love with me. And she seems to have dismissed any ideas she ever had about my being the masked murderer of Belgrave Square."

"But what happens now? I mean, if she's in love with you, she's going to become impatient with merely being taken to dinner."

"Ah, but my sweet, innocent wife, you see you don't understand the politically ambitious mind. Mona may be in love now. But after a time, when she realizes I'm in love with you and a hopelessly faithful husband, she'll grow tired of being in love and start thinking of me in terms of a political pawn, somebody she can move on that elegant political chessboard she presides over at Number 3 Pelham Crescent. She's already bored with Reggie Hamilton. And I'm politically eligible, so to speak. So our relationship is certain to devolve into a coldly practical political partnership, and the only thing you'll need be jealous of is Mona basking in my political glory."

She said nothing for a moment. It was a reasonable explanation; she had hoped for one and she got it. But it was perhaps too reasonable for comfort. And even if it were entirely true, she simply didn't like the sound of it.

She got up and went over to the window to look out at the moon-spangled moat and, beyond, the silver fields.

"What's wrong?" he said from the bed. "You don't seem exactly euphoric about that arrangement?"

She turned.

"I don't like the idea of her promoting your career."

"But that's *Mona's* career. She's in the business of making and breaking careers. She runs a very good salon, she knows everyone who's anyone, and she's very good at what she does. And since you refuse to come to London . . ." He spread his hands.

"But I hate Darlington House!" she exclaimed. "Can't you understand why?"

"Of course. But I'm still lacking a wife who will entertain for me. I don't blame you; you love it down here, your interests are here, you'll have the hospital to work on, so there's no point in your coming up to London and trying to do something you don't enjoy and, frankly, probably wouldn't in any case be especially good at. So you can stay here and Mona can entertain for me. Besides, it will tend to keep her mouth shut."

She sulked. She didn't like giving up any part of her role as his wife, particularly to Mona Morley.

He extended his hand.

"Now come over here to bed. I'm feeling sybaritic as the very devil."

"I'm not in the mood," she snapped.

There was a long silence. It was the first time she had even dreamed of refusing him since their marriage, and she could see he was angered by it. "You're beginning," he finally said, "to sound uncomfortably like Caroline."

With that, he turned off the light by the bed and rolled away onto his side.

She stood in front of the window, silhouetted against the moon, which spilled past her into the bedroom. She was shocked by his remark, but she had to admit there was truth in it. She must not start behaving like his first wife. She must not and she would not. Besides, as much as she disliked the idea of Mona Morley having anything to do with her husband, she thought he probably was right, that she couldn't compete on Mona's territory. She didn't have the skill or the desire. And even though she now was a countess, in class-conscious London society she would always be thought of as a nurse. So perhaps this was the best way, after all.

Besides, as he had said, it would keep Mona from talking.

She came over to the bed. "Darling," she whispered.
"What?"
"I'm sorry."
She felt his hand take hers and pull her gently down onto the bed and into his arms.
"I love you," he whispered as he began kissing her neck.

• • •

When she awoke the next morning, he had already left for London.

She rolled over in the great bed, savoring with sweet pleasure the memory of his lovemaking, made all the more enjoyable by their preliminary argument. She looked out the leaded windows at the sky, which was cloudy but still, to her, beautiful. A cold mist was hovering over the fields, obfuscating the countryside with white, giving it the flavor of a delicate Chinese landscape. She drank in the porcelain beauty, then looked around the bedroom. It too seemed incredibly beautiful this morning; the hammered silver sconces on the paneled walls, the sturdily elegant Jacobean chairs with their grospoint upholstery, the huge French armoire. She saw it all with new eyes because she felt so renewed herself. She wondered for a moment if perhaps they had conceived a child. What a marvelous thought that was! She ran her hand over her stomach and prayed it had happened. That was what he wanted. A child would bring them even closer together and end forever the potential menace of Mona Morley.

Mona. She thought about Mona, and her happiness began to dissipate. If she could only believe what he had said about her; if only it were true that their relationship would turn out to be nothing more than political. But was that likely? Her nagging doubts began to return, burrowing into her consciousness like maggots. If she could fully compete with Mona, she could scotch the doubts forever; but, she was forced to acknowledge, she couldn't. He had said it himself, that she shouldn't try something she probably wouldn't be especially good at. And yet, why couldn't she? She was, after all, a countess. She was rich. She had jewels, gorgeous clothes, a great house, fine carriages, a Rolls-Royce. She was said to be beautiful. Perhaps she had been wrong in staying at the Abbey, evincing hardly any interest in the normal pursuits of the nobility, entertaining no one but the locals, wearing hardly any of the clothes Charlie had bought her. Charlie had a soft spot for the glitter of the world; she remembered his comment during the ball. She had never been much interested in it, aside from the interest of a spectator, but perhaps that was why he was apparently beginning to stray.

Getting out of bed, she ran in her bare feet across the cold wood floor to her dressing room. This was octagonal in shape, a Gothic caprice built by the second earl a century before, a small jewel of a room. The eight walls were mirrored, each glass held in a beautifully carved wooden frame simulating a Gothic arch, the motif continuing above the doors into the ceiling, which was a delicately groined vault. Behind six of the mirrors was a closet (the other two mirrors being doors, one to the bedroom and the other, opposite, to the bath). She opened them all to look at her immense wardrobe, which Charlie had bought for her in Paris. Rows of exquisite gowns, shelves of shoes, box after box of elaborate hats; she had yet to wear a third of them. She ran into the adjoining bath and washed her face. Then she slipped out of her nightgown and put on her underthings. Returning to the octagonal room, she picked out her favorite of all the dresses: a gorgeous bone-colored gown with a delicate lace overskirt that hung down the back in a languid reversed triangle, terminating in a teardrop pearl. She put it on, then its matching pumps, and viewed herself. Elegant. Taking out the leather jewel case Charlie bought her in Florence, she opened it and examined the contents. Pearls. Three strands of enormous pearls that had belonged to Caroline but which now were hers. She had never worn any of Caroline's jewels except for the emerald engagement ring, but now she took them from the case and fastened them around her neck. Exquisite. And the matching pearl bracelet? Yes. she would try that too. Clipping it onto her wrist, she was feeling more like a countess every moment. She searched through the jewel case again and spotted the two diamond star clips

Charlie had bought her at Cartier. They were her favorites, and she fastened them to the dress. Then, quickly, she piled her long hair on top of her head and pinned it in place.

Closing all the mirrored doors, she looked at her eight reflections.

She turned slowly, examining herself from every angle. She was, she decided with pleasure, rather stunning. She certainly was younger, fresher, and prettier than Mona Morley. Much younger.

"*Verbum sapienti*," Sir Andrew had said the night before. "A word to the wise." She had been a fool to be afraid of Darlington House because of its unpleasant associations, too timid to face London society because she was plain Margaret Suffield, the nurse from Chewton Mendip. She no longer was plain Margaret Suffield. She was Margaret, countess of Darlington, and she was very possibly losing her husband. That was the reality; her fears and guilts were phantoms.

She returned to the bedroom and rang up Peter Sims in London. She had met the young Cambridge graduate once, and spoken to him several times on the telephone; now he could be useful. He too was politically ambitious, she reflected, as she waited for the call to be put through to the Albany. They were all politically ambitious. "Power," the first Lady Darlington had said to her that first afternoon so long ago, "that's what it's all about." Power, which made people deceive. Power, which was her true rival. Mona Morley could help Charlie become foreign secretary. That was her wedge, her weapon; and if she, Margaret, wanted to keep Charlie, she would *have* to compete on Mona's territory.

Sims sleepily answered the phone. Margaret said, "Mr. Sims, I may have to contact my husband this evening. I believe he said he would be at Mrs. Morley's?"

Sims replied that, yes, indeed, he would be at Mrs. Morley's, that she was giving a musicale. Could he deliver any messages to His Lordship? She thanked Sims, said there were no messages, and rang off. So he *was* going to Mona's after all! And he hadn't told her. Since it was Sunday, she knew Sims probably wouldn't be seeing Charlie that day, so if she went up to London late she could avoid seeing Charlie and surprise him at Mona's. That would be perfect. She would surprise them all.

She sat down on the bed, pleased with her decision and itching for battle. She would get Mrs. Blaine to help her pack; she could also do her hair, though she would have preferred a professional. It occurred to her that if she was going to play this game, she would need to hire a private maid. Being elegant was, she knew, hard work, and Maud, who was incompetent anyway, had quit after her mistress's death.

There was a knock on the door.

"Come in," she called, and Mrs. Blaine walked into the bedroom.

"Oh," said Margaret, getting up, "I was about to ring for you. Would you help me pack? We're going into town this afternoon."

Mrs. Blaine stared at her gown. "To town?" she said. "And what, might I ask, are you doing all rigged out at this hour of the morning?"

Margaret smiled and turned around for inspection. "Do you like it?"

"I do, indeed. But you haven't answered my question. And why are we going to London all of a sudden?"

She lowered her voice mischievously. "To fight off the wicked witch!"

"Ah, go on with you. There's no witches in London, now that Her Ladyship's passed on."

"Oh yes there are," replied Margaret, "and the name of one of them is Mona Morley."

Mrs. Blaine raised her eyebrows knowingly. "Oh I *see*. A little trouble with His Lordship, perhaps?"

"Perhaps. Can you help me out of this dress?"

"Now wait a minute. Since you're already all tarted up, you might as well stay that way. You've got a visitor."

"At this hour of the morning? Who?"

"His Lordship's brother."

She had begun unfastening the dress, but now she stopped. "Arthur? What could he want?"

"I have no idea. He's in the drawing room."

For some reason, she felt frightened. Arthur? She hadn't spoken to him since his father-in-law's funeral, and then he had been distant, as always. Why was he suddenly here at Ellendon Abbey?

She composed herself and said to Mrs. Blaine, "Tell him I'll see him shortly."

She went back to her dressing room to take off the jewels and change out of the elaborate gown. Somehow, she felt uneasy about facing Arthur in such grand attire.

• • •

By the time she came into the two-story drawing room with its great leaded windows, she was no longer frightened. She had never liked Arthur, and he had never liked her. But he was her brother-in-law now and she would not be afraid of him. He was standing before the window when she entered the room, and she was surprised to see he was dressed in a tweed suit—surprised, because Arthur was not the tweedy type, and customarily dressed more in the fashion of a London dandy.

"Good morning," she said.

He turned. "Good morning."

She crossed the room and extended her hand to him.

"I'm surprised to see you this early in the morning. And I'm even more surprised to see you here."

He took her hand and kissed it, and she noticed he looked rather nervous, though trying to keep up a show of nonchalance.

"I came down yesterday afternoon and spent the night at the Three Lions."

"Why didn't you stay here?" she asked, taking a chair.

"Let's say I wanted to be by myself, to think."

"About what?"

He looked around the room. "Oh, life in general. My childhood. Ellendon Abbey. I was feeling nostalgic."

She didn't believe a word of this, but was determined to remain civil. "And how is Angela?"

"In the hospital. She's expecting at any moment."

"And you're here in the country?" asked Margaret, amazed.

"Angela can have the child without my help, thank you."

"I'm aware of that, but I should think you'd want to be near her."

"Let's say I thought it more important to come down here and prepare for my child's future."

She had no idea what he was talking about, and as he seemed nervously hesitant about getting to the point, whatever it was, she asked if he would like some breakfast.

"I had breakfast at the inn," he replied. "By the way, I found out some interesting facts last night at the bar. It seems there's a stranger in town. A Mr. Ridley, I believe is his name. He's rented the Billings cottage and has been seen about for some time now. He's a bit of a mystery here, but some people think he's a detective. Interesting, isn't it? Do you have any idea why a detective would be staying in Rockhampton?"

He looked at her.

"Perhaps he's on a holiday."

"Perhaps. But I have another theory. I think he's observing you."

She felt a rush of panic. "That's a rather odd theory, Arthur. And a rather unlikely one, too."

He laughed. "You are a cool one, aren't you? Well, my dear sister-in-law, you're going to need all your sang-froid from now on. You see, I *know* what happened the night Caroline died. Or rather, was murdered. How did you manage it? Put the pillow over her face and smother her? That's always a good way. But, no; you being a nurse, probably picked a more scientific method. Am I right?"

She remained silent for a moment. Then, quietly, "Whatever gave you this monstrous idea?"

"I deduced it in the best Sherlock Holmes tradition. I reasoned to myself, who had the motive? And the answer was always you. Then, who had the opportunity? And here, of course, the answer was again you. And just recently, everything I had been thinking was confirmed by the one man who knows what really happened that night: Paul Rougemont."

She was startled, but said nothing.

"Paul is in London," he continued, "and has been for some

time, I suspect. He's been sheltered by his girlfriend or wife or mistress—her status seems a bit hazy. At any rate, I've talked to Paul. He's quite indignant at being accused of Caroline's murder. He had no reason to murder her. But he suggests *you* did, and of course you did, didn't you? He says Caroline was very much alive when he left her and that you had ample time to save her. But you didn't. You didn't because you didn't *want* to save her. It really was simple, after all. All you had to do was not give her her medicine and no one would suspect because everyone would blame Paul. However, *I* suspect."

"You can't hope to substantiate a single word of this madness," she said quietly.

"No, perhaps not, but I think the odds are favorable that you won't enjoy my spreading this story to the police."

He was right, of course. With the police already watching her and with Mona having threatened to go to the home secretary, an accusation from a new quarter—particularly one so close to Charlie—would place both of them in a serious position.

"I think," she said, "it's distinctly peculiar you'd believe a criminal like Paul before your own sister-in-law, not to mention your brother."

He looked at her contemptuously.

"My dear Miss Suffield—oh, excuse me, Lady Darlington!" He performed a mocking bow. "Let us not confuse family ties with loyalty, no more than we should confuse, for example, noble marriages with nobility. I have no more loyalty to you or to Charlie than you do to me. And as for your new status? Well, when a duke marries a mining heiress, she is still a miner's daughter beneath the coronet. You may be a lady now, but I choose to think of you as the sweet young nurse who came to Darlington House some time ago"—he emphasized the next words—"with but one thing in mind: to seduce my brother, murder his wife, and become the second Lady Darlington. All of which, I concede, you've accomplished in fine style."

He smiled. "Oh yes, I'll give it to you. You're most clever. You would be touched to hear the way they talk about you in the village: the 'sweet' Lady Darlington, the 'kind,' 'good,' 'generous,' 'charming,' 'lovely' Lady Darlington. Oh, the adjectives ooze out of their mouths like treacle, until one becomes bilious. You've fooled them all in brilliant fashion. You've even fooled Charlie, though he always was a dimwit about pretty women. You haven't, however, fooled me."

Silence. Be calm, she told herself. Calm.

"And assuming what you say is true, which it isn't, what do you intend doing about it?"

"Ah, as to that, that brings us to why I'm here this morning." He had been leaning against the lid of the ebony Bechstein. Now he moved away from the piano, pulled a chair up beside her, and sat down, leaning conversationally on the arm. "You see, I have no desire to tell the police what I know. There's no point at all in that, except for the rather abstract one of satisfying the law, or some such nonsense. No, I'm willing to protect you, but in return for the protection you must do something for me."

"Assuming you had anything to trade, which you don't, what would that be?"

"Why, murder Charlie, of course."

Silence.

"You're insane," she said quietly.

"I'm quite sane, thank you. You've murdered once with great success, so I'm convinced you can do it twice. Charlie has gotten everything simply by being born before I was, which is bloody unfair. You murder Charlie—neatly, of course; we won't want you caught at it, but I assume you know your business— and I become the sixth earl. I won't deny I'm desperately hard up, with no prospects of relief, so the Darlington fortune will be a convenient way out of my dilemma. Charlie's enjoyed it long enough; now it's my turn. As for you, well, you will be the dowager countess, a very lovely dowager countess, I might add, with a handsome income, a social position of sorts, and unlimited opportunities to land another wealthy peer in the time-honored tradition of my mother-in-law, Lady Bridgewater, who I understand has already doffed her widow's weeds and was recently seen dining at the Savoy with a rich French count. You're much younger than Violet and twice as pretty, so I'm sure you ought to be able to catch a marquess at the very least." He paused. "The alternative, of course, is that I tell the police I think they should begin investigating you instead of Paul, who, incidentally, is more than willing to testify against you to save his own neck. Perhaps they couldn't convict you, perhaps they could. For instance, no one bothered to perform an autopsy on Caroline's body. At the time there didn't seem to be any reason to, but now there just might. They might exhume her body to see what really did kill her; whether she died of heart failure, as you claimed, or perhaps something else."

Exhumation! A farfetched notion? Perhaps. He was doubtless probing, testing, hoping to startle her into some damning revelation. He was watching her face closely as he talked. Still, she couldn't take the chance of dismissing him too lightly. She had to stop him. She had told the police she'd not had time to give Caroline any of the digitalis, but of course she had. Not much, true, and she had no idea whether now, after so many months, the medicine would be traceable. But she didn't dare take the chance; if they did find a trace of the digitalis, they would have a lie that in itself could immediately compromise the rest of her story and, inevitably, Charlie's position as well. She had to stop him.

"At any rate," he went on, "it would be unpleasant for everybody, wouldn't you say?"

"Arthur," she said, "I won't even attempt to deny this absurd notion of yours. And you're a miserable judge of character if you think I would ever do anything to injure my husband, much less *murder* him. But even if this wasn't the case, your plan wouldn't work anyway. Because, you see, I'm going to have a child."

Arthur's bravado vaporized. He looked down at her thin waist, then back up to her face.

"You're lying."

"Not at all. So even if Charlie were to die tomorrow, which I pray he won't, his child will inherit the estate. If it's a girl, you'd get the title, but I doubt you're as interested in that as the money, family tradition not being your special interest. I'd suggest, therefore, that if you're really having money problems, instead of concocting ridiculous fantasies and trying to blackmail your relatives, well, as a humble nurse and former wage-earner, might I recommend you to go out into the world and look for a job? And in case you decide to spread your vicious little story about me, a respectable bride with child, I think you know where sympathies will lie."

She watched him. He was confused, she could tell, but he was trying to save face. It had been a lie, of course, a desperate lie to shut him up, and one that inevitably would, in time, catch up with her if she weren't fortunate enough to conceive a child. But she had to take the gamble that she would be able to. And certainly the lie had achieved its immediate purpose. Arthur stood up and forced a weak smile.

"You . . . you won't say anything to Charlie about this, I hope. I really was playing a sort of joke. . . ."

"You meant every word of it," she said. "It was a childish idea and a filthy trick, but if it had worked you would have been happy as a lark. Don't try to weasel out of it now."

"No," he said, giving up, "you're quite right. I won't try to weasel out of it. And I did mean it. It's not the first time in my life I've made a serious miscalculation." He thought a moment. "Might I use your telephone?"

She was surprised by his request.

"Of course. Use the one in the library. Are you going to ring up the mysterious Mr. Ridley and tell him to come put me in irons?"

"Not exactly. I've . . . well, abandoned that plan for Plan B. I think it was Clausewitz who said if one attack fails, always have an orderly retreat in reserve. Maybe it was Napoleon. At any rate, if you'll excuse me?"

He hurried out of the room, cursing himself for not having thought of the one obvious flaw to the plan—that the woman might be pregnant. And if not, he couldn't wait for the passage of time to disprove it. Now he had badly compromised himself— *God knows what Charlie will do to me if she tells him,* he thought—and there was only one alternative left. He'd need to work quickly. He had already wasted too much time working up his nerve to attempt Plan A.

He hurried into the library and closed the door. Then he got the local operator and placed a call to Inspector Hadley Mayhew of Scotland Yard. As he waited for the call to be put through, he told himself there was at least one compensation—he could still collect the eight-thousand-pound reward for information leading to the arrest and conviction of Paul Rougemont.

• • •

When Margaret rang Charlie up that noon to tell him what Arthur had tried to do (but not to tell him she was taking the London train a half hour later—she was still determined to surprise him), he could hardly believe it. "You mean," he said, "he wanted you to murder *me?*"

"Exactly. It was a ridiculous idea, but typical of Arthur. Then he'd inherit your estate. I think he's really convinced I'm a cold-blooded killer hiding beneath a mask of sweetness—or at least he was—and I suppose he thought I'd jump at the chance to save myself. Thank heavens I thought of a way to stop him."

"What?"

"I told him I was going to have a child, so he couldn't get the estate anyway, which seemed to take the wind out of his sails. Then he got out as fast as he could. Still, it was frightening."

"Yes, I can imagine. Blast Arthur! He bloody well *would* like to see me packed off in a coffin. He's always hated me ever since we were children. But what bloody cheek to ask you to do it for him!" At the same time, he thought it was probably no cheekier than his asking Margaret to do away with Caroline. If only the woman *had* been killed by Paul! And if only he hadn't needed to involve himself and Margaret in her death. But now the "perfect crime" that he thought he had committed was beginning to shows its depressingly imperfect elements. First, the police. Then Mona. Now Arthur. They were all a bit wide of the mark, of course, but they were sniffing closer all the time, and how much longer could he and Margaret continue to out-maneuver them?

"Darling?" It was Margaret's voice. "Are you there?"

"Yes. Sorry, I was just thinking about Arthur."

"Don't be too upset, please. He seems convinced he made a fool of himself." Silence. "Darling, do you love me?"

"Yes, of course." His tone was irritable.

"I wish it hadn't been a lie. I mean, about my being with child."

"Yes, I wish so too. But I'm glad you were quick enough to think of it."

"You sound angry."

He wasn't angry, he was frightened; and he wished she would ring off so he could think.

"One doesn't normally jump with joy when one's brother tries to do one in," he snapped.

She rang off. Unexpectedly. He looked at the phone with surprise, then replaced it on its hook. He had been short with her, and she was hurt. Well, it couldn't be helped. He was in no mood to talk about love.

For the first time in his life, Charles Avalon, the fifth earl of Darlington, was beginning to know the clammy feeling of terror.

She was more than hurt; she was wounded.

Did he have no idea of the torture she was going through to protect him? She had even tried to play down the whole Arthur business in an effort to spare his feelings, and yet all he did was snap at her. She needed constant reassurance of his love. She couldn't help it; the very basis of their relationship made it necessary, and now that there was Mona, she needed it even more.

Still, after she rang off she began to feel somewhat ashamed of herself. He was, after all, as tense as she, she supposed. She was being unfair to him. She decided to ring back and apologize. But when the call was put through, Rogers informed her he had left the house a moment before.

"Where did he go?" she asked.

"He didn't say, milady. He looked a bit disturbed."

"Yes, thank you, Rogers."

She rang off again, wondering where he had gone and regretting even more her temper. Then Mrs. Blaine stuck her head through the door to tell her it was time to go to the station.

• • •

Inspector Mayhew had just returned from church with his family when he received a call from Scotland Yard. It was Wilson. He told his superior they had gotten a call from Lord Arthur Avalon. "That's Darlington's younger brother," said Wilson.

"Yes, yes, I know. Go on."

"He told us Rougemont had contacted him a while back to try and make a deal with the insurance company over the emeralds."

"Why didn't he call us sooner?"

"He said he wanted to wait till he found out where Rougemont was staying."

"And did he?"

"He says he's at the Schooner Pub, Bankside. He thinks the owner's daughter has been hiding him. We're about to go there, but I wanted to report to you first."

"Good. All right, bring him in. I'll be at the Yard shortly."

He rang off, delighted at this news. Paul's continued evasion of the police had become a distinct embarrassment to the inspector, as well as to the Yard, and it was a relief finally to have a solid lead on his whereabouts. Not only that, but apparently he had the jewels as well.

As he hurried out of his house back to his automobile, giving his wife a hasty peck on the cheek in transit, it occurred to him that at long last he could call off the men he'd had watching Lady Darlington. They had been expensive, and it seemed the woman was to reveal nothing more exciting than her gardening skills.

At least he assumed he could call them off. The supposition was based on capturing Rougemont with the jewels. He thought it likely that the man would break down and confess to the murder as well, once he had been picked up with the emeralds. He had been in hiding for months, and it was the inspector's experience that the average criminal, after undergoing a long period of hiding, was usually almost relieved to be caught and could be induced to make a confession.

Besides, in the last analysis, he really didn't think a man with the position and character of the earl of Darlington could either commit a murder, or marry someone who had. He was, after all, a peer of the realm, and the pages of English history—the inspector prided himself on being a scholar in these matters—recorded few noble criminals, or at least, criminals who had been caught and brought to trial in the House of Lords. There were the duelists: Lord Mohun, Lord Byron of Rochdale, and the earl of Cardigan, the last the dashingly idiotic hero of the Charge of the Light Brigade. There was Earl Ferrers, who was hanged in the eighteenth century for the murder of his steward. There were the bigamists—in the eighteenth century, the eccentric duchess of Kingston (or countess of Bristol, as she was revealed to be at her trial); and Lord Russell in Victoria's reign. But these were merely the exceptions that proved the rule that peers simply did not commit crimes.

So the inspector really couldn't believe that the handsome earl of Darlington, a noble peer, could ever have killed his wife.

It simply wasn't done.

• • •

As the string quartet launched into the final movement of the first *Razoumovsky* Quartet of Beethoven, Mona Morley's eyes wandered around her drawing room. Its size had been doubled by opening the doors to the adjacent room, creating a sitting area the length of the house, and her guests—approximately three dozen of them—were seated on chairs or on the floor, listening to the four musicians at the end of the room. It was one of Mona's unpolitical evenings, so most of the people were either members of, or on the fringes of, London's artistic and literary world—a pousse-café of intellectual types. There was a young poet fresh out of Oxford; several unproduced playwrights

fresh out of money; a woman novelist fresh out of readers; and
a Valkyrie-sized German baroness who composed motets (for
which there was not much of a market). These were Mona's
"amusing" guests, whom she invited for their conversation, wit,
or eccentricity rather than accomplishment. However, Mona
always took pains to cultivate the successful, being no champion
of permanent lost causes, so there were also present two playwrights whose comedies were currently selling out on the West
End; a bearded novelist who was the critics' darling; and Sir
Frederick Barchester-ffrench, the most fashionable portraitist in
London, and the star attraction of the evening. Sir Frederick's
appearance was anything but Bohemian. Like the style of his
portraits, which was flashily con brio, Sir Frederick was a fas-
tidious fashion plate, realizing that sartorial splendor was one
entrée to the world of rich commissions. Even now, he was
surrounded by three wealthy ladies who were obviously eager
to be transformed by his facile brush into elegant beauties
(which, judging from the faces of two of them, would require
every trick the Master could call upon); and Mona was amused
by their unsubtle approach, which, she knew, would do them
little good. Sir Frederick had become so rich he could pick and
choose his clients. And since the forty-year-old, gimlet-eyed
bachelor had the reputation of being a satyr as well as a brilliant
portraitist, he usually painted only beautiful women whom he
might be able to seduce during the lengthy sittings. From what
Mona had heard, he was generally quite successful.

But her mind was less on Sir Frederick or her guests or the
Beethoven than on the absence of Charlie. He had yet to appear
at the musicale, and since he had promised her he would come,
she was confused and not a little annoyed by his absence. In the
weeks since the death of her husband, Mona had, as Charlie had
told Margaret, progressed from an infatuation with the earl to
the point where she was now quite deeply in love with him.
He was the first man she had ever been in love with, and
romance, coming, as it had, relatively late in life, had struck her
with even more than its usual force. She doted on the man. She
was continually maneuvering to be with him, but Charlie was a

hard man to pin down, and as often as not he would either be late for their rendezvous or, as tonight not show up at all. To a strong-willed woman such as Mona, this sort of behavior was most annoying. So far, though, she had swallowed her pride. Tonight, however, she was beginning to wonder if she hadn't been too lenient with him. If he didn't come at all, she decided, she would let him know her displeasure in the strongest possible terms. After all, if being in love meant continually being insulted, then perhaps she should start falling out of love—though she had to admit that might be considerably easier said than done.

The quartet came to a brilliant conclusion, and the musicians were rewarded with enthusiastic applause. Then, as they tuned their instruments in preparation for the next item on the program —the haunting Borodin quartet—Mona's butler appeared in the doorway and announced, "The countess of Darlington."

A hush fell over the crowd. All eyes turned toward the door, since most of the guests knew something was going on between their hostess and the earl. This combined with a natural curiosity to see the nurse who had replaced the first Lady Darlington, and Margaret couldn't have planned a more dramatic entrance or one filled with more expectant suspense. Nor did she disappoint. She had put on again the bone gown, the pearls, and the diamond stars. Her hair she had set in a soft chignon, and the total effect was of an incredibly lovely, fresh beauty of a woman who elicited from that arbiter of feminine pulchritude, Sir Frederick, a one-word encomium: "Exquisite."

Mona's sentiments were not quite as complimentary, but despite her surprise, she came to the door and extended her hand, saying in a pleasant tone that belied her annoyance, "What an unexpected pleasure."

Margaret smiled and lied, "I told my husband I would meet him here."

"But he didn't come," said Mona, truthfully enough.

Now it was Margaret's turn to be surprised.

"Then where is he?"

Mona took her arm and led her into the room.

"I have no idea. But since you're here, you must stay. We're about to hear Borodin. I'm extremely fond of Russian composers; they're so colorful. Ah, my dear, you've already made a conquest. Look!"

Sir Frederick was approaching them. He took Margaret's hand and kissed it, saying, "Mona, introduce us."

Mona laughed.

"Margaret, beware! This man is dangerous. Sir Frederick Barchester-ffrench, who will, in less than one minute, ask if he can paint your portrait."

"I won't ask, I'll insist," said Sir Frederick. "I've heard the new Lady Darlington was attractive, but I had no idea she was radiant." He lowered his voice and said to Mona, "Let me sit with you. I can't take much more of the Three Un-Graces." He nodded toward the women who had been fawning over him, all three of whom were now glaring at Margaret.

"Lady Darlington will sit with me," countered Mona, "and you can sit where you wish." She signaled to the musicians, who began the Borodin. Then she offered Margaret a seat next to her on a small white sofa at the rear of the crowd, where the two of them sat down. Margaret was excited by her successful entrance and not a little pleased by Sir Frederick's praise and attention. But she couldn't believe Charlie wasn't there, and she began casting surreptitious looks about the room, as if half expecting him to appear from behind a potted palm. She decided he must have tried to escape from the room when he saw her; it was farcical, but she couldn't think of any other explanation for his absence. Mona was watching her, and, as if reading her thoughts, she leaned over to whisper, "He really *isn't* here, you know."

Margaret said nothing, but she believed her. And now she began wondering what had happened to prevent him from coming. She remembered his irritation on the phone that morning, and Rogers telling her he had left Darlington House "disturbed." Where had he gone?

The answer was to come in a totally unexpected fashion. The musicians were in the middle of the slow movement of the quartet when Mona's butler reappeared in the room and made his way around the guests to the sofa, where he leaned over and whispered in Margaret's ear, "Milady, a Mrs. Blaine just telephoned. It seems there has been some trouble."

Margaret noticed the man seemed nervous.

"What sort of trouble?"

"Your husband's brother," he said, "has been found murdered."

She stared at him, realizing now, with slowly mounting horror, where Charlie had gone.

Part IV

The room looked as if a maniac had been turned loose in it.

Furniture had been overturned, the silver brushes on Arthur's bureau swept onto the floor, as well as the perfume and cologne bottles and atomizers on Angela's vanity, many of which had broken, spilling their contents on the rug and permeating the bedroom with a sweet odor that somehow made the presence of the body on the floor seem even more eerie. It was lying face-down, and an ice pick was sticking out of its back.

"He was getting dressed to go out for dinner," Wilson said to Inspector Mayhew. "The shirt was clean, and he hadn't yet knotted his tie. We think he came out of the bathroom to get his tie. The man was apparently waiting for him and stabbed him."

"You don't think there was a fight?" said the inspector, looking around at the shambles.

"No. We think that was done afterwards, either as a diversionary tactic or, more likely as far as I'm concerned, in a burst of rage."

"How did he get in?"

"Through the window," said Wilson, pointing to an open window. "It's on the side of the house, and there's a bay window just underneath that makes it relatively easy to reach. There was only one servant in the house at the time—he had discharged most of the staff, apparently because he was hard up—and his wife's in the hospital having a child."

"Has she been notified?"

"No. I called his brother's house. He wasn't in, so I told the housekeeper, a Mrs. Blaine. I thought it best if Lady Avalon were told by a member of the family."

"Yes, you were right. Well, there's nothing more to be done here. Let's go back to my office and talk to the girl's father."

Wilson nodded. Then, taking a last look around the room and at the body, Inspector Mayhew walked over to the door and left.

• • •

His name was Godfrey Hall, and he was frightened. He had been frightened for three months, ever since his daughter Alice had returned from Amsterdam, where she had been touring as the assistant to a third-rate London magician, and told him she had married a man wanted by the police. When he heard that his son-in-law was Paul Rougemont, he had almost killed her. She insisted her new husband was innocent of the murder of Lady Darlington, and begged her father to help her get him back to London so they might at least try to raise some money on the emeralds. He had finally given in, and Paul had come across the Channel from Calais, successfully avoiding the police, which was fairly easy to do since passports still did not exist in most of Europe. He had put his daughter and her husband in the room above the Schooner, where they set up an escape route out the back window across neighboring roofs, a precaution that had paid off that morning when the police broke into the pub. Alice and her husband had gotten away. But now, ten hours later, as Godfrey sat in Inspector Mayhew's office, the burly publican wished they hadn't. Because he had no doubt that it was Paul who had broken into Arthur's home on Portman Square and stabbed the man who had turned him into the police.

" 'e's crazy," said Godfrey. "A bloomin' loony, and it don't surprise me none 'e done it. I thought 'e'd kill *me* a dozen times at least. Full of 'imself, 'e is. Got delusions of grandeur, if you know wot I mean. Thinks 'e's a bloody king wot can do wotever 'e wants and get away with it. But I tell you, Alice 'ad nothing to do with it. I swear on a Bible and my mother's grave. Alice is crazy about the bloke, but she wouldn't 'arm a flea, much less stab nobody with a bleedin' ice pick."

Mayhew, leaning on his desk, tended to believe the man.

"Where do you think they've gone?"

"Australia—where else? Probably 'alf-way to Dover already, and if you're smart you'll watch the Channel boats for the next couple of days. But I'm telling you this only on the condition you'll let 'er off. Alice isn't the best daughter a man could wish for—she's got the theater in 'er veins, and you know wot *that* does to decent girls!—but I wouldn't want 'er to swing for no murders because she'd never do it. It's *'im* wot done it, and 'e's crazy as they come."

Inspector Mayhew wasn't interested in the girl. It was Rougemont he wanted, Rougemont who had killed twice and well might again. He already had notified the Dover police as well as the police of every other port in England. The train stations were crawling with bobbies, and London was being combed. He felt certain he would have him before twenty-four hours had passed.

What the inspector didn't know, and what Godfrey Hall knew but wasn't telling, was that Paul and Alice were already halfway down the Thames on a tramp freighter bound for New York, guests of the skipper who happened to be Alice's maternal uncle. They had planned the trip a week before, having given up on Arthur's ability or desire to make the deal with the insurance company. The last-minute raid by the police had only hastened their departure. And, Godfrey Hall assumed, it had also prompted the side excursion to Portman Square.

Unfortunately for Arthur.

• • •

She kept telling herself Charlie couldn't possibly have murdered his own brother, but she couldn't convince herself. He had purposely let his wife die, after all, and he had disliked Arthur—admittedly with reason—almost as much as Caroline. All of what she now was beginning to think of as her pathetic attempts to see a special nobility in her husband was plain self-deception, a refusal to face facts: he had killed once, he had lied frequently, and—most painful for her to accept—he had married her only to prevent her from ever telling in court what he had done that terrible night to his first wife. It made her miserable to think these thoughts, but she could no longer keep them out of her mind. When Mona Morley had confronted him with half the truth, he had made her fall in love with him to keep her quiet— with the added dividend of acquiring her backing for his career. When Arthur learned more of the truth than he realized, he had murdered him. It was cold-blooded, simple. And yet she still tried to persuade herself it couldn't be true. When she had come home from Mona's she had gone directly to their bedroom— Caroline's old room, with all of its horrible ghosts!—changed into a peignoir and sat up to wait for him to come home and tell her where he had been. She prayed that he would have a persuasive alibi. She prayed he could dissipate her hideous suspicions.

And she was terrified he would not be able to.

He came into the room at three thirty in the morning, surprised to see her. Before she explained to him why she was in London she said, "Have you heard?"

He nodded as he took off his tailcoat. He looked immaculate as always—a hopeful sign. Surely too immaculate to have committed murder.

"I heard about it at the club," he said.

"Was that where you were?" she asked hopefully.

He caught the implication in her voice. "Where do you think I've been? At Portman Square?"

She didn't answer. He came across the room and took her hand.

"Is that what you think?" he repeated.

"I don't know what to think," she replied. "You weren't at Mona's, which was where you were supposed to be—though you didn't choose to so inform me."

"I see. You've decided to play detective."

"Do you blame me?"

He looked at her a moment, then let go her hand and went over to a chair and sat down. "All right," he said, "I suppose I deserve this. Arthur comes to you this morning and tries to blackmail you. You tell me, and I quite naturally become angry. I vanish. Tonight, someone stabs Arthur with an ice pick in what apparently was a monstrously brutal murder. Inference to be drawn: I killed my brother. Now you're waiting for me to give you a convincing alibi. The problem is, I can't give you a good alibi—or rather, one that you're going to like hearing."

"What is it?" she asked tentatively.

"Since yesterday morning, after I talked to you on the phone, I've been with Laura Metcalf."

She wanted to shout with relief. It was so typically Charlie, she knew it was true. To his surprise, she ran across the room and threw her arms around him, kissing him as tears ran down her cheeks.

"Good Lord," he said, "you're probably the first wife who cried with joy when her husband admitted he'd been out with a tart."

"I don't care," she said happily. "I don't care if you were out with a thousand tarts. The important thing is that you weren't *there*."

"Did you really think I could do that to Arthur?" he asked. "I mean, we were hardly chums, and he did try to persuade you to kill me, but I would hardly *kill* him, especially with anything so unimaginative as an ice pick."

"Oh, Charlie. I didn't know *what* to think I've been so miserable. I almost fainted at Mona's when I heard about it. . . . *Can we trust each other? Can I trust you?*"

She looked at him, waiting to hear something that would forever exorcise the ghosts in her mind. He kissed her, then said, "You can trust me. You can trust me about Arthur, and you can trust me about Mona. I know you've at least a million sound reasons not to, and I can only give you one good reason in mitigation. But I do think it's the best of all."

"What is it?"

"I love you."

She looked into his eyes and believed him.

"Then," she said quietly, "I trust you."

And she did.

• • •

The account of the crime in the morning papers served to bury her fears deeper. The police were blaming the murder on Paul Rougemont, whom they were now labeling a "homicidal maniac," and the hunt for the elusive killer was on again with renewed vigor. She wondered now how she could have thought Charlie had done it, even though she remembered that the night before she had been almost convinced of his guilt. She was ashamed of her suspicions, and decided she would make it up to him by trusting him implicitly from now on.

They both went to the hospital to tell Angela, who, the night before, had with ironic timing given birth to a baby boy. They tried to tell her as gently as possible. She became hysterical. She had genuinely loved Arthur, with all his faults, and his death was a devastating blow to her. Fortunately, a nurse was on hand to give her a sedative, which mercifully put her to sleep. Then Charlie and Margaret went to view the baby. He looked nondescript and helpless, as all babies do. And though Margaret perhaps had good reason not to regret her brother-in-law's death, looking at the baby boy she couldn't help but feel sorry for the father who would never see his son, and the son who would never see his father.

The funeral was three days later, and again a crowd filled the stone church at Rockhampton to hear the eulogy, then troop out to the churchyard where, not far from Caroline's grave, Arthur was interred. Margaret, wearing black veils, was made morose by the ceremony and its lugubrious associations. Charlie was sober too, but he noted one thing that gave him a certain sense of satisfaction: at least this time Inspector Mayhew hadn't come down from London. Furthermore, he had learned that morning that the mysterious Mr. Ridley had finally left Rockhampton. So it seemed the police were no longer interested in either himself or his wife, and after having been convinced three days earlier that the world was closing in on him, apparently he was now safe after all. That night he told Margaret that since the police were no longer watching them, he saw no need to continue his attentions toward Mona Morley. "She's abandoned the notion I had anything to do with Caroline's death," he said, "and since I know you are something less than happy about my relationship with her, well, I'll stop."

She was, needless to say, most pleased at this news.

"Besides," he added, "I'm sick to death of her trying to influence my vote. When it comes to politics, the woman really can be tiresomely dogmatic. And it looks to be a very dogmatic summer, politically, that is."

Lord Darlington was right. The budget battle was convulsing all of England. The fight was most heated in the House of Commons, where forty-two parliamentary days were required merely to get the Finance Bill through its committee stage. There was no summer recess that year becaue of the bill. And while the fight raged in the Commons, it was being carried on throughout the country as well. The banking and financial worlds were the first to launch the attack, Lord Rothschild sending a letter protesting the bill to the prime minister, the letter also being signed by other financial leaders. A Budget Protest League was set up, and debates roared. The chancellor of the exchequer, Lloyd George, led the defense of the bill, and on the thirtieth of July he made his famous Limehouse speech, which elicited furious rebuttal from the other side. Mr. Asquith, the prime minister, also joined the fray, addressing a group of city Liberals in July and, in September, addressing with brilliant effect a crowd of thirteen thousand at Birmingham. Throughout all this, the bill continued its laborious progress in the Commons, where a staggering total of five hundred fifty-four divisions was to take place before its passage on the fourth of November. But well before this time, the possibility that the duke of Suffolk had foreseen at Mona's house on the evening of Budget Day was becoming a probability, as well as a matter of general knowledge. On the sixteenth of July, Lord Lansdowne made a speech suggesting that the peers "would not swallow the Finance Bill whole without wincing." And on the next day, during a speech in

Edinburgh, he was rebutted by the young Winston Churchill, whose speech elicited ominous rumbles from the Palace. Indeed, the possibility of the hereditary body, the Lords, daring to reject a finance bill elicited rumbles from every segment of the population. And by the autumn, there were few Englishmen who didn't realize that the issue was not only one between the two houses of Parliament, but between the past and the present—between two ways of life and two ways of thinking.

Through all this, Charlie worked assiduously for the bill and against rejection. With Margaret no longer afraid of either Darlington House or London society, they gave a series of dinners for Tory peers whom Charlie thought to be "fence-sitters," and he believed he was successful in bringing a number of these waverers over to his side. He also spoke to various Conservative groups throughout the country, trying to win party support for the bill. Already popular with the Party regulars from his days in the Commons, now, thanks to the publicity of the two sensational murders in his family, he had become a genuine celebrity—as well as a curiosity—and he drew huge crowds wherever he spoke. Margaret went along on these trips, and her beauty and pleasing manner charmed everyone. The idea that this young, attractive former nurse had won the heart of the romantically handsome earl excited the crowds, for everybody likes a Cinderella story. And by the end of the summer, the duke of Suffolk was willing to concede—furiously—that his former brother-in-law and new wife were making dangerous inroads into public opinion as well as Percy's bloc of rejection-inclined peers. To quiz Mona on why she seemed to be failing so spectacularly with Charlie, he invited her one August weekend to his country seat in Suffolk, Cheyney Castle.

Cheyney Castle was a genuine castle that had once been used as a fortress by Rolfe Cheyney, the thirteenth-century founder of the family. It was a brooding mass of masonry glowering on the cliffs overlooking the North Sea, and while generations of Cheyneys had made the inside a showplace of civilized luxury, no one had been able to civilize the outside, the ramparts of which, Mona reflected as she was driven up to the front entrance in one of the duke's carriages, looked like something from which

Hamlet might have spouted his gloomiest soliloquies. She was not the only guest. The castle was bulging with house guests, all of them peers of the same old-school stripe and philosophy as their host. Their wives, like Percy's duchess, were mostly either fat and dull or horsey and dull—Percy's wife belonged to the latter category. Mona wasn't expecting much of a good time.

She hadn't been in the castle two hours when Percy managed to confront her in the famous Long Gallery, a two-hundred-foot-long picture gallery from the paneled walls of which six hundred years of male and female Cheyneys stared arrogantly out of their gilt frames at posterity. The gallery was empty; and as Percy led Mona down it, he indulged his rage without fear of being overheard—though, she reflected, if the room had been packed it probably wouldn't have deterred him. Percy sincerely had no interest in what his fellow humans thought of him.

"You promised me you'd manage him!" he exclaimed. "You said you could get his vote, and what's he been doing? Going all over England with that damned wife of his, making speeches and causing trouble!"

"I never promised you anything," replied Mona coolly. "Nor most certainly did I guarantee anything. I did think I could manage him, I'll admit. But for the first time in my life I've been utterly wrong about a man."

Her voice took on a mixture of bitterness and sadness, two emotions that were so foreign to Mona's usually icy composure that the duke gave her a searching look.

"What's the matter?" he asked. "You didn't fall in love with him, I hope."

"Percy, your gentle tact never fails to impress me. But if you must know, yes, I'm afraid I did."

"Good Lord, the man really is uncanny with women," replied the duke, not without a trace of envy. "But I can't say it was especially intelligent of you."

"Falling in love is rarely an intelligent act, and falling in love with a politician most certainly isn't. I'm afraid, however, I couldn't help it. He's really incredibly attractive, you know, and for a time we were seeing a good deal of each other."

"And then?"

She shrugged. "And then he lost interest in me. Now, I'm pleased that he did. But at the time I was hurt. And furious at him, I might add. Quite furious."

They walked past a huge painting of the third duke on a horse in the midst of his famous pack of hounds.

"Well, it's damned inconvenient," said Percy. "I mean, that he lost interest in you."

"Somehow, I thought of it as something a bit more than 'inconvenient.' He told me he was truly in love with the nurse, or rather the new Lady Darlington, and that was all there was to it. I suppose if anything is 'inconvenient,' it's that Charles has decided to become a faithful husband."

"Damned odd, if you ask me," said the duke. "He wasn't faithful to Caroline. Of course, I can't say I blame him. She was a howler of a woman, even if she was my sister. Never could stand her myself. But where does that leave us? I mean, as far as putting pressure on him is concerned?"

She had stopped before a portrait of Caroline, painted when she was married to her first husband.

"I have no idea," she said. "It appears, though, that we'll have to abandon it."

"Well, I don't like it. I don't like it at all. He's causing dissension in the ranks."

"Percy, your gift for turning an original phrase never fails to astound me," she said, looking at Caroline's painted likeness and wondering where Charlie had been the night of his brother's murder. "Besides," she added, "with all his fine efforts, he's not going to win, is he?"

"Of course not. But he's become well-known. He's glamorous, he's young. If he voted against us, it's inevitably going to make him look good and ourselves bad. Lochinvar! Sir Galahad on his noble charger, voting for the common man against the evil lords. It can make him a powerful figure in the country. The wonderful Lord Darlington! That's how people will think, damn them. I understate when I say it would be enormously helpful to shut him up, to get him onto our side."

Mona thought this over as she continued looking at Caroline's portrait. Any suspicions she had had about Charlie's involvement with Caroline's death had pretty much been forgotten. She knew the police thought Rougemont had killed Arthur as well as Caroline. She *supposed* they knew their business, after all; and she was weary of playing amateur sleuth.

Still, she wondered where he had been the night that Arthur had been killed.

• • •

In the months following Arthur's murder, Margaret marveled at how full, and fulfilled, her life with Charlie had become. Ironically, it seemed that Arthur's death had brought her and her husband even closer together, if for no other reason than it had seemed to remove the threat of the police from their lives. And then there was Mona, too. Or rather, the absence of Mona. Margaret was now convinced that Charlie had meant what he said about giving her up. She even thought he had given up Laura Metcalf, and this gave her an understandable sense of satisfaction. So their marriage, which had begun under a cloud of fear and guilt, was now thriving under the sunshine of mutual confidence. And there was more: she had thrown herself into the campaign for the Finance Bill, had enjoyed traveling about the country with Charlie as he made speeches in support of it. She also enjoyed entertaining at Darlington House, much to her surprise. And she discovered that while some people still snubbed her—though subtly—many more accepted her. Lord Exmoor, for instance, one of the young Tory peers Charlie had invited to dinner in an effort to bring him over to their side in favor of the Finance Bill, had been overwhelmed by the lovely Lady Darlington and not only promised to cast his vote with Charlie but, to Margaret's amusement, began writing her terrible love poems. There were others, less romantic, who accepted her as a friend. And by the end of the summer, she found herself with a wide circle of acquaintances among the younger set in London, who were more open-minded than their Victorian parents and, coincidentally, more fun.

She had also thrown herself into the hospital project. Sir Andrew had recommended a young architect named Hugh Stafford to design the building, and when Charlie and Margaret met with him they wholeheartedly concurred with the doctor's selection. He was far from a radical designer, but he had taste, a fine sense of proportion, had worked on the design of a hospital in Liverpool, and therefore was well-acquainted with the practical problems he would encounter. Charlie had given a twenty-acre wooded tract of land to the village of Rockhampton for the site, and Hugh designed a lovely Georgian building of red brick that blended superbly with the landscape. The small hospital was to have an outpatient clinic, two wards, a dozen private rooms, and a surgery wing with all the up-to-date equipment. Work on the designs progressed so rapidly that by the autumn they were able to take bids from contractors. Construction was scheduled to commence the following spring.

All of this gave Margaret pleasure and satisfaction. And to fill her cup to the brim, she even had a genuine romantic complication that convulsed her and Charlie with private amusement. Sir Frederick Barchester-ffrench, the fashionable portraitist who had been so struck by Margaret's appearance at Mona's musicale, had bedeviled her to allow him to paint her, and Charlie had finally commissioned him to do a portrait as a gift to Margaret on her birthday, which fell in September. Margaret warned her husband that Sir Frederick had a dangerous reputation. Charlie suavely allowed that he thought that since she trusted him, the least he could do was return the trust, and so she began twice-weekly sittings at the artist's Chelsea studio. During the dozen sittings, he tried every trick he could imagine in an effort to lure her into the adjacent bedroom, running the gamut from romantic gramophone records to offers of mid-day drinks to invitations to luncheons in obscure and ambience-drenched restaurants, all of which Margaret good-naturedly fended off. The result was a spectacular portrait but a disgruntled Sir Frederick, who was more than glad to have done with his uncooperative client.

There was a curious ceremony that September when they hung the painting in the gallery at Ellendon Abbey. Lord Darlington had insisted it go up in the place of Caroline's portrait, which he wished to rehang in what had been—and was now rarely visited—

her bedroom. Margaret hadn't liked the idea; it struck her somehow as a bad omen. But she hadn't put up too much resistance, and the first Lady Darlington was subsequently buried in the west wing. It was intended, Margaret knew, to be an exorcism of a ghost. But as she watched her own portrait going up on the wall of the gallery—its dazzling Boldini-esque technique presenting her in a white dress standing before a small sofa—the ghost of Caroline seemed to permeate the long hall and she remembered that May day she had first met Charlie and he had taken her down the gallery past Caroline's portrait to the bedroom of the "monster," as he had called his first wife. And now the monster was dead, and Arthur was dead, and her portrait was going up on the wall, and she was as happy as any woman could possibly be.

The ghosts whispered in her ear that she was too happy, that the bill for all this had yet to be presented, that the piper had to be paid some day.

She shuddered slightly and was glad when she could go back to the library for tea.

• • •

Angela opened the letter and read it, crinkling her nose with distaste at the scented pink stationery. It was dated the twentieth of September, and read as follows:

> Dear Lady Avalon:
> I read of the death of your husband and wish to convey my sincerest condolences to you. Realizing that your nerves would be in a delicate state following such a tragedy, I have waited some months before bringing to your attention a debt your husband owed me. However, the size of the amount owed is such that I feel compelled to wait no longer, since it is now some months overdue. During the first four months of this year, your husband visited my establishment a total of twelve times, dining on eight of these occasions and consuming a total of nineteen bottles of Veuve Cliquot champagne at one pound, ten shillings, the bottle. Though I do not normally extend credit, at your

husband's request I did so for him, having had pleasant associations in the past with other members of his family. Now I will be appreciative if you will send to me at the above address a cheque for ninety guineas made out to,

[signed] Laura Metcalf

Angela gasped and crushed the letter in her hand. The nerve! she thought. The disgusting nerve of the woman! Rising up from her escritoire, she went over to the mantel and threw the letter in the fire, watching as it curled into flame and thinking morosely of Arthur. She knew he had gone to "that woman's" house in St. John's Wood, but she would never give the creature the satisfaction of paying her bill. Never!

She walked out of the room and went upstairs to check on her baby. He was asleep in his crib, looking angelic, just as Arthur sometimes had looked. She smiled at the child, whom she had named Arthur William in deference to both father and grandfather, and prayed that he would grow up a Christian gentleman and never be tempted to go to St. John's Wood.

• • •

Ten days later, Margaret was seated in the sitting room of her suite at Darlington House having her hair brushed by Edna, her new private maid. Edna was a pretty young girl from the Midlands to whom Margaret had taken a great liking; and as she brushed her mistress's hair, she chattered on about her boyfriend, a young clerk in a draper's shop, who, she complained, was always trying to "take liberties."

"Still," said Margaret, "if he didn't try, I don't think you'd like him half as much, now, would you?"

"Oh well, that's true, ma'am. But it's all he thinks about, really. It's disgraceful, it tis. It seems the young men these days are only interested in one thing, and it's very difficult for a girl to keep her virtue, if you know what I mean. Chester works hard and he has a good character when it's during working hours. But when the sun sets it's like he's Count Dracula all of a sudden, out for blood. All he can think about is you know what. It's a crying shame."

As she rattled on, Rogers came into the room to tell Margaret there was a "lady" downstairs, asking to see her, if she might. Rogers looked more aloof than usual as he said "lady," which Margaret didn't fail to notice. "Who is it?" she asked.

"A Miss Metcalf," he replied. "She wished to see His Lordship. When I told her he wasn't in, she started to leave, then changed her mind. She asked if she might see you, milady."

Laura Metcalf? Margaret was astounded that she was in the house. Yet she was much too curious to see the notorious courtesan not to go downstairs, the dubious propriety of such a move notwithstanding. And as Edna hurriedly pinned her hair, she inspected herself in the mirror, having no wish to be outshone by the former rival for her husband's affections. Satisfied with her appearance, she went downstairs to the Red Room, where Laura was examining the large conversation piece of the Darlington family. She was dressed expensively and tastefully, for whatever Laura's deficiencies in taste about her house, when it came to clothes she had style and knew precisely what she was about. As she turned to look at Margaret, the latter was forced to admit the woman was stunning.

"Miss Metcalf?" she said uncertainly.

Laura looked her over. She seemed favorably impressed.

"Yes. I came to see your husband, but when I found he wasn't in I was too curious to see you to leave. I hope you don't mind?"

The woman was so pleasant, Margaret began to relax.

"Of course not," she said, coming a little nearer and yet surprised at her inability to get too close to the woman. It was undoubtedly a leftover from her parsonage childhood, but she half expected a bug to leap across the room and give her an unmentionable disease if she got too close. "Might I ask what you wanted to see my husband about?"

Laura laughed. "Oh, business. But don't worry; your husband hasn't visited my place since he married you. No, it's your husband's brother, the late Lord Avalon. He died owing me a considerable sum of money which Lady Avalon seems unwilling to pay. So I was about to ask Charlie—that is, Lord Darlington—if he might help me out with her. Is anything the matter?"

She had become alarmed at the look on Lady Darlington's face, which had gone completely white.

"No, it's nothing. I . . ." Margaret felt so weak she leaned against the back of one of the gilt sofas for support. "Excuse me. Did you say my husband hasn't visited you since our marriage?"

How queer the woman is, thought Laura. One would think she'd be delighted by such virtuous testimony, but she looks as if she's about to faint dead away.

"That's right," she said, starting toward the door. "Oh, he was quite peeved with you at one time—that was when the first one was alive, you know, Caroline the Bad, as I came to think of her. He told me he was very upset with you, but he was in love with you even then. I could tell. And ever since he married you, I've lost one of my favorite customers. La, that's life, isn't it? Well, I mustn't take more of your time. Will you tell Lord Darlington to try to get my money out of Lady Avalon? Ninety guineas it is, which is considerable, else I wouldn't be making such a fuss. Are you *sure* you're all right?"

She stopped in front of Margaret, who forced a half-hearted smile and nodded. "Yes, I'm all right, thank you."

"You look like you've seen a ghost, poor thing. Well, I'm off. Quite a house you've got here! If you ever decide to sell it, think of me. It would make a wonderful . . ."

She waved her hand gaily and left the room.

Margaret had seen a ghost, in fact. The ghost of her fears and doubts, which she had thought were dead and buried.

For if Charlie had not been to Laura's since their marriage, where had he been the night Arthur was murdered?

And why had he lied to her?

• • •

The term "Legal London" designates an area in Holborn on the Victoria Embankment that includes the Royal Courts of Justice and the Inns of Court. To anyone but an Englishman, the Inns of Court would be a somewhat enigmatic institution—or rather institutions, since there are four of them: Lincoln's Inn, Gray's Inn, the Inner Temple, and the Middle Temple. However, to the English legal profession they make eminent sense. They are valuable real estate and office buildings, housing the chambers of barristers, the offices of some solicitors and non-lawyers, and providing a few living quarters. They also have the function of educating and qualifying members of the Bar, the aspirant to which is accepted by one of the four Inns as a student. Then, when he has fulfilled the qualifications, he is called to the Bar by his Inn and remains throughout his professional life a member of that Inn and subject to its professional discipline.

South of the Strand lies the Temple, occupied by two of the Inns, the Inner Temple and Middle Temple. The Temple area was first settled by the Knights Templars, and the Temple Church dominates the area both historically and architecturally. There are also lovely gardens and Jacobean-style brick office buildings, in one of which, the Paper Buildings, Charlie was meeting that afternoon with a number of his fellow peers to discuss their progress—or lack of it—against the forces in the Lords that would reject the Finance Bill. They were using the chambers of Lord Despard, an eminent barrister sympathetic to their cause, to avoid interference by any of the vast number of peers who favored the duke of Suffolk's militantly rejectionist stance. In fact, the mood of the meeting had been defeatist because, despite Charlie's efforts, Percy's side still had a clear majority, and the meeting had been filled with the sort of talk that precedes a capitulation. Charlie had said little if anything, listening to the grumbling from a horsehair sofa into which he had slumped, his long legs stretched in front of him, his eyes seeming to concentrate on the toe of his right shoe, which he was slowly wiggling back and forth. Finally Lord Despard, one of the few older peers to have sided with the anti-rejectionists, cleared his throat and said, "I think the time has come for us to take a clear look at our position. If it is impossible for us to stop rejection of the Finance Bill, then perhaps we should consider going with the majority and presenting a united front, which I fear, God knows, the noble house will need to withstand the abuse that's going to be heaped upon it."

Silence as everyone in the room looked at Charlie. The thought of capitulation had been in more minds than Lord Despard's; and now that he had voiced it, they all looked to Charlie to see if he would go along with it.

After a moment Charlie said, his eye still on his right toe, "In the first place, there will still be the Liberal peers who will vote against rejection. So it's not a question of presenting a united front for the Lords as a whole."

Lord Despard nodded.

"I acknowledge that. But the Liberal peers are a distinct minority, and if the Conservatives stand together it will strengthen the position of the House. Useless dissent can only weaken the House and the Party as well."

Charlie hunched himself into an upright position.

"I disagree," he said quietly. "I don't think intelligent dissent is ever useless, and I believe our position is the only intelligent position in this debate. My brother-in-law and his friends are trying to stop the clock, which, of course, is an impossibility. The history of Europe for the last century and a half proves that every time a group or class has tried to stop progress, disaster has followed. The most Percy and the others will gain is a little time—he knows it as well as we do. So I think it's vitally important we continue to dissent, even if we don't have a prayer of succeeding. It's important to show England that not all the Conservative Party or the nobility is for stagnation, and that some of us realize the world is changing. And while I, for one, am far too cynical to think Utopia is around the corner, I think quite probably the change will be for the better." He paused a moment, then added, "Besides, I think we should keep in mind what Disraeli said about England being two nations, the rich and the poor. I like to think of a successful country operating somewhat like a successful marriage. If the partners don't exercise a bit of give and take, the marriage isn't going to work very well. I think the same can be said about the two classes in this country. I don't like to pay taxes. No one does, God knows. On the other hand, my family has taken a good deal from this country for some five generations, and I feel now is the time for it to give something back. So whatever the rest of you decide to do, I can guarantee you one thing: when the vote is taken, I will vote against rejection."

He looked around the room. It had not been an electrifying speech—Charlie's style was far too low-keyed for that. Still, he had made his point. Lord Exmoor mumbled "Hear, hear!" and the others followed suit. Even Lord Despard finally joined the chorus.

Charlie felt satisfied he had successfully carried the day.

• • •

He was not to carry the night so successfully.

When he returned to Darlington House he knew something was wrong. Margaret was waiting for him in the library. She looked strained and tense; and as he kissed her, he said, "Is something the matter?"

She nodded.

"I have an unpleasant feeling it's something to do with me?"

She nodded again.

"Laura Metcalf was here," she said. "It seems Arthur owed her ninety guineas, which Angela won't pay. So she came here to ask you to help her get the money."

"That's typically Laura," said Charlie, feeling relieved as he sat down. "She has the tart's proverbial heart of gold, but when it comes to business she's a combination Rothschild and Baring. Well, I suppose I'll end up footing the bill, but I don't imagine that especially upsets you."

"It wasn't that. She told me, rather by way of making me feel good, I suppose, that you hadn't been to her 'establishment' since our marriage."

He didn't miss the point. "I see. That's a bit sticky, isn't it?"

"It's more than sticky, Charlie." She hesitated before saying it: "Did you, in fact, kill Arthur?"

He laughed.

"For God's sake, Charlie!"

"I know, but it's so beautifully paradoxical. Two hours ago I made a stirring speech about the brotherhood of man. And then I come home to find my wife suspecting me of murdering my brother."

"What can I help but think?" she exclaimed. "You've lied to me so many times, and now *this* lie! Of all the times you should have been truthful with me, it was *this* time! You told me to trust you, and I did. I've trusted you all along. My whole life—my whole existence is based on my trusting you. But I can't trust you if you continue lying to me!"

She had spoken with great force, and he knew this time he had pushed her trust too far. He cursed Laura for having come to the house.

"All right," he said, "I'll tell you the truth. I probably shouldn't have lied to you the night Arthur was killed, but there was a reason for it. The plain fact was, I had no alibi at all."

"Where had you been?"

"Out walking. Quite literally. I walked from one end of London to the other. Oh, I stopped for lunch at a pub in Hampstead Heath, but they wouldn't have remembered me."

"But why were you walking all over the city?"

"Because I was terrified," he said.

"Of what?"

"Of going to the gallows. When you phoned from the country and said Arthur had tried to blackmail you, I began to realize for the first time that there was a distinct possibility I might be hanged, and the thought genuinely terrified me. Oh, it's one thing to talk about committing a crime, and you accept the risk of being caught and won't it be a jolly picnic going to the noose? But when the *reality* hits you: when you think, my God, it really may happen to me—well then, the beads of sweat begin appearing on the forehead. I was scared, and I went out to walk off my fear. I walked hours—the whole day, really. And I finally ended up at the club about midnight—my feet covered with blisters, I might add—to find that my brother had been murdered. Well, I saw immediately I was in a very bad position in your eyes, and possibly Mona's, because I knew the thought might occur that I'd done Arthur in. And here I was without a decent alibi. So I thought of where I might *say* I'd been that you'd believe, and which at the same time you'd probably never check on. The answer was Laura, of course. And now . . ." He spread his hands slightly. "Well, now you've found out. Do you believe me? I've lied to you so many times, I could hardly blame you if you didn't. And yet I hope you do."

She didn't answer for a moment; then she nodded her head in a slow, almost reluctant "yes." But he could see the doubt lingering in her eyes. And he realized that he had probably killed her trust forever.

• • •

That night, she had three dreams.

In the first dream, Charlie was climbing the steps of a wooden gallows. When he reached the top, a hooded hangman placed the noose around his neck. She was watching, trying to stop the procedure but unable to make a sound—she was voiceless. A vicar was standing next to the hangman. She recognized him as Dr. Filbert, the vicar of the Rockhampton church, the man who had buried Caroline and Arthur. He was reciting a prayer which seemed interminable. The hangman was growing impatient. Then, as Margaret silently screamed, he pulled the lever of the trap and Charlie plunged downward. Dr. Filbert continued to pray.

The dream ended. Sometime later in the night, the second dream began. This time she was floating down the gallery at Ellendon Abbey. The windows of the gallery were open and long white curtains were being blown by a silent night wind. They billowed lazily into the hall like the shrouds of ghosts, and as she moved down the corridor they seemed to clutch at her with gauzy fingers. She tried to duck away from them, but she couldn't avoid them. And then one of them wrapped itself around her and she found herself unable to move, as if entwined in some delicate filament with the strength of steel. She struggled, but her movements only ensnared her further. Then she saw Caroline and Arthur coming down the gallery toward her, Caroline in the nightgown she had been wearing when she died, Arthur in the tweed suit Margaret had last seen him in. They, too, seemed to float, and like everything else in the dream they had no color except varying shades of gray. As they came closer, Margaret made one final terrified attempt to free herself from the curtain, but it held her even more firmly. And then she saw that in fact they were hands that were holding her: Charlie's hands. She turned her head in an effort to see him, but he was directly behind her and holding her too tightly to allow her to turn. Still, she knew it was he. She could feel his breath on her neck. She tried to free herself, but his hands continued to grip her like steel claws. Caroline and Arthur were almost next to her now, and she recoiled as they reached out to touch her with their fingers. She began sobbing with fear, trying to scream, but again, as in the first dream, she was voiceless. The ghost fingers touched her, and the dream ended.

She slept without dreaming for a while, though the sleep was fitful. Then the third and final dream began. This time she was standing at the top of the stairs at Darlington House. It was the night of the ball, and Charlie and Caroline were on the landing beneath the Titian Saint Sebastian greeting the guests. As she watched, she saw Charlie draw a butcher's knife from his coat. She screamed, "Charlie, don't kill her—" This time she had a voice. He looked up at her, smiled, and said, "Why not?" Then he plunged the knife into Caroline's back. The guests didn't seem to notice. They continued to file by their host, stepping over Caroline's body, which had slumped to the floor. It was insanely comic: the prime minister, the first sea lord, the king's mistress all casually stepping over the corpse, chattering away as they continued to climb the stairs. Then Arthur and Angela came up. Charlie greeted them, kissing Angela's hand with sang-froid. Margaret called out, "Arthur, Charlie has just murdered Caroline! Can't you see? Hasn't anyone noticed? My God, *look!* She's right there under your feet—"

Arthur looked down and saw the body, then said, "She's absolutely right. You shouldn't have done it, Charlie. Caroline was no plum, but you shouldn't have killed her. It's not civilized, you know. It's not even very English."

She saw Charlie pull another knife from his coat.

"Arthur, be careful," she called out. "He's going to kill you too!"

Arthur laughed good-naturedly. "Charlie's gone a bit far with Caroline, but he wouldn't kill *me*."

And at that moment Charlie plunged the knife into Arthur's back. He slumped to the floor beside Caroline; then suddenly the guests vanished and she was alone in the stairwell with Charlie and the two bodies.

Charlie pulled the knife out of Arthur's back, then looked up at Margaret. He smiled that charming smile she adored so much. Then he began climbing the stairs toward her.

"Oh please don't," she said. "Oh, God, don't kill me too."

"Why not? You're the only one who knows."

She was collapsed in fear.

"You're safe with me, you know that, I'll never tell—I love you, Charlie. Oh God, I love you. . . ."

"And I love you, Margaret." He was at the top of the stairs now, coming toward her slowly with the knife in his right hand. "But if one life is cheap, two lives are cheaper, are they not? And three make an absolute bargain."

"Charlie, don't joke . . . you joke at everything but don't joke at death—"

"Death is the best joke of all, didn't you know? The final, funniest joke of all."

He was standing in front of her now. As he raised the knife to plunge it into her neck, she called him "murderer," and woke up to find Charlie propped up in bed beside her, staring hard at her. He had turned on the bedlamp, and his face was white.

"You were talking in your sleep."

She was trembling. "I had a nightmare . . ."

"You've never talked in your sleep before."

"Oh Charlie," she whispered, "tell me you didn't kill Arthur. Make me believe it. Make me *believe* it."

He looked at her a moment, and his eyes were different from anything she had ever seen before. No, that was wrong—she had seen him look that way once before.

He answered her with a single word: "How?"

That was all he said. He reached over and turned off the light. As he pulled the blanket over him, she stared at the dark ceiling and told herself they were nothing but dreams, that she was imagining nonexistent horrors. But she hadn't imagined the look in his eyes.

She remembered when she had seen that look before.

It was just before the death of Caroline.

• • •

Charlie, like Macbeth, had murdered sleep. Her sleep. The next three nights she continued to have dreams, each time with slight variations, but always ending the same way, with Charlie about to plunge the knife into her neck, at which point she would wake up in a cold sweat. He would be awake, too, she was certain, though he pretended to be asleep. He was lying next to her, thinking God knew what as she stared at the ceiling, too terrified to get up and unable to go back to sleep. During the day she would tell herself the dreams were meaningless, that Charlie had neither killed Arthur nor intended to kill her, but another part of her mind obviously thought otherwise and the fear was materializing in her dreamworld. Even worse, she was talking in her sleep, and he was listening to her. So that, perversely, the dreams might of themselves be creating the reality. For if he kept hearing her call him a murderer, hearing her say he was going to murder *her*, might not he indeed begin to consider the idea . . . if for no other reason than to shut her up? No, she told herself. It was impossible. Yet he had allowed Caroline to die . . . killed her. And though he made no further reference to her talking in her sleep, a chill was developing between them that she knew she was not imagining. It could hardly be otherwise, with her calling him a murderer each night.

She decided she would have to get away from him for a while and told him she going to the country. He made no objection. It was the second week of October. The budget fight was building to a climax in the Commons, and so he would need to stay in town. It was all so matter-of-fact. Yet despite everything, she hated the thought of leaving him with the strain between them yet unresolved. The morning of her departure she told him she would change her mind and stay in town if he wished. But he said she obviously needed a rest and it was better for her to go to Ellendon Abbey for a week or two. Perhaps he could come down on weekends. If not, he would speak to her on the telephone.

The telephone. Weekends. After all their happiness, was it posible this was what their marriage was coming to? She wanted to throw herself in his arms. She wanted to tell him she loved him and was longing to trust him again. Instead, she walked to the door of the library and opened it.

"Margaret," he said.

She looked back. He was standing behind his desk, watching her.

"Yes?"

"I love you."

"I hope you do," she said. "God knows, I hope you do."

Then she went out of the room.

It was the last time she was ever to see him.

• • •

Her second day at Ellendon Abbey, the weather turned unseasonably bad. A bone-chilling rain lasted for almost three days, followed by a blast of cold air that turned the leafless trees into ice-covered fantasies, killed stray sheep, and caused dozens of schoolchildren to be put to bed with severe colds. The elderly were affected too; and by the end of the first week of the bad weather, Mrs. Blaine was in bed with a cold and a one-hundred-and-two-degree fever. Margaret gave her aspirin and told the cook to prepare hot soup and tea for the housekeeper. This seemed to work the first day, when her fever came down two degrees, to one hundred. But Margaret suspected the cold might develop into something worse. Her fears were realized the following morning when she received a call from Dr. Filbert, who told her there were three cases of influenza in the village. That afternoon Mrs. Blaine's fever soared to a hundred four, and there was no doubt in Margaret's mind that the woman had contracted the flu. By the day's end, Beryl, the upstairs maid, was in bed with a fever, and Evans, the gardener, had gone home with one. And the very contingency for which Margaret had most wanted the hospital—but which was coming months before construction was even to be started—now looked as if it were to happen with swift ferocity: an epidemic.

Influenza was a deadly sickness in 1909, and Margaret knew from her nursing experience that there was tragically little that could be done for its victims except to feed them aspirin and make every effort to keep their fever down. The worst that could happen was that the flu would develop into pneumonia, in which case death was almost a certainty. But even without pneumonia, the flu itself could kill. And to prevent the disease from spreading further throughout the household, she transferred Mrs. Blaine and Beryl into Caroline's bedroom in the west wing, where she personally took charge of them, feeding them as much liquid as possible and putting ice packs around their upper bodies to reduce the fever. She had no alternative, though she was, of course, exposing herself to the disease. Dr. Quarles, the only available doctor in the area, was, she knew from her experience with the Evans child, worse than useless. Moreover, there was nothing he could do for the patients that she wasn't doing herself, and she felt she could do it better. Edna, her private maid, volunteered to help her. And the first night in the "flu wing," as the west end of the house was quickly dubbed by the rest of the frightened staff, both Mrs. Blaine and Beryl responded well to their treatment. By seven the next morning an exhausted Margaret felt the situation was well enough in hand for her to leave the patients in Edna's charge and go to her own room to catch some sleep. The weather had turned warmer, which was a hopeful sign, and as she lay down on her bed, not even bothering to undress, she thought that perhaps the disease might yet be contained and the dreaded epidemic averted after all.

Exhausted as she was, she was not to sleep well. The dreams persisted, as they had every night since she had come down from London. Except this time there was a new dream, one so strange and, somehow, so broodingly macabre that it evoked in her a new terror.

This time they were in the graveyard of the Rockhampton church, attending Caroline's burial. Everyone was there: Charlie, Arthur, Percy, Inspector Mayhew, Mrs. Blaine, Mona Morley. Dr. Filbert was reading the burial service as the snow fell. Then the pallbearers began to lower the crested coffin into the ground.

Suddenly, they stopped. The crowd began to murmur, and Margaret stood on her toes in an attempt to see over the shoulder of the woman in front of her what was causing the commotion. Then she saw: a liquid was seeping out of the closed coffin, slowly at first, then more rapidly as the people backed away. The liquid was colorless; now it was pouring from under the lid as if the coffin were filled with it, a miraculous pitcher of the unnamed and somehow malevolent fluid. It cascaded down the sides of the coffin, falling into the empty grave beneath, which began to fill with it.

Arthur stepped forward and removed his right glove. He put his finger in the fluid and, as some of the crowd gasped, placed the finger to his tongue to taste it.

"Digitalis," he said, and Margaret screamed.

Now everyone turned to stare at her, parting to make a path between her and Arthur and the fluid-seeping coffin, a path that Arthur began to walk down, slowly, pointing his finger at Margaret.

"It's digitalis," he repeated, his voice echoing as in some endless tomb. "You said you hadn't time to give her the medicine, but you did. You lied, didn't you, Miss Suffield? Or rather, Lady Darlington. You lied because you murdered the *real* Lady Darlington."

"It's not true," Margaret sobbed, backing away from him. "I *didn't* have time to give her the medicine. She died before I could do it."

"Then why is her coffin filled with it? Shall we exhume the corpse, conduct an autopsy? Not that it's necessary any more, but we'll do it if we have to."

"No, no, please . . ." she stumbled againt a gravestone and almost fell.

"Then tell us the truth!" His voice seemed to bounce off the walls of eternity. "Or are you capable of telling the truth after so many lies?"

"I haven't lied . . . I *did* give her the digitalis, but not *that* much—"

"Finally, the truth. You didn't give her enough to save her, did you? Because you wanted her to die. Admit it, you wanted her to die."

"No!" she sobbed. "I tried to save her—but Charlie stopped me. He wouldn't let me give her the digitalis. He said, 'Let her die.' I tried to get the medicine back from him, but he said 'Let her *die*.'"

Now Arthur stopped, and a cold wind began blowing over the gravestones, moaning sepulchrally as it swirled the snowflakes in a blinding dance. She fell on her knees to the ground, too weak and frightened to stand.

"Then my brother killed his wife?" said Arthur.

"No, no . . . *Paul* killed her—"

"Liar—"

"Then *I* killed her! But not Charlie, please. Not Charlie."

"Make up your mind," said the voice. "Who did kill Caroline?"

Now the wind stopped as suddenly as it had begun, and the snowflakes vanished. A leaden silence filled the graveyard. She looked up to see the crowd turning to look back at the gravesite. She also looked. To her horror, the coffin lid had opened, and the fluid was now pouring out of it. But there was something worse. Caroline was standing beside the coffin. Caroline whose shroud, soaked with the liquid, clung to her body in wet folds. She raised both her arms and pointed one finger at Margaret and the other at Charlie.

Margaret screamed and woke up to find herself tangled in the counterpane, the noon sun streaming through the leaded windows of her bedroom. She was hot, and for a moment as she tried to quiet her wildly pumping heart, she wondered if she had caught the flu. But as she sat up and began to calm herself, she told herself the perspiration on her face was the result of the nightmare. She hated this dream more than the previous ones. It was more grotesque, more . . . insane?

Insane? The idea flickered through her mind like a sputtering candle. Was it possible she was going mad? That the strain of all the months of guilt and fear had snapped her reason? Yes, she knew the insane were supposed never to question their own sanity; yet these continuous nightmares were hardly indicative of a balanced mentality. She ran her fingers through her drenched hair and searched her mind for some way to find peace. She could find none.

She heard a knock on the door and started. Her nerves were shattered, and she told herself she would somehow have to gain control over them. She called, "Come in."

One of the footmen opened the door and told her a Mrs. Morley was in the drawing room.

Mona? Here? At least not at Caroline's grave . . .

"Tell her I'll be out in a few minutes," she said wearily. Then she went into her bath to wash the sweat of fear from her burning face.

• • •

After she had washed and put on a clean dress, she hurried down the gallery to the "flu wing" to check on her patients before seeing Mona. She didn't like the gallery any more. Even now, with the sun streaming through its windows, it was chillingly reminiscent of her dreams, and she half expected the ghostly figures of Caroline and Arthur to materialize in front of the wooden door at the end of the long hall, their ectoplasmic fingers pointed accusingly at her. And as she pushed open the door to the bedroom, the uncomfortable thought again sparked briefly in her mind that perhaps she was going insane. If she weren't, she might as well be, she reflected ruefully. The persistent nightmares were making her waking hours almost as much a torment as her dreams.

Edna was half dozing in a chair by the door when Margaret came in. Then she woke up and put her fingers to her lips. "They're asleep," she whispered.

Margaret looked at the two cots she'd had placed in the bedroom. Mrs. Blaine and Beryl were indeed asleep, though the older woman was restless beneath her top sheet, which Margaret saw was soaked through.

"What are their temperatures?" she whispered.

"Beryl's is still a hundred three, but Mrs. Blaine's has gone down to a hundred one," replied Edna.

"That's good. Perhaps her fever has broken. You'd better change her sheets. How are the icepacks?"

"I refilled them half an hour ago."

"All right. Have you had lunch?"

"No, ma'am."

"Well, change the sheets, then I'll come in shortly and relieve you. There's someone to see me in the drawing room, but I shan't be long."

"Oh, take your time, ma'am," said Edna, cheerfully enough under the circumstances. "I'm in no hurry."

Margaret smiled at her maid and squeezed her hand. "Thank you, Edna," she said. "I don't know how I'd manage without you."

Then she left the room and returned down the gallery to the entrance hall. As she neared the drawing room, she heard someone playing a Chopin nocturne on the Bechstein. The languid music seemed curiously inappropriate in the harassed atmosphere of Ellendon Abbey, though she supposed the rest of the world was going about its business as usual, unconcerned with the medical drama being played out in a remote corner of Kent. When she went into the drawing room, she saw Mona seated at the piano, looking as languid as the nocturne sounded. She stopped playing when she saw Margaret and got up from the piano stool. She was wearing a well-tailored green suit with a diamond-spray pin on the lapel. A smart, veiled hat was on her head. She started to cross the room when Margaret said, "I shouldn't get too near, Mona. We have two cases of flu in the house, and I've been tending them."

Mona stopped, looking alarmed.

"I heard there were several cases in the village, but I didn't know you had it here too. Your servants might have warned me."

"You might have warned us you were coming," retorted Margaret, sitting down at one side of the large room. "But I don't think there's any danger of your catching it if you don't stay too long. I hope I don't sound inhospitable?" She knew she did, but didn't care. She was in no mood for Mona Morley.

Mona seated herself on the opposite side of the room and said, "The reason I'm here is a political one, not social. And since there's flu in this house, I can assure you I shall make my visit spectacularly brief. I've just been to a houseparty at Lord Plymdale's in the next county, and his chauffeur drove me over. Will one of your men be able to take me to the train station?"

"Oh, yes."

"Good. Well, we had a jolly time at Lord Plymdale's. There were a number of Conservatives there, including the duke of Suffolk; naturally, the conversation dealt with the Finance Bill and the Lords' probable rejection of it. Now, my dear, I suffer no delusion about either your sentiments on this issue, or Charles's. We know Charles intends to vote against rejection. The whole country knows it, for that mater. Nor will I try to deny that the Conservative peers would like very much to change his vote, not only for reasons of party unity, but, to put it most bluntly, for reasons of class unity as well. For this reason, it was decided to offer your husband a quid pro quo—what in more vulgar political parlance would be called a deal. Percy will be seeing Charles this afternoon in London. And it was decided that I should come over here to inform you of the situation."

"Why?" asked Margaret.

"Because you have influence over your husband."

"I'm flattered you think so," said Margaret drily. All things considered, her influence with Charlie was currently at ebb tide. She wasn't, however, about to inform Mona of that fact.

"Well, it's no secret to me that Charles is quite deeply in love with you," said the other woman, not without a trace of bitterness. "Which is as it should be, of course," she added hastily. "You've made a most charming wife for him, for which you're to be congratulated. Both you and Charles have become quite popular with the Party regulars and the public these past few months. And that's why the Party leaders feel that Charles would make an excellent foreign secretary when the Conservatives are returned to power."

The two women looked at each other across the enormous room. Then Margaret said, "I take it that's the deal you spoke of?"

"Yes. If he votes with the Party, he will be guaranteed the foreign office. He's wanted it for years, of course. We all know that. I think probably he had given up trying for it after Caroline's unfortunate death, not to mention his brother's. But of course there's actually no reason why the fact that two members of his family were struck down by a homicidal footman should in any way reflect on his capacity to fill high office. And we all feel his appointment would be a popular one with the country. He is certainly eminently qualified for it."

Margaret was silent for a moment, then, "Do you seriously think my husband would betray his political convictions so cheaply?"

Mona smiled.

"Not so cheaply, I'd say. And long experience with politicians has convinced me their convictions are the lightest baggage they carry. Believe me, Charles is no more and no less cynical than the others. It's just that he had given up hope for political office. Now that the leaders are willing to accept him back in the fold, as it were, you'll be surprised how quickly he'll see the virtue of rejecting the Liberal budget. It's really to everyone's advantage. And it's cerainly to yours. If Charles votes against rejection, he won't stop the Lords, and he will be a political pariah as a result of it. Being a political pariah is not amusing, nor is being the wife of one. On the other hand, if he votes with his party and eventually becomes foreign secretary? Well, it would be a heady role for you to play. Very heady. You would be at the very center of power. You and Charles could influence events on an international scale. You're an intelligent woman; you'd hardly have attained your present position if you weren't. I think, upon reflection, you'll see that no matter how romantic a quixotic vote against the Party may seem, the practical advantages of a vote with the Party offer even more romantic possibilities, and more opportunity to do good as well. Charles knows that without political power, no matter how noble his intentions, he will end up a cipher. He's no fool. And I think you know it too."

"You're certainly blunt enough."

"It's too late for anything but bluntness. The Finance Bill is bound to pass the Commons within a fortnight, at which point it will go to the Lords. There's no more time for games. We must all take sides. And we want you and Charles on our side, which we feel is not only the winning side, but the just side as well."

Margaret gave her a skeptical look, and her visitor laughed. "Well then, let's just leave it at the winning side. What do you say?"

She didn't want to say anything. It was his decision, not hers. She knew what she wanted him to do, and it wasn't to give in to Percy's cynical quid pro quo. But she neither would nor—with the current parlous state of their relationship—probably could influence him.

"I'll have to think about it," she said.

"What's there to think about? Don't you want Charles to be foreign secretary?"

Margaret stood up. "I said I would think about it, Mona. Now if you'll excuse me, I must look in on my patients."

Mona's face took on a slightly contemptuous smile.

"Still the nurse *au fond*, aren't you?" She picked up her gloves from the piano. "Well, my dear, I suppose I can understand why you'd prefer keeping Charles from high office."

Margaret bristled. "What do you mean by that?"

"Simply that some women are not well-equipped for life at the top. It's too challenging, socially and intellectually. Some women prefer a less demanding life, a more, shall we say, 'humble' existence?" She drew on her gloves. "It's too bad, actually. I mean, for Charles. His first wife abused her power. It would certainly be a pity if his second wife were afraid of it."

" I would never 'keep' my husband from any office he wished," said Margaret, attempting to control her temper. "Nor am I afraid of life at what you call the top. I recovered from that some time ago. I'll be disappointed in him, however, if he accepts your deal."

Mona crossed the room.

"And I'll be disappointed in him if he doesn't. Not only disappointed; frankly, I'll be amazed. Now, if you'd be so kind as to arrange for my transportation to the station, I won't keep you from your patients any longer."

Margaret nodded with chilly politeness and opened the door. They went into the entrance hall, where a footman was opening the front door to admit Dr. Filbert. The silver-haired, black-gaitered cleric came over to Margaret, who introduced him to Mona.

"How do you do, Mrs. Morley," he said. "I fear you've chosen an unfortunate time to visit our part of the country." He turned to Margaret. "We've had a dozen new cases in the village since this morning."

"A dozen?" exclaimed Margaret.

"Yes, the situation has taken a turn for the worse. I've called Faversham to try to get some medical assistance. They're sending in a doctor and a nurse. We're putting all the patients in the church to try and keep the flu from spreading further, but it doesn't look good at all. If the church fills up, I wonder if we might use Ellendon Abbey?"

"Do you think there'll be that many?"

"There certainly may be."

"Then of course you can bring them here. I already have two cases, you know, but we could handle more, I suppose."

"Excellent. I hoped I could count on you. Then I'll be getting back to town. Mrs. Morley?"

He nodded at Mona, who said, "Perhaps you could take me into town with you? I must catch the train to London."

Dr. Filbert looked surprised.

"I'm afraid that will be impossible."

"Why?"

He looked at Margaret.

"I thought you knew. The town and the entire surrounding area have been placed under a strict quarantine. No one is allowed to come in or go out except, of course, the doctor and nurse from Faversham."

"When did this happen?" exclaimed Mona angrily.

"Just an hour ago."

"But how long will it last? I must get up to London!"

Dr. Filbert spread his hands. "Until the epidemic's over, I'm afraid. It may be as long as a week, perhaps longer."

"This is *most* inconvenient!" Mona sputtered.

Margaret couldn't suppress a smile.

"I was sure we could count on you, Mona. Your being here will be a great help to me. You'll see first-hand how romantic the nurse's calling can be. Even, at times quixotic."

• • •

The epidemic, almost as if it had been gathering momentum, now burst on the village like a flood pouring through a cracked dam. Within four days, there were fifty-seven cases of flu in Rockhampton, and seven deaths had occurred. To make things worse, the heavy rains returned, turning the roads into bogs and the streets into ponds, making it even more difficult to bring supplies and assistance in through the quarantine, and further isolating the area from the rest of the world. Everyone was terrified to go out of their houses, and the village seemed deserted except for the funeral coach carrying the bodies down the rain-spattered main street to the churchyard for quick burial. Then, faces would appear at streaked windows to watch the passing of the dead. Otherwise, curtains were drawn and doors and windows bolted, for the country superstition persisted that death could be literally locked out of a house.

The church had filled rapidly, and by the third day Dr. Filbert was calling on Margaret to take up her offer of shelter for the overflow. Things had also grown worse at Ellendon Abbey. Mrs. Blaine had, happily, recovered and was able now to lend a much-needed hand. But on the second night Beryl, the maid, had developed pneumonia and died at three the next morning. Furthermore, the cook and two of the footmen had come down with the flu, as well as Edna, so that the west bedroom, or "flu wing," was filled to capacity. Now Dr. Filbert wanted to bring eight new patients in, and he told Margaret there would probably be more the next day.

"I'll need cots and fresh sheets," she said. "Can you get them for me?"

"Yes."

"And some help?"

"We're terribly short-handed. I can't promise you more than one or two of the local women."

"We'll take whatever we can get."

That afternoon, the patients were brought into the ancient house and the entrance hall was converted into a ward. The cots were set up in rows, and the tall, carved-teak screens the third earl had bought in Siam forty years earlier were moved from the drawing room to separate the male patients from the female. A fire was kept going in the large hearth, but this only partially heated the great, drafty hall. Still, it was the only feasible place to house the patients.

Margaret set up a six-hours-on, six-hours-off schedule for the attendants, who now consisted of herself, the recovered Mrs. Blaine; Mrs. Gates and Mrs. Drew, two women from the village; two of the footmen at the Abbey; and an extremely reluctant and frightened Mona Morley. Mona hadn't wished to help at all, much preferring to stay locked in her bedroom. But Margaret needed her, and she literally bullied her into puting on one of her old nurse's uniforms and joining the others in changing sheets, cleaning bedpans, refilling the icepacks, and the other extraordinarily unromantic and unpleasant chores that had to be done. The day after the eight patients were moved in to the temporary ward, Dr. Filbert brought in four more, including, to Margaret's sorrow, young Sidney Evans, the gardener's son, who had caught the flu from his father. Sidney had a raging fever of a hundred and five and was delirious. Margaret took personal charge of him, for she knew the boy's chances of surviving were slender and she couldn't bear the thought of his dying. But the added responsibility of Sidney was wearing her down. She could only catch bits of sleep at odd hours. All the highly feverish patients needed their bedsheets changed every half hour; furthermore, they had to be turned from side to side at least as often because of the danger of pneumonia settling into the depressed side of the body. This coupled with the continuous sponging of sweat-soaked bodies, the continuous replenishing of ice packs, and the hundred other duties that she didn't dare leave unsupervised for too long left Margaret, by the end of the fifth day, in a state of near collapse. And to make things worse, five new patients were brought in and Mrs. Drew, one of the two women from the village, came down with a fever and had to be put to bed herself.

The one bright spot in this nightmare was Charlie. He called three or four times a day from London, concerned about the epidemic, frustrated by his inability to come down and help, and, she thought, genuinely worried about her catching the disease herself. She put on as good a face as possible, telling him the situation was under control, which it wasn't. But she was cheered by his concern, and again her love for the man began to reassert itself and the terror of the dreams and her fears began to subside. Her relationship with him had always been a seesaw between trusting adoration and, hopefully, neurotic suspicion, and now the balance was tipping back to the former, happier emotion. She was further elated when he told her he had turned down Percy's offer of the foreign secretaryship. It seemed to confirm what she thought of as the good side to his character, the uncynical, almost idealistic side to the man that she knew was there, though he preferred concealing it with his façade of dry urbanity.

"May I tell Mona you turned it down?" she asked.

"Why not?" he replied. "Tell her while she's changing bed-pans. It will make her day."

She couldn't help but laugh, tired as she was. "Charlie, you'd die if you'd seen her the first day! She was furious at having to 'descend' to the level of the common bedpan. But I absolutely hounded her into working. And I must admit that the last few days she's gotten better. She's really become quite helpful, and thank God we have her."

"Is there any sign of the flu easing off?"

"Well, we hope the epidemic's peaked, but we won't be sure for a few days. Three of our patients are over the crisis, and I'll probably move them into one of the extra bedrooms tomorrow to get them away from the others. Edna's quite desperately ill, though. And I'm terribly worried about little Sidney Evans. We can't get his fever down, and it's been over two days now.

If the fever doesn't break tonight, I think he may not get through tomorrow."

"Does his mother know?"

"I haven't told her it's that bad. I haven't had time, in point of fact, but I wouldn't anyway. Why make her more miserable than she is?"

"Yes, I suppose you're right."

She looked around to see Mona coming into the library. She looked almost as exhausted as Margaret; now she closed the door, leaned againt it wearily and said, "It's Edna."

Margaret closed her eyes. "Dear God," she whispered. Then she said into the phone, "Darling, I must go. It's Edna. I didn't think she'd pull through but still I'd hoped she might."

Charlie expressed his sympathy. Then, just as she was about to ring off, he said, "Margaret, I'm most proud of what you're doing."

It was an unexpected compliment, and somehow—perhaps because of her exhaustion—it touched her profoundly. "Thank you," she whispered into the phone. "I appreciate that, my darling."

She rang off and got up from the desk. Mona was watching her from the door. She said, "What do you appreciate?"

Margaret hesitated. "He said he was proud of what we are all doing."

Mona ran her hand through her bedraggled hair. "I'm glad *someone's* proud. Frankly, I think we should all get the Garter at the very least. Did he say anything about Percy?"

"Yes, he told me he turned him down."

Mona shrugged. "Well, you were right and I was wrong. Again." She walked over to the window and looked out at the leaden sky, which was turning black as night fell. "It's odd," she continued, "but I've been wrong about your husband all along. Did you know I was once in love with him?"

"Yes," she said, "I knew."

"He is the only man I ever have been in love with," Mona went on in a flat tone. "I never was in love with my husband. I rather liked him, but that was as far as it went. But I did fall in love with Charles and I was idiotic enough to think he was in love with me. I suppose I shouldn't tell you this, should I?"

"I don't think it matters now, does it?"

"No, I suppose not. Some women should never fall in love, and I think I'm definitely one of them. It doesn't agree with me." She turned from the window. "He never made love to me, you know. Or perhaps you don't know?"

"I know."

"But he was most attentive. And then quite suddenly it was all over. Poof! He vanished out of my life. It was as if he didn't need me any more." She shrugged. "Well, you seem to have won all around, and it would be less than sporting of me not to offer my congratulations, which I hereby do."

The conversation was making Margaret feel distinctly uncomfortable, since she knew why Charlie had given his attentions to Mona.

"I'd like to see Edna," she said. "Will you come with me?"

Mona nodded and walked over to the door. There, she paused. "Will you answer a question?" she asked.

"Of course."

"That night you came to my house—the night Lord Avalon was murdered—where had Charles been?"

She was instantly on her guard. "Why do you ask?"

"Why? Because it was immediately after that he vanished, and I was dropped like the proverbial potato. I've always wondered what could possibly have kept him away."

As she tried to decide which of Charlie's stories to tell, Mona smiled. "Come now. I know you don't like me. But don't you think that after five days in this place—which must make the hospitals of the Crimea seem like a bank holiday in comparison—we might let down our hair a bit and become friends?"

"Well, if you must know," said Margaret reluctantly, "he spent the evening at St. John's Wood."

Mona blinked with surprise. Then she laughed.

"Marvelous!" she said. "Absolutely marvelous. I should have known. Where else would he have gone? The lure of my company, the lure of Beethoven and Borodin, all paled before the attractions of Laura Metcalf's dimpled flesh. So much for culture, alas! Well, shall we return to the chamber of horrors?"

She opened the door and went back into the entrance hall with its rows of cots. Margaret followed her, wondering if she had accepted Charlie's lie as gullibly as she herself had that night, and further wondering what had been her real purpose in asking the question in the first place.

At two fifteen that morning, Sidney Evans' fever dropped to a hundred two, and he told Margaret he was hungry. She had been sitting next to him for more than two hours, applying cold towels to his head and chest and forcing tea into his stomach. He had been delirious most of the time; now, as his temperature miraculously dropped, he came out of the delirium and Margaret knew he was going to be all right. She gave him a peeled and cored apple, which he quickly consumed. Then, as she rubbed her hand lightly over his forehead, he closed his eyes and went to sleep.

"Thank heavens," she whispered to Mrs. Blaine. "I think he's going to be all right."

"But you're not going to be all right unless you get some rest," said Mrs. Blaine. "Will you let me put you to bed?"

"Yes," said Margaret, wearily getting to her feet. "I'm feeling most awfully tired."

"I should say so! You look like you're about to drop in your tracks. Come on with you, now. I'll be taking you to your room and tucking you in. And don't you worry about the patients; we'll look after them. They're most of them asleep now. Personally, I think the worst of it's over."

She helped her mistress to her bedroom, where she got her undressed, then put her in the big bed. As she started to turn out the light, Margaret said, "Mrs. Blaine, I think you'd best get me some aspirin."

The housekeeper looked alarmed. She reached over and felt Margaret's forehead.

"You don't feel feverish," she said.

Margaret's eyes were closed.

"But I think I will be soon. I've been feeling ill for some hours now. I was bound to get it sooner or later, I suppose. I'm just thankful it was later. Will you and Mrs. Morley take charge of things?"

"Of course we will, poor dear. And we'll take charge of you, too. I'll fetch the aspirin."

By the time she had returned to the bedroom with the medicine, Margaret had a temperature. And by noon the next day, it had developed into a raging fever. Now Mrs. Blaine was giving her the same treatment she had been giving Sidney the night before, forcing liquids into her, packing ice around her body and filling her with aspirin. She was perspiring heavily, soaking her sheets so quickly they had to be changed every half hour. By six that evening, when Mona came in to relieve Mrs. Blaine, the housekeeper looked genuinely frightened.

"I don't know what to do for her," she whispered. "She's got it as bad as any of the others! She looks like Edna did, just before she passed on, poor soul."

Mona looked at Margaret, who was turning from side to side, her eyes closed, her voice a mumble.

"What's her temperature now?" she asked.

"A hundred five. That was a half hour ago, the last time I checked. It's been high all afternoon. The poor thing's delirious and has been saying weird things, talking about a dripping coffin, or something." She shook her head sadly. "I know how she feels, having been through it myself. It's no picnic, for sure."

She left the room and Mona sat down next to the bed. The epidemic had been a harrowing experience for her, and she was as exhausted as the others. But she was rather glad she had gone through it. She had discovered resources in herself she hadn't known existed, and she took a justifiable pride in what she had done. She admired Margaret, too, though the admiration was grudging. It was galling to Mona that Charlie preferred the nurse to her, but she had to admit Margaret had strength, energy, and a straightforwardness that, in a devious world, was unusual—at least to Mona, and certainly she had achieved miracles in the past few days. As Mona watched her, she nervously wondered if she would catch the disease too.

An hour later, Margaret's fever dropped to a hundred three and she seemed better. She was even able to eat some bread along with her soup. As she sat up, Mona asked her, "What is this business about a coffin that's dripping?"

Margaret gave her a startled look. "What do you mean?"

"You kept mumbling about some coffin that was overflowing with digitalis, whatever that is. You made it sound like a tea-kettle boiling over. Were you having a nightmare?"

Her hands were trembling, and it wasn't only from the flu. "Yes, I have bad dreams sometimes. Did I say anything else?"

Mona smiled. "Guilty secrets from the fevered brain?" She smiled again. "No, it's all right. You didn't say anything."

Thank God, Margaret thought, sipping her broth. Thank God! If she had said anything in front of *Mona*, of all people! She wanted to tell her to go away, to return to the other patients, but she didn't dare. She couldn't afford to give the impression she *did* have "guilty secrets." She would have to wait for Mrs. Blaine and pray she didn't become delirious again.

But she did. At ten the fever surged again, this time with such ferocity that Mrs. Blaine, who replaced Mona at midnight, thought she might not last the night. However, by dawn the fever had subsided again, and though Margaret looked half-dead and was almost too weak to move, Mrs. Blaine thought she had survived the worst.

As she lay in the pillows, her face chalky. she whispered, "Mrs. Blaine?"

"Yes, dear?"

"Will you stay with me?"

"Of course."

"I mean, I don't want Mrs. Morley . . ."

Mrs. Blaine nodded. "I understand."

A few minutes later, she thought she had dropped off to sleep. But she hadn't. She whispered again, "Mrs. Blaine?"

"Yes?"

"Do you think if a person has done something evil—very evil—he can be forgiven?"

Mrs. Blaine smiled and leaned over to pat her hand. "Ah, child, if you were only a Catholic now, you'd know anything can be forgiven as long as you confess and go to mass enough times.

And perhaps contribute a little extra money to the Bishop's Fund. You know."

Margaret smiled weakly and didn't say anything for a while; then, for the third time, she whispered, "Mrs. Blaine?"

"Yes, child."

"If I die, will you tell my husband I've always loved him very much?"

"Ah, go on with you, talking that way! You're not going to die—you're over the worst of it, and I don't like that morbid kind of talk."

"I know. But in case . . . will you tell him?"

Mrs. Blaine's forced cheerfulness sagged a little, and a troubled look stole over her kind face. "I will do that, my dear. I'll tell him."

Again, Margaret smiled.

"Thank you, Mrs. Blaine."

• • •

She died at nine-thirty that evening.

Conclusion

Two weeks later, Lord Darlington was ushered into the Scotland Yard office of Inspector Mayhew, who got up from his desk to come over and shake hands. Charlie was in a sober mood. Again, the mourning band was on his coat sleeve, but this time the mourning wasn't mere show. The inspector expressed his condolences. Charlie said a brief "thank you," then inquired why he had been asked to come to Scotland Yard.

"Please sit down," said the inspector, indicating a chair in front of his desk. Charlie sat. The inspector picked up a cablegram as he returned to his chair.

"We received this cable from the New York City police this morning," he said. "Paul Rougemont attempted a bank robbery in Brooklyn two days ago and was shot. They took him to Bellevue Hospital, where he died last night. Before dying he confessed to the murder of your brother, Lord Avalon. Apparently he and the girl had arranged passage on a freighter to New York the week before. When your brother turned him in to us, it apparently angered him enough to decide to kill him before getting on the boat. The girl, by the way, is living in Brooklyn and has had a child by Rougemont. The emeralds, unfortunately, seem to be gone forever. He sold them to a New York fence—though he refused to give his name—and apparently he sold them for a fraction of their value. I'm afraid by now they've been broken up and the individual jewels resold separately."

Charlie nodded. "I'd given up any idea of recovering them," he said. "The insurance claim has been settled and the money is going into the construction of a hospital I'm naming for my late wife. My second wife, that is."

"Yes, I'd heard that," said the inspector. "A fitting tribute to Lady Darlington." He cleared his throat, and Charlie wondered why the man looked so nervous. Finally, the inspector said, "The cablegram informs us of something else that is frankly rather embarrassing to bring up under the circumstances."

"Which is?"

"Rougemont admitted killing your brother, but he insisted he did not kill your first wife. He claimed the late Lady Darlington went into your first wife's bedroom and smothered her with a pillow after he had already left Darlington House."

Charlie looked at the inspector coolly. "And did he suggest why he thought my wife did that?"

"His theory was she figured if she could get rid of your first wife, she could become the second Lady Darlington. And when Rougemont chloroformed Lady Caroline, the nurse saw her opportunity and took it."

"Tell me, inspector," said Charlie evenly, "Do you seriously believe a woman like my late wife, who gave her life in the service of her fellow human beings—do you seriously believe a woman like that could smother her own patient, no matter how compelling the temptation?"

The inspector turned slightly red.

"Well, no, but of course we felt it necessary to bring the accusation to your attention. Naturally, we shall carry the investigation no further. It would be pointless in any case, since your wife is deceased. Still . . ."

Charlie stood up. "Then I think there's nothing more to be said. This man Rougemont not only killed my first wife and my brother, now he's attempted to besmirch Lady Margaret's reputation. He's done quite enough, and I'll fight with every weapon I have anyone—including you, inspector, and the Yard—who spreads this disgusting calumny further."

"Of course, your Lordship, you have my word nothing will be said about this. . . ."

"I'm sure. Then I'll bid you good day, inspector."

He walked out of the office, leaving Inspector Mayhew not only shaken but rather ashamed at having wounded the earl by telling him the cable's contents. He sighed and put the cable in the manila folder marked "Lady Darlington." Then he stamped "Case Closed" on the cover and buzzed his secretary for a cup of tea.

• • •

"You really loved her, didn't you?" said Mona two nights later. She was wearing one of her most beautiful gowns, a delicate pale-blue velvet creation from Mr. Worth that showed her shoulders and neck to best advantage. She had put on her handsomest diamonds, and a diamond-and-sapphire clip fixed to her hair held a sinuous aigrette in place. She was sitting opposite a tail-coated Charlie at the small, round dinner table in her intimate white dining room at Number 3 Pelham Crescent. The room was illuminated softly by candles; through the tall windows they could see the first snowflakes of the year drifting down on London.

"I loved her very much," replied Charlie as he cut into his squab.

"I was able to know her so much better during the epidemic," continued Mona. "I was terribly impressed by her dedication and courage. She was never afraid. Of the flu, that is."

"Margaret was a brave woman. She was never afraid of anything."

"She was afraid of you."

He had put a forkful of squab in his mouth. Now his eyes shot up and looked across the table at her as he continued chewing.

"What makes you think that?"

Mona folded her hands gracefully.

"The things she said while she was delirious. She said a great many fascinating things, actually. She talked about your character, for instance. It seems there was a certain ambivalence in her mind about you. She wanted so much to believe in your goodness, but she was having some difficulty, you see. Because of Caroline, of course."

He cut another slice of squab. "I'm afraid I'm not following you, Mona."

She laughed. "Oh come now, Charles. The charade is over. I know everything. I've known it for several weeks. Since, in fact, just before Margaret died, so there's no longer any need for pretense. Besides, it's such a chore after a while, and I'm certain you must be thoroughly bored with it yourself by now. After all, it's been months, hasn't it?"

"Just what is it you think you know, Mona?"

"That you murdered Caroline. It was murder, you know. I've checked it out with my solicitor, and he's assured me that anyone who intentionally prevents medication being given to a dying person is guilty of murder. Medication, for example, like digitalis. Not being a medical person, it was only a vaguely familiar term for me. However, I asked my doctor about it's meaning, and I must say I'm most pleased with my newly acquired knowledge. Education is, as they say, not only ennobling but of practical value as well."

She smiled.

Charlie placed his fork on his plate and wiped his mouth with his napkin. "I see you're up to your old tricks again, Mona. You know, if you continue saying such unpleasant things about me, I'll have to pay a visit to my own solicitor."

"Or murder me?" she asked, almost playfully.

He said nothing.

"You see," she continued, "Margaret was having nightmares. She had been for some time, actually, and I must say they were quite vivid. But there was one in particular that was especially colorful, and when she became delirious she let out enough of it so that only an idiot could miss the point. And, as I think you're aware, I'm no idiot."

"What did she say?" asked Charlie. "I think you can understand a natural curiosity on my part."

"Oh yes. It all had to do with digitalis, which was apparently cascading out of Caroline's coffin in the dream like a veritable waterfall. And someone was threatening to exhume Caroline's corpse, which put Margaret in a perfect sweat of fear. Why do you think exhuming Caroline would worry Margaret so much, Charles? Do you think they might find something they hadn't expected—for instance, this digitalis? Margaret *had* told the police she'd not been able to give Caroline any. But what if she had?"

Charlie shrugged. "That doesn't seem to make much difference, one way or the other."

"Perhaps. But it seemed to make a difference to Margaret. At least, in the dream. For someone then accused her of having lied to the police. And she said, and I quote her most accurately, 'I *did* try to give her the medicine, but Charlie stopped me. He said, "Let her die." ' Interesting, isn't it? And then she repeated it: 'He said, "Let her *die!*" ' It paints a lovely picture of what must have gone on in Caroline's bedroom that night."

Charlie laughed. "It certainly does, and a very dramatic one too. But I don't think the police would be particularly impressed by your version of what a dying woman said in her delirium."

"I think they might be extremely impressed. Particularly if I told Percy, and we persuaded a number of influential friends to insist on an investigation. And the press? Well, when they'd get wind of it, they'd have a fine time, wouldn't they? And they'd certainly provoke an exhuming of Caroline's body. Oh, I think we could interest the police. And my testimony might just be enough to place the noose about your most handsome neck."

"It's certainly turning out to be an enjoyable dinner, Mona. I can't tell you how delighted I am you invited me."

"Isn't it fun? You know, Charles, I've been quite dazzled by your virtuosity. The way you worked everything out so beautifully with Margaret. I mean, using her love for you to keep her quiet. Marrying her so she couldn't testify against you. You're to be congratulated. But you realize, of course, that one must pay for one's crimes eventually?"

"One would like to think one doesn't," he replied. "Not that I'm admitting any of this. Personally, I think you'd be laughed out of Scotland Yard. But I assume you've spun this fantasy in an effort to extract something from me. I'm fascinated to hear what you're after."

She toyed with her diamond bracelet.

"I want to be Lady Darlington. That way, you'll never have to worry about *my* testifying against you."

"That's very thoughtful of you."

"There's more. I also want to be the wife of the foreign secretary. So I want you to accept Percy's deal and vote for rejection tomorrow in the Lords."

Silence. Charlie sipped the Pouilly-Fumé. "You want a great deal, don't you?"

"I do. And I expect to get it. You made me fall in love with you, Charles. Now I know why: to shut me up when I half-stumbled on the truth before. But it's a very cruel, very un-chivalrous piece of business to make a woman fall in love and then abandon her. Almost as cruel as preventing a nurse from administering life-saving medication to one's dying wife."

"What if I refuse?"

Her face looked beautifully reposed in the candlelight as she said, "Then you may very well hang."

He said nothing, but continued watching her across the table.

"I'd hate to do it, Charles," she went on. "But I would."

"Oh, I'm sure you would."

"So think about it. Life, death. It's simple enough. I will be outside the Lords tomorrow, waiting. If you vote for rejection, well, then I think it would be splendid if you took me to the Savoy for dinner. It could be a sort of celebration of our impend-ing engagement. And if you vote against? Well, I shall go directly to Whitehall. Would you care for some more squab? It's really most deliciously tender, isn't it?"

"Very," said Charlie. "But I'm afraid you've spoiled my appe-tite, Mona."

"I'm terribly sorry. I probably should have waited till after dinner. Some more wine, perhaps?"

Charlie smiled. "I'll take that. In fact, I think I may get roaring drunk."

Mona laughed and rang the bell for her butler.

• • •

He didn't get drunk, and he didn't sleep. He spent the night thinking of Caroline, whom he had killed. Margaret, whom he had loved. And now Mona. Caroline: vicious, arrogant, and dissolute. Margaret: kind, loving, and courageous. And Mona? An icy machine. A calculator.

He wondered if having Mona for a wife might not be the worst punishment of all.

• • •

The next day as many people as could gain admittance thronged the anterooms of the House of Lords, swarming through the vaulted entrance hall past the long row of Gothic coat-hooks (each one labeled, as in a school, beginning with the royal dukes, then progressing all the way through the peerage from Lord Aberconway to the marquess of Zetland), pushing by the life-sized statue of the young Queen Victoria on the coronation chair, buzzing with rumors and speculation about the vote on the Finance Bill, which everyone apparently sensed would mean the end of the noble house's actual power. Leading off the main anteroom was the chamber itself, built, paradoxically, in 1847 after the first Reform Bill had already begun to clip the wings of the peers. It was a small room, only eighty feet long, floridly Gothic in the Victorian interpretation of that ornate style, bathed in red light from stained-glass windows, the walls lined with statues of the Magna Charta barons. Along the walls beneath the barons ran red-leather sofas, facing each other; between them was the curious "woolsack," a big red pouf on which sat the lord chancellor. At the end of the room, beneath a huge gilded canopy, was the throne, resplendent symbol of a power long since vanished in all but its ceremonial functions.

As the vote began, Charlie sat in his accustomed seat, occasionally exchanging glances with one of his group, all of whom seemed to be looking to him for moral bracing in the nervous moments before commitment. The duke of Suffolk, he noticed, was watching him also. And he had seen Mona Morley in the anteroom.

As the vote droned on, he thought about Mona, Margaret, and murder. It was almost amusing, actually. He had come so close to pulling it off. But when Margaret had died . . .

His name was called: the Right Honorable the fifth earl of Darlington. He got to his feet. "How votes the noble earl?" he was asked. "For or against rejection of the Finance Bill?"

He looked around the chamber and said, loud and clear: "I vote against."

There were cheers from his men, stony silence from the vast majority of the peers. He sat down, a smile on his face. Mona would be on her way to Whitehall soon. He had no doubt she would go through with it.

But, he thought, at least Margaret would have been proud of him. It was, after all, a rather noble thing to do.